Time of the Eagle

of the

SHERRYL JORDAN

Time of the Eagle

AN IMPRINT OF HARPERCOLLINS*PUBLISHERS*

Eos is an imprint of HarperCollins Publishers.

Time of the Eagle
Text and illustrations copyright © 2007 by Sherryl Jordan
All rights reserved. Printed in the United States of America. No part of this book
may be used or reproduced in any manner whatsoever without written permission
except in the case of brief quotations embodied in critical articles and reviews. For
information address HarperCollins Children's Books, a division of HarperCollins
Publishers, 1350 Avenue of the Americas, New York, NY 10019.
www.harperteen.com

Library of Congress Cataloging-in-Publication Data
Jordan, Sherryl.
    Time of the eagle / Sherryl Jordan.— 1st ed.
       p.   cm.
    Sequel to: Secret sacrament.
    Summary: Avala, the daughter of Gabriel Eshban Vala, dreams of becoming a
healer like her mother, but she is instead destined to bring about the Time of the Eagle,
in which tribes hunted by the Navoran dictator will unite and win their freedom.
    ISBN-10: 0-06-059554-X (trade bdg.)
    ISBN-13: 978-0-06-059554-8 (trade bdg.)
    ISBN-10: 0-06-059555-8 (lib. bdg.)
    ISBN-13: 978-0-06-059555-5 (lib. bdg.)
    [1. Fantasy.] I. Title.
PZ7.J7684Tim 2007   2006019371
[Fic]—dc22

Typography by Andrea Vandergrift
1 2 3 4 5 6 7 8 9 10

First Edition

For Kael

May you grow to be a finished person,
knowing wholly who you are, having absolute peace,
totally embracing your path and your destiny,
and knowing the All-father as
your Friend.

Acknowledgments

Like *Secret Sacrament* (the story of Gabriel), this story about his daughter, Avala, arose out of a time of personal difficulty and pain. And again, as with Gabriel's story, many friends gave support and encouragement. My special thanks go to Caroline, who first persuaded me that *Time of the Eagle* must be written; and to Jean, whose friendship and encouragement keep alive the writer-spirit in me. Deepest thanks go, again, to my editor, Antonia Markiet, without whose wisdom and guidance Avala might have given up her battle, and I the struggle the write it down. But there was joy, too, in the writing of this novel—the pleasure of the company of old friends not visited for several years: Salverion, Sheel Chandra, Ashila, and the eternal spirit of Gabriel, the healer.

Sherryl Jordan
Tauranga, New Zealand
June 2006

TERRITORIES
of the
Navoran Empire
And of the
Shinali Igaal
And Hena Nations

N

S

KEY:
1: City of Navora   2: Citadel
3: Taroth Fort   4: Mt. Sharnath
5: Exit of Catacombs
Miles:

5   10   15   20

Hena Lands

Hena Lands

Desert

Marsh

Hena Lands

Marsh

Desert

Igaal Lands

Dead forest

Place of the Gathering

Himeko Mountains

Oakwei River

Anjee River

Nyranjeera Lakes

Fertile Lands were once Shinali by Navora

Shinali Camp

Ravinath

Exily River

Owel River

Igaal Camp

Port Timano (Navoran)

Coastlands to west

Napangardi Mountains

Forested hills

Igaal Lands

Coal leaves from Port

Navoran coal mines

Fertile country Navoran farms and crops

Caves where Shinali hide

plains

Navoran Port

farms near Craigie

Last Shinali Land

3

Taroth Pass

old coastal road

1

5

Sherryl Jordan

Contents

The Main People in My Story

Shinali

Ashila	My mother, and our tribe's healer
Yeshi	Our Chieftain
Zalidas	Our Seer and Holy Man
Avala	Myself

Navoran

Gabriel	My father, who died before I was born
Salverion	Grand Master of Healing, at Ravinath
Sheel Chandra	Master of Mind-power, at Ravinath
Taliesin	Healer at Ravinath
Delano	Poet at Ravinath
Jaganath	Emperor of Navoran Empire
Embry	Navoran army commander, friend to the Shinali
Boaz	Second-in-command to Embry

Igaal

Mudiwar	Chieftain to my Igaal tribe
Ishtok	Youngest son of Mudiwar
Ramakoda	Oldest son of Mudiwar
Chimaki	Only daughter of Mudiwar

Hena

| Atitheya | Son of Hena chieftain, pledge-brother to Ishtok |

First Scroll

Prophecies & Cords
That Bind

1

I was the first child born to a hunted people, in the first winter of their flight.

My earliest memory is of being carried on my mother's hip across barren plains, with wild mountains all around, and of rough tents made of skins stretched across sticks planted in the dust, of hunger and thirst and a feeling I did not like or understand, but which I know now was the fear that shadowed my people, as a wolf shadows a wounded deer. Always we were moving on, always looking behind us, always afraid to rest.

My people were called the Shinali, and by the time I was born there were only a few of us left, for we had fought many battles with many enemies and lost much. Early in my life I came to realize that the tribe held me high in their hearts, and I thought it was because my mother, Ashila, was the healer, with skills that meant the difference between life or death. But later my mother told me who my father was, and I knew why I was beloved. My father was Gabriel Eshban Vala, from the stone city of Navora, far to the south of our journey-lands.

Things were not good between my father's people and my mother's, for the all-conquering Navorans had stolen nearly all the Shinali lands and left us only one little plain. When my parents first met, my people still had that plain. Navorans were not allowed on our land, but my father came, for my mother invited him. He, too, was a healer, famous and honored among his own people; but when he chose to sit at the feasting-fires of the Shinali, it cost him dearly. His own people turned against him and against us. In the end they drove us off our last land, imprisoned us in a stone fort, and would have killed us all; but my father saved us and traded for our freedom with his life.

A hard freedom it was, for the Emperor in the stone city wanted us all dead. All my childhood life we wandered, staying only a little season in each place, afraid of the bands of soldiers we saw sometimes, far out in the desert or in the mountain passes, searching for us; again and again we moved, living the life of the hunted, until I was fifteen summers old. And then we found a valley, protected and hidden by a ring of mountains, and there seemed to be a shield of peace; and the awful fear that had hung across my people all the years suddenly lifted, and they knew a kind of contentment. For the first time in my life I stayed in one place for more than six full moons, and the river and mountains and hunting grounds and places of gathering became familiar and loved.

It was there, in that peaceful valley, that the day came for the celebration of my sixteenth summer. It was a day high in importance, for in our tribe when she is sixteen a girl becomes a woman, and the whole tribe rejoices and honors her and welcomes her as a new person. The sixteenth borning-day is always celebrated in summer, when food is plentiful, so there can be a big feast.

Because in our tribe women are the healers, my mother was teaching me her ways, and my work it was to gather herbs along the riverbanks and from the mountains. That afternoon of my sixteenth borning-day I went gathering, leaving the women and children to prepare gifts and special food for my celebration feast. Always I gathered alone, though I knew to be watchful, for battalions of soldiers still searched for us. And the Hena and Igaal peoples—age-long enemies to us—drove us off with arrows and spears when they found us sometimes on the edges of their lands. But I had not seen any enemies during my gathering-times, until that day.

That day I walked beside the great river we call the Ekiya. I went to the very end of the ravine, to the edge of the desert lands, the only growing place for the *eysela* flowers, from which we make medicines for the wiping out of disease. I had gathered almost half that were there, when I went back to the river for a drink, for the day was hot.

I drank quickly, glancing often across the baked grasslands to my right, for beyond them lay enemy lands, the country of the Igaal. I could see no sign of human life, and the peaceful hills seemed to dance in the haze of heat; yet a feeling of danger swept over me. It was an impulse familiar to my people, and we never ignored it. Quickly I bent to pick up the gathering-bag at my feet, and in that moment heard the throb of many hooves. Then I heard distant shouts. From the south they came, the riders hidden by the rocks guarding the entrance to the gorge. Snatching up my gathering-bag, I looked for a hiding place.

To my left soared the walls of the ravine, the river snaking between them. The nearest bend was far away, with no hiding place between. The hoofbeats were close. Clearly I heard the yells of men racing their horses to the water. Not far into the ravine was a wide rock higher than the others, flatter and sloping upward where it jutted out over a deep pool. I ran to it and, holding my breath, slid over the edge into the still water below.

Silent, icy green engulfed me. I swam under the overhanging rock into the deep shade and found myself in a shallow cave, chest deep in water, the rocky roof close to my head. Even then I was not much afraid, for I thought that they would ride on, following the river as it turned northward. Shivering with cold, I waited.

The pounding in the earth slowed, and there were sounds of iron-shod hooves striking stones. From above came the snorting of horses, and men's voices. I heard the crunch of boots on stones as the riders dismounted. Their voices rang across the water, echoing back from the cliff on the far side of the ravine. A little way to my right, hands reached down from overhanging stones, to drink as I had done. Some held strange water flasks made of metal, which they filled. Farther along, where the river widened into stony shallows, horses dipped their heads and drank.

Clearly I heard the men's words. They were not Igaal hunters but soldiers from the stone city. I recognized many of their words, for their language was my father's, and my mother had taught it to me. Then I heard the word *Shinali* and knew they spoke of my people. And then I was afraid, a high lot afraid. I still remember their words, for that day, every hour of it, is carved deep into my knowing. Some of their words I did not fully understand, but here record all that I understood or guessed was their meaning.

"They won't be around here," one of the soldiers said. "If they were, they'd have been found by now. They'll be a hundred miles away, up north by the marshlands, I reckon."

"We should have killed them years ago, when we had them locked in Taroth Fort," another said. "Or we should have kept them all as slaves. Then we wouldn't be off on raids like this, to get slaves from the Igaal instead."

"What I can't understand," said someone, "is why the Emperor Jaganath, with all his powers, can't find the Shinali."

"Maybe you could ask him why, sometime," said someone else, and laughed. "If you dare. Personally, I'd rather confront a pit full of vipers."

"Maybe the Emperor's not the only one with powers," said a different voice, bright to my mind. "Maybe someone's protecting the Shinali. Years ago, before the Citadel came under Jaganath's control, some of the old masters there used to have great powers. I remember my father talking about it. The old masters disappeared when Jaganath took over, and everyone said they were murdered, but I think—"

"If you fought as wildly as you dream, boy, you could go and fetch the Igaal slaves all by yourself," another said, and they laughed.

"It is nothing to laugh about, this work we have to do today," said a different voice, older, gruff, and weary. "There's no glory in putting helpless women and children to the sword—nor much victory in carrying off a few terrified slaves. When I first joined the army we were proud, as soldiers. I'm not proud now of what I do. And I don't wish to hear jokes about it."

"That's mighty close to treason, Boaz, my friend," someone warned.

"It's not treason to wish for the betterment of our Empire," replied the one called Boaz . "Nor is it treason to wish for the end of a reign of fear."

They were silent then for a while, and I could hear only the talk of men farther downriver.

Then a different voice, quite close, asked, "Are we coming back this way, after the Igaal raid?" The speaker sounded young for a soldier, and his voice shook. I wondered if he was afraid.

"No, lad," said someone else. "We're only going this way so they won't see us approach. When we leave with the new slaves we'll stick to the middle of the plains, where there are no hiding places if they try to escape."

"Does this water have to last till we're home again?"

"According to the scouts' report, there's a river by the Igaal camp. Don't worry, boy. You won't die of thirst."

"It's the Igaal arrows you need to worry about, not water," said another, and there was laughter again.

All along the riverbank toward the plain, horses and men drank, their dark outlines confused against the dazzling light. Through the voices I heard the jingle of harnesses and the stamping of hooves. I watched and listened and waited, quivering with cold and fear, and praying to the All-father that they would soon depart. Then I heard boots on the rock directly above. The soldier stood very still for a while, and I heard him sigh deeply. I heard something drop and slide on the rock, and he said a word

8

I did not know. A water flask flashed downward just in front of me, plopped into the pool, and sank.

I heard him walk up to where the rock was flat. There were scuffles and sounds of metal grating on stone, and I supposed he was unbuckling his sword and taking off his heavy armor and clothes. There were comments and jokes as his friends cheered him on. Someone warned, "Don't dive, Embry; there might be hidden rocks."

In the dimness below, I prepared to hide underwater. I heard the man sliding on the rock, saw his bare feet, then his white legs as he lowered himself, yelping at the cold, into the pool; then I sank down, down, my breath locked, my long hair wound tight about my free hand so it would not betray me.

Opening my eyes, I looked through the emerald silence and saw a naked form, pale as a filleted fish, flashing in clouds of bubbles. Several times he dived, sometimes frighteningly close, and it seemed an age before he found his flask. I waited, ago-nized, hungering for air. Suddenly, unable to wait any longer, I shot upward, gasping. When I opened my eyes the man was still in the water, laughing and yelling, waving his flask above his head. Then he saw me.

Shock showed in his face. He swam slowly, looking at me, frowning as if puzzled. I stared back, perfectly still but for my right hand sliding down to the knife in my belt. In those few heart-beats I saw that he was a little more than thirty summers old, his face and forearms burned red by the sun, his shoulders pale. He was beardless, with a long crooked scar on his chin. His eyes were green; his wet hair, almost shoulder length, was light as straw. He was the first Navoran I had seen up close, and I wondered if my father had looked like him.

Above, someone yelled, "Come on, Embry! We're going."

A heartbeat more he looked at me; then, to my astonishment, he smiled. Not a fleeting smile, but a wide, warm smile, as if he suddenly recognized an old friend and was glad.

"Coming!" he yelled, looking up at his companions again. Without a backward glance he swam along to the shallows where the horses had been drinking, and clambered ashore.

I listened, trembling like a rabbit before the blade falls. I heard the man's bare feet slapping on the rock as he ran back to his belongings. Then I heard boots on the rock, and the soldier thanked someone as they helped him strap on his armor. I strained to hear. But he said nothing else; nothing about me. There were sounds of men mounting their horses, and more commands. Then there were the sharp sounds of horses crossing stones. For a short time the ground throbbed with their going; then all was quiet.

Still I waited in the water, my hand clenched about the bone handle of my knife. At last, stiff with cold and with teeth chattering, I pulled myself out of the water and looked across rocks and the wide grasslands to the east. Across the brown plain a dark smudge marked the battalion, already vanishing in dust and heat.

I watched until it disappeared, then, with shaking hands, I spread the gathering-bag on a flat rock and pressed the water out of it, hoping the herbs within were not ruined. Putting it over my shoulder, I began to walk home. I walked quickly, running at times on the hot stones, avoiding the soft dust in between where footprints could be tracked. Yet despite my caution, there was a peace in me, for I remembered the soldier's face, and how the light about him had shown no hate, but only a brief joyfulness I could not understand.

It was afternoon's middle when I came to the place where the ravine widened suddenly into the green valley, and I saw my home. Children played outside the tents, and in the river beside the dwellings the young men swam naked, wrestling one another, laughing. Smoke rose from the smoke-holes in the tents, carrying the fragrance of bread-cakes. Beyond the dwellings rose the mighty peaks of the Napangardi Mountains, brown and desolate in the summer's heat. A group of men approached the tents from the foothills, carrying bows and spears, and bearing the carcasses of three deer.

Walking quickly, I passed the place where the boys played in the river, and they called my name and shouted things about working up a good hunger for the feast. Hurrying past the first tents, I entered the largest home in the center of the camp, the dwelling I shared with my mother, the clan's holy man, and the chieftain and his family.

It was dim inside, but I could see, around the shadowy edges of the tent, the elders and smallest children sleeping through the afternoon heat. Several women were gathered on the far side of the hearth, their heads bent over a garment, their fingers busy with bone needles and fine leather thread. They did not see me but went on with their work, laughing and talking quietly. I knew the dress they were finishing was for me, for the celebration tonight.

My mother, too, was there by the central fire, sharpening some healing-knives. A sunbeam fell on her from the smoke-hole above, lighting her with smoky gold and shining on her smooth braided hair. Her face was beautiful, and there was strength in it, for she had endured much. But there was always a sadness in her eyes, even when she laughed. She did not hear me approach, but went on sharpening the knives. Deadly those blades were, if in the wrong hands; but I had seen her cut out tumors with them, slice away festered flesh, and take out babes who could not be born—and all those she cut felt no pain, and afterward they were healed and made whole. It was my dream that one day my skills would equal hers.

I put my gathering-bag on the hearth, and she looked up, startled.

"Avala! You should not be in here! Outside! Quick!" Laughing, she jumped to her feet and tried to usher me outside. "You know the custom!" she said. "We're preparing gifts in here, and your new dress! And what are you doing, out gathering? You should be resting, enjoying yourself, thinking on the great thing that we celebrate, tonight."

"I have something to tell—" I began, but she pushed me along the riverbank, toward a place where my friends were sitting, talking.

"My love, this is a rare day!" she said. "Your birth, above all others, is celebrated. Enjoy the day. Spend it with your friends."

"I saw soldiers today," I said, and she stopped, the laughter fading from her face.

"I saw soldiers, Mother. And one of them saw me."

The color drained from her cheeks. "Tell me," she said.

So I told of the day's happenings, and all the time I felt her fear rise. When I had finished she said, "Yeshi must be told this straightaway. Oh, Avala! What a thing to happen on this day!"

"I feel that we're in no danger, Mother," I said, but she called to the boys in the river.

"Tell the chieftain we have a thing he needs to know!" she called. "Tell him to come quickly!" Then she turned to me, and there were tears in her eyes. "I had been so glad, this day," she said. "But now I'm thinking we'll have to gather all our belongings together and leave, tonight, lest the soldiers come back. Your feast may have to be another time. Come, we'll meet with Yeshi on the grasslands. It's better that only he knows, at first, and after he can decide whether to call a meeting of us all."

She took my hand and we walked together toward the hunters. Always I had seen my mother's hand steady and strong, but now her fingers trembled, and she was cold in spite of the summer heat.

2

I have no wish to see what Jaganath will do to this Empire I have loved; neither can I bear to think of its future collapse. However, I believe that when the eagle returns in full strength, it will bring not destruction, but a cleansing, and the restoration of what was best.

I also believe you are the voice, the cry, that calls the eagle and begins the reformation. Your last words to me were that the weed had entangled us both; I prefer to think that you and I are in the wind that blows across the field of wheat; that we fly freely above the storm and, in spite of the chaos, play out our destined parts in the fulfillment of a great and splendid prophecy.

—Excerpt of a letter from the Empress Petra to Gabriel, during the Shinali internment in Taroth Fort

"I'm thinking we don't have to worry, Mother," I said as we walked toward our chieftain. "The soldier, he was not full of hate. I'm not afraid of what happened. We're all still safe."

"I trust your words, Avala, but this is for Yeshi to decide," she said.

Already the boys were nearing the hunters. We saw them speak to Yeshi. Then they ran back to the river, and the chieftain hurried on to us, ahead of the hunters.

Yeshi was not a tall man, nor imposing as people said his brother Tarkwan had been, but he was strong and unafraid, and he held our people's welfare above all else in his heart. Like all Shinali men, he wore his hair long, decorated with leaves and beads of bone. About his neck was the sacred bone *torne*, sign that he was chieftain. It had been worn by Tarkwan before him, and by their father before that, and by all the chieftains in time gone.

He reached us, and my mother said, "Avala has a thing to tell you, Yeshi. It is a high lot important."

Again I gave an account of the day. When I had finished speaking, Yeshi asked, "Are you certain you were not followed home, Avala?"

"I am very sure," I said. "I'm thinking there's no reason to be alarmed. The soldier I saw had no hate in him. They all went on their way, far east to the Igaal lands, to capture slaves. We are in no danger. I have it in my knowing."

"How could you tell that the soldier had no hate?" he asked. "Could you see into his heart?"

I said, hesitantly, "This is a hard thing for me to explain, Yeshi. The soldier who saw me, he looked surprised, but he smiled, and it was as if he knew me. His soul-colors, they were blue and green, and those are colors of peace. There was only goodness in him. He would not betray me. Or any of us."

A long time Yeshi looked at me, weighing my words. I had not talked openly before of this gift of special knowing that I had. My mother was aware of it, and my grandmother, but no one else.

"Ashila, what is your word on this matter?" Yeshi asked. "Did you know your daughter could see soul-colors?"

"Avala has had this gift of Seeing since she was small," my mother replied. "Gabriel had the gift, and so do I, in a smaller way. In our daughter the gift is strong."

Again Yeshi was thoughtful for a long time. At last he said to me, "I'm thinking that what you say is true, Avala, and not only because you have the gift of Sight. I believe you because I have it in my own knowing that all soldiers are not against us. When we were prisoners in Taroth Fort, some of the Navoran soldiers were kind to us, for they were not at ease having to keep us in that place. One man, especially, was kind. He became a good friend to Gabriel. His name was Embry. Perhaps there are still soldiers who think of us with favor."

At the soldier's name, my heart leaped. "Embry?" I said. "That was the name of the soldier I saw! Embry! Two times they said his name."

My mother touched my arm. "This soldier's face," she said to me, "what was it like?"

"Halfway to being old," I told her. "He had no beard. His eyes were green like willow leaves. His hair, it was pale like the desert sand. He had—"

"A scar on his chin, here?" said my mother, smiling, tracing a zigzag mark across her own skin.

"Yes!"

She bent her face in her hands, and I knew that she walked in the old days, kept and treasured in her knowing. At last she said, wiping her eyes, "Surely the All-father's hand is covering this day! Embry, of all men, will not betray us. He and Gabriel, they both did things to win our freedom—things that were a high lot brave."

"I remember those things," said Yeshi. "It is true, Embry will not betray us. I'm thinking we will stay here, so long as we see no more soldiers. Thank you, Avala. I will speak with the elders of this, and with our priest. Meanwhile, we will hold the feast in honor of your borning-day, and welcome you as a new woman

to our tribe, and we shall not worry about this day's happenings." He smiled and placed his hand on my head, as he often
had when I was a child.

There was comfort in his touch, as well as strength, for I
loved Yeshi a high lot. As he looked at me, I remembered childhood days when he had taken all of us children out onto a plain,
and given us little bows and arrows he had himself made, and
taught us to shoot. At other times he had told us stories of our
past, of the land and the life we had lost. It was Yeshi who told
us of the eagle, symbol of our people; and how one day we would,
like the eagle, rise up in power and be a great nation again. Always,
he had cared for the warrior-spirit in us.

"You're a special daughter to us, Avala," he said.

He drew me to him and embraced me, and I felt the hard
shape of the bone *torne*, the amulet he wore. I remembered Yeshi
showing me the *torne* when I was a child, telling me that the
carving on the bone was the face of the man who would do a
great thing for our people, and start us on the journey to being
a great nation again. I still remembered his words. "It's the face
of your father, Avala," he had said. "Before we even saw his face,
we knew him, for he was in our prophecies. Yet we did not realize, when he was among us, who he was; we only knew it later,
when we found out what he had done for us, for our freedom.
Now his life is legend, and we keep him in our knowing, as hero
and brother and friend."

As Yeshi drew away now, I glimpsed the carving again, the
profile of the man's face, strong and fierce and far-seeing, his
long hair blended with the wings of an eagle in flight.

* * *

17

As night fell all the people gathered about the chieftain's tent, and the ceremonies for me began.

My mother and some of the women elders came and took me down to the river. There in the darkness I stripped off my clothes and bathed while the women chanted Shinali prayers. The washing was sacred, signifying the setting aside of childhood. When I came out of the water my body was dried and anointed with oils from wildflowers, and my mother put the new dress on me. Beautiful that dress was, made of fine strips of white leather, and in the bright moonlight I saw that it was painted with eagles and stars and the curving, interweaving symbol that was our sign for dreams. New shoes were put upon my feet, and they, too, were made of white leather and painted with stars.

As the new clothes were put on me, my mother said, "Beloved daughter, we put on you the garment of womanhood. May your ways be peace, may you nurture and guard those weaker than yourself, love those who are kin and those who are strangers, and live in gratitude for all things."

Then my long hair was combed, and thin portions plaited down the sides and decorated with carved bone beads. A hard time they had, plaiting my hair, for it was unruly and curling, as my mother said my father's had been. I thought of him many times that night, and wished he were there. Then I would see my mother's face, shining and full of love and pride, but still with that sadness in her eyes, and I knew that she also was thinking of him.

When they had finished dressing me, we all turned and faced the tribe, waiting in the firelight by the tents. Two people came to us across the dark grass. My grandmother came bearing a small lamp, symbol of wisdom's light, and with her was our priest, Zalidas. I had always been a little afraid of him; I felt that he expected me to do great things for my people, as my father had done, and his unspoken hopes were a heaviness on me. Yet with all the tribe, I honored him, for he had held my people together through sixty long summers, through battles and betrayals, sicknesses and near destruction, through captivity and escape; and his songs kept our dreams alive.

He was here now to paint my face with holy symbols, and he held a little tray bearing the things he needed. He stopped in front of me, and my grandmother held the lamp high, saying, "May wisdom light all your words, Avala, and all your ways." She smiled, and I felt a great love from her.

Then she moved the lamp close, so the priest could see to paint my face. Before he began he prayed to the All-father to guide his hand. While he prayed the night wind tore at the little flame, and made strange lights dance across the priest's bone necklaces, and on the sacred paintings on his robes. Then he began to paint my face with a piece of antler dipped in colored clays mixed with fish oil. My heart beat fast as he painted the images, and all the women behind me chanted quiet prayers, for what he painted was meaningful, like a prophecy for my life.

It was strange to be so close to Zalidas, and I could hear him breathing as he painted, and see yellow flecks in his heavy-lidded eyes. He was shaking a little, for he was very old and frail, and often in pain. Red he used, on one side of my face, and blue on the other. On my brow he painted something in black, then in

19

white. When he had finished he said a traditional blessing-prayer over me, and gave me a flat piece of polished silver, a little bigger than my palm, so I could see what he had done.

On one cheek pranced a red horse, and on the other a blue eagle flew. On my brow, painted in black, was a sword crossed with an arrow, and about the weapons was a circle in white. Signs of war. Strange signs for a healer, I thought, and looked at the rest of my face. Between the gleaming marks of paint, like two pieces of summer sky, were my blue Navoran eyes. Always they startled me, when I saw them, for they were a high lot strange against my brown skin, though my skin was light for a Shinali. I saw my straight eyebrows, almost meeting above the high bridge of my nose. My nose, too, was from my father, strong and beaklike. My image looked mysterious, fierce with the painted signs of war. I was not sure I liked my face, and I certainly did not like what Zalidas had done.

As he took the mirror from me, he said, "The horse is the sign of the Navoran Empire, Avala, for Navoran blood runs in your veins; the eagle is sign of the Shinali blood in you; and the Navoran sword crossed with the Shinali arrow are signs of the day when you will fight for our lost lands. But outside the arrow and the sword is a circle, sign of unity and the fullness of time, for in you, in your mixed blood, the arrow and the sword are also met in peace."

He blessed me, then my grandmother took my left hand, and my mother took my right hand, and they led me over to the people. Yeshi was waiting for me at the entrance to his tent. One side of it had been raised on poles, and mats were put outside on the grass. The feasting-fires were not far off, and the fragrant smoke drifted across us, and the flame light glimmered on the people on the edges of the gathering. Though so many people were crowded there, the silence was complete. Over their heads, beyond the mountains, a round moon rose.

Yeshi held out both his hands, and mine were placed in his. To my surprise, my chieftain was near tears, and he did not speak the usual words of welcome for a new woman.

"This is a high night for me, Avala—for all my tribe. It has been a gift for us, great beyond telling, to have had among us the child of Gabriel. And it is a new gift, to have a woman among us, now, who has his blood in her veins."

He kissed my brow, and the bone *torne* swung between us, golden in the lamplight, its shadow black across his robe. My heart thumped painfully, and I thought how it was always like this—the image of my father golden, shining, almost holy, and myself lost somewhere in the shadow of him. I loved my father dearly, and I loved Yeshi, but I wished that tonight I would be seen for myself, just as Avala, new Shinali woman.

He smiled and began the formal greeting. "I welcome you, Avala, to your old home, to the tent you have always shared with us. You walked out of here a child. You walk in here a woman. I welcome you with honor and with love."

Then my grandmother gave me the lamp, and I took off my shoes and went into the tent. The feasting-mats had been laid out, and the lamps upon them shone on clay bowls of leaf salads and boiled fish, and hollowed gourds of water. The meat would be brought in later, but before we ate there was to be the giving of the gifts. I sat at the far end of the mat, and people came in. My mother was the first.

She sat in front of me and placed into my arms a rolled sheep-skin garment. It was very old and worn. I shook it out and saw that the smooth side of the sheepskin, the outside of the tunic, was painted with canoes in a river.

"Long years I have kept it for you," my mother said, and her eyes were moist. "It was made on our own land before the days of the Wandering, when we had sheep. The paintings, they're not good. The artist was in a hurry. He had been canoe racing in the river with Tarkwan, and their canoe had won. After, the children and young people wanted him to paint canoes on their clothes, for he was their hero. He was hurrying to finish, so he could walk on the Shinali lands with me. It was the first day I saw his face."

The words fell softly on my heart, as beautiful as first snow, and I asked, "My father, he did the paintings?"

My mother nodded. Taking the garment, she turned it over and touched some strange signs I did not understand. "The first letters of his names," she said. "Gabriel Eshban Vala."

For a while I could not speak, for tears. At last I said, "I thank you, with *sharleema*, for giving me what my father's hand has touched."

My grandmother waited behind her, at the head of the whole tribe in a line, so my mother moved aside. My grandmother's gift was a set of healing-knives, with bone needles for sewing up wounds. I recognized the knives my mother had been honing that afternoon. "My hands are not steady anymore, for using these," Grandmother said. "But with them I taught your mother to heal, and she is teaching you. Look after them well, for they mean healing and life."

Many gifts there were, some of them treasures people had

saved all the years of the Wandering. I felt overwhelmed, marveling that they thought so much of me. The final gift was from Yeshi, and always it was the same, in these rituals: he told of the history of our people.

He was sitting on the edge of his sleeping place, the most important place in our tent, and everyone was sitting before him. Behind him, fixed to a screen of flax woven over wood, hung our tribe's most valued possessions: the war drums and spears of the old warriors; and suspended above them, steel bright and shining like gold in the firelight, was a fine Navoran sword. A great treasure it was, for it had been left to us by my father. And under the sword, wrapped in leather for safekeeping, was a precious Navoran letter.

Smiling, Yeshi called me to sit beside him. Everyone became very quiet, even the children, and Yeshi began his story. As if to me alone he told it, though I had heard the story more times than I could count, and all the tribe knew every word, for the story was always exactly the same, so we all would hold it in our knowing. And this is what he told.

> *"In the beginning, when the first winds blew across the earth, and the leaves unfurled on the first trees, and the father of all deer grazed the plains, and the first eagles flew, the All-father made us for this land. We increased, walked strong upon the earth, and were at peace with all things. A mighty nation we became. Our lands spread from the sea in the west to the sea in the south, and, in the east, to the great range of the Napangardi Mountains. In the north our lands were bordered by lakes and the long river that runs from the*

mountains to the sea. We called ourselves the Shinali, and wished only to live on the land, fishing and hunting and keeping sheep. But in the far north and east were deserts and marshes, territories of the Igaal and the Hena, and they fought us many times for our pleasant lands.

"Then, two hundred summers gone, a new tribe came to our shores, a tribe with pale skin and hair like wheat and eyes the color of the sea. In big boats they came, with sails like the wings of giant seabirds. The Shinali tribes who lived by the sea became friends with them, and traded with the newcomers, and gave them the white shining pearls from the shells in the sea. But the newcomers desired those pearls above all else, and soon they fought the Shinali for them, and sank the Shinali fishing boats, and drove the shore people far inland, and built their own stone city beside the sea. They called the city Navora.

"More Navorans came, and the stone city grew, and other cities were built along the coast. The stone city became the center of a great Empire, and the Navorans grew in numbers and in might. Then they wanted more land for crops and for their herds, so they fought us for our inland places. We fought and lost many battles, and over the course of summers and lifetimes all our lands were stolen from us— all but one small plain, between the mountains and the city made of stone.

"In that hard time we were given a prophecy, a promise from the All-father that a day will come when we will join with those ancient tribes who once were enemies, with the tribes of the Igaal and the Hena; and we will rise up together to fight the Navoran conquerors, whose Empire is great and whose army is yet unbeaten. And our people then will win back their stolen lands, and take up again the life they lost. The time foretold, the time of final battle and of victory, is called the Time of the Eagle.

"But while we lived in hope on that small plain, the last of our own land, the Igaal and the Hena came down again from the north, and on one side we fought them, and on the other side we fought the Navorans. Even the Navorans were afraid of the Hena and the Igaal, for they came in multitudes that could not be counted. So the people from the stone city built a fort in the place in the mountains where the northerners came through, and they made it strong with their army, and guarded the pass. Taroth Fort it was called, and we lived in its shadow. And our chieftain in those days was Oboth, father of Tarkwan and Yeshi.

"But the Time of the Eagle seemed yet a long way off, and we were a small nation trapped between two mighty foes, so it seemed to us a wise thing to make a treaty with the Navorans, since they guarded the pass that kept us from our northern foes. The Navorans made that treaty with us, and said we could keep our last little plain for all time. So for many summers there was peace.

"In that peace-time the Navorans were ruled by the Empress Petra, and she kept the treaty strong. But the stone city needed land for growing food, so we sold a little of our plain, and Navorans made their farms there, and lived by us in peace. But still we hoped for the Eagle's Time; and while we hoped there came a man to us, beautiful of face *and heart, from the city of stone. His name was Gabriel Eshban Vala.*

"Gabriel dreamed Shinali dreams, and honored our ways, and loved a woman among us, called Ashila. He knew of our prophecy, for his wise ones had told him of it. For in this man's time, in the stone city, there was much that was wrong, and an evil man, called Jaganath, was rising up in power. And this Gabriel who came to us, who was healer of bodies and minds and hearts, he, too, hoped for the Eagle's Time, for it would mean the end of the wrong in his Empire.

"But the evil spread fast. Oboth died, and Tarkwan became chieftain, and in his days the treaty was broken, and Navoran soldiers marched upon our land, and we were forced to fight for what was ours. And because we fought, our last plain was taken from us, and we were made prisoners in Taroth Fort. Gabriel was with us, and he and Ashila, they healed our battle-hurts, which were many and deep. But Tarkwan they could not heal, not his battle wounds or his broken heart, and he died. And in our time in Taroth Fort, when our children died of hunger and thirst and illness made us weak, the evil man from Navora, Jaganath, had it in his mind to kill us all. But the Empress Petra wanted us to live, so she fought Jaganath, and we were caught in the middle of their terrible fight. Gabriel, too, was caught, but his heart, and the heart of Empress Petra, they were close. And while we were in Taroth Fort, Gabriel called upon the Empress to help, and she sent him a letter, and that letter gave us freedom.

"But on that day of our liberation, Gabriel was summoned to the city of stone. He had done a secret thing beyond our knowing, and traded for our freedom with his life. We did not know, when we set out on our journey to far lands and to hope, that we would not see his face again; but after two full moons we knew, and mourned for him. And we mourned another thing: the joy went out of our freedom, for we realized that the new Emperor in the stone city was Jaganath, and he was pursuing us, for he feared the Time of the Eagle. And so began the Wandering.

"But with every rising of the sun the ancient prophecy burns anew in our hearts; and with every rising of the moon we dream of our lost land. For the land is our life, our hearts' home, our place of belonging. In it lies our freedom and our peace. So we wait for the day of our return. We wait for the Eagle's Time."

With the end of the story, the formal part of the night was over.

The roasted meat was brought in, and we were ready to feast. Zalidas spoke a blessing over the food and over us, and then, for the only time in my life, I was allowed to fill my bowl first, before the chieftain.

I don't remember that we ever had such a feast before, except for Yeshi's wedding night when I was four summers old. We ate until we could eat no more, then the musicians played and we danced to the pipes and drums while the elders clapped in time to the music's beat. We worked up a high lot of excitement with our leaping and whirling, and the drums echoed back like heartbeats from the mountains. When we were all worn out the musicians put their instruments away, and it was time for the priest's final blessing on me.

He was standing where Yeshi and I had sat for the story, with my father's sword above him. I stood before him, with the whole tribe gathered behind me, pressed close. There were only us two standing, the priest and I, for his blessing was like a foretelling for my life, and was for my ears alone. But as I waited a fear went over me that he would say things too heavy for me to bear. With all my being I was aware of my father's sword, of the letter from the Empress Petra, of the vast, wondrous heritage my father had given me, and I hoped I could be worthy of it.

Zalidas began with the traditional blessing, and I bent my head, my eyes closed. I felt the weight of the priest's hands on my hair. I felt, too, the pain in him, his great weariness. "All-father, put your hand on this daughter's life," he said. "Keep her in your love, in the knowledge of you and all your ways."

He hesitated, and I waited for his whispered personal blessing. But he lifted his hands from my head, and I glanced up. He had stepped back and was clutching his chest, his eyes rolled upward. I thought he was ill. Beside us, Yeshi leaped to his feet. Suddenly Zalidas began chanting. A strange chant it was, low and haunting and powerful, such as he used in trances when he moved in other realms and saw into the deep mysteries of things. He was reciting an ancient prayer, talking to those long departed from this world.

Spellbound, afraid, I watched him. I saw a white light about his head, and a shifting in the shadows all around. A look of rapture came over him. He seemed to grow, to shine, to gather about himself powers and presences that blessed and uplifted him, until he seemed strong and potent, and the years fell off him; and there was no pain, only a great glory and a communion with things otherworldly and high. All this I understood in my heart, and the hairs rose on the back of my neck. I wanted to flee, but the priest's hand shot out and gripped my wrist. At the same time his chant became a song. He sang of war and of peace, of fields of fire, and the shadow of a mighty eagle's wings.

As his voice died away there was a profound quietness in the tent, except that some of the old ones sobbed. I was trembling, for he still held my wrist, and I could feel the power in him. I thought he had finished, but he suddenly cried out in a loud voice: "Gabriel, our beloved son, began the Eagle's Time, but his daughter, she shall finish it! He bought our freedom, but she shall bind us together with the tribes of the Hena and the Igaal, those who once were enemies, and she shall unite us into a great army that shall win us back our land! This day the Eagle begins its flight! This day its rise begins! This day, with this daughter, blood of the new and blood of the old, child of love out of nations that hate, child of war and child of peace, Daughter of the Oneness, blessed cord that binds."

And he gripped my hand more tightly still until I cried out with pain. Then, suddenly, he relaxed his hold. His eyes closed, and the light about him seemed to diminish. All of him seemed to shrink, to become again a frail old man.

I helped him to sit down, and he smiled fondly, as a grandfather might, and thanked me. Then he said, quietly and calmly, "This day it begins, the Oneness. I bless you, daughter. I bless you, for through you it comes."

I knew his words were meant as a blessing, but I felt the awful weight of them, and was afraid. Also—though I am ashamed, now, to speak of it—I doubted in my heart that Zalidas was right. Then my mother led me away, out to the river where I could be at peace. She kissed my cheek, and left me there alone.

30

For the rest of the night I sat looking at the river and the eastern mountains until the sun came up and set the peaks aflame. It flooded the valley with fire, and turned the waters of the river scarlet like blood. Then I thought on how my father had died to carry out his destiny, and I shook with fear lest Zalidas had been right, and I was to be a child of war; and that my way, like my father's, would lead to suffering.

As the sun rose, my mother came out and sat by me on the grass. Behind us, the camp was awake. We could hear children playing, and people talking. Women came down to the river to collect water in jars and to wash the bowls from last night's feast, but they stayed far from us. The sounds of ordinary life seemed strange, for all had changed for me.

"It is a heavy thing, to learn one's destiny," my mother said.

"I thought I knew what mine was," I replied. "You told me once that our destiny is always to do with what gives us highest joy. I have that joy now, helping you and Grandmother with the healings, making medicines. I want only to be a healer."

"You will be a healer," she said, "if you heal the hearts of our enemies, and help us all to become one. Healing is more than stitching up cuts, my love. And peacemaking, I'm thinking it's the highest kind of healing of all."

"But am I to be a peacemaker?" I asked. "Or am I to go and gather up an army, and march it off to war? I'm not knowing what Zalidas meant. I'm not even sure he said the prophecy over the right person."

"What do you mean, love?" she asked, looking at me, surprised, shading her eyes from the early sun.

"Did he speak the prophecy over me, over Avala, healer and new woman?" I asked. "Or did he speak it over the daughter of Gabriel? Sometimes, Mother, I don't know who I am, who I'm supposed to be. Some of the boys, they say that . . . that it's not fair, the way I'm favored. And I'm thinking that what they say is true. I'm thinking that no one sees me for *me*, for who *I* am. Even Zalidas favors me, and that's why he said those things last night. He said them because I'm Gabriel's daughter. He wasn't being fair. I'm not a warrior. I'm not even a good speech-maker. How will I persuade the Hena and Igaal to fight with us—if that's what I'm supposed to do? I think Zalidas made a mistake."

"If what Zalidas said is true," she said, "you will find the vision in your own heart. You will know your destiny for yourself, not because a priest told it to you. You're confused now, but when the time is right everything will be made clear to you. Meanwhile, hold close to your friends, who love you, and shut your ears to envy. Anyone who is different finds life hard. Your father, he felt alone at times, and some of his people were jealous of him, too. Sometimes he didn't know who he was. He called himself a Navali once, when he didn't know if he was Navoran or Shinali."

We laughed a little together, and I felt comforted. "I suppose I'm a true Navali," I said, "since I'm half Navoran and half Shinali. Yet when I saw the man Embry yesterday, that was the first time I've seen a Navoran close. He was supposed to be my enemy, but he was not. He was my father's friend, a friend to Yeshi, to you, to all of us. Men like him, like my father, have loved our people. Surely there are more like them. All Navorans can't want us dead.

Yet we flee from them like rabbits fleeing from a fox."

"The Navoran with highest power is the Emperor Jaganath," she said. "What he commands is done. And he wants us dead. The prophecy of the Time of the Eagle is not forgotten in Navora, certainly not forgotten by Jaganath. He knows that if the prophecy is fulfilled, he will lose everything. So he wants to wipe out every chance that the Eagle might rise. He wants to wipe out our race."

"And we want to wipe out the Navoran race," I said. "Which one of us is right? Or are we both wrong? Can we not live in peace, side by side?"

"Not all of Navora will be destroyed, in the Eagle's Time," she replied. "The prophecy also speaks of a Navoran remnant that will survive, a group of dwellers near our Shinali land, who will live in peace with us, and make a new way. I believe that Gabriel's mother, your Navoran grandmother, is among those people. The Time of the Eagle is not about destroying the nation that stole our lands, though many of us have lost sight of that; it's about making a new life for all of us. Then, we will all live in peace, side by side. That part of the prophecy is a great comfort to me."

"Are you ever afraid, Mother, that the Emperor Jaganath will find us? That the prophecy *won't* come true?"

"Even great prophecies are not set in stone, but depend on human beings to work them out and fight for them and bring them into being. And human beings are frail. We are all afraid at times. Even your father knew fear."

"Was he afraid of his destiny?"

"Yes, at times he was. Sometimes our destiny is hard, my love, and costs us much. But it is always to do with the things we love most deeply, and there is always joy in it, somewhere. Don't worry about how you will carry out the task ahead; your path will unfold before you, one step at a time. You don't have to search for your destiny; it will find you."

She caressed my cheek, moving her thumb around the painted Navoran horse, and I knew she was thinking how like my father I was. Always there seemed to be two loves in her eyes when she looked at me; she saw my face, and loved it, and she saw another face, behind and beyond, that she loved above all else. Other men in the tribe had wanted her for wife, for she was a high lot beautiful, but she never went to them. She was my father's, then and now.

"May I ask you something, Mother?" I said.

"Anything, love."

"You and my father, why did you never marry? You had time, in Taroth Fort, and Zalidas, he would have blessed it."

She looked away, over the river, her eyes full of sunlight and far things. "We wanted to marry," she said. "But Tarkwan would not give his permission. He said there would be no blessing-rituals until we were free again, that there could be nothing blessed in captivity. And yet your father and I, we were blessed, and we were married in our hearts."

Suddenly someone called to her, and people ran toward us from the tents.

"Ashila! It's Zalidas! He's collapsed!"

Zalidas had a high fever, and although my mother did all she could for him, by morning's middle he still lay unknowing.

34

People walked about quietly, new fears mingling with their wonder at the prophecies spoken last night. Only the children played as usual. I went to sit with my friends on the grass, needing to talk about everyday things, but conversation stopped when I joined them. No one would look at me.

Then one of the girls said, "When will you go, Avala?"

"What do you mean?" I asked.

"When will you go on your long journey to the Hena and the Igaal?"

"I'm not knowing the answer to that," I said. "Maybe not for many summers yet."

One of the youths said, "If Zalidas spoke all those words over me, I'd be wanting to rise up like a warrior, and go this very day."

"I'm not a warrior," I said. "I'm a healer. I don't like fighting."

One of the young men stood up. He was Neshwan, and he had been a small child in Taroth Fort. He remembered that place, and he hated the Navorans a high lot. Across his bare chest was tattooed an eagle in full flight, its talons spread for attack.

"Did you tell Zalidas that?" he asked, with a scornful smile. "Is that why he collapsed? His precious warrior-woman doesn't want to fight?"

His companions laughed. Three companions he had, and they were all hotheads. There was mockery in their laughter, in the way they looked at me. In that moment I realized that it was not only resentment in them, but hate. It shocked me, and I stood up to go, not knowing how to deal with it.

One of the girls, my friend Santoshi, stood with me. She was nearly two summers older than me and had a loyal heart.

"Don't be listening to him, Avala," she said softly. "He's jealous, because he wishes Zalidas's words had been spoken over him."

"I'm not jealous," said Neshwan, overhearing. "Why would I be jealous of someone who's done nothing all her life except sit in the sunshine of her father's honor? You've had an easy life, Avala, with all the old ones falling over themselves to please you, because you were *his*. I'm not speaking against Gabriel; he was a good man, and I remember him like a light in a dark time. But you have done nothing, and they hold you up—"

"Enough, Neshwan!" shouted Santoshi, startling me, for she was usually quiet. "It's not true, what you say! Avala, she's healed us time and time again. She has her father's gifts, and she uses them. What have you ever done, except go off on hunts and killed rabbits and deer? Does that make a warrior of you?"

"You didn't complain, when you ate the meat I got," he replied. "And my hunting bow does make a warrior of me. What will Avala's herbs and poultices do, in the Time of the Eagle? Will she rush about the battlefield with her ferocious bundles of herbs and brave little bandages?"

His friends laughed again, and some of the other boys and girls stood up beside me.

"My father had only his healing power," I said, "and he accomplished great things."

Neshwan snorted, and turned away. "She's not worth arguing with," he said to his friends. "She's hiding behind her father again."

They sauntered off, and some of my friends shouted rude things after them. I turned away and began walking back to the tents. I realized I was weeping and was furious with myself for it.

I wiped my arm across my face and smudged red and blue paint across the sleeve of my new dress.

Santoshi came with me, putting her arm about my shoulders. "He's a snapping wolf cub," she said. "Don't be worrying about him."

"Is it true, Santoshi?" I asked. "Do I hide behind my father? Do people love me just because of him, because of what he did for us?"

"No, of course not!" she cried. "You did not choose your father. We'd love you even if he was a one-eyed hunter who couldn't shoot a stag at two paces."

"You say that because you're my friend," I said.

"Yes, I am your friend. *Your* friend, not your father's friend. I didn't know your father, so I see only you. I see a friend I admire for her healing power, for her gentleness, for her truth which is arrow straight. I see a friend who many times gives her last strength to heal the sick, who is so tired after that she cannot crawl to her own bed. That kind of strength, it's more than the strength it takes to draw a bow."

"But I might be needing bow strength, now," I said. "Zalidas said I have to go and do great things. I have to be a warrior. I can't. I want to be a healer. I wish Zalidas had not said those things last night."

Santoshi put her hands on my shoulders, stopping me. "You say you can't do great things," she said. "I'm thinking that you already do them. As for Zalidas and his heavy sayings . . . Well, there's something I want you to know, that I've not told anyone before. When I had my sixteenth borning-day feast, Zalidas told me I would one day suffer a high lot, but I would grow strong

37

because of it, and I must never lose courage. With all my heart, I wished he hadn't said that. He also said—to cheer me up, I think—that I would marry that little weasel, Taiwo. I didn't see that as a blessing, either."

We laughed, leaning on each other, for she and Taiwo were betrothed now, and a high lot in love.

"Come to the river, and I'll help you wash away that paint," Santoshi said. "The blue eagle and the red horse, they're already meeting on a battlefield, on your face."

I crouched beside Zalidas and felt the waves of pain that came from him. His eyes were closed and he seemed asleep, but he moaned at times, his eyelids moving as if he dreamed. On the other side of him sat my mother, wiping the sweat from his face with a damp cloth. She gave the cloth to me, and placed her hand under his head, on the back of his neck. She became very still, her eyes closed as she sought out, in her inner knowing, the deep pathways of his pain; and from her fingertips she sent a light that eased and revived. It was beautiful, watching her heal. This skill she had taught to me, and it was better than a hundred herbs for pain, for it wiped out all feeling for a time and brought complete freedom from suffering. Many of her ways she had passed on to me, but some of the secret healings, taught to her by my father during the terrible weeks of their imprisonment in Taroth Fort, were still known only to her.

Soon the priest's breathing became slow and deep, and he slept like a child.

"What is wrong with him?" I whispered.

"It's his heart," my mother replied. "It put a big strain on his body last night, when his spirit moved in the realms of the All-father."

People were coming in quietly to rest, for it was the middle of the day, and the sun was intolerable. Even my friends came in this day, to rest alongside the elders and smallest children, and my mother told me to rest, too, since I had been awake all night. So I went to my sleeping place and lay down.

The sleeping places were laid out along the outer floor of the tent, under the walls, and were never walked upon, for they were sacred to us. The most important place was Yeshi's, and we lay in order of rank out from him. Next to him were his wife, and then Zalidas, and then my mother, as healer, and me, with my grand-mother on my other side. But this day Zalidas was by the central hearth, where my mother could wash him easily and give him medicines. Though I was very tired, at first I could not sleep, and lay for a while looking about the tent.

Above the sleeping places the deerskin walls were painted with scenes of my people's life from the days when they owned their own land: images of children fishing in a wide river, flocks of sheep, deer hunters, and a large thatched mound in the earth that had been the tribal underground home. The scenes were painted in detail, lovingly, and I thought on Yeshi's story, and how our ancestral land was our place of belonging, our hearts' home.

I slept, and dreamed of looking after sheep. But in my dream a wolf came, and I had to fight it with my bare hands. But while I wrestled with the wolf, my face came close to its face, and I saw that it had my blue eyes. I woke sweating and shaking. Though everyone else was still asleep, I got up and changed out of my

39

beautiful dress and put on my old one, woven of wool. It was frayed now, and the paintings on it were faded. I went over to my mother, still sitting by Zalidas.

"I'm going to collect the rest of the *eysela* flowers at the far end of the gorge," I said. "They're too precious to leave, and they won't last many days in this heat."

She looked suddenly anxious. "Take care, love," she said. "I know that if ever you have the All-father's protection, it is surely now—but even so, take care."

I got our gathering-bag and made sure I had my small knife in my belt. The tunic my father had painted I put into the bag, for evenings could be cool, even in high summer. At the tent entrance I put on my shoes, and my mother came to say good-bye.

On an impulse, I pressed my hand to my chest, then placed my palm over my mother's heart. "My heart and yours will always be together," I said.

She looked surprised, for it was the age-old Shinali farewell, not used unless the parting was to be long. But she, too, made the farewell, and though she smiled I felt a sudden and sharp sorrow in her.

Then I walked away.

Soon flies the Eagle, swift as fire, gathering in its shadow the might
Of those who once were foes; then in oneness we shall fight,
And the fields of the destroyers shall turn to fire,
Their city be destroyed, and their empire
Shall cease.
And by the ashen fields and city felled spring up two mighty trees,
Roots separate, yet branches held in unity, two nations free,
All wrongs made right, all things restored
And every spear and sword
Laid down in Peace
In the Eagle's Time.

—Song of Zalidas

I t was sunset when I reached the far end of the gorge. Walking
across the churned dust and the prints made earlier by the
soldiers and horses, I thought of the Igaal people, and how they
would now be mourning the battle-slain and those taken in slavery.
I reached the place of the eysela flowers and removed the precious tunic from the gathering-bag and put it on, for already the
air was cool. Then I took my knife from my belt and bent to pick
the remaining flowers. At last I had them all and stood and looked
about me at a world aflame.

To the west the sun quivered red as blood on the brow of the
purple mountains; beside me the river flowed like molten brass;
and in the east the lands burned with fiery light, glorious beyond
words. A great quiet hung upon the earth, a kind of holiness,
and I lifted my eyes and saw an eagle drifting high. And as I

gazed upon the bird and the vast enemy lands all around, I thought of the time to come, the time of the great prophecy. And while I thought on these things my vision changed, and it seemed that the eagle grew and covered all the earth, and fire flew from its pinions and claws, and the skies shook with the thunder of its wings; and I saw the huge armies of Navora and the mighty city crumble and fall like a field of wheat before the fire. I saw, out of the ashes, two trees grow: a tree from our new-won Shinali lands and a tree from the Navoran farmlands nearby; I saw Navorans and Shinali together grow crops and tend the lands, and a new people springing up, the eagle's wings spread wide across them in promise and in peace. And I knew, in those moments, that the words of our priest, Zalidas, had been true: that the Time of the Eagle was at hand, and I would play my part in it. As the vision ended wonder came over me, and I was no longer afraid or tormented by questions. I was sure at last that my part would be revealed, and that when the time came for me to act, everything I needed would be given to me.

Slipping my knife back into its sheath, I lifted my bag higher onto my shoulder, ready to go. The awe of the vision was still strong on me, and peace enfolded me like a cloak. I was about to turn away, to begin the long walk home, when I noticed a ragged shape on the stones ahead, between the river and the plain. I went closer, and saw that it was a man. Very still he was, as still as death, and a cloud of flies hovered over him.

I thought that perhaps it was a soldier fallen from his horse. But as I drew near I saw that he wore no soldier's uniform. He wore leather trousers such as our men wore, and an open coat badly torn. His hair was cut short, and under the dust and sweat on his face, I saw that his brow and nose were tattooed with zigzag marks. The tattoos were the same on both sides of his face, and were strangely beautiful, though the lines were violent and sharp. He was of the Igaal people.

He was on his back, very still, his eyes closed. Tied to his belt was the end of a lion's tail—his trophy, no doubt, from a hunt. But he had paid dear for it, for there were deep cuts down his chest where the beast's claws had sliced through his tunic and his skin, right to the bones of his ribs. The flesh on his left thigh was torn also to the bone. Flies swarmed over his injuries, and I brushed them away and lifted his coat to feel his heart. His skin was very hot, slick with blood and sweat, and his heart beat faintly.

I was still holding up his coat, wondering what first to do to help him, when he shot out his hand and grabbed my wrist. Arrow swift he was, and strong, though I knew his strength would not last long.

"You take an awful liberty, Shinali woman," he said, opening his eyes a slit, and looking at me.

"Not as much liberty as the lion," I replied.

"It paid for it." His voice was rough and guttural and, although his accent was strange to me, I understood his words. I understood another thing, also, as I crouched there, his fingers about my wrist in the same place where, not long before, Zalidas had held me: I suddenly knew how it could be that I was the Daughter of the Oneness, the link between my people and those who were age-old enemies; and it seemed to me then that all my life had been a preparation for this moment, this act of mercy, with this man.

"I'll bring you some water," I said, pulling my wrist free, for already his strength was gone. "Do you have a waterskin I can fill?"

He lifted his right hand, feeling for something behind his belt, and I noticed that in order to do so he had dropped a knife, curved and bloodstained. For the space of two heartbeats I was afraid. Half closing my eyes, I studied the light about him. I saw no violent reds, only a shadow of great grief shot through with pain.

"Lost it," he said, not finding his waterskin. Then he collapsed back, fatigued.

"I shall have to take you to the river," I said.

With care I removed the *eysela* flowers from my bag and spread them out in rows on a long flat stone. I was glad the sun was gone, for in the cool of the evening they would not wither. When the bag was empty I spread it out on the ground beside the man.

"If you can move onto the bag," I said, "I'll drag you to the water."

Groaning, sometimes crying out words I did not know but that I guessed were Igaal curses, he struggled onto the bag. I picked up the handle behind him and began to haul him over the stones. He was a big man, tall and large boned, though there was no fat on him. He helped all he could, though sweat poured into his eyes and down all of him, and I could see that he was on the edge of fainting. After a little while we stopped, both of us breathless, and the man lay flat on his back, a pulse thumping wildly in his throat. I thought he had fainted, but after a time he spoke.

"Horses I've ridden and once, in a time of dire need, a donkey," he said, "but never have I ridden a woman's gathering-bag. I hope my brothers never find out."

I laughed, wiping my arm across my face. "My mother won't be impressed, either," I said. "It's her best bag."

Then I bent and picked up the thick handle again.

By the time we got to the river the man had fainted, and the cuts in his chest were pulsing blood. I soaked the hem of my long dress and wrung it out over his lips. Revived enough to move again, he scrambled on his hands and knees to the water. A long time he leaned over the pebbly shallows, scooping water into his mouth with his hand. Then he washed his face and head, and rolled over onto his back and let the water run over him. The river gurgled on, stained with his blood.

"By the sweet goddess Shimit," he said, laughing, "I've died and gone to paradise."

"You'll die in truth if I don't stop that bleeding," said I. Wading into the stream, I began to haul him ashore. Suddenly he gripped my wrist, and I was alarmed at the force in him.

"Death won't claim me yet," he said, "not before I return home. You'll take me there, Shinali woman."

"I'll take you to my tribe," I said. "Nowhere else."

"To my home," he said. "I saw the soldiers. I have to know what happened to my tribe."

"Let me go," I said. "My people are camped just at the end of the gorge, near the river. It won't take long for me to run there. I'll bring men to come and help you. This I swear. My people—"

"Your people are dogs! Speak no more of them! I know about your people and their weak and foolish ways. I want nothing to do with them. But you—you are here, now. So you will take me. *You.*"

Then I did see the reds of violence about him, and tried to pull free. But he jerked suddenly on my arm, and I fell into the shallows with him. Struggling, I bit and kicked, and he lifted his knife, and I thought he was going to kill me. Then something crashed across my head, and I knew nothing for a time.

Pain pulled me back. I opened my eyes and saw the night sky bright with stars. He had hauled me onto the shore and was lying beside me, leaning up on one elbow watching me. He seemed much revived. There was a tightness about my neck, and I put up my hand and felt a thick leather thong, and realized he had used my belt for a noose and tethered me like an animal. My knife, too, was gone.

I staggered up and tried to run, for I thought he was not strong enough yet to hold me; but he had tied the other end of my tether about his own wrist, and as the cord between us went taut, the noose about my neck tightened and I fell, choking and half strangled, onto my knees. I pulled it away so I could breathe. Then, dizzy and sick, I sat down as far from him as my tether would allow.

"If you want to breathe," he said, getting to his feet, "stay close."

"I did not lie to you," I said, desperate for him to understand. "My people will help you. They want—"

"Your people want our hunting grounds!" he said. "They lost their own lands, now they want ours! Don't try to deceive me,

Shinali woman! Now come."

I stayed where I was, and he pulled on the cord. Choking, I got up and went to him.

"Walk in the river," he said, leaning heavily on me and hopping on his good leg. The smell of him mingled with the ache in my head and the bile in my throat, and I hoped I would not get sick. We went down into the shallows, and I realized he was making sure my people could not track us when they came.

I looked back, thinking of the precious flowers laid upon the rock, and of the gathering-bag abandoned on the stones, stained dark with the man's blood, and of my mother finding them. An awful grief washed over me as we faced the Igaal lands and began our long walk. Then my vision came to me again, and an echo of the old priest's words. I remembered that Zalidas had talked of a blessed cord that binds, though I did not think he meant this leather tethering cord about my neck.

A cold wind moaned across the grasslands, which were silver-blue beneath the moon. I shivered underneath the tunic with my father's canoes, even though I could feel the heat of the man's arm across my shoulders. Heavily he leaned on me, and I could feel his body shaking, hot with poison fever. It was a marvel to me that he could still go on. He was breathing hard, and we had spoken few words. Suddenly he stumbled, almost taking both of us to the ground.

"I'm thinking you should rest now," I said.

He shook his head. Moonlight glimmered on the black stains on his coat, and I knew he was bleeding again. We had crossed the grasslands and were at the foot of the hills on the other side.

As we struggled up the first hill the man swayed, and I thought he would collapse. But he went on, groaning with every move, his eyes closed as he summoned strength. Slowly, slowly, we climbed another hill, then we were among trees. I smelled pine and felt the needles cool and smooth under my thin deerskin shoes.

Again the man stumbled, and this time I helped him ease himself to the ground. He lay on his back in a small hollow between two trees, and in the pitch blackness I could barely see him. But I could hear his groans, his anguished breath. I went as far from him as I could, before the noose about my neck pulled to choke me, and looked through the trees at the low hills. Already the wind, rustling and tossing the long silver grasses, had swept away our footsteps.

I went back to the man and knelt beside him. As my eyes got used to the darkness I saw the shape of him more clearly. He was shivering, though when I held my palm close to his chest I could feel his fever-heat. In the shadows not far from my hand gleamed the bone handle of his knife, the smaller handle of my own beside it, and I wondered if I could remove mine from the sheath without his knowing.

"Your people," he said suddenly, opening his eyes, making me draw back. "They have horses?"

Briefly I thought of lying, decided against it. I shook my head.

"Then we'll stay here till sunrise," he said. "Sleep, Shinali woman."

I lay down as far from him as possible.

"Close," he said. "I'm cold." He pulled on the leash and I moved closer to him, feeling the pressure of his hand on the leather near my throat. In the close atmosphere of our shared hollow, the stink of his blood and stale sweat washed over me in waves, and I almost retched. Also, I could smell the lion's tail still tied to his belt. Though I knew my curiosity might displease him, I asked him why he had been tracking the lion.

He sighed then, and was silent. I felt pain in him and a huge, overwhelming sorrow.

"The lion killed my wife," he said, after a long time. "She went down to the river with the children, carrying water jars. It attacked one of the children, and . . . My wife, she saved the child. Several were injured, but only she died. Six days I tracked the lion, across the plains and in the mountains. It killed my horse one night when I was sleeping in a cave, guarded by fire. I followed it on foot after that, then I killed it."

I said, very low, "My father, he died to save some people, too. We say that such a person is honored in the realms of the All-father, and that the All-father loves them a high lot because their love was more to them than life. You and your wife, you had children?"

"Three," he said. "If they still live." He scarce could speak for pain, and I understood the terrible need that drove him to go home.

I slept and had strange dreams of fiery fields, battles, lions, and a huge eagle overshadowing all. When I woke the sun was creeping through the treetops, flicking down spears of light upon the man still asleep. When I sat up the leash slipped through his fingers onto the ground between us. The other end of the noose was still tied about his wrist, and his knife lay loosely in his hand. Slowly I removed the knife, all the while watching his face. His eyelids did not flicker. In utter quiet I cut the leather thong binding me to him. For a while I crouched there, still holding his knife, torn between the urge to flee and the strange certainty that all this was within the All-father's plan for me. In the end I replaced the handle of the knife across his upturned palm, then sat down near him and removed the remains of the noose from about my neck.

The man moaned in his sleep. In the morning light I saw that his skin was gray. Around the exposed bone on his leg the tissues were swollen and going black, and pus ran freely down to his foot. The wound was covered with dust, and flies were already busy about it, and about the scratches on his chest. Maggots writhed in some of the wounds, and revulsion and pity went through me. He was breathing painfully, fitfully, his skin slick with sweat, and I knew the poison had spread into his blood. I knew I must try to heal him, and do it now.

I lay down again, facing him with my head close to his. He was still on his back, and I lifted my hand and laid it lightly on his brow, feeling the heat of him and the strange raised lines of his tattoos. He did not move. Closing my eyes I shut out all but my knowing of him, of his agony and fever-heat and grief. Slowly, so attuned to him that even my breathing matched his, I overlaid with light the poisonous force that ran through all his wounds. Into his limbs and torso and head I sent the light, and then deeper, into his veins and heart and through all his pain, through his unspeakable weariness and grief and fear, healing him, making him strong again.

50

With sudden violence he moved, rolling across me and pressing something cold against my throat. "What were you doing, Shinali woman?" he hissed.

I could not speak at first. I was confused, crushed by the weight of him, my spirit still wandering in the deep places of healing. Then he asked his question again, and I realized that it was the blade of his knife across my neck. Sweat dripped off his chin onto my face, and I could smell his breath.

I managed to say, "Healing you."

He must have noticed that the noose was no longer around my neck, and that the leather tied about his own wrist had been sliced clean through, for he sat up and leaned back, staring at me in astonishment. Then he laughed and shook his head, and struggled to his feet. Staggering, he went and looked between the trees at the grasslands.

I lay still awhile, disconnecting my forces from his, gathering back my strength. In the kind of healing my mother and I did, we gave a high lot of our soul force to the sick. I suspect, too, that we took some of their pain into ourselves while we healed, in exchange for our wellness, for I often ached after such healing, and felt feverish. This time I felt very weak, and it was a while before I was able to go and stand beside the man. The grasslands remained empty, with no sign of my people come to look for me.

"Your healing," he said, his eyes still on the land, "is it *munakshi?*"

"I'm not knowing that word, *munakshi,*" I replied.

"It means magic," he said. "It means a person who is different from others, or a curse, or a powerful good, or a strange thing past understanding. You, I think, are *munakshi.* Tell me, why didn't you escape when you had the chance?"

"Because without help you will die. You said you made fire. Do you still have flints?"

He felt inside his coat and withdrew a small package. "Yes," he said. "Why?"

"If your foot gets worse it will have to be cut off. The skin all around the wound, it's dying and will die a little more each day until your whole leg is dead. If I can heat my knife, I'll cut away the bad flesh and stop the poison."

"You have a crone's worth of knowing, in that half-ripe head."

"My mother is a healer. She's teaching me."

"Are you a good learner?"

"Wait, and find out," I said.

Smiling to himself, the man put the flints back inside his coat, then placed his arm about my shoulders. "There's a lake in the hills, half a morning's walk away," he said. "We'll drink there and rest, then I'll think about letting you slice off bits of me."

We began walking, and it was pleasant there in the forest shade, though the ground was uneven and walking was very hard for the man. But he was greatly restored after the night's sleep and the healing I had given him, and we walked more quickly than yesterday. I, too, felt refreshed, though I was hungry, and longed for a drink.

"What is your name, Shinali woman?" he asked after we had been walking for a while.

"Avala," I said.

He stopped walking, took his arm from across my shoulders, and faced me.

"I am Ramakoda, eldest son of the Igaal chieftain, Mudiwar,

52

of the Tribe of the Elk," he said. "I swear to you, Avala of the Shinali, that when I have been home, and know what has become of my children, and regained my strength, then I will take you back to your own people."

He made a strange sign toward the sky, then, though it must have pained him, he bent and lifted up a handful of soil. He pressed the soil to his brow, to his lips and heart, then let it trickle onto the ground near his feet. "This I swear," he said, "by Tathra, god of the sun, and Shimit, goddess of the earth."

Then he put his arm about my shoulders again, and we went on.

By the time we reached the lake, Ramakoda was almost past knowing where he was; the poison in his blood was taking hold, and he shook with fever and could barely stand. I lowered him into the shallows and helped him drink, then washed his face and head and splashed water over his dust-caked wounds. Then I dragged him to a shaded place under the trees, where the ground was flat and the grass was clean, and where I could do my healing. Without a word he gave me the packet of flints and my knife, and collapsed. But I could see his eyes open a little, watching me, and I said, "If you wish, I can stop the pain while I cut away the badness."

"More *munakshi*?" he asked.

When I nodded, he added, "I'm not knowing if our priestess would be pleased. But she's not here to curse you. For myself, I don't care. Heart's truth, I'm about finished."

On the stony shore by the lake I made a fire. For binding cloths I cut long strips from my hem and washed them, then spread them on clean stones to dry. I searched under the trees for healing herbs and found a plant I knew. I pounded its long leaves between stones, then put them near the binding cloths. Then I washed my knife in the river and heated the blade in the flames. If hot enough, it would seal the bleeding flesh as I cut, and make the healing clean and quick.

Though he seemed already unaware, I put my hand under his neck, on the top bones of his back, found the ways of his pain, and closed them. Then I got the knife and did my work.

All through the healing he did not wake. I was binding up his leg when he spoke my name, and I looked up to see his eyes wide open and full of alarm.

"Have peace. You will soon be able to move again," I said. "The numbness will go. To stop the pain, I had to stop all your feeling. It will come back soon enough."

"When will you begin the cutting?" he asked.

"I have finished," I said. "I am binding you up, now. When you can sit I'll be able to bind up the cuts on your chest. They too are clean, and have stopped bleeding."

"Finished?" he repeated, not believing me. He tried to lift his head to look down at the wounds but could not yet move. Fear and astonishment flashed across his face.

I went to the lake, came back with my hem wet, and pressed the cloth against his parched lips. "You can drink properly as soon as you're able to move a little, and to swallow," I said. "I'll give you some leaves to chew then, as well, which will help clean out the last of the poison."

"I can feel the ground under my head," he told me, the look of fear giving way to wonder. "I can hear and speak and see, but from the neck down I can't feel, can't move. I'm in a mighty bad position, Shinali woman."

"You would be if there were enemies about," I said, and placed the binding cloths across his chest, to keep flies from the mended wounds. Then I went to wash his knife in the lake. I passed the blade a few times through the fire to cleanse it completely, then returned it to the leather sheath at his side. I burned the few bloodied cloths in the embers, checked the bindings on his leg, and sat down by him to rest, my fingertips pressed lightly into a hollow of his neck to feel the pulsing of his blood. "Already your heart works more easily," I told him, "now that the breeding place of the poison is gone. Time to come, your leg will heal well. You may always have a limp, though."

"I would rather limp on the earth than not move on it at all," he said. "I'm owing you much, Avala. Not just for the healing with the knife, but for the stopping of pain. It's a wondrous way of healing you Shinali have."

"Some of the healing is Navoran," I explained. "My father was Navoran, and a great healer, one of the best in their Empire. My mother, too, is a healer. I am twice blessed."

"A Navoran father!" he said. "That explains the blue eyes. Curious I was, about those. How is it that a Navoran high in honor came to marry a woman of the Shinali?"

"They met when he went onto our Shinali land," I said. "It was in the last season my people lived on their own land, before they were imprisoned in the fort. My father's name was Gabriel. He went on our land one day and met my mother. She was collecting fire sticks. She invited him back to the Shinali house, and into her heart. When my people were prisoners in the fort, for making the Navoran soldiers angry, he was with them. He was like no one else. My mother's face, it still shines when she talks of him, though he died before I was born."

"You're a strange mix, half-breed," he said, with the ghost of a smile, and closed his eyes.

5

The sun was at its height when we staggered out of the forest and I saw a stretch of grassland with a river on the far side. Near the river were dark patches that I knew were the tents of the Igaal camp. A vast camp it was, with many dwellings spread along the riverbank. The sky to the left of the dwellings was black with birds.

Seeing his home, Ramakoda gave a low cry and almost fell. I struggled to hold him upright and felt an awful grief in him. We went on, and with every step my astonishment grew at the size of the Igaal camp. "Your people are a very great nation," I said after a while, afraid and awed.

Ramakoda grunted and shook his head, a smile briefly crossing his face. "Not my nation, Avala," he said. "Just one tribe of it. A small tribe, compared with some."

Although he leaned now on a stout stick as well as on me, his wounds were bleeding freely under their bindings, and he was close to collapse. Suddenly he signaled me to stop, waving his hand toward his home. I noticed four horses approaching us from the camp, three of them bearing riders. We stopped, and I wanted Ramakoda to sit and rest while we waited, but he insisted on standing to greet his people. He moved apart from me a little and leaned only on his stick. I wished his arm was across my shoulders still, for I felt separated and alone, and fear gnawed at me while I waited for my enemies.

At last the horses stopped in front of us, and the three men dismounted. I realized that the fourth horse had been brought for Ramakoda. I studied the men as they greeted him. The oldest of them was gray haired, with a wide necklace of animal teeth. The riders were all fiercely tattooed across their foreheads and down their noses, though the old man's markings were the most elaborate, and in the center of the tattoos on his brow was a symbol of an elk. Each man wore a coat of light leather that reached almost to his knees. The coats were not laced up as our Shinali garments were, but crossed over in the front and held closed with wide belts. Their shoes were of animal skin, very finely stitched. The gray-haired man limped to Ramakoda and placed his hands on his shoulders. He touched his forehead to Ramakoda's in greeting, then drew back a little and looked at him. They both had tears in their eyes.

"You are in time for many funerals, my son," said the old man. "We were attacked by Navoran soldiers, and there was a hard battle. Many were wounded. But in the end the soldiers won, and took a great number of us for slaves." His voice was cracked and broken, and he could barely speak for emotion. Ramakoda just looked at him, and the old father told him that nine and twenty had died in the battle, and he spoke several names. Ramakoda made no response. Then the old man said, "And those taken in captivity are forty and two. They are Chetobuh, Nambur, Olikodi, Tanju—"

Ramakoda gave a low cry, and fell into his father's arms. The other two riders stepped forward, and somehow the three of them got Ramakoda onto a horse. He was still conscious, though he slumped forward over the horse's neck, his breath ragged and agonized. I thought that, in his anguish and grief, he had forgotten me; but he said, "The Shinali woman, she was healer and helper to me. She is *nazdar*."

I had no knowing of the last word he said, but I supposed it had a meaning good for me, since one of the men reached down and hauled me up onto his horse in front of him. I had not been on a horse before, and I leaned forward over the animal's neck and clung to its mane, terribly afraid of falling. Yet we went slowly, for Ramakoda was near to fainting, and his father rode close by him, talking to him to keep him aware.

Then we reached the camp, and the man I was with gripped my arm and swung me down from the horse. Staying close to Ramakoda, I looked at the enemy people who had gathered about us, silent, staring, their tattooed faces streaked with tears. Behind them were tents beyond numbering, stretching for many arrow flights beside the river. Beyond them, out on the level grasslands, were a large herd of goats and many horses. On a flat piece of ground by the riverbank the carrion birds flapped and screamed as they fought over chunks of flesh on the stones. I realized what flesh it was, and horror swept over me.

Ramakoda's father said something to an old woman, and she came and led me away to one of the tents. At the door she told me to remove my shoes, then we went in. It was cool inside, for there was no central fire, and the tent was deserted. I was led across soft carpets to a place near the back wall, where the old woman rolled out bedding for me, and indicated that I was to lie down and rest. She went away, and I sat on the bed and looked about me at the tent walls, at woven hangings strange and wonderful, with jagged patterns that wove about one another, and colors bold like blood and wheat and raven's wings. Carved wooden chests stood about the floor, and there were graceful urns and cross-legged stools with tasseled cushions, iron-wrought lamps, and other pieces of furniture astonishing to me. Astonishing, too, was the size of the tent, for the walls rose straight up and were many sided, and the roof was a separate piece rising to two peaks where the great poles stood. The whole place was wonderful, rich, and colorful beyond anything we Shinali had. A musky fragrance hung about the tent, pleasant but unknown to me.

The old woman came back and gave me a bowl of warm broth. She crouched down by me while I drank it, and we watched each other warily. I saw that she had a tiny tattoo on her brow just above her nose, and wore her hair pulled tightly back and knotted on the back of her head, in a way unfamiliar to me. Her hands were calloused from hard work.

"My name is Avala," I said, attempting friendliness. "I'm a healer."

"So Ramakoda told us," she replied. "Though your people are our enemies, he has it in his mind to ask that you be *nazdar*. So you are safe."

"I'm not knowing the meaning of *nazdar*," I said.

"It means under protection. More than guest, more than friend. If it is agreed to, you will stay in Ramakoda's family tent as kinswoman to him."

"Will you tell me what happened to Ramakoda's three children?" I asked.

"One as good as dead," she said, "and two sons taken in slavery."

Then she went away, leaving me to rest. I lay down, not expecting to sleep, because of the strangeness of my situation and the danger of being deep in enemy territory. Also, it was strong in my knowing that my own people would be searching for me, and that my mother would surely be desperate. I remembered Ramakoda's sacred vow that he would soon take me home, and it was my only comfort. I slept at last and dreamed that I could hear my mother weeping. When I woke the tent was in darkness, and I could hear people sleeping about me. Again I slept.

When next I woke it was day and there were sounds of busyness outside the tent, and I could smell cooking. From the distance came the bleating of goats. I was alone. A clean dress had been put out for me on a cushion at the end of my bed, and on a woven rug nearby stood a large pot of water with some clean cloths for washing. There was also a small metal bowl with some charcoal embers in it, and some pieces of wood that gave off a pungent smoke, not unlike the musky scent that hung about the tent. I did not know what it was for, though it was placed next to the pot of washing water. Everything seemed alien, and I yearned again for home.

All around the tent were many chests or boxes covered with

rugs, and set with pottery lamps filled with oil, but yet unlit. I saw bedding rolled up and placed at one side against the walls, and there were urns filled with water or grain, and boxes carved and inlaid with colored woods, that contained jewelry or knives. Uninterrupted, I examined everything and discovered that most of the large chests contained heavy clothes of many layers padded and lined with fur. There were chests storing boots and horse equipment and extra rugs, and narrow boxes containing Igaal arrows. I discovered that the musky fragrance came from the wooden chests, either from the wood itself, or from spices the Igaal put in their clothes.

As I ran my fingers across the wondrous carvings and beautiful urns and rich rugs, I remembered the tattered flax mats and chipped bowls and buckled iron pots that were all my people had to call their wealth. I remembered Ramakoda's words about his tribe being only one small tribe of many tribes, and for the first time I realized how impoverished my people were, and how pitifully few.

Saddened by the new things in my knowing, I stripped and washed myself all over. I washed my hair, too, and it felt good to be clean again. I dressed in the Igaal garment, a dress long like my own, with wide sleeves to my wrists, but this was made of fine leather and not of wool. It was not painted as our garments were painted, but all around the hem and sleeves a pattern had been cut out with a sharp knife, and it was beautifully done. The pattern in my dress and the patterns in the tattoos I had seen were similar. The dress, too, smelled of the musky odor.

Crossing the floor, I waited awhile before the tent doorway, saying a prayer to the All-father. I needed courage, for it was strong in my knowing that I was alone in enemy territory, though so far I had been treated well. My hand shook as I lifted the tent flap and stepped outside.

Blinking in bright sunlight, I saw that it was about day's middle. Again, the vastness of the Igaal camp astonished me. It was ten times, at least, the size of our entire Shinali nation. Under the trees along the riverbank large mats were spread, and people sat on them, eating a meal. Beyond the tents the birds were gone, the skies and stones silent and empty. Herds of goats roamed, shepherded by children.

There was a shout, and one of the children pointed at me. Then they all were still, looking at me. Everyone stared, and no one smiled. Afraid, I forced myself to look back at them. And in every face it seemed that a tent flap came down, shutting me out. Cold as winter stone their faces were, set hard with years of hate and bitterness and scorn.

Longing for the faces of those who loved me, I was about to flee back into the dark safety of the tent when a man stood up and came toward me. He was Ramakoda, though he was much changed, clean and strong. He limped but did not use a stick. I smiled, glad to see his friendly face, though layers of sorrow were laid across the grief already on him.

Reaching me, he stopped. "Come, Avala," he said with gentleness. "I have a boon to ask my father, on your behalf."

Trembling, I went with him to a long flax mat nearer the river. Over thirty people sat there, and I recognized one of them as the old man who had come to meet us. He was sitting cross-legged, before him a bowl of steaming meat and a plate of torn flat bread. As Ramakoda approached, the old man stood up and faced us. I noticed that he stood with difficulty, relying on a sturdy stick for support.

Ramakoda whispered to me to do as he did, then he went and knelt on the edge of the mat before his father, his forehead to the ground. I thought it strange that a son should kneel to his own father. I knelt beside him, my forehead, too, bent to the earth. Then Ramakoda lifted his head and spoke.

"This woman is Avala of the Shinali," he said. "She has shown me great kindness, and came with me freely to give me help and strength. She healed me, and you have seen the measure of her skill. It is my wish that while here she is protected, and that she stays in our tent as my *nazdar* kinswoman, until the time when I can take her back to her own people. I ask your favor on this."

For a long time we knelt there while all around were silent, waiting for the chieftain's judgment. I realized that this was the formal asking that would decide my fate. My heart thundered as I stared at the long thin legs of the chieftain before us. He wore trousers of leather, carved down the sides in patterns, as my dress was carved. I saw that one of his feet was crooked, an old break in which the bones had never been set aright. Once I lifted my gaze to his face and saw that it was very lined and full of pain, and his short gray hair stuck out about his ears.

At last the chieftain said, "I cannot bless the presence of an enemy in our camp, especially an enemy from the Shinali, whom we despise. But she has my protection, since she gave you aid. She may stay today, but tomorrow she must go."

Ramakoda bent his head, then stood up. I, too, bowed my

head and thanked the chieftain, then Ramakoda took me to sit on the far side of the feasting-mat. He gave me a bowl of meat and told me to help myself to the platters of bread and cress and cooked roots. The food smelled strange to me, and I learned later that meat and vegetables were cooked in pits dug into the earth, covered over with leaves and hot stones.

The meal continued, and people began to talk, though it seemed to me that their conversation was strained, and there was no laughter. There were many other mats spread out along the riverbank, where the air was cool, but I heard no laughter from those groups, either, for all were grieving for loved ones lost to slavery or death. I heard no talk of the ones who were absent; men spoke of a hunt they planned, and of a new canoe they were carving, while the women talked of the clothes they had to make before winter, or the things they wanted to trade from one another, jewelry or clothing or toys for their children. No one spoke to me save Ramakoda.

During the meal I said to him, "I was told about your two sons taken as slaves, Ramakoda. I'm sorry."

"There were many taken," he said. "Every family in the tribe has suffered loss. I swear by Shimit, if I was chieftain here, we'd be going to Navora now to get them back."

"Would your father ever do that?"

"No. He used to be a great warrior, but he's old now, and wants only peace. He pays a high price for this, what he calls peace."

I said nothing, sensing a deep anger in him.

After a while he asked, "Later today, would you sew up my

65

cuts? Our priestess wanted to treat them, but I said I would have you do it, and no other. She warned me of dire consequences, but I shall risk them."

"Of course I'll sew up your cuts," I said. "Tell me, where is your priestess?"

"She's the one beside my father," he said.

Looking across the mat, I saw an old woman rocking slowly back and forth, the air about her filled with the sharp shadows of pain. Both her feet were bound with strips of cloth, deeply stained.

"Her name is Gunateeta," Ramakoda said. "She doesn't do much healing anymore. Last winter she was lost in the snow for several days, and the cold killed her feet. Now she can barely walk. My father wants her to teach one of the women her healing skills, but she is bitter and short-tempered, and no one wants to work with her. Soon we will have no healer."

I looked away from the holy woman to a youth with striking patterns on his coat. He was the only one with painted clothes, and though he had an Igaal tattoo on his brow, he seemed different from the other youths. He was good-looking, with hair curling in heavy ringlets cut shoulder length, and his soul-colors were mauve and blue, the finest hues.

"My youngest brother, Ishtok," said Ramakoda, seeing where I looked. "He is our pledge-son."

"What does that mean?" I asked.

"The Hena are a divided people. Tribe fights tribe, and some of them fight us, while others are friendly. Many summers ago we were attacked by a Hena tribe and had almost lost the battle

when another Hena tribe—enemy to the one that attacked us—
came to our rescue. Afterward, when we had won the battle, the
Hena chieftain who had helped us and our chieftain swore
always to be at peace with each other. As a pledge of friendship,
the Hena chieftain sent one of his sons to live with us for five
years, and Mudiwar sent Ishtok to live with the Hena tribe.
Ishtok came home to us three summers ago."

"Who is the man he talks with?"

"That is my other brother, Chro. Chro fought well in the battle against the Navoran soldiers, so they tell me. My other two
brothers were taken for slaves. The woman next to them is my
sister, Chimaki. Her husband died two summers ago, of fever.
They had no children. She is second mother to my youngest
child."

"I'm not understanding," I said. "What is second mother?"

He explained, "In Igaal clans, every close kinswoman to a
child is considered its mother. Its birth mother is called its first
mother. If—if my youngest child lives, Chimaki will be her
second mother."

He went very still, and grief went through him again, hard
like a sword. It is strange how I felt his feelings, the same way I
felt my mother's or those of other people I loved. I think we were
bound together by fate long before we met, Ramakoda and I. He
said, of his youngest child, "Kimiwe is five summers old. During
the battle she was knocked into a fire. She's dying of the burns,
but death comes slow."

"Where is Kimiwe now?" I asked.

"In the healing tent, with the others wounded in the battle.

The healing tent is Gunateeta's domain, and only she may go in there, for it is full of the spirits she calls upon to help. Gunateeta tells me that Kimiwe is beyond knowing, though she still breathes."

"Many times I've helped my mother heal burns," I said. "My father taught my mother to heal burns the Navoran way."

He looked at me, astonished. "Sewing up cuts I can understand, and giving plants to fight poisons," he said. "But burns . . . Well, they're another matter. You can heal burns, Avala?"

"I'm knowing what to do with burns," I said, "though it's not the healing that is hard but keeping out poisons afterward."

"If you stopped Kimiwe's pain, and tried to do the healing, she would have a chance at life."

"And if I try to heal her and she dies?" I said. "What will you do to me?"

"There would be no blame in you. She is dying anyway, so you cannot make her worse. If you only take away her pain, I would be thankful. I know your healing well, Avala. I'm willing for you to do this thing, if you are willing."

I hesitated, not because of the child, but because of what these people might do to me if I failed, no matter what Ramakoda said.

"I already owe you my own life, Shinali woman," he said. "And you have agreed to do more healing on me. If I ask too much, I am sorry. My daughter is all I have left of my family. She is heart of my heart."

"I'll do my best for her," I said at last, "if your father, and all your people, will swear to let me go in peace, no matter the

68

outcome. I'll not be trapped in a thing that might kill me."

"You were trapped in such a thing the moment you first knelt by me, to help me," he said.

And then I remembered the words of our priest, Zalidas, and the hope I had that first hour with Ramakoda, when the lands about me burned with light and the ancient prophecy hung in the skies as clear as an eagle's wings. I thought that perhaps, in the All-father's knowing, my true work in the Igaal lands lay yet before me, and my healing of Ramakoda was only the beginning.

"I have never been trapped with you, Ramakoda," I said. "But I still would like your father's blessing on anything I do here, among your people."

"Then I'll ask for it," he said, "when the feast is over."

I noticed that some people had not joined in the feast—five people who stood over the mats with the food, waving large fans made of branches. They kept the flies off the food, but I wondered that they themselves never stopped to eat. No one spoke to them, and they were ignored. I asked Ramakoda who they were.

"Slaves," he said, putting down his food bowl and licking his fingers clean. "They eat when we've finished."

"Where did they come from?"

"The Hena. After battles, we keep prisoners for slaves. And we trade for slaves, when we meet with other Igaal tribes."

"Why is there hatred between you and some of the Hena?"

"It's the old conflict—they try to steal our lands, so we fight."

People were beginning to leave, now that the meal was over, and Ramakoda stood up, saying, "I'll go and talk with my father, and do battle with Gunateeta over my daughter. Wish me luck, Shinali woman."

He limped around to the place where his father was. The holy woman was still there, with a few other members of the chieftain's family. Again, Ramakoda knelt before his father. I could not hear what he said, but it made the people turn around and stare at me. The holy woman, standing just behind the old man, pointed at me and said some angry words, but I could not make them out. People who were leaving began to turn back, to find out what was happening. The chieftain raised his hand and said, very loudly so all could hear: "Who will heal your child, Ramakoda? Choose carefully."

Ramakoda replied, "I choose the Shinali woman, Avala, as healer for my child. And as healer for myself, as my cuts need to be sewn up."

The chieftain gave a command, and a girl brought him a bowl of water. In utter quiet he washed his hands then flicked his fingers hard, shaking off the drops. The bowl was taken away, and people stood around in silence, waiting. They all were watching the holy woman. She spat onto the ground and hobbled away.

Ramakoda bowed again to his father, then came back to me. "The healing of my youngest child, it's yours," he said.

"Your holy woman is not pleased about it," I remarked. "Nor your father, I'm thinking."

"He does not like crossing Gunateeta. He needs her to pass on her skills, else we shall be without healer and priestess when she dies. So he tries always to keep the peace with her, and she knows it, and holds a little power over him. It is the only power she has, these days."

"Why does he not command her to teach what she knows?"

"He has, but she said the spirits were angered and would depart unless she chose freely the one to follow in her shoes. And who can argue against spirits?"

"You argued against them," I said, "in asking for my healing for your child."

"I love Kimiwe," he said. "Love is stronger than fear." Suddenly he grinned, and added, "Besides, Shinali woman, I'm counting on your *munakshi* to protect us."

6

When I was with the Shinali I had the opportunity to help their chieftain, an old man called Oboth, who was in a great deal of pain. I did not heal his illness, for that is incurable; but I did ease his suffering for a time. I felt then that, of all the pains I had ever eased, the soothing of Oboth's was the most wonderful. In the eyes of my nation, Oboth and his people were my enemies, and yet with them, with the Shinali, I felt only a great peace, even a sense of belonging; and the healing of Oboth was like a greater healing, a healing of age-old enmity and wrongs, a breaking down of walls that were more than pain, more than one man's disease. It was a healing of hearts, his and mine.

—Excerpt from a letter from Gabriel to his mother,
kept and later gifted to Avala

I was nervous, afraid, and worried about the priestess; yet when I knelt beside the child Kimiwe, there was nothing in my mind save pity. She had been terribly neglected. My mother had taught me that cleanliness is vital in healing; it was a thing my father had told her. Yet the child Kimiwe had not been washed or treated in any way, so far as I could tell, and I marveled that her burns had not become infected. Awful wounds they were. Her chest was burned, part of her hair, and one side of her face, though her eyes were spared.

I had her placed on a clean mat near the entrance in the chieftain's tent, in good light, for the skies had clouded over and it was dim inside. Then I asked for a fire to be lit and water to be boiled, and for the sharpest, finest blades to be brought to me. I asked for the best tendons for thread, fine bone needles, clean cloths, and herbs for making poultices. My request for the plants caused some alarm, for herbs were the priestess's specialty, and she wanted nothing to do with me. Somehow Ramakoda got from her what I wanted, though I sniffed and tasted all the leaves he brought, to make sure my healing would not be deliberately hindered.

The afternoon was half gone when I was satisfied that all was ready. The honed knives, passed through flame for cleansing, were laid out on clean cloths beside the child, the poultices were prepared, and the child herself carefully washed. Then I asked all to go, save Ramakoda.

For a time I sat by Kimiwe while her father sat on the other side of her, and I prayed and got my mind and heart in harmony with the child's. Then I leaned over her, my hands on either side of her small body, and pressed my brow to hers. Healing and ease I sent through her, like white light going ahead before I began with the blades. She was all-unknowing, yet I poured light into her mind, too, so that even her dreams and memories would be healed while I worked. Then, no longer aware of anything but the task before me, I washed my hands and began. First I carefully cleaned the burns, then, slicing as thinly as I could, removed strips of flesh from her thighs, which were not burned, and laid them over the raw places of her chest and face. I sewed the new pieces of skin in place and laid across them clean cloths soaked in healing herbs and oils. Over the new wounds on her thighs I placed healing poultices, and bound her well. Then once more I leaned over her, pouring through her all the healing force I owned, and I kissed her face where she was not burned, and said a prayer for her.

I sat back, suddenly flooded over with weariness, and saw that it was night, and it was raining, the drops drumming softly upon the tent roof. Someone had placed burning lamps all around us. A cup of water was put into my hands, and I looked up to see the pledge-son, Ishtok. He crouched by me, his hands linked between his knees, his eyes on little Kimiwe. His clothes smelled damp, and in the lamplight golden raindrops fell from the curling ends of his hair and ran down his skin.

"Your healing, it is different from ours," he said, glancing up and smiling. It was a slow smile, warm and lingering. "It is different from Hena healings, as well."

I sipped the water he had given me, and wondered if he knew the change he had made to my pulse. He was beautiful; no doubt all the girls were in love with him. And perhaps he had left broken hearts in the Hena tribe.

"Ramakoda told me you lived with the Hena," I said. "I would like to hear about the ways they heal."

"I'll tell you tomorrow. You look tired. I hope you don't mind, but my brother Ramakoda wants you to sew up his cuts, while you're about your healing. I'll help, if you would like me to."

So Ishtok helped me as I washed the needles and got more clean tendons, and sewed up Ramakoda's wounds. The cuts had stayed clean, for Ramakoda had kept them clean himself. Ishtok said nothing as I put my hands behind Ramakoda's head to stop the pain, but while we stitched up the deep cuts he glanced often at Ramakoda's face, as if he could not quite believe that his brother felt nothing. I noticed that Ishtok's hands were marked with many small scars. I mentioned them, and he said, "I'm a wood carver. I learned the skill with the Hena."

"You should take more care," I said.

"I think not," he replied, "with a healer like you to stitch me up."

I had never blushed in my life until that moment, and I covered it by getting up and going to ask Ramakoda's sister, Chimaki, for fresh binding cloths.

The next morning I woke late to find that the rain had gone and the day was fine, and only Kimiwe and Ramakoda were in the tent with me. He was sitting by his daughter, watching over her. As I checked her burns Ramakoda said, "She slept peacefully all night. But she woke before, and said '*Bani*.' It is the Igaal word for Father. Then she slept again."

"She's healing well," I said. "Next time she wakes, give her water to drink. She is badly in need of it. Before I go I'll mix more medicine to stop her pain, and I'll show you how to look after her. You don't need to take me home, Ramakoda. I'm well used to traveling on foot, and your daughter's need of you is greater."

He said nothing, and I continued, "It will be a few days before you know if the healing has worked or not. If poison gets under the new skin, it will come away and she will be as hurt as before. Worse, because her thighs will be wounded as well, and all for nothing. Let no one touch her but yourself, always wash your hands first, and keep everything here clean. The smallest bit of dirt under the cloths will spoil everything."

"I'm wanting to ask you something," he said, his eyes on the child's face.

"I'm knowing what it is," I said. "But my people will be thinking I'm dead, Ramakoda. I want to go back to them. Besides, your father said I have to go today."

"That he did, and I will keep my vow, and take you home. Please show my sister, Chimaki, how to look after my daughter."

So I showed Chimaki, and she was quick to learn. "I'm thinking I would not mind being a healer," she said, smiling sideways at me, almost shy. "Perhaps, on one of Gunateeta's better days, I might ask her to teach me. But I would rather learn from you." Like Ramakoda, she was tall and big boned, with a pleasant face and an easy way about her. Her long hair was twisted up in a knot such as all married Igaal woman wore, and she had a fine tattoo on her brow. She loved Kimiwe well, and I was sure that the child would heal swiftly under her care. But that afternoon, as I helped Chimaki give Kimiwe medicine for pain, the child vomited and wept, and was a high lot distressed. I took away her pain in the secret ways my mother had shown to me, then sat by her awhile, undecided. I yearned to go home, to put my mother's mind at rest, for she would be frantic with worry about me; yet I also wanted to ease this child's long journey through her pain. While I crouched there, anguishing over my decision, Ramakoda came and sat by me.

"I have asked my father if you may stay a few more days," he said. "And that sits well with him, for he is impressed with what you have done in your healing of me. But the decision is yours, Avala. If you wish to return home now, I will take you."

I covered my face with my hands. Again I heard Zalidas's words, heard him call me the Daughter of the Oneness, who would unify all the tribes for war; and felt the great heaviness of his prophecy. I remembered my mother's words that our destiny is always to do with our highest joy, and how healing was my dream. Again I felt torn between the two, the healer and the child of war, for it seemed to me that they could not be the same thing. I felt confused, destined to walk a road I could not understand. Then suddenly I realized that there was not one road stretching before me this day, but two. One path led home with Ramakoda, leaving open the hope for future friendliness between our two peoples—a path where I would put off finding my destiny until a time to come, a time when I might feel more prepared, more worthy, to be the Daughter of the Oneness. It was the path of delay and self-comfort, an easy path. But the other path was the place of beginning, of stepping out into the darkness, of putting out my hand now toward my destiny, no matter how unprepared or confused I felt, or how afraid. This was the hard path, the frightening path. But perhaps it would be more frightening to never know—to return home now and miss what may be my best chance to begin my destiny. Maybe my only chance.

At last I took my hands down from my face.

I said, "I will stay until Kimiwe is truly well."

Relief shone on Ramakoda's face. "May Shimit bless you every day you live," he said. "I will not forget this, Avala. From this day on, my tribe and yours are at peace."

That evening Ishtok asked me to sit by him on his family's feasting-mat. As he offered me a platter of meat so I could fill my bowl, he said, "I promised to tell you about the Hena healers, though I'm thinking that their ways are not as good as yours. I've never seen anyone stop pain the way you do."

"The way I stop pain, that is a Navoran skill," I said.

"Ramakoda told me your father is Navoran, and that your blue eyes come from him."

"It's true," I said. "My father was a healer, honored among his people. My mother, too, is a healer, and he taught her some of his ways."

"It must be hard for you, having two bloods," he said. "Don't your people hate you for being half Navoran?"

"My father was their hero. He did great things for my people. But it's still hard, having his blood. They expect me to be a high lot brave, like him."

"And are you?" he asked, with a sideways look and that slow smile. "Brave, I mean."

"What do you think?" I said, returning his smile.

"I'm thinking you must be," he said. "It was brave, what you did to Kimiwe yesterday, knowing she could die if you made a mistake. It was brave, helping an enemy hunter. It was more than brave, going with him into his camp, when you knew his people would hate you."

"You don't hate me."

"That's a truth. But most of the people here do. Shimit's teeth—you're Shinali *and* Navoran! How much more horrid could you be?"

We laughed, and I liked the quietness of his mirth, the way his shoulders shook while he made soft laughter. I remembered

Santoshi and how she and I often laughed together, and I wondered what she would think of Ishtok. I stole a long look at him and saw that the humor still lingered about his eyes, and there was an easiness about him, an openness, that was rare among the youths I knew. I thought Santoshi would like him, too, if she ever met him; his soul, like hers, was arrow straight, and there was no falseness in him.

We were quiet for a time, eating, and then I asked, "Why do your people hate mine? I can understand why you hate Navorans, but the Shinali have done nothing to you."

He chewed thoughtfully for a while, then said, "We heard how your people made the treaty with Navora, and gave them some of your last bit of land. My father says you gave away your spirit and deserve what happened to you. Myself, I know nothing about your people, as I knew nothing about the Hena before I went to live with them. It is easy to judge from a distance, out of ignorance, but judging fairly, with truth—well, that is harder, and may cost some effort."

"Tell me about the Hena?"

"They live in the far north, on the edges of the marshlands. They live off fish and marsh birds, and make boats out of reeds. When they move to new territories, they fill each boat with belongings, and carry it slung between two horses. They also carry sick people and little children in the boats that way, when they move.

"When they settle in a place, they build huts out of mud plastered over reeds. There are many Hena tribes, and they fight one another often, because there is not much good land. Some tribes live just by raiding others and stealing their smoked fish and grain, if they've managed to grow crops. It's a hard life, the Hena life. It is made lighter by music and songs, and they are fine dancers. Their storytellers are their priests, and in their stories the Hena history is kept alive.

"My Hena tribe has a priest who is also a seer and prophet. His name is Sakalendu. He is not like our old Gunateeta, who is really only a healer. This Hena priest, he lives face-to-face with the gods and is wise beyond the ordinary wisdom of men. He foretells droughts and floods, and other angry acts of the earth, and gives his people time to prepare for them. He also tells the meanings in dreams. He works with the healer, a woman clever with plants and with the knife, but she cannot do the things you do. She uses mud often, to cake broken limbs until the bones heal, and to stop pains in the elbows and knees. She also uses mud for skin complaints. And she is an excellent midwife. But many people are afraid of her, for she has a bad temper. The Hena women yell at their men, and at their children. They are even worse with one another. It was something I never got used to."

"Don't Igaal women get angry?" I asked.

"Yes, but even in anger an Igaal woman must never raise her voice, especially to her husband."

"The women in my tribe would find that difficult," I said, making him smile.

He asked, "Do you have a husband in your tribe, Avala?"

"No. My tribe, it's very small. It's hard for us to find husbands and wives now who are not of our own kin."

"We would find that hard in this tribe, too," he said. "We choose husbands and wives at the Gathering, every other spring.

All the Igaal tribes meet together and trade for slaves and horses, and exchange goods, and choose marriage partners. Why don't your people do that?"

"We don't have many tribes," I said. "We are only one. All the Shinali in my home tribe, they are the nation."

He stared at me, and I felt the disbelief in him. "Shimit's teeth!" he breathed. "Is that your heart's truth?"

"Heart's truth," I said. "Too many fights with too many enemies have killed nearly all of us."

"Who do you trade with for horses, carpets, other things?"

"We don't trade. We don't have carpets or beautiful chests for our belongings. We have few things, because when we move we must carry everything ourselves, without the help of horses. When our things wear out or break, we cannot replace them. Always, my people long for their own land again, and to build another house such as we had, and to have a place to keep sheep and weave clothes and make pottery. We're not truly wanderers like your people, Ishtok. Our land is all we had. All we want."

We fell silent, finishing our food. He was frowning a little, creasing the small tattoo between his brows. Straight his eyebrows were, dark and fine as falcon's wings, and the tattoo made a graceful link between them.

"At your Gatherings," I said, "how many tribes are there?"

"About twenty," he replied. "Many are larger than ours. We cover the plain like stars in the sky."

"Aren't you afraid Navoran soldiers will see you all, and attack?"

He laughed softly. "There are so many of us," he replied, "we'd all only have to spit, and we'd drown the Navorans. They don't dare come near us."

"If men choose wives at the Gathering, they choose people they're not knowing very well?"

"If a man chooses a wife at the Gathering, she comes to live with his tribe for two turnings of the seasons, until the next Gathering, and if they still want to marry each other, then they marry at the Gathering. But if they don't please each other, she returns to her own family. But our Gatherings last sometimes for two full moons, so we come to know each other well enough to be sure."

"And you, Ishtok? Have you met a girl you want to marry?"

"In my Hena tribe, I met someone," he said. "Her name is Navamani."

"It's a beautiful name."

"She's a beautiful girl. But I don't know if it's my destiny to marry her."

"Didn't you ask the Hena priest if it was your destiny?"

"No." He grinned. "I was afraid to, in case he said it wasn't. Do you know your destiny, Avala? Sorry—foolish question! Of course you know it: you're already living it."

I could not help smiling, for he spoke more truth than he knew.

I finished eating and put down my bowl. To the west, the coppery sun quivered as it slid behind the far mountain peaks. I thought of the evening I had met Ramakoda, and seen the vision in the skies of the eagle and the burning fields. Ishtok, too, watched the sunset, his eyes half closed.

"It's my favorite thing in all the world, the sun," he said.

"I think the moon is more beautiful," I said.

"No—the sun is best! It warms the earth; its light is life to us. It unfurls the leaves on the trees, calls up the grains and the herbs, and opens up the flowers. Your moon can't do that."

A slave came and cleared away our bowls, and Ishtok stood up to go. Standing with him, I said, "There's something I want to ask you."

"Ask anything you wish," he said.

"Before I go," I said, "I must speak with your father about something that is a high lot important. I want all your people to hear it."

"The only time we all gather to hear a talk is at a council meeting," he said. "Women are not permitted to speak at such meetings, though they may attend if Mudiwar says so. Would you like me to speak on your behalf? That would be acceptable."

"Thank you, but I need to say the words myself. Will you persuade your father to listen to me?"

"I will try, but it will have to be at the right time, when I know for certain that you are in his favor. What you ask is against Igaal custom." He gave me a strange look, puzzled and wondering, but asked no questions.

"I'll tell you when I'm ready to talk to him," I said, "and would be grateful if you would ask him then."

Before dark all the women went down to the river to bathe, and I went with them. Only Chimaki talked to me. When we had bathed, we put blankets about our bodies and went back to the tent to dress while the men went to bathe. I discovered what the bowls of charcoal and sweet-smelling wood were for: after dressing, the women stood over the bowls and wafted the sweet smoke up into their clothes and over their bodies, so they smelled good even in the worst of summer's heat. Chimaki told me that when they were traveling in the desert and had no water for washing, they used only the smoke baths. She also said they had strict rules about men and women not seeing one another naked. I thought of the youths swimming naked in the river by my people's camp, and of how at night we all stripped by our beds and washed before going to sleep. We were not ashamed of our nakedness, and honored one another, and did not stare. Even the youths and us girls, we did not stare at one another—well, not openly, anyway. I preferred our freer Shinali way.

As darkness fell the men and boys came back, and we all sat together on the soft carpets to talk and tell stories. Ishtok came and sat with me. I was quiet, thinking of home, and he must have taken my silence for sorrow, for he said, with a high lot of gentleness, "It's hard, being cut off from your own tribe. There were many times, when I was with the Hena, that I wished I could commune with my father. I got so desperate once, I even tied a message to a hawk's leg and tried to get the bird to fly to my father's camp."

"What happened?" I asked.

"Well, it was a good message. I'd drawn my smiling face on a scrap of rabbit skin, so my father would know I was well. The hawk ate the message before it left the Hena camp."

We laughed, and I accepted the bowl of drink he passed to me. It smelled pungent and strong, and I sipped it cautiously. He said, "It's called *kuba*. It's what's in the shared bowl they all pass around."

"It's better than your goat's milk," I said, giving it back to him. "But not by much."

Grinning, he drank the *kuba* himself.

Slaves were lighting the lamps. People went and got their bedding, and spread it out. I noticed that if anyone walked on the blankets, it was no matter. Also, with the Igaal, there were no special sleeping places, and people lay down where they wished. Ishtok came back with his bedding and mine, and spread our blankets out side by side. Ramakoda made his bed on the other side of Kimiwe. Chimaki, too, was nearby. We all got into our beds, and it felt strange to me, having Ishtok there so close. I felt suddenly shy. Every night of my life, until this time with Ramakoda and his people, I had slept with my mother on one side and my grandmother on the other.

The slaves put out all the lamps but one, and people talked quietly before they went to sleep. I was awake a long time, thinking of home.

I thought of how Yeshi's tent would be silent, the air heavy with worry and grief for me. These three days and three nights they would have worried and searched for me, all along the gorge and riverbank, and out toward the Igaal lands. My heart traveled out to the gathering-bag I had left on the stones by the Ekiya River, and the precious *eysela* flowers laid out in rows beside it. The bag had been stained darkly with Ramakoda's blood, after I had used it to drag him to the river. Did they think the blood was mine, and that a wild animal had taken me, maybe dragged me to the river for killing? But then I would not have laid the flowers out tidily, in rows. What a mystery my disappearance must be, to them! And my mother and grandmother—what did they think? Did they believe me dead? Or would their hearts tell them that I was alive? I wished I had the gift my mother said my father had, of sending words from his mind through fields and trees and stone, to people he loved. With all my heart, I wished I could tell her that everything was well with me. I wished I could tell her that, in the days to come, I would strive to do what Zalidas had foretold, and be the Daughter of the Oneness.

7

My birthing time, my dying time, the mother I have and the father I
have, each day of my life, my dreams, and my one true destiny—
all were chosen and ordained for me by the All-father,
before ever I drew breath.

—Shinali proverb

The next morning, when I had finished changing Kimiwe's
bindings, I went down to the river, which seemed to be
the gathering place for all the women. They were washing clothes,
slapping them against the smooth rocks to clean them, and the
men were working under the trees nearby, carving their new
canoe. The women were laughing and talking, and children played
in the shallows by them. But suddenly the laughter stopped,
and we saw old Gunateeta hobbling out of her healing tent. She
was wearing all black, and there were ashes in her hair and on her
face and clothes. The women in the river stood up to look at her,
and the men stopped carving.

Mudiwar went over to the priestess, and she spoke to him for
a while. Then he went to the men by the canoe and said something to them I could not hear. Six of the men went into the healing tent and came out carrying three bodies. Filthy those bodies
were, covered in blood and pus and other fluids, and two of the
bearers retched as they carried them. Even from where I stood,
a stone-throw away, I could smell the stench. I sorrowed for the

people still in the healing tent. As soon as the bodies were brought out, women began wailing; a high-pitched, trilling sound strange to me, full of a wild and frightening grief.

People came running from all the tents, and a great crowd went down straightaway to the funeral ground. I lingered on the edge and watched for a while. Bizarre funeral rites they were, sickening to me. While Gunateeta chanted and prayed and limped around waving long trailing banners red as blood, men began chopping up the bodies of the dead. The birds were already there, waiting. Arms and limbs of the dead were cut up and the flesh stripped off and laid out on special stones for the birds to devour; but some of the organs and the bones were kept, wrapped in red cloths and buried with the heads on the far side of the ground, under pyramids of stones. Tall sticks stood in the stones, bearing funeral flags marked with prayers and sacred signs.

I did not stay till the end, but went back to Mudiwar's tent and sat by Kimiwe. That day there was no midday feast, and Kimiwe told me that people fasted on funeral days. She was talkative, cheerful, and healing so rapidly that I expected to go home very soon. In the afternoon Mudiwar and his family came into his dwelling. Many of the women were still weeping. Ishtok came and sat by me, his face solemn.

"My father is worried about the others in the healing tent," he said quietly. "Gunateeta is in so much pain, she forgot half the prayers on the funeral ground. She is no longer being a good healer. It's a serious matter for us."

Even as he spoke, the chieftain came over.

"Shinali woman," he said. "Show me this healing you've done on my granddaughter."

It was the first time he had shown interest in Kimiwe's healing, and as I obeyed I was aware of people gathering around us. While the chieftain examined her wounds, Kimiwe smiled shyly up at him. She said, calling him by the Igaal name for grandfather, "It doesn't hurt anymore, *Mor-bani*."

"No hurt at all, little one?" he asked gently.

Kimiwe shook her head. "I want Avala to look after me all the time, *Mor-bani*, not the grumpy lady. I don't like her."

"Then I shall have to go and see the grumpy lady, as you call our esteemed holy one, and hear her words on the matter," said the chieftain, and then he went out.

By this time there were many people gathered outside as well, talking quietly, their faces astonished and fearful. Straight to the healing tent the old man went, and the people followed, falling over themselves in their eagerness to see what would happen. I stayed behind and was binding Kimiwe's burns again when Ramakoda came in.

"Avala! My father's calling for you. Come—now!"

I hurried out, and he took my arm and almost dragged me to the healing tent. "My father's gone in, even though it's forbidden ground to him," he said. "Name of Shimit, things are happening this day!"

As we neared the healing tent the crowd parted to let us through. Then the entrance to the tent was in front of me, and I was choking in the smoke that poured out, pungent and suffocating. The chieftain's shoes were in the entrance, where he had kicked them off. From inside he called my name again, and he sounded angry. Ramakoda prodded me and I went in.

Darkness and fetid heat engulfed me. I retched at the stink of human sweat, blood, urine, vomit, and suppurating wounds. The buzzing of flies filled the air. In a fire pit in the floor burned something earthy and foul, its fumes too stinking to breathe. I could hardly see but after a while made out the sick lying in their filthy clothes on the dirt floor. Many were moaning quietly, and some entreated the chieftain for mercy; others were silent, near death.

Coughing a little, Mudiwar was standing on the other side of the fire, and Gunateeta was sitting near him, slouched over on a little stool. Noticing me, she jerked upright, her face cold and furious. She opened her mouth to speak, but Mudiwar spoke first.

"A long time you've been looking after these sick ones, Gunateeta," he said.

Her eyes, red-rimmed from the smoke, flicked upward to his face. "Yes, and death has not claimed many of them," she said. "I've held it off, Mudiwar."

"You've also held off life," he said. "I've seen Kimiwe. Her burns are healing well, and she is almost as she was before the fire. To my mind, her healing is better than the healing I see here."

"Your mind is the mind of a chieftain and a warrior," Gunateeta said. "Your mind cannot see the spirits of death coming and going. You cannot judge healing."

"I can tell whether people are alive or not," he said. "I may not see the spirits, priestess, but I see plenty else. Come."

He turned and went out. I rushed after him. All the people

90

were watching us, waiting for the chieftain's words. He said nothing, waiting for Gunateeta.

At last she emerged, bent and limping, and wreathed in smoke. Blood seeped through the dirty bindings on her feet, and I felt sorry for her.

Mudiwar said to her, with some gentleness, "Times past, Gunateeta, you were a good healer, and I honor you for that. But I think your healing power has become trapped behind your own pain, and now you need healing for yourself."

She looked at the far hills, and gnawed on her lower lip.

Then Mudiwar said to me, "Shinali woman, can your *munakshi* heal the sick in this tent?"

"I'm not knowing anything about *munakshi*," I replied. "But I can heal. The ways I worked on Kimiwe, they were learned by my mother from a healer from Navora. A very great healer. There is no *munakshi*, only a high lot of knowing."

"I thought the Shinali and the Navorans were enemies."

"One Navoran was our friend."

"Strange, that a Navoran soldier caused my grandchild's hurt," Mudiwar remarked, "and a Navoran skill heals her. Those blue eyes of yours, they come from that Navoran healer?"

"He was my father," I said.

"So, we shelter two enemies in one skin," he remarked. I thought he was angry, but to my surprise when he spoke again he sounded kind. "I'll turn a blind eye to the bloods in you," he said, "if you will use your *munakshi* to heal my people."

I hesitated, my heart in turmoil. How long would it take to clean up the healing tent and those inside, and to do the healings for them? Three days? Four? Too long, already, I had been away from home. While I was silent one of the men called out.

"We'll not have *her* heal our sick!" he cried. "Not a Shinali with Navoran blood! You may turn a blind eye to the bloods in her, my chieftain, but I cannot! And neither would my son, who lies in Gunateeta's healing tent! He'd rather die than have that half-breed touch him!"

Other men called out in agreement, and women nodded in support.

"Go home, Shinali she-dog!" someone yelled.

"If that Shinali witch goes in my tent," said Gunateeta in a low voice, "Shimit will surely curse us all."

"How can Shimit curse us?" cried Mudiwar. "We're already cursed! Two and forty of our kin gone in slavery, almost as many others dead, or dying in this tent. Is not that a curse? Is there anything worse to fear?"

They were silent, angry.

Mudiwar lowered his voice and said, "Consider another thing, my people: consider that Shimit might have sent this Shinali healer to us, for such a time as this. To spurn the Shinali healer now may be to spurn the gift of the gods themselves."

"She is no gift, my chieftain!" called out an elderly man. "It was her father's people who caused us this sorrow! As for her Shinali blood—it's the filthy Shinali that draw the soldiers out here to our lands, like wounded dogs tempting out the wolves. If the high chieftain in the stone city found the Shinali he hunts for, he'd stop attacking us!"

"The Shinali dogs asked for their trouble!" cried someone else. "Like weak pups they suckled the Navoran wolves, and now they pay the price for their stupidity! But we pay it, too! Us, and all the Igaal tribes, and the Hena—we all suffer, because of the Shinali fools! I say we kill the witch. Tie her to a stake out in the desert, and let the Navoran soldiers find her. Then they'd find all her people, and have all the slaves they want, and we'd be left in peace."

Mudiwar banged his stick on the ground again, but no one took any notice. The whole tribe was in an uproar, and the sound of their hatred toward me was overwhelming. Terrified, I thought I would be torn to pieces, there and then. But Ramakoda raised his arms and stood beside his father, and there was quiet.

"Igaal!" Ramakoda cried. "My people! This talk is not worthy of you! Let me ask you a thing. Which tribe of us, of the whole Igaal nation, is without fault? Which tribe has all people who are wise, who are strong in truth, who walk in honor with the gods? Which tribe has no thief, no liar, no deceiver, no breaker of the laws? Tell me—which tribe?"

He glared on them, was tall and fierce and strong. Quietly, but clearly so all could hear, he went on, "There is no such tribe. Every tribe of us, every clan, every family, has good and bad. And the Navorans are the same. And the Shinali. I say that this Shinali woman with us now—this healer, this friend to me, my *nazdar* kinswoman—she is a good Shinali. I am proud that she healed me, for she healed me well. I am proud that she heals my daughter, for Kimiwe is a new child now. And I will be proud to see my father open up this healing tent, and let this Shinali healer do her work inside. If any of you do not agree to let her touch your kin, then speak now, and you may go in and get your kin, and bring them out and take them to your own tents. Then tomorrow, or after a few tomorrows, you can set them free to fly with the birds. But let us give some of them a chance at life."

There was total silence.

Ramakoda bent his head to his father, and stepped back.

Mudiwar coughed a little and said, "Before I saw the work of this Shinali healer, I spoke a word. Now I speak another word: she is to help my people in this tent. She will be given all that she needs, and you will do anything she asks of you. And Gunateeta will pray to the gods for us all."

There was a fluttering of hands as people covered their mouths in shock. Some cried out in astonishment and fear. Then Gunateeta spoke.

"My chieftain," she said, "you cast me off as healer, so I will take you at your word. Never again ask for my help. Never ask for my advice. Never ask for my prayers. And when the Shinali witch has gone, never ask for my forgiveness."

Then she hobbled away, her stained robes billowing about her, to her own small tent on the edge of the funeral ground.

Disappointment swept over me, that I would not soon be going home, after all. Despite Ramakoda's fine talk, I was about to argue, to say I needed to return to my own tribe, when someone moaned from inside the tent. An awful moan it was, full of desperation and pleading and pain; and my heart melted, and I knew I could not go.

"I will help," I said to Mudiwar, "but I need someone to work with me. May Chimaki help?"

"She may," said Mudiwar. "And Ramakoda, since he is your *nazdar* brother and is responsible for you. May Shimit also be with you, Shinali woman."

I looked at Ramakoda and was surprised to see him smiling.

"So, the sick are in our hands," he said. "I wasn't expecting to turn healer this day. I hope you realize I'm about as clumsy as a cow with a bow and arrow, when it comes to needlework."

But there was nothing clumsy about Ramakoda, I found. He and Chimaki worked with carefulness and were gentle. We had two-and-twenty people in the healing tent. Seven were beyond my help, and I simply washed them and eased their pain, then asked their loved ones to bear them away to their own tents, so they could pass peacefully through the shadow lands. Then we washed the fifteen sick who remained, changed the fouled bedding they lay on, and cleaned their wounds. When everyone was clean and had been given a little water and medicine against festering, then I began the healings.

Never had I been faced with so much human agony. Though Ramakoda and Chimaki were excellent helpers, I longed for the company of my mother and grandmother, whose wisdom and skills had always been my guide. Now, without their help, I felt very alone, unsure, and afraid because all decisions lay with me. My hands shook and I felt sick with nervousness and fear. Once, seeing how I trembled, Ramakoda asked if I was ill.

"No," I replied, "but I'm afraid. I've not had to mend wounds like these before. I'm afraid I'll make people worse, not better."

"Even a clean and comfortable death is better than what they had before," he said softly. "You cannot make them worse, Avala."

His words encouraged me, and I worked better without my fears to hinder me. By the time we finished our healings, the place was transformed. The sick were lying in tidy rows in fresh bedding on new flax mats on the floor, clean water bowls beside them. There was no fire, only a large pitcher filled with fresh water from the river, for the thirsty. A new door was made in the other side of the tent, and the summer breeze swept out the flies and disease and brought in clean air and healing. And it was quiet. The silence spoke loudest of all of the hard work we had done, for the sick lay free of pain at last. So we let in the ones who loved them—their husbands and wives and children and mothers and fathers—and then the quiet was broken only by tender words of comfort and love and joy.

Pleased, unutterably weary, I went to the chieftain's tent and washed, and changed into a clean dress. Then I went down to the river and sat alone to renew my strength.

About me blew the smells of the Igaal evening meal that was being prepared, the scent of bread and the pit-cooked meat, and I ached with longing for more familiar smells and the cooking fires of home. Chimaki came down and sat by me, and I was glad for her company. She gave me a small bowl of tea, and I drank gratefully. Before us the half-moon rose, yellow as a gourd in the violet skies.

"The people, they're saying you are a better healer than Gunateeta," she said. "Mudiwar is well pleased with you. He has spoken with those you healed, and they say they felt no pain while you did your work on them. It is strong magic."

"Thank you, Chimaki. But today's healing, it was not magic, but the skill of two women and a man. You and Ramakoda, you both worked with a high lot of gentleness. I was glad that you were with me."

"I think my father is going to ask if you will stay a few days more, until those you healed today are further along in their journey to wellness," she said. "If you're willing to do that, I'll help if you like."

"I'll stay another day or two, and teach you all I can," I promised, and she smiled at me, her face bright with gratitude.

"Tell me something, Chimaki," I said. "The healing Gunateeta did, did it ever work?"

"In time past, she was cunning with herbs," Chimaki replied. "She could heal fevers sometimes, and was a good midwife. But when it came to injuries or battle wounds, she asked the spirits to help her. Maybe they did try to help, but she could not hear them properly. When Ishtok came back from the Hena, he tried to talk to Gunateeta about their ways of healing, but she got angry and said her ways were good enough. Now we have seen your ways, and I think they are better than any, Hena or Igaal."

8

My one or two extra days with the Igaal stretched into four, then five, and still I stayed, reluctant to go until all the sick were safely over their fevers and infections. Only one more died, who was beyond my help. Once I went to Gunateeta's tent and asked her if I could heal her feet, or at least stop her pain, but she swore and threw her medicine bowls at me. Apart from that time I did not see her.

I got to know the members of Mudiwar's family, especially in the evenings when they gathered in his tent to talk and drink *kuba*. I learned that Chimaki was the wise one of the family, and that everyone went to her for advice; and that although Ramakoda was honored because he would be chieftain one day, he also caused dissension because he was not afraid to stand alone in his opinions. I noticed that his brother Chro grieved deeply and openly for those in the family taken in slavery, and he would not let anyone put away the sleeping rolls that remained, unused, against the walls, a reminder always that there were kinsfolk missing. But my favorite of all in Mudiwar's family was Ishtok, with his ready wit and easy way of being. I had never been able to talk with a youth the way I could talk with him, and we passed the evenings discussing the Hena and my people. Often, during our conversations, he carved. He made toys for the children, clever dolls with jointed limbs, and horses that would walk down a gentle slope, and smooth wooden rings for babies to chew on. All the children adored him for the gifts he gave.

One night, when it was a full moon and we were sitting out by the river, just he and I, he asked, "What will happen with your people, Avala? Will they always be wanderers, dreaming of their lost lands?"

"We have more than dreams," I said. "We have a prophecy."

And there, under the shining moon, with the music of the river running by, I told him of the Time of the Eagle, and of the day when all our tribes would become one. But I did not tell him of Zalidas's words over me, or that I was the Daughter of the Oneness. Yet when I had finished speaking he looked at me long and hard, his moonlit eyes half shadowed by his curls, and said, "I'm thinking that you play a part, Avala, in the making of that unity. You must have wondered at your being here, a Shinali healer in an enemy Igaal camp, winning our hearts with the good that you do. Is that why you came—to begin the Oneness?"

"It is a part of it," I said. "But finding Ramakoda and bringing him home, that was not planned by me."

"You believe in destiny, then? In the workings of the stars?"

I looked up at the night sky, at the uncountable sparks of light, all in their appointed places, all on their great sky-journey above our lives. "I believe in it," I said.

He, too, looked up, and said, "Do your Shinali people have names for the stars?"

"We do. That big row of stars over our heads, running east to west, we call that Nakula, the Pathway to the Sun. And that big star burning alone, that is Zathiya. Do you have names for them?"

"Yes, and stories saying how they got there." He lifted his arm and pointed to a place in the sky near the moon. "See that little red star there?" he said. "We call it the star of destiny. See it?"

I could not. "Come closer," he said. "Look along my arm. It's there, between those two near the moon. Can you see it yet?"

My chin was on his shoulder, and I was looking straight along his arm, but still I could not see it. I turned my head, saw his face close, his beautiful moonlit eyes brimming with quiet laughter.

"There is no red star!" I said, drawing back.

"No," he said, with a wicked smile, "but I got to smell the fragrance of your hair."

One night, during that time, I had a dream. It began as something wonderful and strong. I dreamed that I was flying high in glowing skies, riding on the back of a giant eagle; but then ominous clouds gathered about, black jagged clouds shaped like Igaal tattoos that wrapped about me, trapping me, and I lost the feel of the eagle's wings, and knew only darkness and wild forces all around, and a terrible helplessness and fear. I awoke troubled and went straight to the healing tent, thinking that a dreadful thing had happened to those still there. But they were well, and kept on getting well, and after a time I put the dream far back in my knowing and forgot about it.

All my strength, in those days of healing, came from my faith in the prophecy of the old priest, Zalidas, and from my certainty that here, in these days, the Oneness had begun. It was like a mystery within me, a marvel, and it gave my spirit eagle wings. Often in the healing tent I stopped what I was doing, flooded by the astonishment that I was here, in enemy lands, doing a work of healing and restoration, and being honored for it. I was sure that every healing, every pain wiped out, was another thread in the cord that would unite the Igaal with my people.

There was joy in those days, too, apart from the happy times with Ishtok. There was pleasure in seeing the faces of the Igaal women soften and smile as they thanked me and touched my sleeves, which was an expression of gratitude with them. Some put small gifts into my hands. They began to open up the tent flaps of their hearts, and to talk freely with me. One day the chieftain, Mudiwar, came to watch me heal and afterward asked me to cure the old foot wound he had. I could not heal him, but I took away his pain for a morning, and he went on a hunt with the young men and tracked a deer, and came back laughing, full of victory, and walking without a limp.

With growing excitement I thought of my meeting with Mudiwar and my telling of the Time of the Eagle. I imagined my return home with Ramakoda, son of the Igaal chieftain, and how he would greet our chieftain, Yeshi, and how they would offer each other gifts, beautiful cloaks and furs and knives. I thought of the great feast to celebrate my return, and of the speeches and words that would seal the allegiance between our two peoples. I thought of how someday, time to come, I might go with Ishtok to visit his Hena tribe, and tell them of the Time of the Eagle;

101

and of how we all would be drawn into one huge army, and march in triumph to take back the Shinali lands. Visions filled my head and my heart, and I felt a great peace like a cloak about me, and believed it was the All-father's hand overshadowing me.

In that peace, I went to Ishtok and asked him if he would arrange the council meeting with his father. "I have already spoken to him of it," said Ishtok. "He did not say yes, or no. I will ask him again. I know he favors you a high lot, since all the sick are well, and you have taught Chimaki many of your skills. Also, Ramakoda is already making preparations for the journey back to your own people. You have not many days left with us." He smiled, but I felt a sadness in him and wondered if he would miss me.

The next morning a strange wind blew from the south, warm and unpredictable and fitful. We Shinali call that wind the *shoorai* and believe it brings change. When it blows children become wild and unruly, things go wrong in hunts, animals are restless, and sometimes great and good things have their beginnings. I felt the blowing of the *shoorai* wind and hoped that it was a good omen for this day.

While the midday feast was being set out I went to see Ramakoda. He was sitting under a tree making arrows, binding the feathers onto the ends of the long shafts. They were beautiful, Igaal arrows, for the feathers were dyed deep blue, and they were bound on with red-stained cord. Our Shinali arrows were dull by comparison.

"I've been here fifteen days," I said, "and I've done my heart's high best for your people. The sick are all out of their fevers, and Chimaki can make any medicines that are still needed. I want to go home, Ramakoda."

He stopped winding the red cord about the arrow shaft and looked up. "I've been waiting for these words, Shinali woman," he said, smiling. "I'm ready for the journey, too. I have gifts for your chieftain, and I've finished packing our saddlebags. I hope you won't mind riding a horse."

"So long as we don't race," I said, laughing.

"I thought you'd want to gallop like the wind," he said. "But it's as well; I've a gentle mare for you, guaranteed not to bolt. We can leave in the cool of this evening, before the meal, and be on the far side of the hills by nightfall. We'll ride under cover of darkness, and be with your people by sunup. But first, we must speak with my father."

"Ishtok has already arranged a council meeting," I said. "After we have eaten, I have something to say to Mudiwar. I want all your tribe to hear it."

"Women don't speak at Igaal councils," said Ramakoda. "Not even Gunateeta in her better days."

"Ishtok is hoping that your father will allow it, since I have healed so many of his people."

"We shall see," said Ramakoda.

He placed a cloth over the feathers and the work he was doing, so the wind would blow nothing away, weighting it all down with stones. Then together we went to the feasting-mats. I sat with his family, with Mudiwar and Ishtok and Chimaki and the others I had got to know.

I was too excited to eat. Excited, and fearful. As always Ishtok

103

sat by me for the meal, but for once we did not talk much. Whenever our eyes met, his face became grave, his gaze full of understanding and empathy. He, too, had known the weight of being ambassador in an alien tribe, of vital gatherings and talks. It seemed an age before the meal was over. Usually old Mudiwar stood up and banged his stick three times on the ground, as a sign that the meal was finished and everyone could disperse; this day a slave came with a small gong hanging vertically in a framework of sticks. There were charms tied about the gong, small carvings, and flags with black sharp-angled signs on them. The flags fluttered in the gusty wind, and the charms clattered as the chieftain banged the gong with a special stick. At the throbbing the people stopped talking, and those on other mats turned to face the chieftain and his family. Those far off came closer and sat on the grass under the trees, where they could hear. When everyone was settled Mudiwar stood up.

"The Shinali woman has healed many of us," he said, "even snatching some of us back from the shadow lands. We owe her our thanks. My son Ishtok has said that the Shinali woman has a word for us. It is not customary for a woman to speak at a meeting such as this. But neither is it customary for a Shinali to be in our camp, or for us to have a healer of such skill. I will permit her to speak."

A ripple of surprise went through the company, and Mudiwar raised his hand for silence. Then he sat down. He was holding his long stick and had Gunateeta's holy red banners tied to it to keep out evil spirits. Ishtok had told me that the priestess was dying, else for this important gathering she would have been here, too. Ramakoda gave me a nod, and I went and sat beside the

104

chieftain, not facing him directly, but turned so that all the people would hear what I had to say. The faces before me were grave,
expectant. I wished I could stop shaking. So much hung on this
hour, on my words.

Mudiwar said, "Our ears, they are listening, Shinali woman.
Speak."

For the space of a few heartbeats I bent my head, asking the
All-father one final time for wisdom. All about me was a deep
silence. And in that silence a huge peace came upon me, a power,
and I felt again the force of all that Zalidas had spoken over me,
that last night at home. All the fine words that Yeshi had said of
my father, they uplifted me. Every fond touch from the elders,
because I was their hero's child, every story of our past, of our
future, our vision of final liberty—all of it bore me up, as if on
wings. I could hardly breathe, for the awe. Taking a deep breath,
I lifted my head. The *shoorai* wind blew about me, steady for the
moment, empowering.

"In the beginning," I said, "when the first winds blew across
the earth, and the leaves unfurled on the first trees, and the father
of all deer grazed the plains, and the first eagles flew, the All-
father made my Shinali people for our land. . . ."

And so I told our history, and there was not a sound in all that
company while I spoke. Even when I came to the part about our
prophecy, and told how my people and the Igaal and the Hena
would be united, there was no sound. Of my father I told, of the
Emperor Jaganath, of the time of my people's Wandering. I finished, my words carrying clear and strong in that vast quiet: "But
with every rising of the sun the ancient prophecy burns anew in
our hearts; and with every rising of the moon we dream of our

lost land. For the land is our life, our hearts' home, our place of belonging. In it lies our freedom and our peace. So we wait for the day of our return. We wait for the Eagle's Time."

For a few moments there was silence. Then the murmuring began again, and some of the people shouted. They sounded angry. I could not tell from Mudiwar's face what he thought.

Ishtok lifted a hand, and his father nodded to him to speak. Ishtok said, "I ask you to remember, my father, that I have told you of the seer-priest with my Hena tribe, whose name is Sakalendu. He foretells a time of change to come, that will alter all our world. The All-Sweeping Wind, he calls it. This belief does not belong only to the Shinali but to the Hena as well."

Again, people talked behind their hands.

I said, "I remind you, Mudiwar, that this prophecy is known also to the Navorans. My people have, as chief treasure, a letter from the Navoran Empress to my father. It has words about the Eagle's Time, and how it will mean a new life for the Navorans, too, and an end to the evil in their Empire. Three nations believe in the Eagle's Time—my people, and the Navorans, and the Hena."

"Avala speaks true," said Ramakoda. "I hold this prophecy to be a true foretelling of what might be, if we all will bend our bows to it."

"If we were meant to be a part of it," called out an old man, "wouldn't Gunateeta have told us?"

"Old Gunateeta couldn't foretell water boiling over a fire," said one of the youths, and there was laughter.

Mudiwar banged his stick, and we waited for him to speak. At last he said, speaking directly to me, "As I see it, Shinali woman, this prophecy is all about your people getting back their miserable bit of dirt. You think I care about that?"

I was dumb, trying to think of a reply.

"It's about more than that, my father," said Ramakoda. "The Time of the Eagle would mean the end of Navoran supremacy."

"Since when were the Navorans supreme over us?" shouted an old man. "We live free. Let the Shinali fight their own battles. They got into their mess with the Navorans—let them get themselves out of it!"

There were shouts of agreement. Then Ramakoda spoke. "You say that the Navorans aren't supreme?" he said, looking across to the old man who had last called out. "You say we live free?"

"We've always been free, my son," said Mudiwar, and the elders nodded their heads.

Ramakoda stood up. "Have you all forgotten, so soon?" he cried. "Have you forgotten our kinsfolk taken in slavery? Our women and children still captives in the stone city? The ones who died fighting to save them? Have you forgotten how, not many winters past, we fled time and time again before the soldiers who hunted for us? Have you forgotten already this summer's battle, and the two and forty of our kin who were captured? And you want to be satisfied with this, and call it freedom? Where's their freedom—the ones who are slaves? Where is the freedom of your wives, your husbands, your brothers, your sisters, your children? Where is the freedom of my two sons? Where's the freedom of those who walk already in the shadow lands? The ones who sit among us now, with pieces sliced off their bodies, some of them blind or lamed? Is this our freedom?"

The tribe broke into an uproar, some agreeing with him, others shaking their heads. Mudiwar banged his gong, but it was a long time before they were quiet.

"My son Ramakoda asks if we have forgotten," Mudiwar said. "I have forgotten nothing. Always there have been wars. The Hena we've fought, times past, and the Shinali. Now we fight the Navorans. Time to come, there will be new enemies. We heard this night, from Avala's own lips, that once the Shinali were a great nation, and it's the fault of the Navorans that they are a small tribe now, with nothing. But I say it's the Shinali people's own fault. I say they are diminished because of their own stupidity and weakness. They were the only ones who signed a treaty with Navora, the only ones to trade off some of their precious land, the only ones to live in the very shadow of the stone city. That is why they lost their soul strength—they gave it away. Well, we will give away nothing. We will fight for what we have, if we are attacked. We will defend ourselves. We will guard the freedom that we have. But we will not be wiped out because we are foolish."

"My father, the Shinali are not foolish," said Ishtok. "They are a people who have been much wronged against."

"The Shinali *are* fools!" shouted Mudiwar. "They made a treaty with traitors! They got nothing but trouble for it. Now they have a crazy dream, and they want us to believe in it. Well, I will not. I will not invite the full wrath of the entire Navoran army down on our heads, and risk wiping out our nation, just so the Shinali can sit in their own dirt. I will not be a fool and lead my people to calamity, just because a prophet coughs up a crazy dream. I will not get caught up in the madness of the Shinali, lest we all

108

end up like them—a wasted tribe of outcasts, with nothing but regret and foolish dreams.

"I will not talk of this matter again. I have wasted enough breath on it. This is my final word." He struggled to his feet and banged his stick, the sign that the meeting was over. People began to talk, to stand up to go. I sat where I was, numb. In disbelief I saw the Time of the Eagle fade like smoke, blown away by an old man's word.

Then Ramakoda called out, "There is one more word yet to be spoken, my father! It is a word of gratitude to Avala, for what she has done for us. You can ignore the freedom her people's prophecy offers us, you can ignore the call to rise up like a warrior in the fight against Navora, but you cannot ignore the good she has done in our camp in these past days. There is a word of blessing, of thankfulness, that needs to be spoken, before I take her back to her own people. This day I will take her, at sundown. I ask, my father, that you speak of our gratitude. That much, at least, you owe her, as chieftain of those she has healed."

Gradually, people sat down again. Only Mudiwar and Ramakoda remained standing, both of them angry. Suddenly foreboding came over me, and I saw again the jagged clouds of my dream, plunging down to suffocate and entrap. In deepening dread I listened to Mudiwar.

"The Shinali woman has healed our loved ones well," Mudiwar said. "For many days our priestess has withdrawn to her own tent, leaving the Shinali woman's *munakshi* strong and unhindered. I see it as a sign: that although Gunateeta remains our priestess, the Shinali woman is our healer now. She will live here among us as our slave and take over the care of all our sick. That is my word, and I have spoken it."

The clouds swarmed about me, heavy, unbearable. Ramakoda took my arm, pulled me to my feet. I clung to him, heard him say, his voice raised and distraught, "My father, when the Shinali woman helped me, on the way to these my own lands, I swore to her that I would take her home to her own place and her own people. I swore it out of the thankfulness of my heart. I swore it in a holy vow. I cannot go back on it."

"Write your vow in the dust, my son," said Mudiwar.

Through the violent shades I saw Ramakoda go to the ground at the edge of the feasting-mat. People moved back to give him room. I saw him kneel down, and with his forefinger he drew a circle in the dust. Through the circle he made two lines, crossing. "This is the circle of my life," he said. "The long line signifies the force between the god of heaven and the god of earth, and the line across it signifies my vow."

Mudiwar went over and moved his stick over the lines Ramakoda had drawn, until no sign of them remained. Then the *shoorai* wind came, wild and fitful, and swept the dust smooth.

"As your father and your chieftain, I wipe out your vow," Mudiwar said. "The Shinali woman remains with us."

Ramakoda stayed on his knees, though he raised himself and cried out, "We can't force her to stay, my father! Many times she could have escaped, on our way here. But she stayed with me, freely, out of goodness. She remains free, with the right to return to her own people. I promised her that. I swore it. I made my vow by the goddess of the earth and the god of the sky. It stands, sure as the earth, sure as the sky. It was my vow."

"You made it, and I have unmade it," said the chieftain. "I

swear the unmaking, by the same gods who made me chieftain, and by my blood, which is older than yours, and by my word, which is more powerful than yours. The unmaking is done. And the Shinali woman is now ours. Say no more. Go."

Ramakoda stood, staggered a little, staring down at the dust. He looked shocked, devastated, his authority unmade, like his vow.

Trembling, my words rising, tumbling, I went over to Mudiwar and said, "I am not staying. I'm going back to my own people, with or without your blessing. You don't understand. By doing this, you are—"

While the words were still in my mouth, he lifted his hand and smacked it hard across my face. I fell sideways and collapsed. I lay there, stunned, the taste of blood and unfinished words bitter in my mouth.

"Never lift your voice to me again!" the chieftain shouted. "Not to me, not to anyone, not even a child or an animal. From this time forth, you are a slave."

Then he walked away, limping badly again. Quickly, people got to their feet and went away. Those who yesterday had smiled at me in gratitude now turned from me as if I were an outcast. Ramakoda walked off toward the place where the horses grazed. I scrambled up and went after him, calling him, demanding that we speak; but he got on his horse and left me standing there, shouting my anger and fear to emptiness. Desolate, I stood gazing back at the feasting-mats. The slaves had begun to clear away the remains of the food. Women were gathering their children together, taking them down to the river to wash after the meal. They laughed and played and splashed one another as they washed, their day unchanged. All about me people went about their work again, and everything was as before. Shocked, wandering, I went past the place where the chieftain's fateful words had been given. Two fateful pronouncements: the spurning of our Shinali prophecy, and the forbiddance of my return home. I glanced at my feet, at the earth where the mark of Ramakoda's vow had been made and then wiped out. And all was changed, for me. *All*.

Slowly my gladness in these past days was all undone; and more slowly still, but with devastating sureness, my love for the Igaal people, my hope in the great prophecy of our unity, my belief in my own part in it, trickled away like blood into the dust. And then there was nothing left, nothing but uncertainty and disbelief, and the bitter rage of betrayal.

9

I went back to Mudiwar's tent and sat on the floor. I was shaking, and my heart felt like a stone. After a while I got up and
took off the Igaal dress I had been given, and put on my old
Shinali dress with its faded paintings and frayed wool, and my
own worn-out shoes. I searched through the beautiful carved chests
until I found a bag for traveling, and a small pouch of flints. From
another chest I took a waterskin and a straight-bladed knife. I
did not consider the taking of these things theft, but only pay-
ment for the healings I had done. Beside one of the lamps was a
large wooden bowl containing flat bread the Igaal had baked on
hot stones, and I wrapped all the bread in a cloth and put that,
too, into the bag. Finally I rolled up the sheepskin tunic my
father had painted, ready to put into the bag for traveling. For a
while I stood there, touching the wobbly canoes with my fingertips, thinking of all he had done for my people, to save them, to
prepare the way for them to become a great nation again. Was
his sacrifice also for nothing?

Angry and grieving, I sat down again and waited for Ramakoda to return.

Evening fell, and I missed the meal. Slaves came into the tent to light the lamps, then went out again. I was alone but for little Kimiwe, who slept. The boys were racing horses, for I could hear galloping, and people calling out, and much laughter. Near dark Ramakoda came in. He sat on a wooden chest in the lamplight, his hands over his face.

"I don't know what to say, Shinali woman," he said hoarsely.

"You could say you are going to help me escape," I said. "I'm ready to go."

He dropped his hands and looked at the bag, at my Shinali clothes.

"I can understand your anger," he said. "I—"

"You have no knowing of it!" I cried. "You could never have knowing of what I feel, unless I had called my people as you lay helpless in the desert, and we had taken you back to our camp and made a slave of you. But even then you couldn't know, because you have done nothing, *nothing* for my people, while I have poured out for the Igaal all my healing strength, all the best that was in me. I gave them our prophecy, our hope for the future of us all. I gave your people life—I gave *you* life, and your daughter—and I'm rewarded with slavery."

He must have been deeply offended that I raised my voice to him, but he showed no anger. He said, very quietly, "It is no longer in my hands, Avala. My father has spoken."

"You may bow to his will—everyone in this camp may bow to his will—but I won't. I'm returning home, Ramakoda, whether you take me there or not. The way is not difficult. And I can walk quickly, and make the journey in little more than a day." I added, to hurt him, "It won't take long, without a wounded hunter to support."

He was silent for a long time. Then he said, "If you try to escape they will bring you back. You cannot get far; you'll be followed by men on horseback, and by the dogs, and when they bring you back you'll be punished. They'll whip you."

"Then I'll refuse to heal your sick, and even your father will see no point in my staying here."

"I think even someone with your stubbornness will soon tire of doing nothing all day. But if you accept our ways, you will find that life with us is not so bad. You will always be under my protection and will continue to live here in this tent as my kinswoman."

"You swore that I would return to my own place, Ramakoda. You swore it. You're the chieftain's eldest son. You'll be chieftain when he goes. Yet your words, your vows, mean nothing. I won't stay in a place where vows mean nothing. We Shinali have a word we use when making a vow, or saying words strong in our heart. That word is *sharleema*. What is sworn with *sharleema* is sworn for all of time. What is asked for with *sharleema* must be given, for it is asked for with the whole heart. Gratitude spoken with *sharleema* means gratitude for all time to come. Our Shinali words hold power. And I swear this: I will return to my own people, for you Igaal have been treacherous and unthankful, and I don't trust any of you. I will go home. I swear that, with *sharleema*. I'll go home tonight, or die trying."

"You won't die," he said. "But you'll be brought back."

"No one will know I'm gone, unless you tell them."

"I won't tell anyone, Avala," he said. Sighing heavily, and moving slowly as if he was unspeakably weary, he got up and went toward the tent door.

"I wish you farewell," I said, and he stopped and turned around. "I hope the All-father stays with you, Ramakoda. And with Kimiwe. I have held you both in my heart, as friends."

"Whatever happens, Shinali woman," he said, "hold it in your heart, too, that to me you are a sister, loved as my own, and always shall be. And when the time comes and I am made chieftain of these people, we will seek out your nation, and join with you in your battle against Navora. That I swear, and when I am chieftain my swearing will not be wiped out."

Then he left the tent. I rolled out my bedding and crawled in, hiding my packed bag under the blanket with me. When the moon was high the others came into the tent. No one saw that I was ready to escape, for I had the blanket pulled high about my neck to hide my Shinali dress. Ishtok came over to me and crouched a few moments by my bed, as if he wished to speak; but I kept my eyes closed, pretending sleep. Him, too, I blamed. They all were traitors.

It was a long time before the talking stopped, and people rolled out their beds and crawled in, and there were snores and the deep sighs of people asleep. Without a sound I got up, picked up the bag, and crept out.

It was a new moon, fine and sharp as a crescent Igaal blade, and for that I was glad, for the night was dark. The tents rose about me, black against the stars, and the rushing river sounded loud. Soundless on the dust, I crept among the tents and out toward the grasslands. Before me in the western skies hung the great line of five stars, which we call the Nakula, the Pathway of the Sun, and beneath them stretched the brief plain and the distant forested hills.

I was almost past the last tents when shadows rose from the ground before me, and an awful growling and barking started up. The dogs! The cursed dogs! I whispered to them, spoke soothingly, for they knew me well; but the devils barked and growled, and several bared their teeth. I thought of running but was too afraid, not trusting them, for most of them had wolf blood. Then people came rushing from the tents to see what the noise was about, and there were angry shouts, and much Igaal swearing. I was taken back to Ramakoda's tent and roughly thrown in. He stayed on his bed, and I thought at first he did not hear the commotion. But he said, as I lay down on my own blankets, "You will have to plan better than that, Avala."

For the rest of that night I lay awake, too angry and afraid and frustrated to sleep. Stupidly, I thought the botched escape would be ignored, since I did not even leave the camp; but the next morning Mudiwar spoke in a low voice to Ramakoda. I was getting the tangles out of Kimiwe's hair, and though I tried hard to listen, I could not hear their words. After, the chieftain went out and I heard the gong summoning the people together. Ramakoda would not tell me what it was about, but he sighed often, and after a while he told Kimiwe to stay in the tent and called me out with him.

All the people were gathered by the river. The chieftain was standing before them, and indicated for me to go and sit directly in front of him. Then they all fell silent, and he said, in heavy tones: "Last night you attempted to escape, Shinali slave."

I replied, "Last night, chieftain, I attempted to keep a sacred vow that was made to me."

Behind me people talked, and some called out in anger. The old man shouted for peace. "You have no voice in this gathering!" he said to me. "The only voice is mine. And these are my words: you will be punished for your disobedience. Twenty lashes. I will carry out the punishment."

Terror rose in me and I tried to stand, to flee, but I was held by angry hands.

"Bind her," said the chieftain, and a man came forward with a flax rope.

Then a voice called from the back of the crowd. "I claim the right of *somanshu*."

It was Ramakoda's voice, and it was followed by talking again, and loud cries. I turned to see Ramakoda striding forward, and people trying to stop him. Someone called out to Ramakoda, "There's no need, Ramakoda! She's only a Shinali!"

But he came forward, and without looking at me said to his father, "I claim the right of *somanshu*. I have that right, since the Shinali woman lives in my tent as my guest."

"She's not your guest," said the old man, and he shook with rage. "She is your slave."

"You have wiped out a vow I made with my lips, my father," said Ramakoda, "but you cannot wipe out what is in my heart. I owe Avala my life, and the life of my youngest child. Avala is not slave to me, but guest and kinswoman. And so I claim the right of *somanshu*. Unless, of course, you wish me to draw a sign of *somanshu* in the dust, so you can wipe out that sacred law, also."

The silence was so deep and wide, I could hear the river flowing, and the whirring of a bird's wings as it flew over us. Then the old man said, his voice quavering with rage or grief, I could not tell which, "Then I accept your right. But I've already said that I'm the one who will carry out the punishment. Will you ask for someone else to do it?"

Ramakoda said, "Not many hours ago, my father, you said your word is more powerful than mine. And so it is. The punishment is yours to carry out, the right to be punished is mine."

And so it was that I was spared, and the Igaal chieftain was forced to whip his own son. Ramakoda made no sound while it was done, but the old man wept. And three things came of it, that whipping: though they did not speak of it, there was a deep rift after, between the chieftain and his eldest son; there was a rift, too, between me and the Igaal people, for they blamed me for the chieftain's punishment upon his son; and the third thing that happened, that anguished me, was that I realized I could not risk another failed attempt at escape, lest more stripes be cut into Ramakoda's back. Next time, I could not fail.

Days went by, and the new moon came and went, and a terrible despair took hold on me. Everything I had believed in had gone. I was left empty, hollow like a reed flute. I no longer knew what I wanted. Escape seemed impossible, for I was never alone; by day the children shadowed me, and by night the dogs were my guards. The yearning for my home, for my mother and my own people, was like an ache in the core of me; but I did not think that I could face them again, now that I had done my work as

Daughter of the Oneness, and failed, and that the Igaal chieftain had spat on our great prophecy. My whole life, the reason for my being, was wiped out, and all Zalidas's fine words over me seemed like a mockery.

Even my slavery seemed a joke now, since none of the Igaal came to me. The healing tent was empty, the medicines unused, yet Mudiwar commanded that I stay there every day, dawn till dusk, since that was my place. I was glad no one came to me for healing, for I did not truly care anymore about the Igaal people, and the tent flap of my heart was closed to them.

I did not speak to anyone, even Ishtok. At night he still placed his sleeping things near mine, as a sign that he remained my friend, but I refused to talk to him. One night while I wept he reached his hand across the dark and stroked my hair. I longed to take his hand and press it to my cheek, to feel the warmth and comfort of him, but in my bitterness and grief I pulled away and kept quiet and pretended to sleep. Cruel to him I was, and to myself, in my great misery.

Then one day a hunter was carried into my healing-tent. There had been a bad accident in the mountains, and he had got an arrow through his belly. His companions had pulled the arrow out, but the barb had torn his innards and dragged some of them outside his skin. He was screaming when they brought him, and straightaway I tried to ease his pain, placing my hands on the back of his neck to block the pathways of his pain. Chimaki was with me, already lighting the fire to heat up the knives and needles and tendons. But the man kept on weeping and moaning, and the white light from my hands would not flow, and all my powers seemed scattered and undone. I could not help him. Chimaki came and sat on the other side of him, her face anxious and bewildered.

At last I withdrew my hand from the man's neck. "I can't stop his pain," I said, distraught. "We'll have to work quickly. Call Ramakoda and some of the men, to hold him."

It was a cruel healing, and the hunter moaned and howled until he fainted, and I could hardly see what I was doing, for sweat and tears. After, he got poison fever. That night I lay beside him while he groaned, my mind fixed upon the healing force that should have poured through all of him. But the force went nowhere, and I grew exhausted while his pain and fever increased.

Three days later, in awful agony, he died. As I heard the axes dividing him for the birds, I wept. I wept for him, for myself, for my huge, unbearable failure in all things, even in my skill to heal. As I mourned, there came a memory of a time far back in my childhood. It seemed that again I was in Yeshi's tent with my mother, and I was watching her heal an old woman. I had been ten summers old then, and just beginning to learn.

I remembered watching in awe as my mother moved her hands over the old woman's head and down the back of her neck, easing her pain. It was a wonder to me, to see the woman's face as she relaxed, and to hear her moaning cease. And my mother's face— Ah! How beautiful that was! I remembered her smile as she smoothed the old woman's brow and hair, and sang softly to her. Full of love my mother's face was, love that lay across her like a light and poured from her heart and her hands and leaped like gentle fire from her fingertips. Then my mother had noticed me there, and she had lifted her hand and stroked my face. Power had come from her. "Always remember, Avala," she had said, "that the greatest thing in healing is love. I always knew that, in a corner of my heart; but your father, he helped me to know it with all of my being. Love can heal all manner of hurts, and go where medicines and knives cannot."

As I called this to my knowing I bent over in the Igaal healing tent and wept. It seemed such a simple thing, to love. Love I had, somewhere in me, but it was lost behind the huge rage at my enslavement, and Mudiwar's rejection of the great prophecy, and beneath the overwhelming sorrow and anxiety and resentment that ached in me with every heartbeat. With every bit of my will I tried to put those feelings aside, to summon up a kind of warmth toward the Igaal. But I could not. My heart was closed, and I did not know how to open it.

I was still bent over, grieving and desolate, when Mudiwar came in.

"You refuse to stop my people's pains, Shinali slave," he said.

"None of them come to me for healing," I said.

"A hunter came, and you let him die. That's why they won't come. Now they're afraid of you. What trickery is this?"

"It is no trickery, Chieftain," I said. "My *munakshi*, it has gone."

"Gone? Gone? How can it go, unless you refuse to take it up?"

"I don't know," I said. "Heart's truth, I tried to heal the hunter."

"You did not try!" he raged, banging his stick on the mat. "Until you do your work properly, you shall not eat. You shall not sleep in my tent, and you shall not speak with anyone save those you are to heal. Chimaki will not help you. See if that will help you find your *munakshi* again!"

122

"How can I heal people, if they won't come?" I asked.

Ignoring that, he stormed out, thumping his stick beside him.

And my heart, it was closed more tightly still, and love was locked away.

So I lived apart in my healing tent, going out only to drink at the river, or to use the toilet pits on the other side of the funeral ground, or to wash. In the evenings I went out to bathe when the women went down for their washes. On the third evening, when the others were not watching, Chimaki whispered to me that she had hidden some clean clothes behind a fallen tree high on the bank. I found them when the women were gone, the clothes and a comb, and a package of bread and meat. There was also my own Shinali dress, and the tunic my father had painted. I wept as I took them back to my tent, thinking of my last night with my own people, of the sacred bathing-time in the river, and the new dress my mother had put on me. Then, I had been loved.

That evening, alone in my healing tent, I combed my hair and put on a clean dress, and looked at myself in the blade of one of the healing-knives. As I looked I had the strange feeling that I did not know who I was anymore. Was I Shinali, or was I Navoran? Or was I neither, a half-breed, not worthy of either of the bloods in me? Maybe the All-father had seen into my heart, my doubting, unloving heart, and had been angry with me, and so had taken away everything I treasured—my family, my tribe, my happiness, my ability to heal. Now I was a slave in an alien place, and would anyone here ever love me?

I thought of Ishtok, and how he had always put his sleeping-things by mine when I had been in their tent; did it mean that he favored me? I looked at myself carefully in the knife and wondered what he saw when he looked at me. I tried to see myself anew, from his eyes. Did he think I was beautiful?

I remembered a talk I had with Santoshi once, when I had been thirteen summers old and she had been fourteen. From her childhood she had been admired, and many of the boys favored her. She had been plaiting my hair for me, and I had asked her, "Tell me truly, Santoshi: am I pretty?"

"Ah, now, that's a thing I'll have to think hard on," she had replied, laughing, turning me to face her. Then she became serious, frowning as she studied my face. "I've heard the old ones say that you look like your father," she said thoughtfully. "More like him than like your mother. They also say he was a beautiful man, so I suppose that you, too, are beautiful."

"The truth," I said. "As you see it."

She sighed. "To be true, Avala, your nose is too big, your eyebrows too fierce, and your chin has a little dent in it that makes you look too strong for a gentle-hearted healer. If I didn't know you better, I'd be afraid of you." She was always arrow straight. But she had added, in her laughing way, "But your eyes are amazing. Any one of the boys would love you, for your eyes."

But as I looked at my eyes now, in the narrow knife in the Igaal healing tent, I thought how my blue eyes had caused only hate in this camp, and the people did not care who my father had been, or who I was. Even Ishtok, did he truly like me for myself, or did he talk to me just because he felt sorry for me, because he knew what it was to be alone in an alien place? That was surely it, I decided; he was simply being kind.

Sighing, I put down the knife, and my hand brushed the tunic with the wobbly canoes. With my fingertip I traced the signs of my father's names, that he had painted. He, too, had been in an alien place, when he had been with my people. Had he longed for his own Navora, as I longed now for my Shinali place? Or was his love for my mother enough to wipe out his homesickness? Or had he suffered, torn between two peoples, two ways of life? For the first time I realized how great his love had been, that he had chosen the Shinali, even all the way to death.

In the evening of the seventh day Ramakoda came in. He sat down and for a time just looked at me, saying nothing. I stared at my hands, ashamed of the way they shook, for I was hungry and weak, despite the food Chimaki managed to smuggle to me. I hid them under my armpits, and looked out the tent flap at the evening skies. The clouds were all on fire, and the river ran like blood between the darkening lands. It was an evening like the one when Ramakoda and I had first met, and I had seen the vision in the skies. A hundred summers ago, it seemed, and the vision had vanished away.

"I'm worried about you, my sister," he said. "My father says you refuse to heal, but I also know that no one comes to you."

"I couldn't heal them if they did come," I said. "The gift, it's gone."

"There's more than the gift gone," he said, very gently. "Your spirit, it's wandering in a desert place."

I looked away. "True," I said. "But I didn't send it there myself."

"I have been talking with my father," he said. "He has given permission for you to live in our family tent again, since you are still *nazdar* kinswoman to me. You may eat with us and live as

125

you did before. He has commanded the people to come to you for healing, even if it is only for bindings for their cuts and medicines for their fevers. He commands you to do what you can for them."

I said nothing. Was I supposed to be grateful?

"I have also been talking with Ishtok," Ramakoda added. "We have worked out a plan for your escape."

Emotions flooded over me—joy, and fear, and again that awful, unbearable weight of failure.

"I know you are always being watched," he said. "But there is one time, one night in the year, when no one will be watching. Ishtok will help you."

I bent my head low, and he asked, smiling, trying to see my face, "Are you not happy, sister of mine? I thought this news would give you joy."

"It does, in a way," I said. "But . . . The work I did here, it was for nothing. It will be hard to go home and tell people I have failed."

"Because Mudiwar won't march on Navora, with your people? Is that what you're meaning?"

"Yes," I said. "I thought this was my chance to persuade your people to join with mine."

He put his hand under my chin and made me look at him. "You *have* persuaded us," he said. "You are looking at the chieftain who will join his people with yours, and who will fight beside you for freedom for us all."

"But you might not be chieftain for many years," I said.

"Name of Shimit, Avala, what do you want me to do—kill

my father, fire up my horse, fly around to the hundreds of tribes scattered across the land, round them up, bring them back here for a battle feast at tomorrow's dawn, and all of us march on Navora in the morning?"

I could not help laughing. "You've forgotten the Hena," I said.

"Ah—the Hena. Yes, well, I shall need another half a day," he said, smiling. Then he added, serious again, "This is what I *can* do, Avala. Next spring at the great Gathering of the Igaal tribes, I will tell of the Time of the Eagle, and light the fire in my people's hearts for freedom. I will also tell them that when they see your people encroaching on our lands, they are not to drive them off, but to welcome them, because a Shinali healer once saved my life, and the lives of many in my tribe. And when I am chieftain, I will find your people, and we will fight side by side. I swear that, with *sharleema*."

I smiled, my heart leaping at the words of affirmation and hope, and at the old Shinali vow.

"In the meanwhile," he said, lowering his voice, "I will tell you the plan Ishtok and I worked out, for your escape. That one time when you will not be watched is the night of the first snow of winter. We have a big feast to appease the gods and bring a friendly wintertime. It's a good feast, lots of *kuba*, lots of storytelling and dancing, and plenty of eating. The feast goes on for two days and a night, and at the end of it we all sleep. Even the little children and the dogs. It's a symbol, that long sleep, of the earth's sleep in the wintertime. And when we wake we dance a special dance, a sign of the spring to come, when the whole earth

127

is awakened, and we move on to fresh pastures and hunting fields. But that sleep in the beginning of winter . . . Well, we call it the Feast of Forgetting."

"And I could go, during that time?"

"Yes, you can go in that time, Avala. It is not the way I wished it, taking you home myself, with gifts for your chieftain. But this way will have to do, for now. Ishtok will go with you to the other side of the forest. Then you'll just have the grassland to cross, and the ravine. No one will even notice you've gone, for a day at least. By then you'll be home."

Home! Joy flooded through me then, and I wanted to jump up, to dance, to hug him. Instead, I hugged myself. I thought of how my mother's face would look when I saw her again, of Santoshi. How wonderful, to be with them again! To see Yeshi again, and my grandmother. Then an awful thought came to me, and I said, "But what if they've moved? What if my people have moved?"

"I have thought of that, too. If they are not there, you can come back. No one will have missed you."

"But then I would never find them," I said. "And I would be a slave here for the rest of my life."

"I have no way of controlling what your people do," he said. "Shimit knows, I have enough trouble trying to have my way with my own tribe. All I can offer is a chance for your escape. Will you take it, or not?"

"I'll take it," I said.

Second Scroll

Ways of Empowerment

10

For the land is our life, our hearts' home, our place of belonging.
In it lies our freedom and our peace.

—From Yeshi's story

Autumn came, and Gunateeta died. For fourteen days the Igaal mourned for her, and the elders cast sticks on the ground to see who would be the new holy one, but the sticks showed nothing, and no one was chosen. Mudiwar limped about looking worried. I kept out of trouble, and Chimaki and I healed all who came to us. Though the deeper ways of healing and easing pain were still gone from me, my skill with herbs and needles and knives remained, and that I passed on to Chimaki. Now she was the healer and I her helper, and I think because of that more people came. We were kept busy.

Although it was autumn now, there was no rain, and Mudiwar said we must move to fresh grasslands for our herds. So everything was packed up, and the belongings loaded onto horses, or onto flat sleds that were dragged. One morning before dawn we left, traveling south. A slow journey it was, for most of us walked, and everyone carried something, even the children. The people sang as they went, glad to be going to a new place; but I was sad, for the move tore me farther from my own people and meant that on the night of my escape, in winter, my journey home would be long.

Near evening we reached a forest and camped under the first trees for the night, wrapped in blankets on the ground. The next morning we went deeper into the trees, following the river inland, and crossed the water at a place where it was shallow and wide. There, we set up our tents. Five days we were to stay in that place, for it was close to Navoran territory, and Mudiwar wanted only to refresh our herds before traveling far north, across the deserts.

On our third evening in the forest, when everyone else was talking and telling stories, Ishtok sat close to me and said, his head bent near to mine, "I want to take you somewhere tomorrow, Avala. Sleep in your clothes, have your shoes nearby. I'll wake you before dawn."

One thought swept over me: escape! Seeing the look in my face, he smiled a little and shook his head. "Not home, yet. Freedom for one day. Will that be enough for now?"

I nodded, and he got up and went to talk to someone else.

That night I thought I would never sleep. But suddenly he was shaking my shoulder, his lips close to my ear. "Avala! It's time."

Before I slipped from my blankets, he was rolling out under the tent wall, for our beds were close to the edge. Quickly, fumbling in the dimness, I pulled on my shoes and got my father's painted tunic from under the roll of my pillow. My hands shook, and my heart beat so wildly I thought the others would surely hear it, and wake. Then I crawled out under the tent flap.

It was very dark outside, for the tops of the trees blocked out the stars. Only the dim walls of the other tents glowed, from the low lamps still burning within. Two of the dogs rose from the shadows and would have barked at us, but Ishtok was prepared for them and threw them pieces of meat that kept them quiet. Then he took my hand and led me out between the tents. We passed the last of them and then stumbled in the darkness among the trees, to the edge of the forest. Ishtok's horse was there, tethered under a tree, already saddled for a journey. Beyond the last trees I could see the vast plain and, black against the stars, the jagged peaks of far mountains.

"Where are we going?" I asked, my voice quiet though we were far from the tents.

"Not to your people, I'm sorry," he said. "I can't do that, not today. Today my father would know, and flog me, and never forgive me. The time for your escape is at the Feast of Forgetting, as we planned. But there's somewhere else I'm taking you, for a day. Someplace else that will mean a high lot to you."

"But won't you be punished, even for this?"

He mounted his horse and leaned down to offer me his hand, to help me up. "Probably," he said. He tried to pull me up behind him, but it was a while before I managed to clamber onto the beast, and we laughed a lot, quietly. I settled there at last, and it was strange to be so close to him, my face brushed by his hair.

"Put your arms around my waist, and hold on tight," he said. "We'll start off slowly, and go easily. I won't let you fall."

I did as I was told, and he picked up the reins and clicked his tongue, and his horse moved off. I was glad it only walked, for I was afraid of falling off; but when the trees were behind us, and the forest grass gave way to the dust of the plain, Ishtok kicked the horse into a trot, and soon after that into a gallop, and I clung to him more tightly. Soon the forest was far behind us, and I asked him, shouting above the pounding of the horse's hooves, "Where are we going?"

He shouted back, over his shoulder: "To your Shinali land!"

At first I could not believe his words. Then joy swept over me, wild and sweet and unexpected, and I laid my cheek against his back, and hugged his waist more tightly still. Briefly he laid one hand across both of mine, and squeezed, and we went on.

The sun came up, warm on my back. The mountains rose before us, their slopes tawny, still bare from summer's blast. Desolate they were, with a wild, bleak beauty. Above them the blushing skies were cloudless, and there were eagles in the heights. Glancing behind me, I saw the plains stretching out on either side, empty and peaceful; and, far behind us now, the forest where we were camped. The wind scudded clouds of dust across the plain and was cool on our faces.

I looked to the front again, over Ishtok's shoulder, to the mountainous wall marching as far as the eye could see, to the south and to the north. Slightly to our left was the Shinali sacred mountain, Sharnath, important in the springtime rituals of our lost life, its summit golden in the sun's first light. Directly ahead of us was a shadowed cleft through the ranges.

"Taroth Pass," said Ishtok, pointing to the cleft. "It's the one pass through the mountains, by the place called Taroth Fort. I've heard the old warriors talking about it. In days long gone the fort was put there to keep my people out, and to stop them from fighting with your people, who had the treaty with Navora. They say the fort is deserted these days. I hope so, or we'll have to turn back fast, and trust to Shimit that no one sees us."

I, too, was worried about the fort, but for other reasons.

Ishtok stopped the horse, lifted his waterskin, and drank, then offered it to me. "I've got food, too, in the saddlebag," he said. "We can eat later. You can have your first meal on your own land."

"I'll always be grateful for this day, Ishtok," I said. "You don't know what you do."

"That's a truth," he said. "I hope I'm not leading you to your death. I'm hoping you'll be able to walk on the edge of your land. But it'll be Navoran crops and grazing fields by now, for sure. If there are people there, we'll only look, then get out. Fast."

"Even a look will be enough," I said.

He kicked his horse into a trot again. Quickly I slipped my arms about his waist and held on, enjoying the rhythm of the ride, marveling that we went so wondrously fast across the earth. As we neared the pass I saw the entrance clearly. The walls were steep and high, and I saw why it had been easily defended in days long past. It was the only place in the mountains wide enough for an army to quickly pass through. Today there were no soldiers that I could see, and we seemed alone in the wide, brown world.

The sun had not yet reached its height when we entered the dark shadow of the pass. A warm wind blew through, smelling of the grasslands beyond. The floor of the gorge was very flat, the cliffs towering on either side. Our horse's hooves echoed strangely, and sometimes we heard the sharp, high cries of birds far above. Once I shouted a Shinali battle cry, herald of the greater battle cries to come, but Ishtok told me to hush. He was a high lot afraid of meeting soldiers, though I felt no danger. About halfway through the gorge we passed a high waterfall that tumbled down steep rocks to become a narrow river. It rushed along to the left of us, its waters roaring and echoing along the high cliffs. The pass was almost straight, and as we came out at the other end, the view of Taroth Fort unfolded before us. Then an awful dread came over me, for it seemed that all the agony of my people hung about that place, and it was heavy with the heaviness of death.

Huge that fort was, its grim walls soaring as bare and bleak as the mountains all around. Four great lookout towers stood on the corners, and there was no way in save by the two high gates. The gateway was higher than an Igaal tent, and when closed the gates would have been impregnable, in days gone by; now they were broken, the remaining wood hanging in rotting planks from the big rusted hinges. And beyond the fort, its grass still summer brown, was the Shinali land.

"It's bare!" I cried, astonished. "After all the battles and the killing, the Navorans have done nothing with it."

We rode farther on, past the towering walls of the fort, alongside the river, on to the edges of the land. It lay before me empty, flat and unspoiled, as if waiting for our return.

Without a word Ishtok turned and offered me his hand, and swung me down from the horse. He, too, dismounted, and I heard him take the horse down to the river's edge. I waited, breathing in the tranquil beauty, the warm scent of the grassland. Then Ishtok came, leading his horse, and we walked together onto the plain. Not far onto the land I stopped and took off my shoes, so I could walk barefoot on the beloved soil. Ishtok took my shoes and followed a little way behind me. On I walked, and on, cherishing the dust, the shining river, the trees, the luminous Shinali air. For the land was still ours, untouched, and that was a marvel to me. A breathlessness was there, a sense of expectation, of waiting. As I walked I thought of all the stories I had heard, in those travel-worn tents of the Wandering; I thought of the story Yeshi had given me that last night with my people, and the songs and prayers of old Zalidas. And then it seemed that they were stories and songs no longer, but something more; and I saw, slow as if outside our time, images of warriors in battle, their faces marked with paint of blue and white, their great war-bows bent, their mouths open in the Shinali war cry. Soldiers there were, too, with bronze armor and shields on which red horses pranced, and white plumes on their helmets and shoulders. The earth trembled, and I heard the throb of drums, the clash of steel, and saw the silver flash of swords, and the bright flights of arrows. The scenes of battle faded and passed.

I saw flocks of sheep, and children minding them, and women sitting by the river with looms, weaving. Sound of flutes and pipes, and people dancing in rain. And old men chanting, their voices cracked and dry, torn by the ancient wind. Then battle again, and a house burning, burning, and darkness, and people walking away. The smell of fire, and the sound of something clanging, like metal cooking pots. Then this stillness, this waiting.

I knelt on the ground, and then lay on it, my cheek against the earth, my arms spread wide. I wept and prayed and sang, and then lay quiet, feeling the earth beneath, the memories of generations layered in the sacred dust.

When I stood I saw Ishtok nearby, his face taut with worry.

"Don't go too far out, Avala," he said. "If someone comes, we're dead."

"There's no one around," I said. "Look—nothing but grass, and memories." I caught sight of the farms on the other side of the river, the strip of land my people had sold to the Navorans.

"My Navoran grandmother lives there," I said. "I wonder which farm is hers?"

Ishtok chewed his lower lip, nervously. "I hope you don't want to visit her," he said.

Smiling, I turned to go back. But at that moment I caught sight of something a little farther along, about halfway along the plain. "I think that is where our house was," I said, shading my eyes from the sun. "There's something standing on it."

I began walking toward it, and Ishtok came with me, still leading his horse. I felt the tension in him, the fear that we walked openly where Navoran eyes might see us, and I took his hand and gave him my peace. For peace I did have, out on that land, despite all that had happened there. There was a presence in that place, a joy-wildness, as if it lay under the All-father's hand, secure in his safekeeping. For the first time I understood, with all of my knowing, why my people longed for this land, this windswept plain, this place of belonging: it was Home.

We reached the mound in the earth and discovered that it was a garden. It was enclosed by a low wall of river stones, and wildflowers grew within, and herbs. And in the center, high on a pole, streamed a white flag, and on it, in blue, a graceful sign of looped and interlacing lines, decorative but simple, without beginning or end.

"A Navoran banner," said Ishtok, and I was surprised at the anger in him. "Shall I tear it down?"

He would have leaped over the stones at once, but I put my hand on his arm. "Wait! That blue symbol painted on it, it's Shinali. It's our sacred sign for dreams. And it means more, for it's the sign that the spirit world and the earth world are both the same; that a word foretold in the spirit world will have its full form in this one."

Astonished, we stood staring at the banner flying over us with its brave sign, at the bright garden.

"Whoever painted the sign was a friend to your people," said Ishtok. "But why would they plant flowers where your house was?"

"The house, it was used as a funeral pyre the night my people left this land," I said. "Most of the house was underground, with a roof of grass. All my people lived in that one house. After the last battle they put all the dead Navoran soldiers and the dead Shinali warriors in the house, and set the roof on fire. Someone has covered over the bones, and filled the hollow, and made it a sacred place. But who would know what the dream-sign means, unless they were Shinali themselves?"

"Perhaps someone from your tribe came back," said Ishtok.

"No. No one has walked here from my tribe, until today. It must have been a Navoran, perhaps from the farms. Perhaps my grandmother. But I don't know how she would know our dream-sign."

We began walking back, and I noticed small things on the

ground—a child's shoe, and a bone spoon, both weather worn and old. There were arrowheads, too, and many small, perfectly round stones. An image came to me, swift and dark, of people fleeing at night, bundles in their arms and on their backs, and children dragged along by their hands, crying.

As we neared Taroth Fort dread came on me again. As if he knew, Ishtok said, gently, "We'll ride past, Avala. You don't even have to look at that place."

"I want to go in," I said. "I understand, now, what the land means to my people. I have shared their peace, their joy. I need to understand their pain, too. Will you come with me?"

He took my hand, and we approached the gateway. For a long time we stood there, looking in on the abandoned courtyard. All around the mighty walls were built wooden rooms, fallen to ruins, and the dust was littered with grasses and the bones of wild animals. We went in farther, and the eerie silence of the place was full of ghosts. It seemed that all the pain of my world had been trapped there, and the screams of women and tormented yells of men and the crying of children had sounded but a moment ago, and been suddenly cut off, and the walls and the stones and the bitter dust still held the echoes.

Ishtok and I did not speak, but he tied his horse to a pillar on the edge of the courtyard and came with me while I looked around. In the courtyard was an old well, a broken bucket on the rim. I dropped a stone down, and it fell many heartbeats before it hit the bottom. There was no water. Not far from the well the ground was blackened from a cooking fire of years long past. I remembered my mother saying how they had starved here, and what little food they had been given was moldy and bad, while the soldiers who had guarded them had feasted well.

I went up some steps into what must have been the Shinali sleeping place, for there were a few blankets abandoned there, covered in rust brown stains. There was a child's little wooden horse in the dust, and a buckled metal cooking pot, and other things abandoned on the day of leaving. The place was open to the courtyard on one side, but on the walls people had drawn charcoal pictures of their life. I could not bear to look; the sorrow of the place, the despair, was like dust choking me. Ishtok put his arm about my shoulder, and we went outside into the sunny courtyard.

"My parents slept in one of the towers," I said. "My mother said it was the tower on the southwest corner. That one over there."

"If you want to go up, I'll come with you. If you want me to."

"I don't know, Ishtok. It's hard, being here. This place, it's where my father lived his last days. Where so many of my people died. Where Tarkwan, our great chieftain, was tortured, and where he died. There is so much pain here. And yet I also want to be here, to know, even if it breaks my heart."

He lifted his right hand and briefly stroked my cheek with the back of his fingers. "I'm here to mend it," he said. "That is what I wanted to do, today. To mend your heart. To make it strong."

I wept, and we went over to the tower together. The door was rusted off its hinges, and Ishtok threw it on the dirt behind us. Then he followed as I climbed the narrow, spiraling stairs.

Never had I been on stairs before, and there were many. And the walls were close, leaning in, suffocating. The air was stale, the dust unmoved since the day my father and my mother had walked

141

down these stairs for the last time. High above us a wind blew in the heights, moaning and whining like a wounded animal. Up we went, and up, resting sometimes, leaning on the curved stone walls. At last we came to the top, and a little wooden door. I turned the handle, and it swung almost silently open. We went in and for long heartbeats stood there, lost in amazement at what we saw.

The room was eight-sided, with eight stone pillars holding up the wooden beams of the roof. And between those pillars, all around, were wide windows open to the sky. Through those windows the whole world could be seen. Going over to the window ledge, we looked down. Though the window ledge was of solid stone, and wide enough to safely sit upon, the sudden spaciousness, the distance to the lands below, made me dizzy. I could see all the way to the sea. Clearly, I saw the land my people had lost, with the silvery river down the very center of it, and the tiny bright oblong that was the garden where the house had been. I saw the green and yellow squares that were the Navoran farms, the land of my Navoran grandmother. Beyond the farms were low green hills and trees, among them a gleam of white walls and towers, the wink of sun on something polished. I realized it must be the place where my father had learned his ways of healing. Past the hills, hazy with smoke and too far to see clearly, was the stone city of Navora.

As I leaned on the window ledge I looked at my hands, and it seemed that I saw my father's hands, for he, too, had stood in this place, and leaned on these stones, and looked down upon the country he loved. His presence was in the air here, in the wind that blew in from the sea. A long time I stood there, touching the stones he had touched, feeling him only a heartbeat away, a finished breath beyond.

Lost in the thought of him, I moved around the windows, and saw an old well-worn road going to the coast. Then sorrow swept over me, for my mother had told me of that road, and of how she had stood long summers past and watched my father walk away along that shining dust, and known she would not, in this life, see his face again. Overcome with grief, I bent my head in my hands. Too many feelings rushed over me, too many images, pictures built of stories my mother had told, fleeting awakenings in my knowing, quick visions of times past and people gone. For a moment I heard shouts in the courtyard behind us, and the clash of steel as soldiers exercised. The sounds echoed around the old walls, then were gone. Somewhere below birds cried; it was the sound of a child screaming. And in this room sighs and whisperings, and vanishing joys too sweet to bear. In this room I had been made.

"I am ready to go now, Ishtok," I said, wiping my face on my hands.

We went back down to the courtyard. The sun had already slipped behind the towering western wall, and the courtyard was mainly in shadow, and cold. Shivering, we got the horse and left the fort. Outside the gates we scanned the land and coastal road, looking for soldiers, but saw none. We were totally alone, the fields and roads bare, the only dust raised up by skittish winds.

We drank at the river and filled our waterskins, and Ishtok got a package from his saddlebag. "I almost forgot. Your first meal on your own land," he said, smiling as he passed me a hunk of bread and cold meat that he had brought. "If you feel like eating now."

"I do," I said. "The fort was not the end of my people's history, and the best part of the story is yet to come. I'd like to eat on our land, and have the first of many feasts."

We sat on the edge of the grasslands and I gave thanks to the All-father, and we ate and drank. The silence there, the radiance of the land, was breathtaking. One last time I walked on it, out just a little way, and knelt and said a prayer. I lifted up some of the dust, and looked at it in my palm, wishing I could take it with me. And then Ishtok came with a little leather bag no larger than my palm, and crouched by me and held the bag while I trickled in the dust. "I knew you would want to take some," he said. And his smile, the tenderness and understanding in his eyes, healed my heart.

"You make up for all the wrongs your people have ever done to me and mine," I said. "Thank you, with *sharleema*."

"It was my joy to give you this day," he said.

He closed the bag with a fine leather thong and placed it about my neck. For many heartbeats his hands stayed there, on my neck, his fingers lightly caressing my skin. Then, smiling a little, he turned away and whistled to his horse, and we mounted for the journey back to his people's camp.

I looked back one last time upon the Shinali land. The sun was low, its brightness blinding. It seemed that the Navoran places were already on fire. I blew a kiss toward the farms where my Navoran grandmother lived, then turned and slipped my arms about Ishtok's waist, and we left.

Slowly we went at first, so we would raise no dust to betray our presence. But halfway down the gorge Ishtok kicked the horse into a trot, and I held on to him more tightly, my hands clenched in front of his waist. He placed one hand across both of mine, and held it there all through that journey.

Cold it was, on this far side of the mountains, and we traveled in purple shadow that stretched out on the flat lands before us, the far edges torn into the shapes of the jagged peaks. Beyond the shadow the world was gold.

It was near the middle of the night when we arrived back, and the whole camp was awake. There were cries of relief, and Ramakoda came to greet us both, shaking his head and half smiling, and I was sure he knew where we had been; but Mudiwar roared at us to go to his tent and wait for him there.

That night Ishtok and I were in a mighty lot of trouble. Mudiwar had thought that Ishtok had taken me home to my people and was furious with him. "You never, *never* go away for a day like that again!" he shouted, in front of all the people gathered about. "Where did you go?"

"Just out on the plain," said Ishtok. "Just riding."

"Ramakoda went out looking, and did not see you."

"We were in the shadow of the mountains."

"Near the mountains? Name of Shimit, were you trying to get yourself killed? There's Taroth Fort there, on the other side, and Navoran territory! Did you not think of soldiers? You're a fool, a fool! You could have been captured—or you could have led the soldiers back here, to us! You have placed all of us in danger. You should be horsewhipped, you and Avala. What have you to say in your defense?"

"Avala has done a great many good things for this tribe," replied Ishtok, quiet and calm, unmoved by his father's wrath. "All we have given her is slavery and pain. I gave her a day of freedom, that is all."

"A day of freedom?" raged Mudiwar. "She's a slave, not a trained falcon you can release when you feel like it!" Then old Mudiwar's eyes narrowed, and he said, almost spitting out the words, "Did you take her to the Shinali bit of dirt? Because if you did, I'll kill you, and after that I'll take away your horse."

Ishtok said nothing.

Ramakoda came forward through the people crowded into the tent and said, "They are home safely, my father. Ishtok is right; we have done a great wrong to Avala, and perhaps this day a part of it has been put right. Let it be."

Mudiwar turned on Ramakoda then, a terrible rage in his face. But suddenly the old man threw up his arms and said, "Oh, Shimit take the lot of you! I'm tired. I'm going to sleep."

One of the slaves rushed to spread out his sleeping-furs, and people smiled at one another, relieved, and got their bedding. Ramakoda said something quietly to Ishtok, and it must have been a warning, because for once Ishtok did not place his bed next to mine. Lamps were put out, and people began to snore. I lay thinking about the day, holding it in my knowing, treasuring it, even the terrible moments, the echoes, the pains, and the stupendous joys. I thought of Ishtok lying not too far away in

146

the dark, and remembered his understanding and his warmth, the feel of his hands upon my neck, the nearness of him. Gratitude flooded through me, for the great gift he had given me that was this day. At last I slept, holding in my hand the little bag of Shinali dust, and dreamed of the shining land.

11

The fiery leaves of autumn faded and fell, then winter breathed its cold across the land. By then we had moved back to our former camp. We had not traveled farther north, for Mudiwar was not well, and the journey would have been too much for him. Now that it was colder, the thicker clothes were taken from the large wooden chests in the chieftain's tent, and I was given long winter dresses and shoes and a white coat of rabbit fur. Kimiwe said the clothes had been her mother's, but Ramakoda made no comment.

Mudiwar's illness worried me. At times, when he exerted himself, he could hardly breathe, and his lips were always blue. Worn out, he went to bed early each night, and lay listening to the stories and jokes, but not taking part. One evening I went and sat by him, and put my hand on his chest. I could feel the rattle of his lungs, and his awful struggle to breathe.

"Do your *munakshi* on me, Shinali woman," he growled, between labored breaths. "I command it."

"Such healing cannot be commanded, my chieftain," I said. "But I will try."

But though I stilled my mind and heart and prayed, and tried to visualize the healing light flowing through my hands to him, the power did not come. I tried to feel love toward him, to awaken a fondness, as if he were a grumpy but honored grandfather; but I felt nothing. His was the word that kept me here against my will, his command the cause of all my sorrow and pain, and I could not wipe that out.

"I'll get some medicine for you," I said, removing my hand.

As I stood to go to my healing tent, he said, "Useless Shinali witch! I don't believe you've lost your power! I think you do it out of spite! You're like all your people—a stinking parasite, a leech on the nation that shelters you!" Then he collapsed, exhausted.

In my healing tent I got the medicine for him, then sat alone awhile in the dark, shivering, lost in grief and doubt and a terrible longing for home.

Then came the day of the first snow, and there was excitement as the people prepared for their Feast of Forgetting. For the first time in my stay with them, they were to eat inside their tents, and Kimiwe told me they would eat inside all winter long. But the food was still cooked in pits outside, and the men did the cooking, wrapped in their furs against the fierce wind. Beyond them, the youths put up a low tent for sheltering the goats at night, and to keep them safe from wolves. The oldest goats had been killed for the feast.

While everyone else was busy outside Ramakoda came to

me with a bag he had made, and told me to hide it under my sleeping-furs, with my coat and anything else I wished to take. "There is food in the bag," he said, "enough for the day's journey. I can't tell you how much I wish I was going with you, with all the gifts and goodwill that you and I both had dreamed of. You'll always be in my heart, Shinali woman."

There were things I wanted to say to him, but some of the men came in, calling for him, and he turned and went out.

When the feast began I sat alone with my back to the tent wall, watching what was going on. All night the people ate, and laughed, and sang songs and told stories. At times the musicians banged drums and the women clapped, and the men got up and danced. They did not paint their faces the way we Shinali did but wore masks carved out of wood, stained with garish colors. Several times Ishtok came and sat with me to talk, but Chimaki was with me much of the time, and he said nothing about our plan.

All the next day I waited while the feast went on and the *kuba* flowed. I did not eat much, for I was too excited, thinking on my escape. While Chimaki was talking with the women, Ishtok came and sat by me.

"I've hidden my bow in your healing tent," he said quietly. "I've put my coat there, too. When it is dark outside I'll give you a signal. It will mean that I am going to get my things, and that after a short time you must leave, too. I'll be waiting for you at the western side of the tents. Don't try to say good-bye to anyone, lest they are questioned after, and punished for not telling Mudiwar. Only Ramakoda and I know you are going."

"Will you be punished?" I asked. "Mudiwar will surely know you helped me."

"Mudiwar is already far gone with *kuba*. By tonight's middle they'll all be far gone. I'm going to pretend I've drunk too much, so that if anyone does remember I disappeared for a time, I can say I fell over on my way back from the toilet pit, and fell asleep in the snow. It happens. You're not afraid, are you?"

"I'm terrified. What is the signal you'll give?"

"I'll flap my arms like eagle's wings."

We smiled, and he put his hand inside his shirt and drew out something wrapped in fine leather. "Talking of eagles," he said, "I have something for you."

Unwrapping his gift, I discovered a drinking cup, beautifully formed out of wood. The bowl itself was perfectly smooth and round, but underneath it the wood was carved into an eagle, its wings spread wide and sweeping upward to hold the bowl. The bird was shaped as if it were just coming down to land, and its lowered talons and the tips of its tail feathers formed points for the cup to stand upon. For a few moments I could not speak; never had I been given such a gift, except for the tunic my father had painted.

"It's beautiful," I said at last. "I'll treasure it, Ishtok, as long as I live. Thank you, with *sharleema*." I touched his sleeve in the Igaal way of showing gratitude, and in the dimness I saw that his eyes were wet.

Softly, he kissed his fingertips and laid them against my cheek, then he went back to the dancing. Long heartbeats after, I felt his touch on my skin, the warmth and gentleness of him. So many times, since our journey to the Shinali land, we had been close, and many times I had thought that he would kiss me. But he never had, nor had we spoken of our feelings, and I supposed it was because I would soon be gone, or because he had made promises to a beautiful Hena girl called Navamani. As I watched him go back to the dancing now my heart ached, and I thought how fine he was, and how much I would miss him after this night.

Bending my head low over the cup he had made, I traced the eagle's wing, and thought of the eagle on the bone *torne* Yeshi wore. The images blurred, combined, both unspeakably precious to me. I wrapped the cup in the leather again, and, when no one was watching, put it carefully in the bag hidden behind me, under my bedding, close to the tent wall.

Ramakoda came and sat with me for a few moments. He brought me some food. As he gave me the bowl he said, "Go well, sister of mine. We'll meet again, in the Eagle's Time."

"I live for that day," I said. "Thank you for all that you have done for me, Ramakoda. For being an older kinsman to me in every way, for protecting me and helping me."

"Not as much as you've helped me," he said. "But for your help, my bones would be bleaching out by the Ekiya, and Kimiwe would be flying in the wind. I owe you a great debt, and will never forget it."

"My heart and yours will always be together," I said and touched my hand to my chest, then to his.

"They surely will," he said. "Shimit go with you."

Then he stood up and went back to the dances.

Chimaki came and sat by me, leaning her head on my shoulder. My heart ached, thinking I would not see her again.

152

"You're a good healer, Chimaki," I said. "If anything ever happened to me, you'd manage well on your own. You know the medicines to give to Mudiwar. If his breathing gets hard, make him breathe over steaming water with leaves in it from the *inagha* plant."

"Nothing will happen to you," she said.

Darkness came, and more hot meat was brought in, and more jars of *kuba*. There were more dances, prayers, and rituals, and I half-listened, drifting in and out of sleep, for none of us had slept much the previous night. I woke suddenly, disturbed by the lack of noise. They all were sleeping, many of them snoring, men, women, and children lying every which way on the rich carpets, beyond knowing, thick furs pulled roughly across them. Even the slaves slept, and the brazier fires burned low, their glow flickering across the furs and flushed faces, and on the drinking cups and empty food bowls stacked high on the wooden chests. I could not see Ramakoda or Chimaki, though Kimiwe slept near me, a doll clutched in her arms.

Across the dim tent someone got up and stumbled over the sleeping forms toward the door. He turned and looked at me, and I saw that it was Ishtok. He flapped his arms like wings, then went out.

My heart thumped painfully. I longed to hug Kimiwe, to say good-bye to her, but I simply kissed her cheek while she slept, then dragged my bag and winter coat from under my furs. I was already wearing new boots Ramakoda had made me, and the warmest winter dress I had. Shaking, sick with apprehension and joy, I lifted the tent flap and rolled outside, dragging my bag after me. The other tents around were powdered white under the moonlight, and were quiet. There was no one but myself outside. I could smell smoke from the cooking pits, and could hear the river rushing southward into the night.

I pulled on my coat and laced it up, then took the mittens from my bag and drew them on. I pulled my hood over my head, and placed my bag over my shoulder. My breath was white in the moonlight, and the cold made my face ache. It had stopped snowing, and a moon, sharp as ice, blazed among the bitter stars. I turned westward and began walking.

I walked quickly, my steps crunching on the snow between the sleeping tents; no one came out. Once a dog barked, hearing me, but a man sleepily swore it to silence. On I went, past the last row of tents. Ishtok was there, on the edge of the plain, his fur coat black against the snow. His bow was across his back, with a quiver of arrows. He said no word but turned toward the plain, and we began walking. On and on through the winter whiteness we went, into the silence and the west. Running east to west were the five stars we Shinali called the Pathway of the Sun, and we followed their direction. Often we turned and looked back at the camp spread along the riverbank, but there was no one about. We did not speak.

We were halfway across the plain before Ishtok relaxed and said to me, with a grin, "This is your freedom, Avala, forever this time. What does it feel like?"

"A high lot joyful," I said. "But sad, too."

He took my hand, and I wished I were not wearing mittens, so I could feel our hands palm to palm. He was not wearing a hood, and there were flecks of snow in his black curls. He did not speak again, and we walked quickly across the moonlit plain. An age, it seemed, since I had ridden across this plain in front of an Igaal rider, with Ramakoda moaning beside us. I looked back at the tents; already they seemed like another world. Ahead were the forested hills. I could see the tree trunks stark against the snow ahead, but they were layered with white above. Then the plain was behind us, and we were in the shadows under the trees.

Letting go of my hand, Ishtok took his bow, and got an arrow in readiness. "Wolves," he said. "Maybe bears. We'd make an easy prey. Keep very quiet."

It was easier walking in the forest, for little snow had fallen through the branches, though the ground was dark. Through the treetops I glimpsed a sky already turning gray. Once we saw two wolves, their eyes yellow and their breaths misty, and Ishtok yelled at them and they fled, vanishing like smoke among the trees. He had not even lifted his bow, though I was glad he had it.

Too soon we were through the forest, facing a wide plain pink from the dawn, with mountains on the other side and a black river cutting through the white. The Ekiya.

"Here's where we say farewell," said Ishtok. "You will be safe; the soldiers never come in the winter. But go quickly."

I pressed my hand to his breast, over his dark fur coat, and spoke the Shinali farewell. He placed his hand over mine, and bent his head until our brows touched. He was much taller than I. His breath blew like mist about my face, and was warm. Briefly his lips brushed mine.

"May all the gods go with you," he said.

I wanted to say things to him, deep things, but did not know where to begin. Then suddenly it was too late, and he was backing away, trying to smile, failing. Behind him the sun rose red in a stormy sky. Clouds, black and heavy, were tumbling in from the north.

"Go well!" he called, and waved once, then turned and vanished among the trees.

A long time I stood looking at the shadows that had swallowed him. Then, from far in the forest a wolf howled, and I turned and began walking across the wide white grasslands. The sun was lost again behind heavy cloud.

By the day's middle I had reached the ravine carved by the wild Ekiya through the mountains, and the river tumbled out to meet me before plunging northward to the plains. I stopped and ate some of the meat Ramakoda had packed into my bag, for I had eaten little at the feast, and drank from the waterskin he had given me. Not far to my left was the sloping rock, slick with ice, that I had hidden beneath when the soldiers came. So long ago, it seemed.

Once more I looked back across the plain toward the Igaal lands, but saw no one following. Already it was snowing again over the forest, and the air was like ice. I thought of Ishtok, no doubt already in his bed again, perhaps asleep. I wondered how long it would be before they would notice I was not there. I tramped on, the river booming beside me, its tumultuous voices echoing down from the high cliffs around. This was familiar territory, though made gloomy and bleak by the snow and ice, and it gave me so much joy to see it again—though even this joy, much longed-for and much imagined, was overshadowed by a niggling fear. Trying to blot it out, to feel only the pleasure of my homecoming, I sang Shinali songs, and strode on.

The skies were heavy with impending snow by the time I reached the end of the gorge. I rounded the last bend, my breath stopped, my heart already leaping at that precious sight of home—and there was nothing there.

I stopped, astounded, unbelieving. I rubbed my eyes, went forward a little way, shut my eyes, then opened them again. The valley was there, the river running dark beside the place where we had lived, the Napangardi Mountains white and majestic beyond—but the tents, the tents were gone. The ground was smooth, white with snow, empty. Silent. No cooking fires, no children. No laughter. No welcoming shouts. Nothing.

I stumbled on, sobbing, shaking my head and calling out the names of those I loved, all my worst fears crashing over me. In the middle of the valley I stopped, looked back, looked all around. I was shaking, shocked, aching all through, aching in my heart, my head. I searched the ground, looking for a sign. How could they have gone without leaving a sign? How could they have gone without me? Then it hit me—that maybe they thought the soldier I had seen had not been Embry at all, but someone else who had betrayed me, and that the Navoran soldiers had come back and taken me prisoner. Maybe my people had fled, believing their hiding place no longer safe. But where had they gone?

I turned all around, looking at the many long passes into the mountains, wondering which way they had fled. And then I realized that now they would be a summer's worth of journeying away. There was no way I would find them. They were gone, and I was alone in the world.

I cannot tell the misery I felt that hour as I sat in the snow in the valley that had been home, and wept and wept for all that I had lost. And while I wept it snowed, and a wind came, and my tears turned to ice on my cheeks. At last I got up and faced back the way I had come. Alarmed, I saw nothing but whirling snow and the gorge rapidly vanishing in mist. I could just make out my footprints, half covered already, and began to follow them. I would find shelter in the gorge, maybe even a little cave, where I could wait until it was safe to journey back to the Igaal.

Snow fell heavily, blowing about me in great drifts, and I could see nothing. I stumbled on in the whiteness, my eyes smarting with the cold, every breath an ache. On and on I walked, blind and frozen. Sometimes I thought I saw a shadow, a deepness in the white, and thought it was the river; but I never found it, and there were no cliffs, no sign that I was in the gorge. Then came fear, terrible and overwhelming. At last I found myself pressing against great piles of snow, and realized they were rocks. Feeling my way around them, I found a tiny cleft and curled up there, covering myself with my blanket. There I stayed while the wind wailed and moaned all around, and the snow blew over and weighed heavy on me, and all the world was white.

I slept, and when I woke it had stopped snowing, and a great quiet lay all around. My blanket had frozen, and the snow on it had made a kind of den. Peeping out, I saw an orange sun sliding down behind unfamiliar peaks. Trying not to panic, I said a prayer to the All-father, then ate half the bread that was left, and dozed again.

When I next woke it was day. I was in a valley surrounded by mountains. It had stopped snowing but the skies were brooding

158

and dark, hiding the sun, and there was a freezing wind. Though I was hungry, I dared not eat the last of the bread, not yet. I went on, lost, in deepening despair. The cold went right through me, and I walked with my blanket about me, hitched up across the lower part of my face, and my hood pulled tight about my head; but still my eyes watered and froze in the wind, and my ears ached, and my feet felt like ice.

All around me were jagged peaks veiled by cloud. The wind shrieked and howled, blowing snow and mist about me so thick that at times I could not see my own hand in front of my face. I had journeyed before with my people in the winter, and I struggled to remember what I had been taught, what they had done in such times as this. But my head was full of mist, and my thoughts scrambled like little foxes that would not be caught. I ate the last of my bread, then went on, somehow putting one foot in front of the other, hardly knowing anymore who I was or where I was going. I fell and could not get up.

Strange dreams came, and I thought I was back in the Igaal tent, for I could hear chanting. Strangely, the voices were not rough anymore to my ears but were harmonized and very beautiful. I thought someone knelt beside me, for I felt warmth, and from the corner of my eye glimpsed a scarlet robe; but when I looked there was no one there. I have no knowing of how long I lay in the snow and sleet; but when I lifted my head I saw a steep cliff, almost vertical. I blinked, thinking I was seeing visions; for there was a door set in the icy rock, a door that was huge and beautiful, and the stone all around it was carved with many signs.

Sorrow and hope went over me, and I thought that I was already in the shadow lands, and that the door was the gateway to the realms of the All-father. I remember that I wept and was afraid, but then I thought that I would soon look upon my father's face, and a kind of joy fell on me. Summoning all my strength, I called out the All-father's name and reached my hand out toward the door. Then, my strength finished, I lay in the snow and waited for death.

12

To my surprise death was warm, blessedly warm. I thought a spirit-being had come for me and was carrying me through the shadow lands, for I was being borne along in strong arms—oddly strong and solid, for a spirit. I tried to open my eyes, but a heaviness lay across them, and it felt as if something was bound about my head. Had I injured myself? Moving a little, I felt fur against my cheek, not the wet, frozen fur of my own garments, but fur that was soft and fragrant with a scent like spices. A huge silence was all around, and the air was warm. I smelled rock and fire. I could hear hoarse breathing, and sudden fear swept over me. I struggled to tear away whatever was over my eyes, and a man's voice said, with great gentleness, "Have no fear. All is well."

An awe fell over me, for his words were Navoran. And I wept then, certain I was in the shadow lands, and that the man who carried me was my father.

"I'm wanting to see your face," I said, barely able to speak for joy.

"Ah—you speak my tongue!" he said, and sounded surprised.

"My mother, she taught me."

He made a sound like a laugh, soft and surprised. "Then we shall understand each other," he said. "We'll be with friends soon, and you'll be looked after. I'm sorry for the blindfold; our place here is secret."

"I thought all knew of death," I said, and he laughed again, heartily, and the sound was rich and real.

"You're not dead," he said. "Though I think you would have been by nightfall, had I not found you."

"You're not my father, then?" I said, and wept again.

"No. Go to sleep, Igaal girl. We've a long way to go yet, and if we don't talk I can begin your healing."

Weary in my soul and in my body, I did sleep, and dreamed strange dreams.

I dreamed of a long winding tunnel with red lights at intervals, marking a strange dark road. I dreamed of a warmth like water trickling into my mind, into the huge spaces of my heart, and with the warmth came strength. There was a sense of welcome, of being known and loved, and of deliverance. Strong wind blew like breath into my face, into my soul, and I wondered if this was death, or a new birth. And then there was only quiet, and rest.

After a time I heard a rustling like leaves in the wind, and opened my eyes and saw a golden light and a dark shape nearby. The light became a lamp, and the dark shape a man. He was reading a book. I had seen a book before, for my mother had a book of my father's, sent to him as a gift when they were imprisoned in Taroth Fort. A long time I watched him read, thinking of my father. The man was wearing a crimson robe with silver stars on the shoulders of it. It surprised me that the robe was like a dress, which he wore instead of trousers, and remembered that my mother had told me that my father had worn such a robe in his own place. The man was fair-skinned, though his long curling hair was black like raven's wings, and he had a short dark beard streaked with gray. I could not see the color of his eyes, for they were cast down upon his book. His hands, as they turned the pages, were a high lot beautiful.

He saw me looking at him, and closed his book. His eyes were brown.

"Ah—you're with us in truth!" he said. He spoke Navoran, and I recognized his voice, for he was the one who had carried me to this place. "Is all your pain gone, Avala?"

I nodded, feeling warm furs about me. I moved my hands, felt that I was clothed in garments soft and smooth, not the thick Igaal dress I had worn. I was clean and dry. I wondered if he had washed and changed me, and my face flamed at the thought. My hands and feet were no longer numb, and all the pains of the cold had gone. Then it struck me that he had called me by my name.

"You have knowing of who I am?" I asked.

Smiling, he got up and went to a door across the room, and spoke to someone outside. I overheard him asking for a meal for me. Then he came back and sat down again. "I know much about you, about who you are," he said. "I'm sorry, but when I found you it was necessary for me to walk in your memories. We should never do this without first asking permission, but you—"

"'Permission'?" I repeated. "What meaning? My Navoran, it's not a high lot good."

"Sorry." He smiled again, and little lines creased about his eyes.

"I'll try to explain so you can understand. You were unconscious—that is, unknowing—when I found you, and I couldn't ask who you were or why you were here. It was important for me to know where you were from. I needed to know if it was safe to bring you here. Do you know what I mean by walking in memories?"

"I have knowing of it," I said. "My mother, she said my father was having that power."

"Your father? An *Igaal* can walk in memories?" The book slipped from his hands and fell onto the floor. He did not pick it up.

"I am Shinali. My—"

"Shinali? But your memories showed Igaal territory, Igaal tents."

"I was being with the Igaal . . . ah, from summer." I struggled to find the right words. Though I understood a good part of the Navoran language when it was spoken to me, I was shy of speaking it myself, lest I made mistakes. But if I made them, he showed no sign, but only listened attentively. I continued, "My father, he was being Navoran. A healer. He was learning in the high white house."

"The Citadel?"

"Yes! My mother, she called it that."

The man stood up, staring at me as if I were a ghost. "His name?" he said. "Your father's name?"

"His name, it was Gabriel Eshban Vala. My name is his, and a little of my mother's, made into one name. My mother's name is Ashila."

For a long time he stared at me, his face pale. Then he said, his voice hushed, "Your father was famous among us. I had been

164

at the Citadel two years when he came, but word soon went about that he was highly gifted. Later, when he came under the wrath of Lord Jaganath, we knew he had taken refuge with the Shinali and was with them in the fort. And we heard of his death. But we did not know he had a daughter. Please excuse me—I must go and tell Salverion. You must speak with him."

He turned to go, but someone else came in just then, bearing a tray with food. The man I had been talking with helped me to sit up, and placed several cushions behind my back. As he bent close I smelled spices again, and as my hand brushed his robes I felt that they were soft as finest down. Later I found out that the robes were made of a stuff called velvet. At the time it was wonderful to me. All was wonderful—the fine garments, the fragrances, the bedcovers so richly embroidered, the beautiful tray he placed across my lap, which was inlaid with different colored woods, and spread with bowls of exotic food. I must have looked astonished, for the man laughed as he stood.

"We'll leave you in peace awhile, to eat," he said. "After, when you're refreshed, you can talk with Salverion. He was your father's teacher, and it will mean much to him to know who you are. Is there anything else you need?"

"Only your name, and the name of this place," I said.

"My name is Taliesin. I am one of the healers here."

"Thank you for being my help, Taliesin. What is this place, inside the door in the mountain?"

He looked amazed again and glanced at the man who had brought my food. In those moments I felt that important words, unspoken, went between them. My face grew hot, and I thought I had said something wrong, or else broken a custom unwittingly.

"You saw the door?" asked the man called Taliesin.

"For a little time. I thought I . . . ah, saw it only with eyes in here." I touched my heart.

For a long time the two men gazed at me, then Taliesin said, "You have some of your father's gifts, Avala. That door is kept hidden, secret. An ordinary person going past would never see it."

"You can make people—how do you say it—never-seeing?"

"Hush now, and eat. I'll come back soon. Please don't leave this room."

Then he was gone, the other man with him. For a while I ate and drank, groaning with pleasure at the deliciousness of the strange things supplied. At last, satisfied, I set aside the tray and got up to explore the room.

It was bigger than the biggest tent I had ever been in. The floors were covered with carpets even more colorful and wonderfully made than the Igaal mats I had admired. Here, too, were many carved boxes, some overlaid with what I later knew to be silver and gold, inset with precious gems. There were beautiful lamps upon stands, and many wondrously carved images of animals and people. There were tables cunningly carved and inset with different colored woods, and piled with books and gorgeous candlesticks and strange but wonderful objects I could not name. On a table near the bed was my bag, the things inside untouched. I took out the cup Ishtok had given me, and stood it on the shining wood. It looked alien in that place, yet as beautiful to me as anything else there.

But the most wonderful thing in the room was the light. The place was filled with a golden and warm radiance, though I could not see where it came from. On the far side of the room high pillars soared beside the stone walls, and between the pillars were spaces open to the world outside. Astonishment swept over me; the world was green, the snows gone. Just outside stood a tree, plump golden fruits gleaming among its leaves. Beyond, the skies were blue. Had I slept so long? I went to lean out into the spaces, to see the world directly below, and my head banged hard on the green hills. Bewildered, I lifted my hand and moved it over the scene before me; they were not sky and tree and hill at all, but images painted on the stone. Marveling, I looked up, and saw that the roof was high, very high, and that light poured down from above, light so shining that it hurt my eyes.

Hardly able to believe what I was seeing, I pushed aside a green curtain and entered a smaller room with a floor of polished stone and steps leading down into a stone pool. The pool was full of water that ran into it from a hole in the wall, and steam rose from the surface. Marvel upon marvel! There were tables bearing soft fabrics, thick and carefully folded; there were shallow golden bowls of small scented cubes, and delicate jars of fragrant liquids. I sniffed everything, even tasted some of the things, since they smelled so good, but they were unpalatable. And then I saw a shining oval surface on the wall, and in it my reflection, clearer than I had ever seen it before. Even in Zalidas's little mirror, my image had been dim in the lamplight, and—on the night that I had seen it—covered with the signs he had painted on me. But now, for the first time in my life, I clearly saw my whole face, undimmed and defined, as clear as the day.

I have to confess I was disappointed. I had always hoped that I had something of my mother's beauty, but my face was angular, my look intent and stern, more like a youth's. My whole body was angular, too straight to my thinking, unwomanly. My long hair was tangled, the little plaits in it half undone, the beads lost. I would have to do something about it, I thought. Sighing, I caught the image frowning, disgruntled, and could not help laughing.

Returning to the room with the bed, I ate some more of the food left for me. While I ate I looked at the wall to my left. In it was a door gorgeously carved, with a red curtain to one side. All the stone walls were painted, mostly with golden patterns as flowing and harmonious as a song. It all was rich, splendid beyond anything I could ever have imagined. I could not tell where I was; deep in the mountains, I had thought, yet this place was surely in the realms of the All-father.

After a while I heard footsteps, and the man called Taliesin came in. "Have you eaten all you want?" he asked, smiling.

I nodded.

"Salverion wishes to see you," he said. "You will need this." He held out a coat made of thick material trimmed with white fur. It was of a color I had never seen before, but I found out later it was purple. He also said I would need the shoes that were placed at the end of my bed. The shoes were soft but too big, and I asked him, as I put them on, where my own clothes were.

"They are being cleaned," he said.

Alarmed, I asked, "And the coat with canoes? The canoes, they are . . . are a high lot good, for me."

"That will not be soaked in water," he said. "Nothing will be spoiled, I promise."

Warmly dressed, I followed him out along narrow passages,

up steep stairways, and through small rooms hung with paintings and woven pictures so glorious I would have stood before them in wonder, had I not had to hurry on after the man. We came at last to an open door and passed outside into a courtyard. All around were the stone walls of buildings, with carved doors and windows with small balconies. Above, the skies were blue, and a wintry sun shone between light clouds swept by high winds. It was warm there, in that protected place, for the air was still and the sun warmed the light-colored stones at my feet. In the center of the courtyard was a fountain in a raised pool, with stone seats all around. To one side was a sundial, and on the other a beautiful statue of a man and a woman with two children. I did not know the names of the things, then, but I was told later what they were. And on one of the stone seats a man waited.

Old he was, with a thin rim of pure white hair that flowed down over his shoulders, and a long white beard. He too wore a long crimson garment like a dress, embroidered about the hem and sleeves with gold. He wore a white sleeveless tunic over the top, embroidered on the front with seven silver stars, and a green band about his waist. When he saw me he stood, and came to meet me.

He took both my hands in his, and for a long time stood looking at my face. His eyes were gray and shining like steel, and his smile was warm; and as he looked at me he shook his head a little, as if unable to believe what he saw.

"Gabriel's daughter," he said, and leaned forward and kissed my brow. "Welcome, welcome to this place. And again, welcome."

His voice was soft and gentle, and his face, though old and

covered with fine lines, wore a look of tranquility and deep joy. I remembered that my mother had told me that this man Salverion was the greatest healer in the world, and that my father had loved him above all others, save her. He it was who had sent my father the book, when he and my mother's people were imprisoned in Taroth Fort. I wondered if I should bow to him, as to a great chieftain; but he drew me to him and embraced me, close and warm, as a grandfather might.

Then we both went and sat down, and he explained to me what this place was. I will not record all my questions and his explanations, for I interrupted him often, especially when I did not understand his words, though he took pains to be clear; I will tell all, as if the Navoran language was as familiar to me then as it is now.

"Sixteen years ago," Salverion said, "our good Empress Petra gave the order for your people to be set free from Taroth Fort. It was the last order she gave as Empress, before she went into exile, leaving the Empire in the hands of a new ruler, Jaganath. It was Jaganath who had imprisoned the Shinali in the first place; and he had planned to have them all killed. He was, and is, a man full of evil, and driven by selfish desires. He has many powers and controls people in terrible ways. He knows only one fear: the Time of the Eagle, and the prophecy that the Shinali people will one day rise in power and bring his reign to an end.

"When Jaganath seized power he quickly claimed total control of everything, before the people had a chance to protest or revolt. He took over control of the Citadel, where your father and many others trained in the best arts of the Empire. Always the Citadel had been the place of highest learning, considered sacred, and set apart from all influence from outside. Even visitors were not allowed inside; its grounds were holy. Some of our masters, our great teachers, had the same mind-powers Jaganath had—power to walk in memories, to understand dreams, to create illusions of things that are not, and to alter the form of things that are. Our powers were, and remain, bound by strictest laws, but for Jaganath there were no rules. We were a threat to him, so early in his reign he took over the Citadel and would have killed us all. But we fled. Many of our disciples—those learning our ways—returned to their loved ones and homes, some of them to far places in the Empire. But seventy of us—masters, and disciples who wished to remain with us—came to this place in the mountains, that was known only to us.

"Many hundreds of years ago people from a great civilization had lived here. Our architects and engineers and artists restored this part of the hidden city, for we knew we would need to stay here for an indefinite time. There is but one entrance to this place—a carved door in the mountainside—and that is blocked from ordinary sight by our powers of illusion. And so we are well hidden, living in this secret place, awaiting the day of freedom when we may return to the Citadel.

"While here we have a great work to do, for we are at war. That war is with Jaganath and his powers, and his terrible desire to find the Shinali people and wipe them out. So afraid is he of the Time of the Eagle, that he searches for the Shinali, has searched long and hard, and will never give up. And so, in order to protect your people, we fight Jaganath in the spiritual battlefields, with the same powers that *he* uses to control and manipulate. We create mists and illusions of bare rock, so that when his spies are near to the Shinali, they see nothing. We put up supernatural walls, we protect, we safeguard. We call it Standing in the Gap, guarding the place between the hunter and the hunted.

"And that is our work, Avala. That is what we do, unceasingly, until your people befriend the Hena and the Igaal and return to Navora to reclaim what is rightfully theirs, as foretold in the prophecy. But that is about much more than the lost Shinali land. Freedom will be won back—freedom not only for the Shinali, and the Hena and the Igaal, but freedom for Navora, too. For we are not free, under Jaganath, and there is much wrong in our Empire that needs to be put right. The great and honorable country that our forefathers began has become an Empire of greed and oppression and persecution. The Empire needs cleansing, renewing, and that shall happen in the Time of the Eagle. That is the full meaning of the prophecy. But for Jaganath, it means simply the end to his power, so that is why he fears the Time of the Eagle, and only that.

"So you see, Avala, your people are not alone in their dreams. We dream with them, fight beside them already, and support and guard them. And, if you can believe it, many people in Navora and in the Empire would support you in your fight against Jaganath, for he is much hated and feared. The Time of the Eagle will be the time of deliverance not only for your people, but for mine as well."

For a long time after he spoke, we sat in silence. I felt that layers were peeled away behind a dream, showing more dreams behind it, more hopes than I had knowing of, and I realized how much hung upon our Shinali prophecy. I realized, too, another thing, that made my spirit leap.

"You have knowing of my people's place," I said, "seeing that you hide them from Jaganath's soldiers."

"Every day, we know where they are."

173

"Can you show me?"

"Of course. Come."

Inside, Salverion led me down a maze of passages, all lit with lamps, to a large room with no windows and only one door. It was brilliant with that strange light from above, and there were no lamps. The high walls were covered with shelves of books. Some of the books were not bound in pages but were scrolled about wooden spindles, beautifully carved. There were ladders placed round about, for climbing up to the higher shelves, and there were chairs and tables placed in the center of the room. Several men sat there, reading. They, too, were wearing long crimson robes, though the sashes about their waists were of different colors. They looked up as we entered, and all stood and bowed to Salverion. He talked with them awhile and told them my name and who I was, and several of them looked surprised, and welcomed me as if I were a friend. In all of them was that same beautiful gentleness, that sense of harmony and joy, that was in Salverion.

Then Salverion explained to me that we were in the library, for they had saved as many books as they could from the great libraries at the Citadel when they left. He took a long rolled paper from a shelf, and opened it on one of the tables, weighting the corners down with beautiful stones obviously there for that purpose.

"This is a map," he said. "It shows all the lands hereabouts, from the southern coasts up to the desert lands of the Hena tribes. Here is the city of Navora. There, Jaganath's palace. These are rivers, these the forests. And these lands—here, and here—

174

were the lands that once belonged to your people. This small part here, between these farms and these mountains, were the lands owned by the Shinali when your father knew them. And his mother, your grandmother, owns one of these farms, and lives there still. . . ."

I marveled, as I looked at that picture of my world, for I saw at last, in the space of a few heartbeats, all the lands we had fought over and lost, and longed to win again. I saw the wide spaces of the Igaal territories, and the vast deserts and marshlands of the Hena. I saw the river I had washed in, and the place where I had stayed in Igaal tents; I saw the mighty Ekiya where it tumbled through the ravine, and the places where I had walked and lived.

"And here," said Salverion, pointing to a place in the mountains far to the north, "here is where your people now dwell. They dwell at the foot of this high cliff, looking down across the deserts to the east. It's not a comfortable place for them, as it's deep in Igaal territory; but it's separated from the city of Navora by many ranges and rivers."

As I stared at that place it seemed that the map vanished, and I saw my mother bending over in the wind, turning meat upon torn flames, her eyes narrowed against the dust and flying ash. In the entrance of a cave she was, and behind her stretched a huge desert, white with snow. She looked cold, sad, and solitary, more than a season older.

"I'm wanting to go home," I said.

"Then you shall go, if that is what you want," said Salverion. In joy I looked up at him. He was smiling, sharing my happiness,

175

understanding my need; but a shadow ran swift across his face, and I felt a sorrow in him, like the loss of a secret hope. I looked at the map again.

"This place we are now, where is it?" I asked.

He pointed to a place in the mountains not very far from where my people had been when I last saw them, at the end of the gorge beside the Ekiya. "Here," he said. "We've named it on this map. It's called Ravinath, which is a very old word meaning 'to guard.'" He hesitated, then drew a deep breath and said, very quietly, "We need to speak further, Avala. I would like to know why you were with the Igaal people, and why there was, deep in your heart, the shadow of bitterness and grief."

Again I looked at him, astonished; his eyes were grave, going deep.

He took me to what I suppose was his private room, for it was furnished with comfortable chairs and lamps on stands, and a table littered with scrolls and books and carved boxes and many things that were alien to me. In one corner was a bed, narrow and raised above the floor, and spread with colorful rugs and cushions. A beautiful tapestry covered one wall, and there were many shelves of books and rolled-up parchments. Humble things, too, stood on shelves: rough pottery bowls, childishly carved wooden animals, and small handmade objects.

He told me to sit in one of his chairs, and I felt almost lost in it, for it was softer and more comfortable than any bed I had slept in, excepting the last. If my amazement at my surroundings amused him, Salverion did not show it; he was courteous and kind, and never made me feel ignorant or out of place, though I felt that I was. And I felt strangely breathless, shut in, for never had I lived with walls all around, out of the feel of the wind and the wild scent of grasslands and river and earth. Already I missed the openness, the sky.

As if he knew, Salverion said, "I know you are not used to walls, so we are preparing you a room on the edge of this place, with a window looking westward across the mountains. Don't look alarmed, my dear; you do not have to stay long. But your people are many days away, and we cannot make such a journey until the weather is settled and clear. Meanwhile, we will do everything in our power to make your stay with us comfortable. Now, when you are ready, tell me of yourself."

So I told him, stumbling in that unfamiliar tongue, but warming to the task in the easiness of his presence. I told him all: about my childhood and our Shinali Wandering; about the soldiers by the river, and my borning-day feast; of Zalidas's prophecy over me; of my fateful meeting with Ramakoda, and of my time with the Igaal. Briefly I talked of my enslavement, the loss of some of my powers to heal, and Mudiwar's tragic refusal to take part in the Time of the Eagle. Lastly, I told of my escape, and the help I had from Ishtok.

When I had finished Salverion asked me a few questions, mainly about the healing skills my mother had taught me, and the way they had been lost. "Most of the powers my mother taught me she learned from my father when they were in Taroth Fort," I said. "Some she has taught me, but not all. Some, she said, are a high lot secret."

"That they are," said Salverion. "Your father was bound by vows never to teach the skills he learned from us. But when he left the Citadel, I released him from those vows. I knew he would share

177

his skills wisely, with another healer who was worthy. I'm glad he found that healer, and that she, too, has found a worthy student. You are a gifted woman, Avala."

"I'm not feeling gifted," I said. "The Igaal, I should have been able to heal them, even when they were bad to me. My father loved an enemy people. I should have been able to love the Igaal."

Salverion smiled, and it was like a blessing on me. "You know the secret of healing, then," he said.

"I know it is love," I replied. "But I failed in it."

"You did not fail," he said. "You say that your father loved an enemy people, and that you, too, should have been able to love your enemies. But your father loved the Shinali for lifelong reasons, very deep, that even I did not really understand. From his childhood his destiny was bound with theirs. And when he finally met them, it was for him like a homecoming. I saw it in him, the pleasure when he mentioned them, when he spoke of your mother. The Shinali were not enemies to him. You, on the other hand, did go to an enemy people, willingly and bravely, and you healed them, believing it was your destiny. For that you were enslaved and starved. The healing that we teach, that your mother taught you, is very much from the heart and the spirit, from the very core of ourselves. And if our heart is hurt, our spirit wounded or weak, then healing is extremely hard, sometimes impossible— even for masters like me, or like your father."

I asked him about my father then, and he told me. Most of it I knew from my mother, but it was good to hear the words from someone else who loved him, who had seen another side of him. "He was the most gifted person I ever taught," Salverion said, in finishing. "Also the most compassionate and just. But he was unsure at times, afraid, hardly believing in his own gifts. And he had his faults. He was outspoken and could be childish at times, if he thought he was right and the rest of the world was wrong. I remember getting quite angry with him once and had to remind myself of how young he was, how unskilled in the ways of the world. I suppose that was one of the reasons I loved him; he was unspoiled, innocent, and incredibly honest. Like you, he struggled at times with the world he was forced to become a part of, with people who were false or unjust. He battled with inner hurts—and, I suspect, in the end, he battled with his own destiny. It is a struggle I think you may share with him, Avala."

Those eyes again, piercing me, dangerous and cleaving as swords. I looked away, tracing with my fingertip the carving on the arm of the chair. My nails had dirt under them. Igaal dirt.

"Do you still believe the words of your Shinali priest?" he asked. "The prophecy that you are the Daughter of the Oneness, the cord that binds?"

I dared not look at him. "My heart, it goes between believing and not believing," I said, studying the Igaal dirt. "When the Igaal let me heal their sick and talked with me, and their hearts were open, then I believed the prophecy. But then they made me a slave. And Mudiwar, he was so strong in his words against the prophecy, I'm thinking he will never join his people with mine. I see now that my belief in the Eagle's Time is not enough, nor the beliefs of all my people, and one old man can stop everything. So I want to go home. My work with the Igaal, the work of the Oneness, it's finished. They killed it. I will do with them no more. Now I will only be Avala, not more, not Zalidas's dream for Gabriel's daughter."

For a very long time he was silent, leaning on the arm of his chair, watching me, his long pale fingers laid across his lips. For some reason I felt ashamed of my words, as if they had been the complaint of a resentful child.

"I am right to want to go home," I said. "I helped them, and the Igaal gave me only hurt and hate. There is no fairness with them. It is over with them."

Slowly, Salverion nodded. "True," he said, "there is no fairness in any of this—not in the way your people lost their land, nor in the way the Igaal have treated you, nor in the burden that destiny has laid on you. But is it truly over with the Igaal, Avala? Is it over in your heart? Or, if you go back to your people now, will there always be unfinished work? Are you sure that Avala and Gabriel's daughter—the Daughter of the Oneness—are not one and the same?"

I bent my head low, not meeting his eyes.

After a while he said, "Sometimes there is only one way to end great wrongs, Avala. That way is through forgiveness."

"I'm not knowing that word," I said.

"Forgiveness means the wiping out of a wrong, as if it never was."

"Are you saying that my people should not come back to get their lands?" I asked. "Are you saying we should just forgive the wrongs? That we should forget what is fair, what is right?"

"There is a time for justice and for putting things right. But there is also a time for forgiveness, for letting hurts go, washing the heart clean, and beginning again."

I took a deep breath. "And it is in your thinking that I should forgive the Igaal, go back to them, and try again?"

"What do you think, Avala?"

For a long time I pondered on his words. At last I said, "I'm thinking I could forgive. It would be hard. A high lot hard. But even if I was going to them with forgiveness, to try again to be the Daughter of the Oneness, there is still Mudiwar's hate for my people, and his last word about our prophecy."

"Hate, even age-old and hard, can be worn down, as a little trickle of water can wear down a rock. And an old man may change his mind. Great things can be accomplished by love. And sometimes all that is required of us is that we be in the right place at the right time. Sometimes our destiny is not worked out over seasons or years, but in a single hour. But when that hour comes we must be ready for it, we must be trained and awake, sword in hand, ready to do the one thing we were born to do. If your hour is with the Igaal, it would be a great tragedy if, when that hour comes, you are home with the Shinali."

"But my hour might be next summer, or the summer after that, or twenty summers away."

"Yes, it might."

"And till then I am to be a slave, alone, my happiness gone, along with my healing?"

"To be a slave, maybe," he said. "To be alone, maybe. But whether you will be happy or not lies within your own heart. As for your healing, that can flow again. That is something I, and the other masters here, can help you with. We can teach you every- thing you wish to learn, everything that will help you to be happy with the Igaal, that will help you to heal them and lead

181

them to their own vision of the Time of the Eagle. We can teach you how to guard yourself against the forces of hate and loneliness, how to be strong within, to guard your inner peace. But only if you wish us to. And I ask you to bear in mind that even the greatest tasks, the greatest deeds, are worth nothing if they are not done with love."

I kept silent, for an awful grief had come over me. I wanted only to return to my people, to look on my mother's face again, and see my grandmother. Was that so wrong?

Seeing my distress, Salverion said, with great gentleness, "No one will blame you if you choose to go home, Avala. I will always think of you with highest love, as I loved your father, simply because of who you are, because you are Avala. Whatever you do will not change that. And you are very young; I know this is an almost unbearable burden for you. Pledging one's service to one's country, above all else, sounds a high and noble thing; yet in reality it is hard, cold, and comfortless as steel. Believe me, dear one, I know what you suffer. Every one of us here at Ravinath knows.

"You have already done a brave thing, already given your best, and more, to the Igaal, to the prophecy. If you return to them it may be for many years. The melding together of two enemy nations is not accomplished in a single season."

"Then what about the prophecy?" I asked, near tears. "What about the Time of the Eagle?"

"Even prophecies must rise or fall upon the free will of those chosen to fulfill them," he said. "Nothing is written that does not depend upon the consent of human hearts, and even God himself cannot move against the freedom of our will."

Anguished, I bent my head in my hands. I felt trapped, caught like a rabbit in a snare, and every way I turned was pain and loss.

Salverion said, "I understand your pain, Avala, your uncertainty. In that, you are so like your father. He, too, suffered self-doubt, and felt torn between two peoples, between duty to one and love for the other. I will go now, and leave you here to think, to make your choice. Take all the time you need. Do only what is in your heart; do it willingly, with your whole heart, with gladness and with love. Anything less will not be fulfillment—not of the prophecy, nor of your own joy."

He bent and kissed my forehead, and went out.

14

I have told you before, Mother, that in the palace and in the dining
rooms of the powerful, I hear and see many things that worry me,
about our Empire and what is happening to it. The old values that
Father cherished are no longer upheld, and there is a great deal of
corruption and hypocrisy. I cannot help remembering my two days
with the Shinali, and how much I loved the simplicity and the peace
and beauty of their life. I am glad you live next to their land, and
that you are open to building friendships with them, though this is
against Navoran law. There is an honesty with the Shinali, a heart-
openness, that I loved. Though I deeply love the Citadel and those
who teach me here, and life here is separate and far above the
corruption in the city, my heart is often out by the river, on
the Shinali land. I feel torn inside, divided in my soul.

—Excerpt from a letter from Gabriel to his mother,
kept and later gifted to Avala

The room I had been given was in a tower with a rounded
wall and a window looking to the west. The window had
folding wooden shutters and heavy red curtains to keep out the
winter cold. There was a bed raised from the floor, covered with
thick blankets and furs and tasseled cushions. On the floor were
rugs softer and more splendid even than the Igaal carpets.
There was not the brilliant source of light from high above, but
there were several lamps on stands. Set into the outer wall was a
hollowed place where a fire burned, and the smoke went up a
narrow shaft to the outside. Beside the fire were shelves of

books, not with words, but with pictures. Perhaps to make me feel at home, someone had placed the cup Ishtok had carved on a round table in the center of the room, and by it a small bowl of dried mountain wildflowers and fragrant herbs. The walls, like all the walls in Ravinath, were stone, richly carved and painted with harmonious designs. It was a lovely room, small and homely, and I knew everything in it had been especially chosen for my pleasure. But that first night there I could not sleep, nor be at ease.

At some time in the night I opened the window shutter and curtains and, wrapped in a thick fur, stood watching the slow journey of the moon. So high was my window, so high the mountain from which Ravinath was carved, that I could see over the western Napangardi ranges to where vast plains lay smooth and blue with moonlit snow. They were the lost Shinali lands, and beyond them was the sea, though that was past my sight. Below, the ground was lost in mist, and directly in front of my window clouds slowly passed, glimmering with moonlight. In the gaps between them were the stars, winking in the bitter cold. At any other time I would have found joy and wonder in such a place, but now I felt only entrapment and fear and confusion.

I was torn, terribly torn, between my own longings and the hopes of many people. And there was another thing that made it hard for me to choose to go back to the Igaal: I realized that, for all my high dreams and my belief that I was, indeed, the Daughter of the Oneness, there was a deep resentment in me toward the Igaal, for the way they had treated me. It was like a huge rock blocking a narrow path, and I could not walk around it, or climb over it, or pretend it was not there, no matter how hard I tried. In the end I always came back to the same hard truth: apart from a few people, I did not like the Igaal tribe and wanted to punish them for the hurts they had given me. But to punish them was also to punish my own people, and myself, for it was to refuse to play my part in the Time of the Eagle. And so, by that open window overlooking the moonlit Shinali lands, I came at last to the hard, breaking, painful place of forgiving.

But even then the final decision was not made. Although I felt freer in my heart, there was still the longing for my own people and home, and the grief that many summers might come and go before I saw them again. Restless and lonesome, craving someone to talk to, I pulled on a warm robe and my soft shoes, and went out.

The passages, though lit with oil lamps on the walls, were dim and very cold. Looking for Salverion, I went back down the stairs and passages I remembered but could not find the distinctive curtain to his door. I retraced my steps, found myself in unfamiliar passages, and discovered narrow stairs winding upward. I climbed them, thinking that at least I might arrive back at my own room. But I did not, and the stairs took me higher and higher, and the passages became narrower, and the oil lamps glimmered on ancient carvings I had not seen before. I shivered, suddenly overwhelmed by terror at being lost, closed in and imprisoned. The stone walls, the high roof lost in blackness, seemed to lean in upon me, suffocating me, crushing me. I fought for breath, wanted to call out, to scream. But then a calm came over me, and I went on, almost as if I knew where I was going, through narrower passages and up more winding and age-worn stairs.

186

I came at last to a door. I put my hands on it; it was warm. I pushed it open.

Warmth swept over me. Unafraid, yet with my heart hammering, I went in, closing the door behind me. The room was round and must have been the highest in Ravinath, for the domed roof was made of the clear stuff I later knew was glass, and I could see the moon and stars. In the center of the room, on a high-backed chair, sat a man well advanced in years. Very still he sat, his face upturned and luminous, his eyes closed, his beautiful long hands turned palm upward on his knees. Moonlight flooded over him. His hair was silver-white, long and waving to his shoulders, his skin darker than mine. He had no beard, but only a white mustache, soft and long. And on his face was a look of profound joy.

Soundless, I went and stood before him. For a few moments I thought he was a statue, for his face was so majestic and still; and the moonlight drained his clothes of all color, so there were only shades of moonlit blue and black. But then, very slowly, he took a deep inward breath, and his eyes opened. Such eyes! Dark they were, and deep, and wise almost beyond bearing. Under their steady gaze I felt naked, torn open to the heart, wholly known and understood. Yet it was not an unpleasant feeling, only strange, and very peaceful. Then the man smiled, and his smile was the most beautiful and loving I had ever seen.

"Don't be afraid, Avala," he said. His voice was deep and tender, with a strange accent. "I am Sheel Chandra. Your father was the son of my heart."

I was silent, overcome with awe. He was as I imagined the All-father to be, all-seeing and all-knowing, and yet all-loving, too.

"What is on your mind, beloved?" he asked. "Sit, and tell me."

There was a cushion on the floor near his feet, and so I sat on it. He wore soft shoes threaded with silver or gold, which shone bright in that flooding light of the moon. "I'm thinking you have knowing of it already," I said.

"I saw you the day you left your people, and you passed like a light out across the desert," he said. "I covered you with protection, then left you in the shadows with the Igaal, for I could not shield two tribes. It is true, I have some knowing of what is in your mind, but I would like to hear it from your lips."

So, in halting Navoran, I told him of myself and of the decision yet before me. Lastly, I talked of the one great dilemma that stood in the way of everything: my almost unbearable sorrow that my mother must believe me dead, and my desperate need to see her face again.

"If I could talk to her," I said, "if I could tell her it is well with me, then I could take up any work, and do it with all my heart. But the way is there for my going to her, and I can't not go, even for the keeping of a high prophecy. I'm sorry. I am bad. And I have a cold heart for others."

"You have just forgiven an enemy tribe for its great wrongs toward you," he said, smiling, "and you think you have a cold heart? There is nothing wrong with your heart, dear one. It is your daughter-love that cries out now, and that, too, is good, since you wish only an easing of your mother's grief. You have great love—and that is the highest of all things. I will tell you this, Avala: your mother, too, is awake this night, and all her thought is turned on you. She is in a good place to receive a message from your mind. You are not able, yet, to reach her on your own; but if you will sit here near me, and let me rest my hand on your head, then I will take you to her in our thoughts. Will you be afraid to do that?"

"No," I said. Then, knowing he knew, I added, "Well, a little lot afraid. Will she be afraid?"

"She may be at first, but then she will know great joy," he replied. "But to reach her, you must be very still, very calm, and go only where I lead. And when you see your mother, do not try to speak aloud, but only speak silently from your heart the things you most want her to hear. Keep your words few, your message simple and clear. It may be that she will not see you, but only be highly aware of your presence. She will hear your words with the ears of her heart. Do you understand all that I am saying, dear one?"

"I'm understanding it," I said.

And so I sat near his feet, my back against his knee, and lifted my eyes to the stars. I felt his hand on my hair, and power came from him, calming me, making me so still within that every beat of my heart seemed huge and slow, and the stars above pulsed with the rhythm that was in me. Then the shining roof blew away like mist before the wind, and I was lifted high, high, and the night streamed cool about me, and the mountains spread like crumpled rocks below, and the desert stretched far beneath, and I came to the place where my people dwelled.

It is hard to talk of this vision, this journey of my soul, of the great oneness I felt with the earth and the air and the stars, for it was a sacred thing and I do not understand it, even now. But I know that out there, under those stars, I saw my mother bowed over on the ground in the lonely night, with a blanket about her, and tears upon her cheeks, crying my name.

Then I was before her, and she lifted her head and her face changed, and a look of awe came over her. But she stayed very still, and said a prayer and waited, her eyes almost on the place where I was. From my heart I told her I was no spirit but was alive and well, and that I would go to the Igaal for a time; and there was a great peace about us, and love, and I saw her stand upright, very straight, her face alight with joy. And then I think—but I am not sure—that I made the Shinali farewell, and my hand brushed her robe; and then there was a withdrawing, a rushing of wind, a huge sense of swinging far and away and down, of passing through glass and stone, down into warmth. Then I was sitting again by Sheel Chandra, and his hand was still upon my head, and my cheek was resting on his knee. I wept quietly, from joy, and we did not speak for a long time.

The skies above grew pink, and the stars faded, and Sheel Chandra sighed heavily and said, "I must take you to your room, beloved, for Salverion has sent Taliesin with breakfast for you, and he'll be anxious because you are not there. But you'll need to help me stand, for my old heart is not so strong these days."

So I helped him up, and he leaned on me as we left that room. He looked suddenly older and alarmingly weary.

"I'm being sorry that I made you tired," I said.

"You can never make me tired, Avala," he said, with a beautiful smile. "I choose to allow myself to become weary, doing the things I wish most to do. I would rather have journeyed with you this night, than have spent the hours sitting on that chair worrying about you." He looked sidelong down on me, his great dark eyes full of humor. "Besides, it was a grand flight, wasn't it?"

"It would have made an eagle joy-wild," I said, and we laughed as we began the long, slow climb down the many stairs.

He leaned hard on me, and I could not help thinking of Ramakoda, and the long walk with him that had begun this strange journey, this great undertaking upon which I could now, willingly and with gladness, set all my heart.

"I will be going back to the Igaal," I said to Salverion later that morning, when I visited him in his room. "My heart, it would be glad if you would help me to heal again, and not lose that power. And I will stay with the Igaal as healer, and love them as much as I can, for as long as the All-father wants me there."

Salverion came and put his arms about me, and kissed the top of my head. "It will be my joy to teach you," he said. "And Sheel Chandra will teach you the great mind-powers. When you return to the Igaal, you will have the highest skills not only in healing, but also in knowing the meaning of dreams, and with the skill to see the future. And when your hour comes, you will have all you need to do what must be done."

"I will try to be a good learner," I said. I added, my head bent, "I will try to not fail, the way I failed Zalidas."

"Hush—no talk of failure, here!" he said. "You did not fail, Avala. Mudiwar chose—at this time—not to play his part. That is not your fault. Please do not feel that we lay a heavy burden on you. If at any time our teachings become tiring or too hard, tell us. We'll send you out hunting with Taliesin, or gardening with Amael, our herbalist. You can even work with the cooks in the kitchens, if you wish, or you may do nothing. But I have a feeling that our teachings will not be hard for you. Taliesin told me you saw the door in the mountain wall that leads to this place. You already have the Vision and the power to heal through our deeper ways. Besides, it is not all hard work, here, as you shall find out. We have here the best actors and artists, poets and musicians in the entire Navoran Empire." He added, his eyes dancing as he used my own words, "I think you will find our entertainment a high lot good."

Everything in Ravinath was a high lot good, I discovered. For the first few days I did not learn any healing skills, but Taliesin showed me about Ravinath, and I met many of the other people there. I learned that there were several masters, or teachers, and they each specialized in the wisdom they taught—some in healing, some in art, others in music, religion, astronomy, science, and literature. Some of the wisdoms I had never heard of, but Taliesin promised that in time to come I would be familiar with them all. Most of the people at Ravinath were students, called disciples. I soon discovered which wisdom each person was learning, for all the artists wore silver sashes with their crimson robes, while the musicians wore turquoise, the healers green, and so on. Taliesin called me Salverion's new disciple when he introduced me to people, and no one laughed or showed that they thought it strange. I was totally accepted, and that amazed me. But not as much as Ravinath itself amazed me.

Like a dreamworld, that place was. There were more rooms than arrows in a quiver. All, except the outer rooms with windows, were radiant with that amazing source of light from high in the arched roofs. Some of the rooms were filled with treasures— paintings, statues, strange and beautiful musical instruments, gorgeous jars and pottery, models of ships, jewelry, and intricate machines to measure time. I thought how much Ishtok would love it here, and how he would marvel at the statues and the machines. There were also many things made of a stuff like ice, that Taliesin called glass, and it was wonderful to me. There was glass in many of their objects: in graceful lamps, painted drinking vessels, instruments of healing, and—most wonderful of all— in a long metal object, bigger than me, which Taliesin called a telescope. It was mounted on a stand and could be swung around to face any direction, like a large all-seeing eye.

The telescope was in one of the highest towers of Ravinath and was by a window overlooking the eastern mountains. That day I first saw the tower, it was clear outside. Opening the window despite the cold, Taliesin put his eye to the narrow end of the telescope, and looked through it. He moved the telescope around on its high stand, and after a while smiled and told me to look but not to move the instrument. "There are animals in that far valley," he said. "Take a look at them. But don't get a fright; they look very close."

Thinking he was tricking me, because I could see nothing but blue sky and snow, I looked. And there, only an arrow flight away, were wolves eating a deer, the snow about them pink with blood. I jumped back, afraid, and gazed in disbelief at the distant valley. The wolves were gone. I looked through the telescope again, and they were there. I could see them snapping at one another, and the young cubs bounding about, awaiting their turn at the feast. Not far away a group of jackals waited to feast on what the wolves left.

I looked back at Taliesin. "How can it be?" I said, shocked. "A little time they are there, then they are not."

"They are still there," he said. "They are so far away, we cannot see them with our eyes. But the telescope uses mirrors and bits of glass we call lenses and makes them appear close. One night when the skies are clear I'll take you to meet the astronomers, the masters who study the stars, and they'll show you the night sky through this telescope. The moon will amaze you. You'll see the mountains on it, and the huge canyons and plains."

"Mountains on the moon?" I said, laughing. "Next you'll be telling me there are people on it, too."

He gave me a slow smile and closed the window.

"If you look above you," he said, "you'll see a model of our solar system."

I looked up, and saw several little balls suspended from the ceiling. "That golden ball in the center is our sun," explained Taliesin. "The blue ball is our world. The little silver one nearby is our moon, which orbits around our world. The other balls are the planets, worlds like ours, but without life."

I studied his face, suspecting a joke. He looked serious. "Our world isn't flat?" I said, incredulous. "It's a little ball like that?"

"Yes, only it's huge, of course."

"Why aren't we all falling off?"

"It's to do with a force called gravity. Our scientists can explain that better than I can. You'll have to ask them sometime."

"I think you're tricking me," I said.

He looked amused. "I'm not. I swear."

"I think you are." To get onto surer ground, I asked, "The telescope, all the things here, why did you bring them? It must have been hard carrying them all."

"We brought the telescope and most of the scientific instruments," he said, "but all the artworks were made here. When we left the Citadel, most of the artists and musicians and scientists came with us, as well as us healers. One day all these things will be taken back to the city. We wanted to keep alive the highest skills and wisdom of the Empire, so that in the Time of the Eagle, when Navora is raised again in peace, it will be raised splendid in every way. The best will not be lost. And next time the wisdom will be shared. It will be a city for all—for Shinali, Hena, Igaal, and Navorans. A free city, a city of peace."

"I was not knowing that the Time of the Eagle meant so much," I said. "I was told it was for us to get back our land. My elders, they talk on battle with the Navorans, of getting back our land, and throwing down the city of stone. You talk of raising it up."

"The Time of the Eagle will be a time of beginning again, for Navora," he said. "Come, I'll show you something."

He took me down the winding stairs to a room with a painting along one wall. I stood before the images, lost in wonder. Three times higher than I that painting was, and twenty paces or more long. But it was not the size of it that caused me to marvel, nor was it the amazing skill with which it had been done, or the colors, which glimmered with life; it was the painting itself, and what it depicted. It was the stone city, beautiful beyond belief.

So many times I had thought of this place, and I suppose I had imagined black stone houses shaped something like our tents, hundreds upon hundreds of them. But nothing I had imagined had prepared me for this, this luminous vision of vast courtyards lined with gigantic statues, enclosed gardens, sweeping flights of stairs, glorious white domes, soaring arches and towers, and long white roads between buildings so beautiful they took my breath away. Beyond the city, beyond the farthest mighty buildings, was the sea, with sailing ships upon it. And to the left, outside the city walls, were gardens and trees, and a white road winding past other buildings, pillared and domed and very grand.

As I looked upon the city it was strong in my knowing that there, on those paths, my father's feet had trod; and his eyes had looked upon those towers, those high and splendid places, and he had loved them. It was my city, too, mine by right of blood. And as I looked and marveled, it seemed that I heard the sounds of it, the talk of people walking on the stairs, the singing of the wind in the high towers, the sharp clip-clop of horses' hooves on stone ways, and somewhere, far distant, the sound of music. And I smelled the sea, sharp and clean and tangy with salt. I shook my head, startled at the clearness of it.

I saw Taliesin watching me, his face thoughtful and grave.

"It's a marvelous painting," he said. "We all needed it, this memory of our city, after we left. We knew it might be a long time before we could return. Already we have been here in Ravinath for fifteen years."

"The city, will you name me the parts?" I asked.

So we walked along the full length of the painting, slowly, while he pointed out the places. "This is the center of the city here, with the huge square lined with statues. This is the temple, and these pillared and domed buildings are the art galleries and theaters and houses of learning. All the roads and steps lead upward to the palace, that highest and biggest place with the towers, on the cliffs overlooking the sea. And along here we have the marketplaces, where goods and food are sold, and here the aqueduct carrying clean water to the city, from the river in the hills. Here outside the city walls is the little temple we call the Sanctuary of Healing Dreams, where Sheel Chandra did most of his work. This large place is the Navora Infirmary, where the sick are healed, and where your father worked with Salverion. And here, in the hills, is the Citadel. This is where he lived— where we all lived—and learned from the masters. It was the Empire's place of highest learning. It is abandoned now, in Jaganath's reign. And past this road, where the painting does not go, is your Shinali land."

I looked back along the great city, and was near tears. "My people, how can they be saying they will throw all this down?" I said. "It is a high lot beautiful."

"It looks beautiful," Taliesin said. "But this whole city is built of stone, stone that was cut and carried and laid by slaves. Even today, Navora could not exist but for the work of slaves. I some-times think that if every slave in Navora rebeled, the city would collapse. Navora may look beautiful, Avala, but it's built on blood, and every stone was placed with pain. Our forefathers who planned this city, they had good ideas, but it all went wrong. The great laws were bent, evil men took power, and the most evil of them, Jaganath, took the greatest power of all. There is no freedom in this city, not for the slaves there, nor for the Navoran people. That city needs the Time of the Eagle. It needs throwing down, or at least it needs cleaning out, and it needs a new begin-ning. People need to be freed, good laws need to be restored, a

197

new life needs to begin. And I look forward to that time, though it will break my heart to see it happen."

"It will break my heart, too," I said, "for it was my father's city. It is half my city. I want the Time of the Eagle to come, and yet in a way I do not want it, if it means that this great city will be gone."

"I think the city itself won't be gone," said Taliesin. "What will be gone is the evil that is in it. The Time of the Eagle isn't about destruction, Avala; it's about restoration, making things over again in a better way. In the Time of the Eagle, after the battle, this city will belong to all people, Shinali and Navoran, Hena and Igaal, and to the people of all the nations who were once conquered and enslaved. There will be no slaves. In your father's time the Shinali were forbidden to leave their land, even to walk in the gardens outside the city. But in the Time of the Eagle you and your people will walk the streets if you wish, free, for the city will belong to you, to all of us. And everything we have here in Ravinath will go back to the city, and will be for everyone. These great places of learning, that for generations were only for the children of the rich, will be open to all. And the Citadel will be opened again. It will be for all those who are gifted, men and women. Knowledge will be shared, and we will learn from one another. Navora will be better, richer, freer, than it ever was before."

I tried to imagine walking in the streets of the city with Ishtok, under the colonnades and gigantic statues; but I could not.

At that moment there was a sound that came from far away, pealing out again and again, silver-toned and beautiful, which echoed and hummed along the old stone walls, and did not stop.

"The bells!" cried Taliesin, and to my surprise he looked alarmed. "They're a warning. We must go quickly to Sheel Chandra's tower. Your people are in danger. We must shield them."

15

When we got to the tower, almost twenty people were gathered there under the glass dome. Most wore green sashes, so I knew they were healers, but a few wore silver, and I knew they were artists, and there was one astronomer. I realized they would all be experts in mind-power.

There was utter silence, for already Sheel Chandra had begun his work. He was as he had been the other night when I had found him here, still and silent as a statue. But this time he was standing, and Salverion and other masters and disciples were with him, as still as he was, their eyes closed, their faces uplifted, as if they listened.

Taliesin pressed a finger to his lips, and signed for me to stay where I was, then he went and joined them. I stayed near the door, though I wished I could move, for they were facing me and I felt conspicuous, worrying that I might somehow block the power that came from them. Like a wind that power was, an invisible force that flowed over and around me, and passed behind through the stone walls and out across the mountains. Then it seemed that the masters grew strangely dim, and mist blew about them, and the air in the tower grew cold as ice. Wind blew my hair across my face, and I wiped the strands away. When I looked again, the tower was gone. The masters were indistinct, dreamlike, and I could see through their pale crimson robes to a frozen lake beyond. Yet the air was clear and still, and the lake shone steel gray under the blue sky, and children played on it. Shinali children.

I stared, hardly able to believe. I could hear the children laughing as they slipped and slid on the ice, and heard someone call to them not to go far out. I turned, saw a forest of pine trees behind me, and people gathering fallen branches and pinecones from under the trees. Behind them, half hidden in the shadowy depths of the forest, were ragged tents. A small fire burned in front of the tents, and people were bent over it. The scent of pine mingled with the smell of roasting meat. The scene was homely, beautiful, and the laughter and shouts of the children, and the sound of the soft Shinali accents, tugged at my heart. I looked for my mother but could not see her. I saw Neshwan and his friends, their bows in their hands, going off along the forest's edge, no doubt to hunt. Then one of the wood gatherers stood up, very slowly, and I saw that it was my grandmother. She had aged twenty years, and all her hair was white. I wanted to call to her, but when I opened my mouth no sound came. She wiped her sleeve across her eyes and looked at the land behind me. Alarm showed in her face, and she turned and called for Yeshi.

I looked where she had looked, and saw a black smudge

moving across the snow. And I knew, then, why Sheel Chandra was here to guard and shield: the black smudge was a large battalion of soldiers.

Terror broke out among my people. Someone shouted to the children, and I heard, weird upon the bright winter air, the high, wild war cry of the Shinali, a warning. Neshwan and his friends rushed back, and other men ran to the tents and got their bows. My grandmother dropped her wood and ran to the lake, calling the children, crying to them to hurry. People stamped out the fire. Others ran out of the tents, bows and spears in their hands, their faces pale with fear. Some were running away through the trees. Yeshi shouted orders.

I looked back along the plain, saw the soldiers nearer, much nearer. A huge company it was, at least five hundred. The pale sun glinted on swords and bows, helmets and shields. Black they were, against the snow, strangely silent, approaching fast.

Behind me, people screamed and shouted, and children wailed. Mothers with babes were fleeing into the forest, some dragging little children by their arms. It was terrible, a scene of utter confusion and frenzy and fear. The soldiers were so close now I could see their faces, their drawn swords. Fast they rode, bloodlust in their eyes, and they shouted and laughed as they neared the forest. Some lifted strange bows to their shoulders, made of steel. They wore bronze armor on the upper parts of their bodies, and white plumes on their shoulders and helmets. Black cloaks streamed from their shoulders, and the red horse of the Empire pranced across their shields.

I looked at the masters again. Still they faced the forest and my people. I could hear Sheel Chandra speaking, his words low and mystical and sounding gray, like mist. And mist seemed to come from him, from his words, flowing out toward the pine forest and my people. But as the mist flowed past me it seemed like water, then like wood. And then I saw that it was trunks of trees, huge and ancient, standing close, their great roots twisted like snakes across the frozen ground. The mist wove about them, coiling about the enormous trunks, along the low branches. And far beyond them, as if in another world, my people were running, crying, and Yeshi was still shouting. I glimpsed Neshwan standing steadfast, unafraid, his bow lifted, an arrow in place. Then he vanished.

I blinked, and stared again. The pine forest and the tents were gone, covered, shielded, lost behind the illusion of mist and ancient trees whose branches and roots were too tangled and close to allow an army through.

I stepped back, moving like a shadow through the gigantic trees. Then the soldiers were there, not an arrow flight in front of me, pulling their horses to a halt, staring, mystified. Afraid, the horses reared back, away from the trees that were not there. Behind them, the other soldiers shouted and swore as they were forced to a sudden stop. A man with red plumes on his helmet and shoulders lifted a gloved hand, and they were all silent, still. He rode back and forth in front of the huge gnarled trees, struggling at times to control his wary horse, his eyes narrowed as he peered between the interwoven branches. Once he looked directly at me, through me, his steely eyes searching the forest depths. The images of ancient trees and mist remained intact, strong. I could still hear Sheel Chandra's chant, and marveled that the soldiers seemed deaf to it. Behind the soldier with the red plumes, his men were uneasy. One of them rode forward and spoke to him.

"These trees were not here before, sir, I could swear to it," he said, his voice low. "God knows I'm not a superstitious man, but there's something unearthly happening. There were natives here. I saw them through my telescope. And it was a pine forest. I'm not a fool, sir. I know what I saw."

"I'm not calling you a fool," replied the other. "I've seen such things myself, in Jaganath's palace. Things that change, things where no such things should be. I have the same feeling now, that I had then, with Jaganath: to get out, fast."

"There's something else, sir," said the other man, pointing to the ground with his sword. "Footsteps in the snow, going nowhere. Children's footsteps." Looking bewildered, he glanced upward into the treetops, as if he expected to see children perched up there.

But the man with the red plumes said a word I did not know, and backed his horse away, and returned to the company. Raising his arm again, he barked an order, and they all turned around and began to go back the way they had come. They left the ground churned and muddy, a scar on the earth's whiteness. And on the other side of the churned earth, their images wavering like smoke as the soldiers passed by, were the masters and Sheel Chandra, standing in the gap, protecting and powerful and majestic.

Then the soldiers were gone.

I turned and looked behind me. Already the twisted old trees were dissolving, and the straight pine trees emerged, magiclike, out of their mist. I saw Yeshi and others, and heard cries of astonishment and disbelief. I saw my mother, her bow in one hand.

Her other hand she put over her face, and she bent her head, as if praying. The fire had not quite been stamped out, and the smoke drifted across her feet. Other people stood about, their faces full of wonder and fear and astonishment. I wanted to go to my mother, but the trees and mist swirled about me, and when I tried to walk to her, there was a huge rock in front of me. Then it was not rock, but the wall of Sheel Chandra's high tower.

I leaned my head against the stone, feeling confused, misplaced, close to tears. I felt someone behind me, his hand on my shoulder.

"They are safe, Avala. They are well," said a voice, and I turned to see Taliesin. He looked very tired, but his smile was victorious. "We shielded them. But it was the hardest shielding ever."

"I know they are safe," I said. "I saw them, there in the pine trees by the lake."

"You saw?" he said, astounded. "You *saw?*"

I looked past him, to where Sheel Chandra sat on his chair. He looked exhausted, slumped forward, his head dropped on his breast. The others stood about him, and Salverion had his hand on Sheel Chandra's head. I wanted to go and thank them but did not like to interrupt. But at that moment Sheel Chandra looked up and turned his gaze full upon me, and I knew that he knew all that was in my heart.

"You saw what happened?" asked Taliesin again.

"All of it," I replied, and could not help smiling at the look on his face.

"By God, I knew the daughter of Gabriel would have some powers," he said, "but I did not think she would know, by instinct,

205

the skills I've taken twenty years to learn!" He added, trying to look disgruntled, but with a twinkle in his eyes, "Some things are simply not fair."

I leaned over the statue on the table, marveling. It was of a woman, life size, but all her parts—her skin, muscles, ribs, lungs, heart, all inner organs, even her skeleton—could be removed, one piece at a time, so I could see exactly where everything belonged. She was carved of wood, and everything was painted. Some of the organs I had seen before, in my healings, and they were the right color. It was a wondrous thing, for even the smallest bones were carved and fitted into place, and the main nerves and blood vessels were made of stuff Salverion called rubber. It was incredibly intricate, and Salverion let me take it to pieces and examine it for several days, telling me the Navoran names for parts, explaining what each organ did, how they were all connected.

"When we lived in Navora," he explained, "my disciples learned anatomy by dissecting the corpses of unknown criminals, or beggars. It was the best way to learn. But here no one has died, and even if they did, we would not use their body for such a purpose. So I had our artists create this model. We call her Ebony, after the tree she is made from. Now most of my teachings here must be done from her, and from models, charts, and books. Your father learned his skills in the infirmary in Navora, and in people's homes when we were called there to heal. You will not be so lucky. It is difficult teaching healing under these circumstances." He added, smiling, "You will never know how well Ebony feels when you put her back together with all her organs and bones in their right places."

"But she will not be dying, either, if I don't do it right," I said, and he laughed.

I learned a great deal from Ebony, especially about the heart and liver and brain and other deep organs I had not seen during healings I had done. I learned about various diseases that could attack organs, and how to treat them. I also heard, for the first time, about the plague the Navorans called the bulai fever.

"It attacks the liver and the brain," Salverion explained. "It is always fatal, and many thousands die from it. There is bulai fever in the city again, at the moment. Sheel Chandra has seen it in his visions. That is why the soldiers came out yesterday, looking for more slaves. It is the first time they have come out on winter raids. Many in the city have died. When we shielded your people, the soldiers were not actually looking for the Shinali, but for an Igaal or Hena tribe to take back as slaves."

"Sheel Chandra, can he see Mudiwar's tribe, and if it is well?" I asked, thinking of Ishtok, astonished at the intensity of the fear that went through me.

"Mudiwar's tribe will be well," he replied. "The soldiers went back with Hena slaves."

My relief must have been obvious, for Salverion said, with a knowing smile, "I did not think you loved Mudiwar's tribe so much, Avala. Or is it only one there, who is tied so vitally to your heart?"

I surprised myself again by blushing. I asked, to distract him, "Why does Sheel Chandra not shield all the tribes?"

"It would be too much for him. Shielding exhausts him, even though we all help as much as we are able. Most of the work falls on him, and it puts an almost intolerable strain on his heart. So, harsh though it seems, we shield only the Shinali, since they are the chosen ones."

"Why do you call them chosen?" I asked.

"Because they are chosen by God to be the ones through whom all our nations will be drawn together in harmony," he replied. "He often chooses the weak people in the world to accomplish the mightiest things. Now, back to anatomy: I want you to pick up Ebony's heart, and tell me the names of the great arteries and veins leading to and from the chambers."

I did as he asked, and he raised his eyebrows at me and looked pleased. "You have an excellent memory," he said.

"I like the heart, it's my favorite organ," I said, still cradling Ebony's wooden heart in my hands. "It would be a high lot wonderful to see a real heart beating. It holds all the life."

"It is indeed wonderful," he replied. "I have operated on a man's heart, made it beat right when it was not beating properly."

I laughed, thinking he made a joke.

"It's true," he said, laughing with me. "He felt nothing while I did it, and lived for five years after."

I stared at him, unsure, still half suspecting a jest. Then I remembered that he was the greatest healer in the world and realized he was speaking the truth.

"I'm being sorry," I said, feeling my face go red. "Touching a heart, cutting it, I did not think it could be done. Not without death."

"Don't apologize, Avala," he said. "Your laughter is good for me. It makes me realize how privileged I've been in my life, and what an honor it is to pass on what I know, to have someone wanting to learn. I won't be able to teach you heart surgery, but

I can show you how to mend a shattered bone or a pierced lung. Now see this bit here, under our Ebony's ribs. . . ."

The lessons went on, and there were many times when I thought he was jesting about some unimaginable piece of surgery, and he was not. His teachings blew away everything I thought I knew about healing, about what could be done and what was impossible. I must have shown my ignorance many times, but he never laughed at me, only with me, and I never felt foolish. He had a beautiful way of making me feel as if he was honored to be teaching me, not that I was honored to be learning from him. Many times when I was bending over Ebony, puzzling something out, I caught him watching me with that gentle smile of his, and I realized it actually gave him pleasure to be teaching me. It was part of the greatness of his spirit, that he so joyfully shared his wisdom. I thought of old Gunateeta, with her pain and misery and refusal to teach what little she knew, and those hard days with the Igaal seemed a lifetime past.

Yet my link with Mudiwar's tribe stayed strong, for I often thought of them, and every night at dinner I drank from the cup that Ishtok had carved for me, and said a prayer in my heart for him and his tribe. When I thought of Ishtok my heart ached, and a longing went through me, and I realized, with a shock, that I missed him more than I had ever missed Santoshi, or Yeshi, or even my mother.

Everyone at Ravinath ate together in a long, splendid hall with a towering roof made of graceful arched pillars, and with a wall of high curved windows overlooking the western ranges. We sat on cushions at low tables, about twenty of us to a table.

Usually I sat by Taliesin, as he had become my friend as well as my teacher of the Navoran language, and my guide through the maze of passages and narrow stairs in Ravinath; but always someone different came to sit at my other side. On my fifth day there a lively man with olive skin, blue eyes, and a warm smile came to sit by me. As he sat down he noticed Ishtok's cup.

"Ah—carved by a true artist!" he said. "Don't tell me you use your scalpels for carving up wood, as well as human beings!"

I replied, smiling, "The cup was made by an Igaal friend, as a gift. The eagle is the sign of my people."

"May I look at it?"

"Of course."

He picked up the cup and studied it, turning it slowly in his left hand. I noticed that he had paint under his fingernails. "By the way, I'm Tulio, an artist here," he said. "I painted most of Ebony's bits. But they're not as beautiful as this cup. The Igaal are fine artists, obviously."

"Ishtok is," I said. "Maybe all of them. They cut out patterns in their clothes, very clever."

"Well, this cup is more than clever. The design is quite stunning."

"I'll tell Ishtok, when I see him again."

Taliesin said, as he handed me some bread and cheese, "You won't be telling him anything, Avala. Not about this place. Ravinath is secret, and it must remain that way, for our protection."

Tulio put down the cup and said, "The Citadel won't be secret in the Time of the Eagle. There'll be a place there for artists like Ishtok. He has a gift. I believe you're gifted, too, Avala. I've heard amazing things about you, that you already know many of the healing skills Salverion teaches."

"My mother taught me," I said. "She was taught by my father, who learned from Salverion in the Citadel."

"I realize who your father was," Tulio said. "I can see the resemblance. Gabriel and I were both initiated into the Citadel on the same day. From the first time I saw his face, I wanted to do a painting of him."

"Would you paint his face, for me?" I asked. "So I know what he looked like?"

"I'll do better than that," he said, smiling. "I've got a portrait. Just a drawing. He sat for me, once, in the Citadel gardens. I kept the drawing, though it's unfinished. Come up to my studio after the meal, and I'll show it to you."

I had been in the galleries where the paintings and statues were displayed, but not in the private rooms of the artists. Taliesin took me there, and Tulio welcomed us warmly, though he seemed in a muddle. He was trying to tidy the place when we arrived and said, apologetically, "I should have told you to come tomorrow. I live in a bit of a mess. I can't keep two worlds tidy, and all my order goes into my pictures."

It was a glorious mess. There were paintings on wood stacked up against the walls, drawings pinned to the closed wooden window shutters, and even pictures painted directly onto the stone walls. There were several stands with half-finished work on them, and tables covered with plates where colors blended and swirled in marvelous confusion. Even the bed in the corner was covered with drawings, half-finished sketches and ideas. All over the floor were cloths splattered with paint, and there were jars of brushes and rows of pots of color. He obviously worked on several pictures at once, and even unfinished they were amazing. One of the pictures was of a fox standing in the snow, so real and alive I wanted to stroke its fur.

Tulio went to a deep shelf with scrolls, and searched among the rolled parchments.

"Ah—here it is!" he said, after a while. He looked about for a table to spread the drawing on, found nowhere clear, and pinned the picture to one of the wooden window shutters. He stepped back, and I saw my father's face.

Beautiful he was, his features clear-cut like a statue's, his hair long and pale and waving to his shoulders. He was frowning a little, thoughtful and stern. His nose was like mine, hooked like an eagle's beak, and his eyes were far-seeing, his brow fierce. Yet there was a gentleness about him, too, a peace. It was in his sunlit eyes, in his slightly smiling mouth. The drawing was in red pastel on brown parchment, and the highlights were worked in white. It was three-dimensional, stunning. But what struck me most was that it was incredibly similar to the face on Yeshi's bone *torne*. Yeshi had always said that the face on the bone was my father's, but I had thought he meant it was a symbol of my father, not a true likeness. Yet the bone had been carved generations ago. Had the carver seen my father in a vision? If so, how inescapable was a destiny carved in bone—or a destiny spoken in an old priest's words? Was there really any choice, as Salverion said there was?

"Well, from that frown of yours, Avala, I gather you're not too impressed with my fine portrait," said Tulio, with a laugh.

I felt my face redden. "I'm sorry; I was thinking on destiny,"

212

I said. "The picture, it's wonderful. I love it. I will hold it in my knowing for all time to come."

"Then you'd better hold it in your hands, too," he said, taking it down and rolling it carefully, and giving it to me. "Take it as a gift, Avala. I know it will be well looked after. While you're here, would you like to see some other portraits? I've got the Empress Petra here somewhere, and a few of her advisors. There's the Lord Jaganath here, too. If I can just find them . . ."

So it was that, in a messy artist's studio in Ravinath, I looked upon the faces of people my father had known—people who had changed the course of his life, and the course of my nation's history.

The Empress Petra was beautiful, but there was a hardness about her, and a sadness, as if the power she held was more pain than peace to her. I thought of the letter in Yeshi's tent, of the graceful Navoran script, unreadable to me, written by her hand.

Her advisors I did not know, but Tulio pinned up the pictures of them, and told me their names. One face struck coldness through me: a middle-age man with dark skin and black eyes, with a pointed beard combed into little curls, and strange signs embroidered on his elegant clothes. He was very handsome, with a look of disdain, almost of amusement, mixed with cold cruelty. The painting was eerily lifelike, the glittering eyes too perceptive. "That one I don't like," I said.

"That is the Lord Jaganath," said Tulio. "Look well, Avala, and hope you never see him in the flesh."

"I'm hoping I do," I said. "He killed my father's brother, and plotted my father's death. He imprisoned my people in Taroth Fort. Words I have, to say to him."

213

Taliesin gave a low whistle. "You're braver than most, Avala," he said. "If you're serious, ask Sheel Chandra to teach you how to fight with the powers of the mind. You will need such weapons, if you intend to tackle Jaganath."

"I'm serious," I said.

"It would take time, even for someone as gifted as you, to learn how to fight Jaganath with his own powers," Taliesin said. "Sheel Chandra is the only one here who could do it—and he's been a master for more than fifty years."

"Then I shall have to stay here awhile," I said, "while I get the knowing of it."

Tulio rubbed his hands together. "Good. I can do a portrait of you. I've been longing for a new face to paint."

As the days passed, the peaceful rhythm of life in Ravinath became my own rhythm, and I felt uplifted and protected, held in the All-father's hand, beloved and blessed. I was given crimson robes to wear, and a green sash like Salverion's, and velvet shoes. All were remade especially to fit me, for I was the smallest there.

Though I was the only woman in Ravinath, I never for a moment felt excluded or uncomfortable; always I was treated with the highest respect, even honor. Often I made mistakes in the Navoran language, got lost in the labyrinth of passages, stumbled into places I should not have entered, and forgot names and was unsure how to address these greatest of men who were teaching me; yet always I was put right with the gentlest of smiles, and deepest courtesy.

And the joy—the joy there was in learning some of those wondrous things my father had learned! And to learn them from the same revered people who had taught him, the ones he had honored and loved, became a happiness almost too sweet to bear.

Mainly I learned from Salverion, and we studied charts and books as well as the wooden innards of Ebony; and when he was satisfied that my knowledge of anatomy was sufficient, he said I could begin learning from some of the other masters about herbs and other basic healings.

Disappointed, I said, "But I was thinking I would learn how to stop pain in its pathways, better than before. I was thinking . . ."

"I know what you are thinking, dear one," he said. "And you shall learn those things, and much more besides. But first, the basics of anatomy. Then healing with herbs. After that you will learn from me again, and I will teach you all those deeper things you long to know. Last of all, you will learn from Sheel Chandra. His mind-powers are the greatest of all the healings we teach here, and the hardest to learn. But for now, the herbs."

Amael was the master of healing with herbs. He was an elderly little man with a mop of white hair, red cheeks, and a ready laugh. To my surprise I enjoyed working with Amael, because for once I could learn from real things, not models or charts. He had a glass room in one of the high outer galleries of Ravinath, where the morning sun poured when it was fine, and the light heated rows and rows of plants growing in long troughs. These plants he watered daily, with great tenderness. I loved the smell of the place, the sense of life and growth in the bright, concentrated light. I realized I was missing the windy grasslands of the plains.

"We do have a garden," Amael explained, waving his hand vaguely toward a small frozen valley far below our windows. "The Garden in the Gap, we call it. I do have herbs there, in the summer, but there isn't a lot of good soil, and the cooks claim most of it for vegetables. So I have this place. I feel like a bird in its high nest, with its little ones."

I smiled. He did look like a bird, hunched over his beloved plants, dropping some kind of powdered plant food over them.

"They have such power in them, these little plants," he murmured lovingly. "This one here, her name is andrya. Distill a little of her essence into a spoon of water, and she will restore rhythm to a heart in spasms. And this little beauty, wild hereswid, she can combat just about any poison known to human beings."

His passion was infectious, and I came to love the study of herbs with him, almost as much as I loved the study of anatomy with Salverion. And there was a wonderful surprise with Amael: he knew my people.

"I visited the Shinali once, when we were at the Citadel," he said. "It was before your father's time. I visited the Shinali and took them packets of seeds and asked about their herbs. The healer then was a woman. Thandeka."

"She is my grandmother!" I cried. "You know my grandmother!"

"I met her daughter, too. A little girl called Ashila."

"Ashila is my mother."

"Ah—'tis a wonderful thing, how the wheels go round! She's well, your grandmother?"

Before I could reply, Taliesin came in. His face was pale, and he called me from the door, urgently. "Avala! Someone has fallen down the stairs. He's badly hurt. Come and see Salverion do some real surgery."

We hurried down the long stairs, along the passages, and up other stairs to a room I had not been in before. It was a small

217

room, its roof high like a cone, and light poured down from above. Under the light was a long flat table like a narrow bed, and a fair-haired man lay on it, groaning. It was one of the disciples I did not know. Salverion, wearing a long white gown, was bending over him, talking to him, and someone else was setting out healing things on a little table nearby. Four other disciples were there, wearing white gowns. Everything was white, the cloths the instruments lay on, the cover over the injured man, the walls, even the bleached and polished boards of the floor.

"Our surgery," said Taliesin. "Not often used, thank God."

Salverion looked up. "Wash your hands, get ready," he said to Taliesin. "I need your help. Stand at the foot of the bed, Avala. I'll explain all I can while we work. Ask any questions you wish."

For a while the disciples were busy cutting the clothes off the man on the table. They kept him very still while they did it, but he still groaned, and his breath rattled a little in his chest. Salverion stood near the man's head, stroking his hair, speaking to him softly.

"I'm making you sleep, Delano," he said. "You may wake at times, and feel pulling and pressure, but it will not be pain. Empty your mind of all anxiety. You are in hands that love you."

Slowly Salverion moved his hands over the man's face. Delano stopped groaning and sighed heavily. I moved closer. Salverion's hands did not touch the man's skin, and I saw light between them, steady and strong, and growing stronger. Delano's face changed, became so relaxed that even the tiny wrinkles about his eyes smoothed away, and he smiled a little. Then he slept, hardly breathing.

Salverion straightened and moved his hands over the rest of Delano's body, pressing on his skin, seeking out the injuries. But he searched not only with his hands; he also worked with his eyes closed, as if he saw beneath the skin to organ, sinew, and bone. Awed, I knew what he checked, for in my mind I saw Ebony, all her inward parts, right through to her spine. Leaning close, the Master slipped his hands under Delano, examining his back. All the time Salverion spoke to Taliesin, who was standing nearby now, clothed in white.

"Ruptured spleen," said Salverion. "Fifth and sixth ribs broken, lung pierced. Fluid in chest cavity. Lumbar vertebrae cracked. Right pelvic bone broken. Right thigh fractured . . ."

The list of injuries went on. How could a man live, with so much broken in him?

At last, his examination finished, Salverion stood and said a prayer. For wisdom he asked, and skill, and for the Sovereign God to mend what his scalpels could not. Then he began the healing.

All that day I watched, lost in another world, the world of Navoran skill at its highest and best. It was wonderful to see the knife in Salverion's hands, to see the sureness of him, the calm with which he cut so deep into Delano that I thought the man would surely die. But he did not, and the blood was wiped away, and main vessels tied, injured parts healed, tissues sewn up, bones set with steel pins, organs and muscles layered back into their places, and skin sewn over. Taliesin's hands, they worked with the

Master's as if they moved to the same music, in total harmony, and the healing was beautiful to watch.

Once Delano opened his eyes and cried out, and in a moment Salverion was moving his bloodied fingers down the back of Delano's neck, over his face, his brow. Then Delano slept again and did not wake, even when they had finished.

Then someone put a bowl of water near Salverion's hands, and he washed the blood from them and took off the white robe, splattered now with crimson, and went and sat in a chair in the corner of the room. Taliesin washed the blood from Delano's body, using water that smelled strongly of antiseptic herbs, going carefully over all the places where the skin had been cut and stitched together again. There were many of those places, and the rest of Delano was mottled with bruising. Then a white blanket was put over him, and Taliesin sat by him to wait until he woke.

The others left, taking the instruments and cloths that had been used for the healing, but still Salverion sat in his chair, and Taliesin in his, and the only sound was the quiet breathing of the man who was healed.

I did not want to leave. I felt that I had witnessed a miracle, and I wanted to stay to see the last part of it—to see the man Delano open his eyes and speak.

As if he knew, Salverion said, "Come and sit here by me, Avala. It may be a while before he wakes."

So I sat by him, and we waited.

Delano woke at last, and in a moment Salverion and I were at his side. Delano smiled a little, and lifted his hand to touch

Salverion's robe. He tried to speak, but Salverion said, very gently, "Say nothing, my son. Just rest. All went well. Taliesin will stay here with you, and later I will come to relieve him. There will be someone with you every moment." The Master moved his hands over Delano's face again and down the back of his neck, and Delano slept. His lips were curved, as if he dreamed of good things. Briefly I touched his cheek; his skin was warm but not feverish. There was a great peace in him, a sense of order, as if every part of his body was well. The surgery I had witnessed, so drastic and extensive, seemed already a long time past, and even now shattered bones were knitting together, torn tissues mending, and damaged organs and veins were being reformed with new life. Wonder overwhelmed me.

Salverion beckoned to me, and we went out. Suddenly I felt shy, awed by this greatest of all healers. Salverion said, with an amused sideways look at me, "We won't know for a few days if I have been successful or not. Even if Delano survives, he may not be able to walk again. So you can wipe that hero worship out of your eyes and come to the kitchens and make me a sandwich. I'm starving."

Twelve days later Delano was walking about, slowly, and managing to eat small meals. I spent most of my spare time with him, for I discovered that he was a famous poet, and I loved hearing him read his work to me. I think he enjoyed the readings as much as I did, for everyone else in Ravinath knew his work well, and he liked having a fresh audience, even if it was only me. He adored words and never grew tired of explaining meanings or

telling me again and again how to pronounce something difficult. Every hour with him added new Navoran words to my
knowing.

His poems were about many places in the Navoran Empire,
for he had traveled much before he went to the Citadel to study
and perfect his gift. From him, through his poetry, I learned much
about Navoran history, about famous battles and the conquests
of nations. My favorite poems were thrilling ballads about small
tribes fighting back against the Empire, and winning, against
impossible odds, by their cunning and audacity and sheer courage.
There were also sad, angry poems about slavery and the wrongs
done to conquered peoples.

"Why do you care so much about slaves?" I asked Delano, after
he had read an impassioned poem about people in captivity.

"Many people from my country are enslaved," he said. "I'm
not Navoran. I'm from an island called Arridor, in the western
parts of the Empire. My homeland was conquered by Navora
a hundred years ago. The Navoran army overran many countries, sending shiploads of slaves back to Navora to build the city.
Many of the disciples here are not Navoran." He got up and
walked slowly to a shelf and took out a large book. He grunted
at the weight of it, and I rushed to help. We spread the book
out on a table by a lamp, and I discovered that on every page
was a map.

"This is an atlas," he said, and opened it to a place where two
of the pages unfolded out to make a single wide map. "This is
the Navoran Empire. We are in this little country down here,
see? That red dot is the city of Navora. This knob of land con-
tains all the Shinali, Igaal, and Hena territories. But farther north,

across these oceans, are other countries. All the places colored red are parts of the Navoran Empire, countries and islands that have been conquered, many of their people enslaved. Among them are these great countries of Amaran, Sadira, Maruthani, and Quadira. And my own dear Arridor."

"What of these lands that are not colored red?" I asked.

"This huge country here in the east is called Shanduria. Navora could never conquer Shanduria; it's one of the biggest and most advanced civilizations in the world. Sheel Chandra is from there. It's an amazing country. People ride huge animals called elephants, which they cover with gorgeous silks and brocades. Elephants have noses longer than you are tall, and feet larger than meat platters."

I did not know whether to believe him. Seeing my suspicious look, he laughed. "Ask Sheel Chandra some time," he said. "Ask him about the golden cities, the princes whose wealth is greater even than our Emperor's, and the ancient temples covered with carvings of gods and goddesses. Shanduria is very old, many thousands of years old. The Navoran Empire is young, by comparison."

"Were you a slave once?" I asked.

"No. But Navoran sailors and merchants told of wonderful artists and astronomers and musicians in those far countries, and when the Citadel was built, those highly skilled people were invited to the Citadel, either to learn or to teach. So we have Sheel Chandra from Shanduria, and our master astronomer, Zuleman, from Sadira. And many disciples were chosen from the brightest young men in the Empire, to come to the Citadel and study under the masters. Among them are Tulio, your artist friend from

223

Amaran, and, of course, my noble self, poet of highest excellence, from the fair land of Arridor." He bowed very solemnly and moaned as he straightened up. We both laughed.

He added, his face grave again, his eyes on the map of the Navoran Empire, "You see the huge significance of the Time of the Eagle, Avala. All these nations will be affected. Countless slaves will be set free, families reunited, whole countries liberated to have their own rulers restored, living without the fear of the conqueror's ships arriving to plunder again, to steal and enslave. This entire Empire will be different, free."

I looked at the tiny dot that was the city of Navora and at the Hena and Igaal lands stretching to the coast, only the width of two of my fingers on this map; then, overwhelmed by old doubts and fears, I looked again at the vast Empire beyond. How could so much depend on my people? How could so much depend on me? Again I felt the weight of Zalidas's prophecy heavy on my shoulders, and the fear that I would fail. And there was another thing added to the heaviness: my renewed longing to be a healer, and only a healer, and the grief that this was not to be.

I closed the atlas and hoped Delano would not see how much my hands shook. He did not. He said, brightly, "I've been writing again. A poem about my healing, how it felt when Salverion took away my pain. Would you like to hear it?"

I nodded, and we sat together by his fire. Many of our rooms had fires, with the smoke escaping up high chimneys to mountain peaks far above, to be blown away in the winter winds. I thought of the Time of the Eagle, and how the Hena people called it the All-Sweeping Wind. I tried to listen to Delano's poem but could

224

not. While he read he scratched his ribs a bit, where the stitched skin healed, and I thought of him on the table in the surgery, with his chest cavity opened up, and Salverion's hands moving over his exposed lungs and heart, doing their sublime healing. Then the map of the Navoran Empire rose up again before me like an omen, obscuring the vision of the work I revered and loved.

"I'm sorry," I said, standing up suddenly. "I have to go and see Salverion."

Delano looked surprised. "My poem is not good?" he asked.

"Yes. But it's made me think of something."

"Well, that's what it's meant to do." He smiled. "Off you go."

Salverion was reading one of his scrolls, but he looked up as I entered, and put the scroll away.

"How is our patient today, Avala?" he asked, speaking of Delano.

"He is very well," I said, sitting on a stool by a lamp. "He's writing again. A poem about your healing, and how it felt for him."

"I look forward to reading it," said Salverion. "But that's not what you came to tell me, is it? What disturbs you, Avala?"

I glanced at him, saw his gray eyes boring into me, reading me. It no longer unnerved me, that he knew my thoughts at times.

I said, "I've been thinking about Zalidas, and his prophecy over me. I've also been thinking of what my mother said about our destiny being always to do with what we love. I believe what they both said, but the things are opposite."

Salverion came and sat in a chair near me. The lamplight fell on his white beard and rim of white hair and glowed about him like a holiness.

"I love healing," I said. "Every night I go to sleep thinking of what I saw in the surgery that day you healed Delano. And then I think of my own healings, that my mother taught me. I think of the healing I did on the battle-wounded in Gunateeta's tent, of the arrow holes I packed, the sword cuts I stitched. I did it well, but I did not mend everything inside those people, not truly. I know that now. They will always be in pain, with parts of their bodies not working properly. The injured livers, they'll give trouble sooner or later. So will the damaged lungs, the crushed bones, the other parts I did not have the skill to properly mend. Maybe the people I healed will die early, or get a simple fever that will break them at last and carry them off early to the shadow lands. I eased their pain, and gave them a kind of mending, and stopped poison from spreading in their veins, but it was not enough. To heal as you healed Delano, that is what my soul hungers for. So why is it not my destiny? Why must my destiny be to bind enemies together, to lead my people into war? It's all too much, too big a thing for me to do. Even if good does come of it in the end, I'm not a warrior. I don't want to kill. Zalidas's prophecy goes against everything I want."

"Oh, my love," he said, taking one of my hands, and holding it between both of his. "Do you really think you're in this on your own? You will have all the help you need, from people and places you least expect. Even your time here, don't you think this is ordained, planned for you before ever Zalidas spoke? And

226

who said you will kill? I heard that you made growling noises about Jaganath the other day, and that you have words to say to him. In that event, it won't be a sword in your hand that you will need, but power in your heart, power in your mind, power in your very words. The kind of power that can be taught to you by only one person in this world, and that man lives here in Ravinath. Your hour, when it comes, might be quite different from what you expect.

"As for your true destiny . . . Your destiny *is* to heal. The Time of the Eagle is not a battle. It's a way of life, a new age to come, a time of peace that will span many lifetimes and nations and centuries. I believe that what Zalidas foretold is true—you are the Daughter of the Oneness, the cord that binds. But the Oneness will happen over a short time, maybe within weeks or months, once it begins, and the cord that binds—well, you already bind two nations together, within your own body. Your healings have already bound you to the Igaal, since you have the promise of Ramakoda to fight with your people, when he is chieftain. Your friend, the pledge-son Ishtok, is a connecting cord between you and the Hena. Can you not see it, Avala? It is happening already. And this part of your life—being the Daughter of the Oneness— is only a part. I know that when you are young a year seems age-long, but when you consider the whole course of your life, even five years are not many. Even the great battle with Jaganath's army will be a brief part, very possibly only a single day. And after it, enduring peace. In that long peace time, that will last for the rest of your life, what will you do?"

"I'll heal," I said, in tears. "But I want to heal as you do, with your light and your power and your love. I want to heal the Navoran way."

"And so you shall," he said, lifting his beautiful old hand, and wiping away my tears. "So you shall."

17

In your latest letter, Mother, you mentioned reading books about
philosophy. You would like the Master of Philosophy, here at the
Citadel. He is not one of my usual teachers, and I have had only
one talk with him. We spoke, among other things, of the meanings
of names, and he told me that his name means Finished Person.
Isn't that a beautiful meaning? I would love to be a finished person,
knowing wholly who I am, having absolute peace, being perfectly
loving, totally embracing my path and my destiny.

—Excerpt from a letter from Gabriel to his mother,
kept and later gifted to Avala

The wind was blowing strong and warm across the plain, and Ishtok and I raced our horses, laughing and yelling. The horses' hooves thundered on the earth, and I looked behind us through the bright summer haze to the Shinali land. Through the haze my people's house was barely visible, its thatched roof pale gold against the summer grass. White dots marked the grazing sheep, and darker dots the children who watched over them. I looked to the front again, over my mare's streaming mane, and saw Ishtok already in the shadow of the sacred mountain. He drew his horse to a halt and called something to me, but I could not hear it. When I reached him he was looking through a small bronze telescope back across the land, toward the farms and the Citadel.

"Salverion has come to visit us, my love," he said, smiling, handing me the telescope. "We must go back." As we began to gallop back a joy-wildness took hold on me, and it seemed that

I flew across the sunlit land, and a great song was in the air, and the river chuckled beside us. Then came a beating of drums, and a shout, and someone called my name.

I woke confused, dragged unwilling from the joy, and the throb of drums became the sound of someone knocking on my door.

"Avala! Wake up! There's something you need to see!"

I staggered up and pulled on a robe, and went to the door.

Taliesin stood there, fully dressed, grinning. "It's a clear night," he said. "It's a three-quarter moon. Perfect. Zuleman is waiting by the big telescope. Are you coming? I'll wait out here while you get dressed. You'll need warm clothes."

Instantly awake, I dressed quickly, then went out and hurried with him down the lamp-lit passages. "I was dreaming that I was looking through a telescope," I said. "It was a little one, and I was on our Shinali land."

"Well, we'll be looking on other lands soon," he said. "Maybe not lands, exactly. Balls of blazing gas, perhaps. Astronomy isn't one of my strong points, and it's years since I've looked at the stars with Zuleman. He'll explain everything. You've met him, haven't you?"

"I've seen him across the hall, at mealtimes. But I've not talked to him."

We went up several narrow flights of stairs, and came to the top of the high tower where Taliesin had shown me the wolves in the snow, through the great telescope. The room was in total darkness, but for the open window with the myriads of stars beyond, with the moon low over the mountains. Before the window were the dark shapes of the telescope and the Master of

Astronomy waiting for us. As we entered, the Master lit a candle.

Taliesin introduced me, and the Master of Astronomy came over and took my hands.

"Welcome, Avala," he said. "I'm so pleased you could come. It's such a clear night, and Erdelan is so close, and the moon is perfect for viewing. We must make the most of these opportunities."

His hands were cold, but his voice, with its strange accent, was warm and deep. He was elderly, elegant, and tall, with a hooked nose and high cheekbones. His skin was brown, and I remembered that he was from Sadira, on the far side of the Empire. His dark eyes shone with wonder and excitement.

"You're about to see the most amazing things in the known universe," he said, blowing out the candle. "I'll just make sure I've still got the moon. It moves out of view amazingly fast."

He checked, his eye to the small eyepiece of the huge telescope, and I glanced at the earth below. Dark patches of tussock poked through the moonlit snow where I had seen the wolves play four months ago, and silver streams tumbled down the black rocks, from the snow melting in the heights. It was spring now, and the mountains and valleys about Ravinath were waking up from their white winter sleep.

"Now," said Zuleman, stepping back. "If you look through this bit here, you'll see the shadowed edge of the moon." He stood back and waited, as thrilled and breathless as a child waiting for someone to open a gift he was offering.

And what a gift, indeed! I caught my breath, totally unprepared for the splendor I saw. The inner curve of the moon was very bright, its shadow dark as the surrounding sky; but on that bright edge, clear and sharp and solid as if carved of shining stone, were the rims of great holes, vast flat plains, shadowed valleys, and the sculptured shapes of jagged ridges and pointed mountains. And farther out in the deep shadow, invisible but for their sunlit peaks, were the blazing summits of far mountains, bright as stars and sharp as broken glass. It was majestic, alien, glorious beyond anything I had ever imagined.

I tore my gaze away and looked back at Taliesin. I was still half blinded by the blaze of the moon. "There *are* mountains there!" I said, and he laughed softly.

While Taliesin looked through the telescope, Zuleman said to me, "You see that model of the planets above your head, Avala?"

I nodded, looking up. The little orbs glowed softly in the moonlight. "Taliesin showed them to me one day," I said. "He said our world is like that little blue ball."

"That is true. With our telescope we can see some of the other balls, the planets. To the naked eye they look just like stars. But when you see them through the telescope, you'll see that they are indeed globes. As is our world."

Taliesin finished admiring the moon and stepped back.

Zuleman stooped over the telescope and looked for another wonder to show me. He said, "Have a look at these stars, Avala. Stars are suns, most of them many times brighter than our sun, but they look small because they are so incredibly far away. Our sun is a star, our day-star, and it lights our whole sky only because we are so close to it. What you see now are suns, untold millions of miles away."

The telescope was pointed to what I thought was a fairly bare patch of sky, but when I looked I saw stars beyond number, some very large and bright, some tiny, some gathered so close together that they looked like glittering mist. The more I looked the more I saw, stars that went on and on forever into the dark.

"Where's the end of it?" I asked, lost in awe. "Where do the stars end?"

"They never end," the Master said. "That's the glory of them. And the mystery."

He moved the telescope again and peered through it. While he searched the stars he said, "I knew your grandfather, Avala. Gabriel's father. I gave him copies of my star charts, which he used for navigation. He was a sailor, a famous merchant, and went on long voyages to seek out fine silks, artworks, and riches from the far reaches of our Empire, which he brought back to Navora. Some of the greatest foreign treasures in our city came from his ships. Ah—there it is! The four moons showing tonight, lined up nicely across. Take a look. This is not a star, but a planet. Another world, round like ours, though unlike ours in other ways."

I looked and cried out in astonishment. I saw a gray ball with four smaller balls—the moons—in a straight line across it. I could see the land, strangely marked in wide lines, and the shadows of the moons as they passed across.

"That planet is many times larger than our earth," explained Zuleman. "It has those four moons, and many others besides that we cannot see. The bands you see are clouds, and the swirling reddish patch is a huge storm that rages everlastingly. We call that world Erdelan."

"Erdelan," I repeated. "A beautiful name for a beautiful world."

Then I asked to see the moon again, and looked at it for a

long time, not noticing that my hands were shaking with the cold, and my feet felt like ice. I was wishing, with all of my being, that Ishtok were here to see this. How he, too, would love it!

While I looked and marveled, Zuleman told me wonders about our galaxy, of how the planets and their moons and our Earth all swing about the sun in a huge cosmic dance, perfect and elaborate and everlasting. Beliefs I had held since childhood, about a flat Earth and the moon sailing like a ship in river winds in the sky, were blown away, leaving me breathless, awed, and with a blazing desire to know more.

At last Taliesin said, covering a yawn, "Enough for one night, Avala! The stars and Erdelan will be there for the rest of your life. We can come again."

I turned to Zuleman and took his hands. "I've seen the most wondrous things this night," I said. "I feel a high lot honored. I wish all my people could see what I have seen. Thank you. Thank you, with *sharleema*."

"It was my great pleasure," he replied. "When we are free, back in the Citadel, this telescope will be for all who wish to use it. You can line up your whole tribe outside my door, and they can see this. I will be happy to teach them all I know. And I hope they will tell me what their priests and astronomers know, and the Shinali names for the stars. We have much to share."

"Thank you," I said. "And thank you for telling me about my Navoran grandfather. It's good for my heart, to find out about my Navoran family. Did you know my grandmother, too?"

"Only a little. Her name is Lena. We'll talk another time, Avala. Our friend Taliesin is almost asleep on his feet. And you have work with Salverion in the morning. Though poking about in pots of herbs and pickled livers can't be anywhere near as marvelous as gazing at the stars."

I thought about that for a moment or two. Then I said, "Heart's truth, your other worlds are wonderful, Master, but not as wonderful as the healing of Delano."

He looked taken aback for a moment, then he smiled, and his eyes shimmered a little in the starlight. "Maybe you're right, Avala," he said. "My other worlds are beautiful, but they are only gas and dust, ice and fire. Nothing, compared with the miracle of human life." He embraced me and kissed the top of my head, as Salverion often did, and Taliesin and I left.

My heart sang as we went down the long stairs toward our rooms. "Your Empire is so wonderful, Taliesin!" I said. "It has discovered so many amazing things. The things I am learning here, the things I'm seeing . . . It's as if I've lived in a tiny tent all my life, and someone has suddenly blown the tent away, and I find myself in another world altogether. Many other worlds."

"You're seeing the best the Empire has to offer," he said. "Until now you've seen only the worst. Now you see that there is much that is good, much worth saving. Besides, it's not my Empire, but yours as well. It's not another world you're discovering, Avala; it's your own."

"So it is," I said, stopping on a stair, astonished at the thought. "It's half my own life I'm discovering, half my heritage. Half my own self."

He shivered and said, "Please don't stand philosophizing for too long. I'm frozen."

"Let's go to the kitchen for a hot drink," I said, suddenly realizing how cold I was, too, after the hours by the open window.

"I'm too excited to go back to sleep."

Taliesin groaned and muttered something about being too old for midnight feasts, but he came with me to the kitchen. As we sat in the warmth by the massive ovens and sipped our drinks, he asked, "How is your work going with Salverion? All winter you've been working with him. You must know how to numb a bit of pain by now."

"I'm learning slowly," I said.

"Very well. I'll test you." He put down his drink and stood with his back to me and his head bent. "Numb my right foot," he said. "Imagine I've got gangrene from the cold, after staring at the stars all night, and you have to amputate. I want it properly numb, and only from the ankle down. I don't want to be totally comatosed."

He grinned and held aside his dark hair, so I could touch his neck.

"It might be a good idea to comatose you," I said, "since then you wouldn't be able to complain."

His grin widened, then he straightened his back, and I moved my fingers down his vertebrae.

"I didn't think you knew the meaning of the word *comatose*," he said. "I'd better be careful what I say from now on. I suspect you understand everything."

"More than you think," I said, removing my hand from his neck, and picking up my drink again.

"What—done already?" he said. "I don't think it worked. I didn't feel a thing." He tried to walk to his chair and almost fell over. I watched him hop to his seat, and tried not to laugh.

"I'm impressed," Taliesin said. "It is indeed only my foot.

236

Salverion must be pleased with you. He'll be sending you up to Sheel Chandra soon."

"After the next full moon," I said. "I'll have the summer learning from Sheel Chandra, and in the autumn I'll go back to the Igaal. Salverion said you'd go with me, as far as their camp."

"I'll enjoy the journey. Much as I love Ravinath, a trek to the Igaal territories sounds like a pleasant change."

I asked, "Where did you live before you came to Ravinath? Before you went to the Citadel? Are you from Navora?"

"Yes, I'm Navoran," he said. The laughter faded from his face, and he sighed deeply and looked down at the cup in his hands. "I have a wife in Navora, and two twin daughters. The children were eight months old when I was chosen to go to the Citadel. Then my training was to last seven years. After that, I was to be free to go and continue healing wherever I wished, living again with my wife and children. But the Lord Jaganath changed all plans. And, when the changes came, I could not give up the work I believed I had been born for. So I came here to Ravinath, though I knew that we might be here for many years."

"Do you ever hear from them? Your wife and children?"

He shook his head, and I asked, "Did Sheel Chandra not take you to them, in your mind? As he took me to my mother?"

He shot me a surprised look. "Did he, now? You were exceedingly well blessed, Avala. No, he did not use his powers to help any of us in that way. We knew, when we came to Ravinath, that we would be cut off from the world and all who loved us. We also knew it could be for a very long time. But we could not risk contacting anyone, for Jaganath has spies everywhere, and ways of forcing people to give up what is in their minds. Not one soul outside Ravinath knows the place exists—except you. You must never speak a word of it. Not to anyone, ever."

"Not even to Ramakoda, or Ishtok?" I asked.

"No, you must not tell even them," he replied. "If one of them was ever taken in slavery, he could possibly end up in service to Jaganath. And Jaganath could walk in his memories, and discover there your story of us. It would undo much of our work in shielding your people—could undo everything, and have everyone here killed."

"I wish Sheel Chandra could shield everyone, and not just my people," I said.

"He often says that himself," said Taliesin, getting up. He forgot his foot was numb and almost fell over again. I put our cups away and offered to help him to his rooms.

"Just give the feeling back," he said.

"I don't know how to do that."

He sighed again and tried to look annoyed, though he grinned. "Just drop me in the dining hall," he said. "It's almost morning. By the time I limp all the way down the stairs to my quarters, it'll be time to come back for breakfast. Next time I invite you to practice your powers on me, remind me to ask you first if you can reverse them."

I did learn to reverse the effects of blocking nerves, and many other things besides. The deeper healings I learned from Salverion were similar to the ones I had learned from my mother—the sending of light through pathways in the body, to heal and ease and restore—but with Salverion I learned to make the healing deeper and more extensive. Because I knew much more about anatomy, I knew where to send the healing light, and precisely what to do with it. It was as if, before, I had been working blindly; now I worked with sharpened vision, and could send the light to exact places, along exact nerves and blood vessels. Also, he told me much about surgery, though I could not put it all into practice. I did do some dissecting, however; Taliesin and some of the other disciples often went hunting for deer or rabbits or wild goats in the mountains around Ravinath, and when they brought back the carcasses for the cooks, Salverion and I were allowed to have the organs. The cooks got used to me practicing with my scalpel on the contents of their casseroles.

There was one sad interruption to my learning; at the beginning of summer one of the old Masters, a musician, had a heart attack and died, and the whole of Ravinath mourned for him. So for the first time I saw a Navoran funeral and joined in the prayers and listened to the wonderful words they said about him who had died. He was buried in a long silver casket in the Garden in the Gap, under the apple trees in the orchard. In the dappled sunlight there in the garden the musicians played some of the music he had composed, and it was so soaring and sublime that I wept at the beauty of it. That music seemed to reveal the spirit of the great Empire my father had loved, before it was spoiled by the shadow of evil.

The death affected Sheel Chandra deeply, for he loved music, and the old musician had been his great friend. So it was decided that I would not begin my training with Sheel Chandra until summer's middle; and, as I had learned all that Salverion wanted to teach me, in the meantime I was permitted to do whatever I wished to fill my days. I worked in the garden, helped Amael with his herbs, and went hunting in the mountains with Taliesin. I spent many nightly hours with Zuleman, looking at the planets and the stars, and learning, and wishing again and again that Ishtok were here with me.

I also spent many hours with the scientists of Ravinath, asking questions. My curiosity became a joke with them, and when they saw me coming they threw up their hands, pretending horror, exclaiming, "Oh, no, not more questions! Can't someone break a leg, and keep her busy with Salverion?" But their joking was always with fond good humor, and they willingly told me all I wanted to know. At last I learned about gravity, the speed of light, the size of our galaxy, and a hundred unimaginable things besides.

When my mind needed a change from stupendous revelations, I persuaded one of the musicians to teach me how to play music. He gave me an instrument he called a zither, and I spent many happy hours making sounds with it.

I also discovered more about my Navoran grandfather, Jager Eshban Vala, and was surprised to realize how famous and wealthy he had been. When he had died, Zuleman had attended the funeral. "Very grand, that funeral was," Zuleman told me. "The Empress sent an envoy on her behalf, and he made a fine speech. Your father was there. He was only a boy at the time. He was supposed to make a speech, too, a traditional ode spoken by every Navoran first son at his father's funeral. Gabriel refused to finish the speech, and caused quite a stir among the relatives. Got into a bit of trouble for it, as I remember."

"Why didn't he finish the speech?"

"I don't know, for sure. But he was always a disappointment

to his father, and they didn't get along. Jager talked about it sometimes, with me. They had the usual family quarrels. I'm not saying Gabriel was wrong, or a bad son, but he was defiant and disobedient, according to Jager. I always thought that Gabriel was simply outspoken. I wasn't surprised years later when I heard that he had publicly, and to his face, accused Jaganath of corruption. We all knew of Jaganath's crimes and misdoings, but your father was the only person who ever dared speak openly of it— and he was only a youth at the time. He put the rest of us to shame, for our cowardice."

"What did Jaganath do, when my father accused him?" I asked.

"From what I heard, Jaganath very cleverly twisted your father's words around and accused Gabriel of treason. That means being disloyal to the Empire. The penalty for treason is death. I suppose that's when your father took refuge with the Shinali, though even that didn't save him from Jaganath's wrath."

"Will no one speak against Jaganath? Are they all so afraid of him?"

"He was always a very powerful and cruel man, Avala. We're sheltered here in Ravinath, so I don't know too much of Navoran politics today; but from what Sheel Chandra sees in his visions, the city's walls have been rebuilt, and the whole place is like a fort. Not to keep enemies out, but to keep people in. Such is the fear people have of their Emperor. I doubt anyone opposes him these days, and lives."

When I was not thinking of mighty things concerning the Navoran Empire or the world or the stars, I began to learn to read and write. Since I was a small child I had been fascinated by the elegant curves and sweeping lines in the Empress Petra's letter treasured by my tribe, and also had loved the book my mother owned that had been my father's, though I could read no word of it. Now I did learn to make out words and meanings from those signs on parchment, and this was a great marvel to me. To help me learn to read, Delano wrote simple poems, some-times drawing tiny pictures to give me clues about their mean-ing; and in my room at night, under the lamplight, I deciphered them by myself.

Often in those reading times I looked up to see the portrait of my father, which I had on my wall, and a joy-wildness went through me, that I had found my place in his world among the people he had loved. A great peace grew in me, and there were no doubts anymore about my destiny as the Daughter of the Oneness, or as a healer. I missed my own people, but even that longing was not the desperate pain it once had been. I realized, with something akin to astonishment, that for the first time in my life I felt truly at home.

But despite my great contentment in Ravinath, there was one ache that would not go away. Ishtok haunted my dreams and my waking hours, and on the edge of every joy, every new discovery, was the wish that he were with me to share it. And it was more than the wish to share; there was, in the innermost chamber of my heart, a hunger to see his face, to see the texture of his skin and know again the touch of him, the smell of him.

I wondered if this was love, and if it was, then perhaps there was only grief at the end of it, since he had never spoken of his feelings toward me; and despite his tenderness at times, I had always sensed that halting in him, as if with me he would go so far and no further. Perhaps he had been promised in some way to the beautiful Navamani. Or perhaps for him and me there could be no future, since I was only a slave and he was the chieftain's son. Yet I could not wipe out the feelings in me, and so I gave them to the All-father for safekeeping in his hands, along with all the other things that were joy to me, and fear, and sadness, and hope.

18

Freedom's truest flag flies unconfined
In the human mind.

—Delano, Navoran poet

"You've learned a great many things since you first came to Ravinath," said Sheel Chandra. "You've seen the greatest art in the world, heard the most glorious music, the finest poetry. You've witnessed surgery by the most excellent physician in the Empire, and he has taught you how to stop pain and to heal brokenness. You've seen through microscopes, marked the life within a seed; and you've looked through telescopes and plotted the pathways of the stars. But the greatest frontier is yet unmapped and remains almost wholly unknown: it is the power in here." He tapped his own forehead, then leaned forward and gently tapped mine. "In here is the greatest wonder of them all."

We were sitting in his high room where we had first met. He was in his chair and I on a stool near his knee.

"Look about you, tell me what you see," he said.

I looked up. "I see the glass roof, and the blue sky, and white clouds," I said. "Along the wall is the window, open. I see far mountaintops. I see stone walls, a wooden floor. And you."

"Now don't be afraid," he said. "Tell me what else you see."

A shadow caught the corner of my eye, and I turned and saw a large wolf. It was a little behind me, near the far end of the window. It began pacing, its claws clicking on the polished floor. I had seen wolves before, but never this close. Its eyes were amber, translucent, edged with black. Its lips too were black, and its tongue hung out a little, from the heat. Its fur was gray and brown, and dust rose from its coat as it paced. I saw the muscles ripple under its fur, the strong tendons of its legs, its powerful throat and jaws. Suddenly it turned toward me. I froze, hardly breathed. The wolf came over to me, sniffed my hand. I felt its whiskers prick my skin. It licked my wrist; its tongue was warm, rasping. I could see its teeth, yellowed and sharp. I heard it panting. It sat down by me, its tongue lolling, as if it grinned. Then, in the blink of an eye, it vanished.

I stared at the Master, astounded.

"A wolf!" I cried. "You created a wolf."

"If you did not know me," he said, "and if you came in here and saw me with that wolf, you would have thought it was real. And if the wolf had snarled at you, you would have been afraid. If it had attacked you, you would have turned to run. But if it had caught you, you would have felt its claws, its teeth, and you would have suffered all the trauma of being killed by a wild animal. In the end your heart would have failed from sheer terror, and from your absolute belief in certain death."

"But you would never create such an illusion," I said.

"No, I wouldn't. But there is one who would, and you have expressed a desire to speak with him."

"Jaganath?" I said.

"Yes, Jaganath. And his illusions are not just wolves, but things far worse. He uses illusions to control people, to strike such fear into them that they will obey his every wish. Even the strongest men in the Empire he controls in this way. He also has the power to walk in memories, to re-create images of loved ones now on the Other Side. He knows all secrets, all fears, all hurts, all dreams. He also has allied himself with demons, with powers from beyond the veil. That is why, when he took power as Emperor, he closed the Citadel and would have killed us all: we are the only ones in the world who can withstand him. I am the only one who equals him in power."

"Are you saying I should never face him?" I asked.

"On the contrary, I think you must face him. You are the daughter of his great enemy, the person Jaganath hated above all others. Gabriel publicly exposed Jaganath for the evil man he was. If anyone ever again faces Jaganath and accuses him of his wrongs, that person should be you. As Gabriel's daughter, as a member of the Shinali nation, and as a free woman in the Time of the Eagle, you must confront Jaganath. And I shall teach you all the power you need. But you must always bear this in mind: that in his presence, nothing is as it seems."

"I almost want to change my mind," I said.

He smiled then, and touched my cheek with his palm. "No need for fear," he said. "We will begin one step at a time. You have your father's gifts, and great power is already in you. You were born for this, Avala. This is your battle. Not for you the sword, the warrior-hordes meeting Jaganath's army. Not for you the

246

arrows and the spears. Your weapons will be entirely different, your battle another kind of fight altogether."

And so he taught me the deeper wisdoms, the unbound abilities of the human mind. I cannot speak in detail of what I learned, for before we began I made solemn vows that I would never disclose the secrets of his power; but I can say that with Sheel Chandra I learned how to discern between what is illusion and what is real, how to create illusions, to interpret dreams, and to shield myself with light so mighty that nothing could pierce it.

But it was not all solemn learning, with Sheel Chandra. He taught me to walk in memories, and allowed me, for practice, to walk in his. And so I came to see his country, Shanduria, and witnessed some of the astounding things I had heard about, months before, from the poet Delano. I saw the strange high temples, totally carved with the figures of holy people; I saw a wide flight of steps going down into a yellow river where people bathed, saffron robes wrapped about themselves, and where there floated flower-covered barges, slowly burning, that were funeral pyres. There were domed palaces where white tigers roamed, and people with jewels and robes more colorful than any I had seen before. But best of all was the procession of the huge beasts called elephants, with their long painted trunks, golden drapes, and on their broad backs the little jeweled chairs in which people rode. One of the elephants carried a man so completely wrapped in gold and jewels, even about his head, that I could hardly see his face. As I watched that procession I heard people cheering and felt the crowd pressing against my back. I was conscious of a woman standing close to me, holding my hand tight. Though I did not see her clearly, she was much taller than I, and I realized I was seeing the memories of a small child. And I did not only see the memories; I smelled the dust, and a heavy scent like spices, and felt the heat beating up from the shining dust. A grinning boy danced in front of me, one hand held out palm up, the other offering a basket in which were several pieces of cut fruit. The hand of the woman I was with put a coin in the boy's palm, and I took a piece of the fruit. It was pale green and very juicy, delicious. I looked up, trying to see the woman's face, and the scene faded.

I took several deep breaths, and opened my eyes. "Why did you not let me see your mother?" I asked.

Sheel Chandra smiled that beautiful smile of his, and humor rose in his great dark eyes. "Leave me some things that are private," he said. "As it is, I have a hard time going ahead of you in my memories, limiting your walk. The Shandurian procession you were meant to see, and the ceremonial elephant bearing the Great Khan on its back—but the face of my mother was meant to remain hidden."

"Your country is wonderful," I said. "I'm honored to see your childhood memories. Thank you."

"It's always a pleasure to share them with you," he replied. "But I do not let you run totally amok through the mansions of my mind. You see only what I want you to see. I put up many walls. With other minds, other memories, there are no boundaries. When walking in memories, we see also people's deepest agonies, their most terrible secrets, their worst nightmares. What is seen in other people's minds could drive us mad. So we set our own boundaries, and walk in memories only with the person's consent, and for a very limited time. Always, it is done only to heal, perhaps to find the core of disease, or to wipe out a terrible fear. No matter how tempted, we must never walk in memories for our own purposes."

Slowly he stood up, and I stood with him, and he leaned on me as we went downstairs for the evening meal. On the way he said, "You had talked of going back to the Igaal in the autumn. Is that still your wish?"

"Why speak of autumn?" I said. "It's months away yet."

"No it is not, dear one. Summer is almost over. You and I have spent whole days—many days—deep in meditation, communing in our minds, exchanging words by thought alone. Time has not existed for us. In another few weeks it will be autumn."

Astonished, I thought on his words. "I wish to go back only when I've learned everything you want to teach me," I said.

"There is one other skill," he said. "It is the ability to travel in your mind the way we did the first time we were together, when we visited your mother. In the time left to us I cannot teach you to communicate directly with people, but I can teach you to discern where they are, perhaps even to see them. It is a skill that will be necessary for you, I think, though to learn it may take until winter's end."

"How terrible," I said, trying not to smile, "to have to spend a few more months in Ravinath."

He laughed softly. "Then we shall begin tomorrow," he said.

249

Suddenly another thought struck me. "I missed my seventeenth borning-day!" I said. "It was in summer's middle."

"Was it, now?" he said. "Then we shall arrange a belated celebration."

So it was that the seventeenth celebration of my borning-day was in Ravinath, and I was a high lot honored. The cooks made a splendid feast, everyone had the afternoon free of studies and work, and we feasted from day's middle almost until dusk. I sat in the place of honor, in the center of the long table under the many-pillared open window, with the summer-browned mountains and the sun at my back. At the feast's end the table was cleared in front of me, and everyone brought me gifts. I was given tiny bags of seeds from Amael, all carefully labeled, and Zuleman gave me a book of star maps, a different map for each month, showing where the stars were, and their names, and which planets were visible. One of the scientists gave me a small telescope made of brass, which slid away into a cylinder not much longer than my hand. "You won't be able to see the moons of your beloved Erdelan through it," he said, "but you will be able to see many things in this world, that otherwise would not be seen."

From Taliesin I received a beautiful Navoran ring, made by one of the silversmiths especially for me. It was a perfect circle made up of seven silver stars, symbol of the Citadel and the seven Wisdoms taught there. Where each star joined the next were two tiny jewels, one green, the color of healing, the other blue, the Navoran color for freedom.

From Salverion I received a folding leather pouch containing

Navoran surgical instruments. There was a little knife, razor sharp and pointed, made of the finest Navoran steel, for the cleaning of wounds and for surgery. With it was a stone for sharpening the blade, and Salverion showed me how to use it. In the pouch also was an instrument to hold wounds open while I cleaned them, and a delicate tool for removing tiny fragments of dirt or bone. There was an ingenious instrument called a pair of scissors, for cutting, and a set of very fine curved metal needles such as Navoran surgeons used, as well as a roll of silk thread for sewing up wounds. One of the Ravinath artists had painted my name on the pouch, along with a picture of an eagle flying over the slender towers and domed roofs of the beautiful Citadel.

All the gifts were exceedingly precious to me, but the most treasured was from Sheel Chandra. It was a golden talisman identical to one he wore himself: a pair of eagle's wings outstretched in flight, and above them, fitted perfectly within their upward curve, was a single eye, its pupil formed of the blue stone the Navorans call sapphire. The symbol was fixed to a golden chain, and as Sheel Chandra placed it over my head he said, "When you hold this sacred sign against your brow and call to me in your mind, I will hear you. And, no matter how many mountains or walls or rivers or seas lie between us, we will commune together in our thoughts."

As if all this were not enough, the musicians played for me, and the poets read, and Salverion made a speech that I will hold in my knowing for the rest of my life.

"Sovereign God brought you to us," he said, in ending. "He gave us the joy and the great privilege of sharing with you the wisdom and blessings that we have. Yet, in the Time of the Eagle, you and your people, with the Hena and the Igaal, shall give us far more than anything we have given you in this place—for you will give us our liberty, and the right to return home."

Sheel Chandra spread the large, fine parchment out on the table in front of me, and nodded toward the map he had pinned up on the wall. "Now, I want you to copy that map," he said, "everything in the Shinali, Igaal, and Hena lands—every mountain, every valley, and every river and forest. Also, all the coast."

We were in the great library, and the light from above poured down on the blank parchment and the pen held in my hand.

"What has this to do with communicating?" I asked.

"You will find out," he said. "First, the map. Make it as accurate as you can, and add anything you know that is not shown on our Navoran chart."

So, for the next seven days, I made my map. A work of art it was, with the mountain ranges detailed and fine, and all the valleys and gorges distinct. I made the map my own, naming the rivers and peaks with the Shinali names for them, and I even marked the hunting grounds my people had found in the Wandering that were rich with deer and wild goats. While I drew, Sheel Chandra came often to watch, but he did not talk to me. Sometimes I did not even realize he was there. While I made my map other disciples were not allowed to use the library, for Sheel Chandra had said I must not be disturbed.

At last it was done, and I rolled up my map and took it to Sheel Chandra in his glass-roofed room high in the tower.

"Ah—a beautiful work!" he said, when I spread the map at his feet. "Excellent detail. Look across those lands depicted here,

Avala, and know that somewhere, in all this vast territory, are your people. And somewhere is your Igaal tribe. Look on your map, draw its landmarks on the parchments of your heart, know it well. And in the days and months to come, I will show you how to fly in your mind, swift as the eagle flies, down those valleys and across those plains and over those mountains, until you find the ones you seek."

It seemed an easy skill, the way he spoke of it then; but autumn swept her gusty winds about our tower, then winter's whiteness fell on the glass roof, and still I sat there before my map, searching, questing, finding nothing.

"Don't despair, Avala," Sheel Chandra said, one bitterly cold day when I was near tears, thinking myself a failure. "This is the hardest skill of all, one even Jaganath does not possess. It is the kind of vision that comes usually when it is unexpected, a flash of insight, a special gift for a moment only. To train your mind to open up the portals of this Sight, to train your spirit to deliberately fly beyond your body and to commune with other minds, is a very great discipline. Be calm, have peace. It will come. One day your mind will fly and you will see your map no longer, but the lands below. You will fly across the place where your people dwell, and you will know."

I thought of the glorious flight with him, that first night we had met, when he took me to see my mother. So effortless, so swift and wonderful, it had been.

"I feel as if I'm flapping around in the mud," I said, "and I want to soar."

But one day, when the snowdrifts were piled on the glass dome, and the windows shook with the force of the gales buffeting them, I did. I was looking at my map, weary, half asleep and half blind from staring, when my focus shifted, and the map seemed to slide sideways. Instantly, I was wide awake. I thought I was falling down and tried to sit upright, but was already straight. With pounding heart and mounting joy, I glanced along the slanting map, saw it become wide and broad, stretching out beyond the walls. Wind streamed over me. Far below, the mountains stretched like crumpled paper, and rivers snaked, blue-black, between the snowy lands. I saw flat plains dusted with snow and ice, and windswept gorges, and slashes of green forest. Swift I flew through the silent lands, down the valleys, felt the icy air rush over me, and in the deep dark gorges heard the winds howl. Over a plain a herd of wild horses grazed on tussock grass, and I thought of Ishtok. Then I was in a valley with steep mountains all around and an ice-dark lake ahead. Beside the lake, snow-powdered tents. Igaal tents. Then, between one breath and the next, I was in one of them. It was Mudiwar's. With every sense, I was there: I smelled the fire burning in the metal braziers, and the lamp oil, and leather clothes and sweat. Mudiwar sat there, coughing, blue-lipped. I saw Ramakoda with a woman beside him who was a stranger to me. She said something to him, and he smiled at her in a way I had not seen him smile before. I had the feeling she was his new wife.

I heard rough laughter, and voices with an unfamiliar accent. There were strangers there, sitting among the people of Mudiwar's tribe. They wore painted garments, and their long hair was thickened with red mud and formed into ringlets or topknots, even the men's. They were Hena. One of them was a man with a striking face, with high cheekbones and a strong mouth, and no hair at all on his head, but with strange signs painted along his brow. I knew he was their priest, Sakalendu; I knew it from the deep, otherworldly look about him, and from his soul-colors, amber and violet and white. Then I saw Ishtok.

With a Hena youth he was, and they were leaning with their heads close, laughing together. Ishtok lifted his head, and I saw his face joyful in the lamplight. He looked so happy, glad to see his Hena family again. I wanted to laugh with him, to share his pleasure. The youth he was with gave him something on a leather thong. It was a stone carving of a fox, and Ishtok put it about his neck, and embraced his friend.

The scene seemed to diminish, to fade. I was looking at the tent again, from above, then it was only a dot among other dots, beside the dark lake. It was evening, and the setting sun blushed pink on the snow. There was a feeling of wind again, of being drawn back, pulled fast along frigid valleys and past lofty peaks. Then I was in Ravinath, in the high room with my map in front of me. A lamp was burning on the floor nearby. I leaned forward and with my fingertip traced the way I had gone, past the ranges that edged the Ekiya Gorge, along the black river, northeastward to the mountains deep in Igaal land. There. There was Mudiwar's camp, beside a lake hidden within a circle of mountains.

I looked up and saw Sheel Chandra watching me. He was smiling, nodding.

"Well done, dear one!" he said. "But it was not your people you found."

"No," I said. "I found my Igaal tribe. They had visitors. Ishtok's Hena family, they had come to visit him. He was talking with his Hena brother, Atitheya."

"You heard him speak Atitheya's name?"

For a few heartbeats I hesitated, unsure. Then, bewildered, I shook my head. "I just know it," I said. "At least, I think I know it. Do you think I'm right?"

"What I think," he replied, "is that your time with us here at Ravinath is finished. You are ready to go out and begin your real work."

19

At last spring sang her joy across the mountains, and the snows began to melt, and the air rang with the shout of many waters rushing downward to the great Ekiya River.

Shaking with excitement, I put aside the crimson dress I had worn and put on my Igaal dress with its patterns cut about the hem and sleeves, the tunic with my father's paintings, and the boots Ramakoda had made me. I was surprised to find that the hem of the dress was higher than it had been the last time I wore it. I went into the tiny bathroom off my room and looked in the mirror while I plaited back my hair, and wondered at the tribal woman who looked back at me.

Returning to my bedroom, I looked about it for the last time. Then I picked up my white rabbit-fur coat, and the travel bag Ramakoda had given me so long ago. In it were my old blanket, Ishtok's cup, the tiny bag of Shinali soil, the seeds from Amael, the surgical instruments Salverion had given me, the telescope, and the map I had made. I wore the ring from Taliesin, and the sacred sign from Sheel Chandra. Everything else I had been given—the portrait of my father, the zither, the books, the Ravinath clothes, everything I could not take with me—was in the wooden chest at the foot of my bed. When I opened that chest again and looked on those gifts, the Time of the Eagle would have come, and I would be on my homeland.

I looked for the last time out my window, at the western mountains where melting snows ran down toward the far Shinali lands, and I said a prayer for courage. Then I went to his rooms to see Salverion.

For a long time we stood gazing at each other, saying nothing, then I put down my bag and went to him, and we embraced. "Remember what you must tell the Igaal, about your time here," he said. "Tell them only that you were in a high and holy place, and your God looked after you and gifted you new powers. It is not a lie." He added huskily, "We shall all miss you. At every meal when we give thanks, we will pray for you. I love you as my own child. Now we must go; they are all waiting. Sheel Chandra told me you found the Igaal camp yourself, with your map and your Vision."

"They are in a beautiful place by a lake," I said. "But it is a long way from here. I hope Taliesin will be safe, coming back alone."

"Without your excellent skills to protect him, you mean?" Salverion said, with a chuckle. "Hold no fears for him. He has more abilities than you know about, Avala."

We went together down the long passageways to the wide road along which Taliesin had carried me, frozen and semiconscious, when I had first come to Ravinath. Before the road there was a huge hall with a lofty vaulted ceiling, bare but for the dozens of torches burning on the pillared walls. It seemed dark and cavernous compared with the glorious inner rooms and halls.

All seventy people who lived in Ravinath had come to see me leave. Taliesin waited there, at the head of them, in that great dim hall. Sheel Chandra was there, with all the others I had grown to love. In total silence we walked down the long, steep interior road, lit by wavering lamps, to the outer door in the mountainside. On one side of me walked Salverion; on the other, leaning on one of his disciples, was Sheel Chandra. Just behind us came Taliesin, bearing my bag and a large bag of his own. And in the darkness behind him, silent but for the soft marching of their feet, came everyone else.

The door was opened, and after the dimness the light was almost blinding. Shading our eyes, we went out into the wind-swept, dusty valley. The snow was almost gone, though gales whistled in the topmost peaks, streaming clouds like tattered flags across the pinnacles. The gusts rushed down the ravines and swept, moody as the *shoorai* wind, across the company behind me.

It was chill, that wind, and I was glad of the coat and boots Ramakoda had made. For the journey Taliesin had exchanged his crimson robes for a black coat and trousers, and a long fur cloak. He waited on one side while I stood on the top step beside the opened door and said my farewells. Each one came to say good-bye, and it was a hard, sad time. I wept, and most of the others wept, and I felt an awful tearing in my heart. Lastly, I said goodbye to Salverion and Sheel Chandra.

Salverion embraced me again, kissing my forehead and hair. "Go well, beloved," he said. "You carry with you the future and the hope of us all. Go with our love, our protection, and our peace."

Unable to speak, I kissed his cheek and his hands, and made the Shinali farewell.

Then it was time to say good-bye to Sheel Chandra. I clung to him a long time, crying so hard I could not speak, though there was much I wanted to say. And that wonderful old man wept, too, and smiled with so much love I could hardly bear it. He spoke over me in his own Shandurian tongue, and though I could not understand the words, I understood well the love and blessing they conveyed.

Then all that great company sang an old Shinali battle song. I don't know how they knew it, but they sang it with a high lot of feeling. As Taliesin and I walked down the steps and out into the valley the words of the song blew about us like a benediction and a promise, and I wept and wept, and Taliesin put his arm about me, and we went on until I could hear the song no more. Many times I looked back and saw them all still standing there, veiled in the blowing dust, with the shadow of the great open door in the mountain rock behind them. Then we went around a bend in the ravine, and they were lost to my sight.

It was a long journey we faced, and each step farther away from Ravinath seemed like a hundred miles to me. I had not known how much I had loved that place and the people there. Knowing my pain, Taliesin said little during that first day's walk. Sometimes he held my hand to help me over bubbling streams, or across steep rocks, and after did not let it go, and the nearness of him gave me strength. Salverion's last words to me resounded in my heart, and I was very much aware of the hopes that lay on me. A year before, such a responsibility would have crushed me; now I touched the talisman from Sheel Chandra, and a quiet courage rose in me. I glanced at Taliesin, and he looked sideways at me and smiled. "You're not alone, Avala," he said, knowing. "You will never be alone."

That first night we camped on the edge of the plain where I had last seen my people. We could see the mighty gorge of the Ekiya River, slashing through the mountains eastward toward the Igaal lands. It was strange for me to be there, and I felt a longing for my people again. At dusk, after our meal, I took the map from my bag and went out onto the plain a little way. Facing the river and the place where my people's tents had been, I closed my eyes and flew in my mind along the lands depicted on the map. Within moments I was flying in the low sun, bloodred as it went down behind the western ranges, and the evening wind was strong and warm. Below me was a long valley, and in it, about halfway along, I sensed a pulse, a beat of human life. I saw my people then, camped in a ravine where a river went two ways. I saw my mother turning steaks on a spit over a small fire, talking to a little child who crouched near her. She said something that made the child laugh, and when my mother lifted her head and the tawny light fell full on her, I saw that she was smiling, and there was contentment in her face.

It was enough, and I left that place, my heart light. When I went back to Taliesin he was sitting cross-legged by our fire, his hands palm upward on his knees, his eyes closed. I waited until he opened them, then I said, "My people are well."

"It's good that you went to see them," he replied. "You might not have much peace for meditation times, back with Mudiwar's tribe."

"It is nearly two years since I last saw my people, in this valley," I said. "My last night with them was the night of my sixteenth borning-day, when Zalidas spoke his great words over me. I did not truly believe him, then; I did not think I could ever accomplish what he prophesied. Now I know that I am empowered."

Taliesin put some more sticks on our little fire and spread out our sleeping-things. He sat down on his blankets and looked at me across the flying sparks. "I'm going to say something to you, Avala," he said. "I say this as a friend, with love. I know you feel the weight of a great responsibility upon you, and that you wear the mantle of one who may change history for many nations. It is a great destiny. But never let pride take a hold, not for a moment. The greatest king may win his greatest battle only because of the obedience of his warhorse. Bear in mind that your success may rise or fall on the loyalty and steadfastness of the humblest friend—maybe even on the service of a friend you may never meet. Be grateful for everyone, everything, and remember that nothing in this world is certain."

His words cut, and I was hurt. Nothing certain? But I was the Daughter of the Oneness! Even Salverion had said that the future of nations was in my hands. I was chosen, gifted. Indignant, I was going to answer Taliesin back, but then fortunately I closed my mouth.

While the night gathered about us, and the shadows in the valley grew black, I thought on Taliesin's words. I thought of my overwhelming sense of destiny, of empowerment, of being entrusted with the freedom of many. Was it pride, this sense of awe at my rare destiny? Was it pride, this certainty that I would indeed accomplish everything I hoped, without too much pain or sacrifice? My father, too, had dreamed of being a healer, and he was a far greater healer than I; yet he also had fought for the freedom of my people, and it had cost him everything. What made me so sure my life's work would be easier than his? Even my work with the Igaal would have ended before it was begun, if I had not been found by those at Ravinath. If I had had my way, I would have given up long ago and gone straight from Ravinath back to my own people. It was only the wisdom and goodness of Salverion and others that had given me the strength to go on. It was only their generosity and greatness of spirit that had empowered me; and all that they had given to me, all that they had taught, had been a gift, freely given, undeserved by me. But for them, I would not even be alive now. I realized, with a deep sense of humility, that Taliesin was right: by myself I could accomplish nothing, and I must never forget it. Finally, I remembered Mudiwar and his fierce refusal to have anything to do with the Time of the Eagle, and I knew that Taliesin was right in another thing, too: nothing was certain.

After a while, humbled and with a deep sense of gratitude, I got up and went around the fire, and kissed Taliesin's cheek. "I'll remember your words," I said. "Thank you."

For three more days we traveled, following the great Ekiya River northward to the place where it had its beginnings in the mighty Himeko Mountains, in the very heart of the Igaal lands. Mudiwar's people were still in the place by the lake, where I had seen them in my first mind-flight using the map I had made. Their camp was almost entirely surrounded by mountains and was reached only by a winding, narrow gorge that went in from the northwest ridge. It was dusk on the fourth day when Taliesin and I reached the gorge, and night by the time we had walked down its winding way almost to the plain. We camped the night hidden behind rocks, but within sight of the end of the gorge. In the morning we shared a small meal, and then it was time for him to go.

As always in good-byes, I was lost for words.

"Remember that you will be protected every moment, Avala," Taliesin said. "If you need us, Sheel Chandra is as close as your next thought."

I wept, for he was my last link with Ravinath. Drawing me to him, he took my face in his hands and kissed my brow.

"Thank you for everything, Taliesin," I said. "You've been a true friend."

"It's I who thank you," he said. "You've been as a daughter to me, and blessed me more than you know. I will be thinking of you every hour."

Placing a hand on my head, he said a prayer for me. "Go in peace," he said, "and in the grace of Sovereign God." Then, quickly, he bent and picked up his bag, and walked away. Near the first bend in the gorge he turned, and we waved to each other. Then he went around the rocks, his black cloak blowing about him, and was gone.

Turning, I picked up my bag and put my winter coat across my arm. The day was warm, and the breeze that came through the gorge was rich with the scent of springtime grass and the pungent odor of Igaal fires. The rocky walls of the gorge were high but only about six paces apart, and the narrowness of the place reminded me of the long walk into Ravinath. Only this time I was walking back to another world, the Igaal world I had left behind over a year ago. Saying a prayer to the All-father, I began walking. As I neared the end of the gorge, where it began to widen onto the plain, I heard a drumming in the earth, coming from the Igaal camp. It was a single horse. I stopped, put down my things, and waited. Suddenly I felt exposed and alone, almost misplaced, trapped between two worlds. For a few panic-stricken heartbeats I did not know who I was—escaped Igaal slave, or free Shinali woman, or Navoran healer. Then I touched the amulet I wore, the eagle's wings with the Navoran stone and the eye that saw all things, held all things in its peace; and I knew myself to be all three, complete and whole and sure. No matter what happened in these next hours, I had all of Ravinath behind me.

The hoofbeats came nearer, and then the horse appeared. I saw who the rider was, and my heart sang. It was Ishtok, his hunting bow across his back.

Seeing me, he drew his horse to a halt. Slowly he dismounted and walked over to me. I had forgotten how beautiful he was. His face had changed, become more defined, and stronger. He had a short beard, and there was a new tattoo above the old one on his brow. He did not look as tall as he had been before.

"Avala?" he said.

"It is I," I said, smiling, feeling a quickening in my pulse. How good it was to see him again!

He laughed a little, shaking his head, as if unable to believe his eyes. At last he said, "You've changed."

"So have you," I said.

He came close and bent his forehead to mine, in the Igaal greeting. Smiling, he rubbed his brow along mine, then lifted his face and sniffed my hair. "You smell different," he said. "You're taller, too."

Then suddenly we were in each other's arms, and he picked me up and swung me about in a circle, and we were both laughing. He was lean and taut, and smelled of horses, leather, and smoke. As he swung me around I pressed my face against his neck and kissed his skin, but I do not think he noticed.

"Where have you been?" he asked, setting me down again but keeping his arms around me. "I went to the valley where you said your people were, but they were not there. Did you go away with them?"

"No, they were gone when I got there," I said.

"Then where were you? Where have you been?"

I said nothing, not wanting to lie, longing to tell him of Ravinath.

Perplexed, he held me at arm's length, studying my face, my dress, my boots. "You're clean," he said. "Your dress, it's hardly worn. Your boots are still like new. You look . . . perfect. Beautiful. Where were you? Were you with another tribe?"

Salverion's words came back to me. I said, "I was in the mountains. In a high place. The All-father looked after me."

"Even your talk is different," he said, frowning, puzzled and unsatisfied. Suddenly he smiled again and drew me to him and hugged me hard. "Oh, it's of no matter!" he said. "You're back. I prayed so hard to Shimit to bring you back. Ramakoda will be pleased to see you. He's married now. At our Gathering last spring he got a new wife. And Kimiwe will go wild, to see you. She

266

cried for five days after you left. And Mudiwar—" He stopped, and his look worried me. "Well, if your *munakshi* has grown a bit, he'll be glad to see you. He's very ill."

"Did he ever find out that you helped me escape?" I asked.

"No. But he was a high lot angry when he woke up after the feast and discovered that you were gone." He mounted his horse, and I gave him my coat and bag, which he put in front of him. Then he offered me his hand, and pulled me up behind him. I slipped my arms about his waist, glad for the excuse to hug him again, and we set off toward the end of the gorge and the valley. As we rode he covered my hands with one of his, as he had done on that long ride back from Taroth Pass and the Shinali lands. He walked the horse slowly, and I hoped it was because he was unwilling just yet to take me to Mudiwar, and wanted these moments to last.

"Is all well with you, Ishtok?" I asked.

"All is well now," he replied.

"Did you think of me while I was away?"

"Not often. Only at every second beat of my heart."

I pressed my face against his back and tightened my hold about his waist.

"Did you think of me?" he asked.

"Only as often as you thought of me," I replied.

We came out into the valley. Like Ravinath, it was hidden within a circle of mountains, and reached only by this one narrow gorge. Snow still covered the peaks and lay in the deepest valleys, and there were many streams and rivulets rushing down into a little lake that lay like glass beside the tents. The tribe was camped on a grassy plain beside the lake's stony shore, and it was a place of quietness and peace. At the lake's southern end a river tumbled in rapids out through a steep, impassable gorge, rushing to the forested hills and on to the sea. The day was still, and I could hear the distant thunder of the rapids.

"It's beautiful here," I said.

"We wintered in this place," he said. "It's well hidden, though some of us saw soldiers go out in the wintertime, when we were hunting in the western ranges. We saw them go back with Hena slaves. It was an anxious time."

"You would have been glad to see your Hena family," I said, without thinking. And I added, because I had to know, "Did you see Navamani, too?"

He stopped his horse and turned to face me. "How did you know they came?" he asked.

A moment I hesitated, then I replied, "I saw it in a vision. I saw you with your Hena brother."

He looked dumbfounded, afraid. Then he said, half smiling, "You're joking, aren't you? You're guessing."

"I know, Ishtok. I saw him give you a leather thong with a stone fox."

His face went pale, and his hand went to his chest, under his shirt. He drew out the amulet, the little carved fox.

"Shimit's teeth, Avala!" he breathed. "You've come back a seer! Where have you been? Tell me. Please. Else I shall think you've been with the gods—or with ghosts."

He looked so disturbed, I could not leave him in his fear. Also, I did not want to live with a lie between us. I said, "I've been with some people who live in hiding. If they were found by the Emperor in the stone city, he would murder them all. They sheltered me and taught me many things. I was sworn to secrecy about them and their place. I should not even have told you this much. Please ask me nothing more. I won't be telling anyone else this, not even Ramakoda or Chimaki. Will you keep the secret for me?"

"I will," he said. "Were they Navorans, these people?"

"No questions," I said. "I can tell you no more. And please don't look so worried, Ishtok."

"I'm not worried. I'm scared witless. You frighten me. Where you've been, the way you are now. The secrets you hold. There's a power in you that wasn't there before."

"I've learned a lot of things, nearly all of them to do with healing. Please don't be afraid of me."

"Too late. I already am." However, he grinned, then turned to face the camp, and we moved on.

"You didn't tell me about Navamani," I said.

"Who?" he asked.

"Navamani," I repeated. "The woman you were in love with."

"Oh, her," he said. "She met someone in another Hena tribe, and married him."

Smiling to myself, I said, "You must have been devastated."

"I was. For the space of one heartbeat, between two thoughts of you."

We were almost at the camp. Children saw us coming and started running and shouting, and by the time we reached the tents most of the tribe was standing by the lake, waiting for us. We got off the horse, and I saw Ramakoda striding over, his grin wide, warm as his welcome. He pressed his forehead to mine, then held me at arm's length as he looked me up and down.

"What a wonder, to see you again!" he said. "You've weathered the winters well. Where have you been, kinswoman? Ishtok rode out to visit you with your people, but you were gone."

"I've been in a secret place in the mountains," I said. "I can't say more than that."

He was silent a while, frowning, his face bewildered and curious. At last he said, "Well, wherever you've been, the gods have looked after you. Come, see my father."

Suddenly I was almost bowled over by a leaping, squealing, long-haired little girl, and I laughed and picked up Kimiwe. She nearly choked me with her hug, and planted kisses all over my face.

"I looked for you every day, wanting you to come back," she said.

I put her down and kissed her cheeks. Her scars had healed well, though there were pale pink patches on her skin where the burns had been, and ridges down her cheeks. She was bald on one part of her head, where her hair had been burned off, but her smile, her irrepressible spirit, were beautiful. Though she had grown, she looked so small, for I had not seen a child in a long time. Then Chimaki was hugging me, and people were rushing about calling to one another in surprise, and the dogs were going mad, caught up in the excitement. Suddenly there was quiet.

Mudiwar was limping out of his tent. When he saw me, he stopped and leaned on his staff, his face inscrutable. A slave rushed up to him and put down a small stool, and Mudiwar sat down. I saw his shoulders rise and fall as he fought to breathe, and his neck and shoulder muscles were tense from the effort. I went and knelt before him.

"Greetings, my chieftain," I said. "I ask for shelter with you and your people, in exchange for my healing work."

"You will indeed work, escaped Shinali slave," he said, his words broken between the struggling breaths. From where I knelt, I could hear the fluid bubbling in his lungs. He was slowly drowning. "You should be punished," he went on. "Why have you come back to us, after so long?"

"The All-father sent me back to you," I said.

"Your god? Or were you sent back by whichever tribe you sheltered with? Does no one want you now?" He began to laugh but coughed instead, a long time. A slave brought a bowl for him, and as he coughed into it I saw blood. At last he sat upright again.

"We know your people were not where you left them," he said. "Ishtok went seeking you. How is it that the storms and snows and wild beasts have not touched you? That you come to us with your clothes clean and fine, and wellness on you like a light? Where have you been sheltering all this time? Who fed you?"

"I was in a holy place in the mountains," I said. "I was well cared for, and taught new skills."

"A holy place, in truth," he said. "Shimit must have guarded you. How did you find us?"

"I had a vision of your place here, my chieftain," I said.

His hooded eyes narrowed, and he thought about that for a while. Then he said, "You say you have learned new skills. Very well, you can heal me. That is your test. If you make me well, you may live among us as a healer and honored slave. If you fail, you'll be whipped, and be no more than a keeper of our dogs."

Again he began coughing, and two slaves helped him back to his tent.

20

For the rest of that day I was with Mudiwar. Chimaki
helped with his healing, and I was glad of her aid, for he
needed ordinary healing first. I made him breathe over a steaming bowl of pungent herbs, and Chimaki and I pummeled his
back until he coughed up all the fluid in his lungs. He cursed
us furiously, for it was a hard time for him, but after, when he
lay exhausted on his bed, I healed him with the deep healing of
Salverion. By the end of that first day, Mudiwar was breathing
easily, the rattle had gone from his chest, and his lips were no
longer blue. He said, with a glimmer in his eye, "Your *munakshi*
has improved, Shinali woman. I don't think I'll have you whipped
after all, for your escape—though if you drum your fists so hard
upon my back again, I might consider it."

That evening the chieftain rested in his bed and was fed by a
slave, while the rest of us feasted sitting on the mats under the
trees on the edge of the lake. I could not help thinking of the glorious eating-hall in Ravinath, with its tall curved windows open
to the mountain peaks; and when Ishtok passed me platters of

meat to choose from, I looked at the Hena paintings on his sleeves, and thought of gold-embroidered crimson robes. The Igaal dishes of clay and wood seemed suddenly alien to me, after the fine-wrought silver and gold we had used at Ravinath, and the high voices of the women and children were startling, after the world of Navoran men. As I looked at the faces around me I saw the suspicion that remained, the mistrust and resentment. I had not expected Mudiwar's tribe to seem so foreign to me, and had forgotten the hate. I looked at Ishtok, and he caught my glance and smiled, and there was fondness in his eyes enough to ease my ache for Ravinath.

While we ate, I was told about the happenings with the clan over the past year. I heard about journeys, of the Gathering of the tribes, and Ramakoda's marriage. I also learned of hardships.

"It was hard, this winter just gone," Chimaki said. "Many old ones got dead bits on their feet, like old Gunateeta before she died. I gave them medicines for pain, but we wished you were here then."

An old woman said, with a sly chuckle and a shrewd look at Ishtok, "One of us, especially, missed you a high lot, Avala—and not because of sore feet."

Ishtok looked embarrassed, and Ramakoda said to me, "Well, we had other visitors, to make up for your absence. Ishtok's Hena tribe came to see us. They had been attacked by Navoran soldiers early in the winter, and many of them were carried off. They spent some of the winter with us, here."

"Avala already knows about the visit," said Ishtok, before I could stop him. "She saw it in a vision. She even knew about the fox amulet Atitheya gave to me. She has visions now, like a seer."

Others overheard, and talk around us stopped.

"Is that so?" asked Ramakoda. "Are you a seer now, Avala?"

"I see some things in dreams," I said.

People were so quiet we heard a waterbird dive into the lake after a fish. Gradually talk resumed, but I noticed that the looks of hate from some people changed to curiosity. Although Mudiwar had never held visionaries high in importance, others in his tribe did. When I checked the chieftain before bedtime, he said to me, "They tell me you're a seer now."

"Maybe," I said. "Your breathing, it's getting easier all the time?"

"You're the seer," he said, grinning. "You tell me."

"I think you'll live to be a great warrior again," I said. Then I bent and kissed his forehead, and he growled and muttered something about women's foolishness, though he looked pleased.

Before I went to bed, I went outside for a while and stood by the lake and watched the moon rise. It was unutterably peaceful. I thought of Taliesin out in the mountains alone, and wished him a safe night, in my heart. He would be almost at the mouth of the Ekiya Gorge by now.

Suddenly there was a quiet movement beside me, and Ishtok stood there. For once he looked uneasy, unsettled.

"What is on your heart, Ishtok?" I asked.

He replied, "You said you can't tell me about the place you went to, and I honor that. But I'm thinking it must have been Navoran. I saw the things you put away in the wooden chest Ramakoda gave you. They were strange, foreign things." I realized he was talking of my map, and the little telescope. Slowly, he lifted my right hand and touched the silver ring I wore on my thumb, the gift from Taliesin. "And this must be Navoran," he said.

I did not reply, and he stayed close, still holding my hand.

"It must have been strange for you," he said. "Even though your father was Navoran, his people are still your enemies."

"Not all his people are our enemies," I said. "No nation is wholly evil, or wholly good. I'm beginning to think that not many Navorans are bad."

"The ones who come looking for slaves are bad," he said.

"Maybe they're afraid to disobey their Emperor," I said, thinking of the soldier called Embry. "If Mudiwar was a very cruel and powerful chieftain, you'd be honor bound to obey him, even if you didn't like what he told you to do. And the Igaal keep slaves, Ishtok. Am I not one?"

He thought for a while, stroking my hand gently, and I felt the little calluses and scars on his palm from his carving knives.

"The Hena priest, Sakalendu, came to visit us, with my Hena tribe," he said. "I talked a long time with him. I told him about your Shinali prophecy, about the Time of the Eagle. He said he has had many dreams this winter past, of a giant eagle flying in high winds, swooping down across the lands, across the old Shinali plain, and over the stone city. He said there are great things spoken of in the stars, signifying that a mighty battle is about to take place. He has gone back now to make the Hena tribes ready."

I was silent, humbled, remembering what Taliesin had said about the success of my work perhaps depending on the service of a friend I might never meet. As I thought of the lone seer-priest in the far-off Hena marshlands, preparing his people to play their part in the fulfillment of our Shinali prophecy, I was swept over by awe and gratitude.

"Sakalendu was right," I said, "there are great things in the stars, huge forces gathering. Not just for the Hena and my people and yours, but for the Navorans, too. The Time of the Eagle is bigger than I ever dreamed it would be, Ishtok. It will change our world forever. There won't be the old strife, the divisions among the tribes, and between us and Navora. We will have a common battle, and a common peace after. But before any of it can happen, there is something I must do. I don't know yet what that work is, I only know that when it becomes clear I must do it, and it may demand all my strength for a time."

He let go of my hand and stood very still, looking across the lake, his moonlit face troubled and unquiet, his dark eyes moist.

"Will you go away again?" he asked.

"In the Time of the Eagle," I said, "I will be with my own people."

"On your Shinali land?"

"It won't be Shinali land. It will belong to all of us."

"And the stone city? How much is that your home? Who are your people, Avala—the Shinali, or the Navorans? Will you be living with your tribe, or in the stone city with your Navoran friends?"

"In the time to come," I said, very low, "I hoped that I would be with you."

"Is hope enough?" he asked, and I heard a bitter edge in his voice. "What of destiny? As a seer, can you foretell that we'll be together?"

"Even a seer can't foretell the workings of human hearts," I replied. "And despite destiny, each of us has free will, the power to choose. I know what I would choose. But what is your will, Ishtok? What do you want?"

He stood in front of me, put his right hand behind my neck, and gently drew me to him. I could hardly breathe, for the longing and ecstasy that swept through me. Slowly, slowly, he kissed my face, first my brow, down along my nose and chin, then both my cheeks. Tender he was, his lips soft, light as moth wings on my skin. On the edge of my mouth he stopped, leaving me aching, wanting; but he put his arms about me and held me very close, his cheek against my hair. I could feel our hearts beating.

He said, hoarsely, "My will, Avala? Fate has never considered my will to be of importance, and the things that I would have kept have always been torn from me. I asked you before if you will ever go away again. You did not give me a straight answer. If I love you, will I be left again without you? Will I be cast off when you go back to your own people, whoever they are? In the Time of the Eagle, will you be lost in the battle?"

I shook my head, having no answer.

He went on, anguished. "I've had loss, Avala. As much loss as I can bear. I was ten summers old when I was sent to the Hena. When I came back here to my father's tent, my mother had died, all was changed. It was no more my home. Then my heart hungered for my Hena tribe again. Just as I grew to love my blood-kin here, two of my older brothers, and kin-children I loved, were taken as slaves. Then you came, and I tried very hard not to love you. You, too, went away, and every day you were gone I grieved, and all the tribe knew it. This is what happens with my loves, Avala—they go, or are taken from me. Since I was a child

I have been lost, not knowing where my home is, or which love will be taken from me next. And now you ask what my will is, about us. Does it matter, my will?

"While you were away you were in another world, a secret world from which I am shut out. In that other world of yours there were many high and destined things, great things to do with the freedom of many people. You're a seer now; you see beyond my father's tribe, beyond even your own Shinali lands. I can't begin to see what you can see, to know what you must know. These are big things, things to do with nations. Things to do with your destiny, with the destiny of many tribes. In the hugeness of all those things, my will is a grain of sand, and what I want is worth nothing more than the scratch of a bird's wing across the sky."

He fell silent, his breaths torn and full of pain.

"That scratch across the sky," I said, "is a tear across my heart. Your will means everything to me, Ishtok. If you wanted me—if I knew you wanted me—I would never leave again."

"That is a promise you can't make," he said. "If your destiny demanded it, you would go, and I would be the first to say you must. I do want you, Avala, and I love you with every breath. But what I want more is for you to be free to do those things you spoke of, that are your destiny. I don't want to complicate your life or make your path more difficult. I won't ask anything of you except your company. If you want more than that of me, you will have to be the one to speak first, to say when you're ready. But know this: I will help you all I can, in this work you have to do. Whatever you do, wherever you go, I will be beside you. In the Time of the Eagle, when you go to your battleground, I will be there with you. And if the gods decree that you die in battle, I will die defending you. I swear this, with *sharleema*."

I nodded, too moved to speak.

Smiling, he kissed my lips, then put his arm around me, and we walked back to Mudiwar's tent.

Above our heads hung the gray world of Erdelan with its four moons and bands of stormy cloud, looking like a great and steady star.

Third Scroll

Winds of War

21

"This is my healing tent," said Chimaki, taking me into the small tent that stood alone under the trees at the far end of the lake. "I wash soiled bindings in the rapids, far from where people take their drinking water, and I keep everything clean, as you taught me to. It is your tent now."

"No, I'm not taking away your work, Chimaki," I said. "You're a good healer. Without your medicines Mudiwar would have died long ago. I will be happy just to help you, if you need me."

So we became healers together, and although I could not teach her the secret healings I had learned in Ravinath, I did show her better ways to do minor surgery and to mix medicines. Together we made pots from river clay and planted the seeds Amael had given me. The tiny silken bags of seeds were as mysterious to Chimaki as were my Navoran healing instruments, but I had asked her not to question me, and she never did. For that I loved her, and for much besides. Everything I had taught her about healing and cleanliness, she had remembered and followed, and it was a joy working with her.

Mudiwar improved rapidly. One day, when I had given him his medicine and was sitting beside him afterward while he dozed, he opened one cunning eye and looked at me suspiciously under the lowered lid. "That wasn't poison you just gave me, was it, Shinali woman?" he muttered.

"If I gave you poison, my chieftain," I replied, trying not to smile, "you'd be greeting your ancestors by now."

He grunted and closed his eye again. I thought he slept, but he said, after a while, "By Shimit, there must be many times you wish me dead."

"I never wish that," I said.

"Why not? Have you given up your mad idea to go and do battle with the Navorans? Ramakoda would go with you, if I was dead."

"I've not given it up, Mudiwar," I said. "I believe in it more strongly than ever. When the time is right the Eagle will fly, and whether you lead your people, or Ramakoda leads them, is a small matter."

"True, since we'd all be dead at the end of it," he said. "My first responsibility as chieftain is to keep my people alive, Avala. Some of us may be enslaved, some slain by Navorans, but most of us are free, and we're still a great nation—which is more than your pathetic bunch of Shinali can say."

"You may be a great nation," I said, "but you are a people oppressed, living in fear."

"You're wasting your breath. Go and do some work. Heal someone."

I obeyed.

Chimaki and I were busy those first days of my return to the

Igaal camp, for Mudiwar's rapid improvement seemed like a miracle to his tribe, and many came who had gangrene and major illnesses Chimaki alone could not have cured. Together we amputated feet and fingers too gone with gangrene to save, and we removed a tumor from a woman's abdomen, and mended the ruptured spleen of a youth who had been kicked by a horse. All our patients survived, and felt no pain, and slowly the tribe's suspicion and hate toward me melted to a kind of grudging gratitude.

It was a peaceful spring, there in the circle of mountains in the great Himeko Ranges. On my free days, when Chimaki and I were not busy in the healing tent, Ishtok taught me to ride. One day, when I could ride well enough to go for several miles, we went out onto the plains north of the Himeko Mountains and lay in the long grass, watching the herds of wandering deer. I had taken my telescope, and Ishtok was intrigued by it, as he was by all things new and different.

"It is Navoran, isn't it?" he said, lying on his back, examining the telescope closely.

"You spend more time looking at it than through it," I said, smiling, lying beside him, looking up at the sky. "Yes, it is Navoran."

"Do they have other things like this, the Navorans?"

So I told him of some of the wonders of Ravinath, without giving away too much about that place. I told him of the machines that measured time, of the great telescope, of the paintings and artworks, the carvings. "You'll see it all one day," I said. "We'll walk the streets of the stone city, you and I, and I'll show you the marvels I've seen."

"Ah—you *were* there!"

"No. I've never been in the stone city."

"You're a mystery, Shinali woman," he said, moving until his arm was about my neck, and I was lying with my head on his shoulder. "A worrying, maddening mystery. Lovable, though."

"I'm glad you added that last," I said.

"If it's true that we're to walk in the stone city one day, you'd better teach me Navoran words. I want to be able to talk with your blue-eyed kinsfolk. Tell me the Navoran words for the things around us. Begin with my favorite thing, the sun."

So I did. I also told him what Zuleman had told me about our sun, that it was a star, our day-star. Ishtok thought about that a long time, then said, "If the night stars are also suns, why is the night dark?"

"The night stars are too far away to light our sky," I said.

"Who told you these things?"

"A wise man. You'll meet him one day."

"Then I'll need to talk to him, for I have as many questions for him as a bird has feathers. Tell me the Navoran words for *sky*, and *day*, and *light*."

Three-and-twenty Navoran words he learned that afternoon, but still wanted to know more. As the sun went down he lay with his lips against my cheek, and asked, "Now tell me the words for *you*, and *I*, and *love*."

I told them, and he repeated them to me in perfect Navoran, and then kissed my eyes and said the words, also in Navoran, "Blue skies I love."

Until the sun set we lay there in the sweet-scented grass,

holding each other, and he stroked my face and hair, but went no further.

It was dark when we got back to camp. We found that we had missed the evening meal, but Chimaki had kept some bowls of meat aside for us. While we ate, Mudiwar frowned and said that the next time we missed the meal, we could starve. Ishtok smiled and said, low so his father would not hear, that one kiss with me was worth starving for.

When I was not helping Chimaki in the healing tent or out riding with Ishtok, I had long talks with Ramakoda, and realized how deeply he longed to unite all the tribes and to put an end to Navoran oppression.

"Could you not do it, without your father?" I asked.

He shook his head. "To defy a chieftain, even if that chieftain is old and beyond reason," he said, "is to commit the worst crime by Igaal law. We will have to be patient, Avala. But you will be pleased to know that I talked with the chieftain of Ishtok's Hena tribe, when they were here, and the Hena are willing to rise up and strike back at Navora. The Navorans have captured many of the wild horses in the far north, leaving few for the Hena. It affects us, too, for we trade for horses from the Hena. It seems that Navoran greed is never satisfied. Now they want our horses, as well as our people."

A pain passed through him, and he sighed deeply, his eyes searching my face. "I trust you with my life, Avala," he said, "yet I suspect you visited the place of our enemies while you were gone from us. I've seen the thing you call a telescope, and Ishtok

287

tells me it is Navoran. Tell me, were you there, in the stone city? Did you see my sons?"

"No, I was not there, Ramakoda. I can't give you news of your sons, I'm sorry."

"But you won't say where you were?"

"No."

He looked out across the lake, for we were sitting on the stony shore, watching some of the children play on floating logs. "My father thinks you were with the gods in the mountains," he said. "You've come back with strong *munakshi*. My wife says you warned her yesterday not to eat the fresh pot of soup she had made. She gave some of the soup to a dog, and it died soon after. You saved many lives. The whole tribe is talking about it. You have a seer's powers."

"It was just a feeling I had, about the soup," I said. "I think one of the herbs she put in it was not what she thought it was. Our plants are different from the northern ones she is used to. This morning I went gathering with her and showed her which herbs we use that are safe."

He looked at me again and lifted his right hand and touched my sleeve in the sign of gratitude. "Then I thank Shimit for your feelings," he said. "May you always heed them. And may we always listen."

Spring blazed into summer, and Mudiwar began to talk of moving the camp to a far place by the Nyranjeera Lakes. But before he made his final decision, I had a dream that changed things for us all.

It was a dream of a bowl of bread. The bread was fresh and

good, but the clay bowl was old and cracked, with jagged bits about the rim. One of the cracks was very deep, and ants came through it and soon were crawling all over the bread. Then the ants went away, and the bread was left crumbling. Soon there were only fragments left, and birds came and ate them. I thought the birds were crows at first, but then I saw that they were the death buzzards, and the bowl was not a bowl at all, but a hollow in the earth, and what I had thought were pale bits of bread were human bones.

I woke sweating, breathless. I knew, within five heartbeats, that the dream was a warning of death, that the hollow in the earth was the valley ringed by mountains, where we camped, and the crack in the bowl was the one narrow gorge leading in; and I knew that the bread was the tribe, and the ants were an invading army. But how close was that army?

Without waking anyone, I pulled on my dress, got the map I had made in Ravinath, and crept outside. The eastern skies were growing light, and the lake lay like a sheet of steel under the dark mountains. On the stones near the water's edge, facing west, I spread the map. For a while I sat in front of it, my eyes half closed. The lines I had drawn, the mountains and territories and rivers, were vague images in the growing dawn. My breath slowed, and I entered that state close to dreaming, though I was awake and alert. I saw through the map, beyond it, and was as a bird flying high, looking down on the great Himeko Mountains, speeding along the gleaming Ekiya, southward. And I saw them, small and numerous as ants: soldiers, riding hard. And with them came a coldness, a sense of impending death. I withdrew, breathed deep again, flew in my mind back to the shore of the lake, to

Mudiwar's camp. My heart was thundering. Midmorning the soldiers would be here.

Trying to be calm, I lifted the amulet from Sheel Chandra, and pressed it to my brow. The gold was cool, but the stone between the eagle's wings was warm. All my mind turned to that great man and the tower in which we used to sit together. I saw it clearly, the glass roof above, the carved stone walls, the window that would be open now, to the dawn skies. I saw his chair, and him there, waiting. He looked as he had the first time I ever saw him, beautiful as carven stone, his long mustache and hair silver, his face utterly majestic and tranquil. His eyes were closed, his hands turned palm upward on his knees. I knelt before him and laid one of my hands upon one of his, palm to palm. He did not move, but I felt the warmth of him.

"Master?" I whispered, wondering if I was as real to him as he was to me.

"What is it, dear heart?" he said. His lips did not move, but I heard his words clearly. Perhaps I heard them only with the ears of my heart.

"Soldiers are coming, Master," I said. "Will you help me shield us, please? To make our tribe invisible?"

"This is not a time for shielding," he said. "This is a time for battle. Many will die, but great good will come of the evil. Do not take up a weapon yourself. Remember all I taught you."

"Will you protect us?"

"You are already protected, beloved, and many will live who otherwise would have died. Go. Do not be distracted. Make haste to Mudiwar."

"Thank you, Master." I bent my head and kissed his open

palm. The room grew dim; my sight of him diminished. There was wind, the feeling of cold streaming by, the grayness of the coming dawn. Then I saw the map before me and felt the hardness of the amulet pressed too close, now, against my brow. I lowered it, placed it within my dress. Quickly, I began to roll up the map. But suddenly, in the space of a single heart pulse, I glimpsed something else on the map. There was a flash of gray light, a vision as from high above, an image of a company of men farther north, also riding hard. No coldness this time, but still a sense of urgency. Mystified, I would have searched farther, found out more, but Sheel Chandra's words came back to me: "Do not be distracted. Make haste to Mudiwar." So I finished rolling up the map, and ran back to the chieftain's tent.

I put the map in the chest of my belongings and stepped over the sleeping people to Mudiwar's bed. Kneeling, I shook his shoulder. "I've had a dream!" I whispered. "A warning. Soldiers are coming."

He sat up, instantly awake. Those nearest his bed, hearing my voice, the urgency in it, sat up blinking, scrambling for their clothes. Others fumbled to light the lamps.

"Tell me," said Mudiwar.

So I told him the dream and my interpretation of it. Around us, people listened, half dressed, their faces pale in the flickering lamps. Before the sun was over the tops of the mountains, Mudiwar had called a council, and the whole tribe was gathered on the stony shore of the river.

"Avala has a word for us about a dream," he said. "It is a warning. We will heed her words."

Then he nodded at me, and I told them all of my dream

and the terrible meaning. I finished with the words, "Soldiers will come through the gorge, many soldiers. They will be here when the sun has not long been up. But do not be afraid; we are protected, and a great good will come of this. Take heart."

There were a few moments of silence, and I felt the doubt, the terror. Then Mudiwar said, his voice echoing across the still lake, "We will prepare for battle! Men will ride to the opening of the gorge, and surprise the invaders, and kill as many as they can before they reach the camp. Women will fight from the tents. The old and infirm, women heavy with children unborn, and children too young to fight, will flee to that cave our hunters told us of, up the western slope. The path is not difficult. The old men will take bows and spears, to defend you if necessary. May the gods be with us all."

We were dismissed, and the gray dawn about the tents became frenzied with people running, children crying, and dogs barking. In Mudiwar's tent chests were thrown open. People were strapping the great, curved Igaal war knives to their belts, and packing arrows into quivers. Children wailed as their mothers got them ready to leave, kissing their faces, crying. Little ones struggled and howled as the older children dragged them out to the long line of those leaving for the cave. Fathers were giving last-minute instructions to their older sons, and the youths were wrought up, excited, afraid, as they strapped on their quivers full of arrows, and tested bowstrings. Seeing it all, seeing the solemn, excited faces, a thrill of fear went through me. I thought of the soldiers I had seen during the shielding in Ravinath. I thought of their heavy bronze armor, their great warhorses, the shields and mighty swords, and the strange steel crossbows. And I looked about me at Mudiwar's people, some of them not much more than eleven summers old, getting ready to fight. I was covering them all with protection, when Mudiwar's gong signaled the time for the men to leave for the gorge.

With many of the women, I ran out to see them go. All the horses were ready, waiting on the shore of the lake, restive with the fear they caught. Incredibly it was quiet, save for the snorting of the horses, and the last-moment farewells, spoken low, and the soft words of encouragement and love. I went to say farewell to Ishtok. He seemed suddenly older, sterner, and I realized, with an awful suddenness, that by this day's end one of us, or both, might be dead or in captivity. The All-father moved in strange ways, and even with Sheel Chandra's protection, nothing was certain. I passed my hands over his face, down his chest, covering him with a light he could not see. "Be safe, dear heart," I said.

Suddenly he hugged me to him, and kissed my brow. We made the Shinali farewell, and he swung himself up onto his horse. Then the men were riding off, their bows and spears glinting in the pale morning sun, their backs straight and proud. As I watched them go I shielded them, too, though it was hard to do it alone. I wondered how many of them would ride back.

Women were hurrying back to the tents, but I ran to the healing tent. I was thankful that it was on its own at the end of the lake opposite the gorge, where it would not be likely to be trampled by the great Navoran warhorses. Even so, I stood before it awhile, praying, protecting it, shielding it. When I went back to the other tents, the healing tent was invisible, concealed behind a line of trees that were not there before.

Back in Mudiwar's tent, the wooden chests had been hauled into a long line across the floor, opposite the tent entrance. They were piled two or three high, making a strong wall, and covered with blankets and carpets. The women would fight from behind it, at least a little bit safe from Navoran arrows. All the women were armed with bows and had knives in their belts.

Trying to be calm, I crouched beside Chimaki. She glanced at me and frowned a little, seeing me unarmed. Then she said, with a fleeting smile, "Of course you can't fight, Avala. Not kill people of your own blood."

"I won't kill," I said, "but I'll rescue as many as I can, and take them to our healing tent."

She nodded, and we fell silent while we waited. The air in the tent was breathless, taut like a bow at full draw.

Then the noise broke out—the clamor of men yelling, horses screaming, and the strange, high shriek that was the Igaal battle cry. About our tents the dogs were going wild, yipping and howling like wolves. I could hardly breathe for the sudden fear that tore over me. The woman on the other side of me wiped her hands on her skirt, one at a time, then placed her arrow again. We both were shaking.

And outside the noise went on and on, screams of men and horses, shouts, and battle cries, echoing round and round the mountains, until it seemed that there were twenty battles around us. Gradually the sounds came nearer. Horses approached; we heard a man's voice, loud and urgent, giving orders in Navoran. Women screamed, and soldiers shouted. A horse thundered close; a sword slashed along our tent. It struck a pole, cut the bindings holding the tent up, and the roof skins fell on us. I could see nothing; all was confusion, terror, people screaming and shouting. I could hardly move for the weight of the tent on me. I smelled burning, and smoke swirled around. I crawled out from

295

under the tent. All around the edges other women were crawling out, some with their bows, some with knives in their hands.

Around us was dust and turmoil and noise. Soldiers and warriors fought from their horses, struggling as the beasts met and clashed; others fought on foot, hand to hand. It seemed there was no time; all happened slowly, and I had time to look. Soldiers rode off with Igaal people across the saddles in front of them, were shot with arrows as they rode, or else their captives stabbed them. Some captives were trampled under the horses as they tried to jump free. I saw an Igaal bowman on foot, aiming at a soldier with an Igaal girl on the horse in front of him; the soldier rushed at him, cut off the man's head while the arrow shot wild. A warrior with a hunting knife fought against a soldier with a sword; the warrior lost his knife and his arm, then fell, screaming, his belly slit. Some Igaal men, wounded, were dragged along by their terrified horses. Fleeing women were hunted down by soldiers on horseback, caught by their hair, and hauled up onto the horses. A youth fell, had only his hunting knife left; a soldier rode over him, and I saw him underneath the hooves, slashing at the horse with his knife. The animal reared, screaming, then fell, pinning its rider under it with the bloodied boy. I saw a woman defend her wounded son, fighting off a soldier with only a cooking pot, using it as a shield. The soldier was grinning, enjoying the sport, his great sword clanging on the pot like a gong, until she tired, and he sliced off both her arms and left her there, while he rode off with the boy. Some people fled into the lake, were ridden down by soldiers, and slain. The lake edge turned scarlet. All the way between our tents and the mouth of the gorge, men and horses lay on the ground, wounded and screaming. Soldiers rode with branches set alight, burning tents. Wounded people tried to crawl away, were trampled by the Navoran horses.

At first I could not move, overwhelmed by the utter chaos, the hopelessness, the huge scale of the suffering and brutality. Then I forced myself to go into it, though I shook and wept, and could hardly see for the smoke and flying dust. I found an Igaal youth still alive, clutching an arrow in his chest; I dragged him between the horses and the fighting men and the dead and dying, over to the safety of the illusion of trees by the healing tent. Then I ran back. There was an old woman, screaming, crawling, blinded by blood from a head wound. I caught her under the armpits, dragged her, too, through the turmoil to the sheltering tent. Again and again I went out onto the plain, saved another youth, a woman, a Navoran soldier, an Igaal warrior. I do not know where I got the strength; I was not even aware of myself. Nothing seemed real. The agony all around, the confusion and terror, were like a dream through which I moved automatically, driven only by the desire to save as many as I could. There was no time to stop pain, or staunch bleeding; only time to drag the wounded out of the way of the horses and swords, to safety.

Some people, like me, were still on their feet; they ran, were swept up and taken. Then it seemed that only wounded and dead were left; everyone else was carried off. There were dead horses and people everywhere. And still the soldiers came, hundreds and hundreds of them, pouring in from the gorge, their swords and deadly crossbows flashing in the sun. So many there were, our valley could hardly contain them. Half blinded by dust, I carried on, discovered, as I dragged away a wounded youth, that there was red mud in his hair, and his clothes were painted. A Hena warrior? Bewildered, feeling more and more that this was a terrible dream, I left the Hena man by the healing tent and went back. It must only have been Sheel Chandra's protection that prevented me from being trampled, or cut down by a Navoran sword; I know that sometimes it seemed that flying hooves missed me by the width of a human hand, and there were times when swords swung so close to my head, I marveled that I was not killed. In the end even fear left me, and I went on dragging wounded from the battlefield, soldiers and warriors alike. At one point I stood up by the healing tent and saw how many I had saved so far: two long lines of them, lying bleeding, groaning, lifting their hands in pleading to me. Some were already dead. The illusion of trees had vanished, my powers too scattered now to sustain it. One more time, I thought, I would go back, then I would leave the battlefield altogether, and remake the shield, and begin the healings.

The battle had moved closer. They were fighting on the edge of the lake, upon the fallen tents, across the scattered cooking fires, over the bodies of the dead. The screams and battle cries and the clashing of blades filled the valley. Smoke rolled across the water like mist; underneath, the lake looked weirdly passive, still. All else was bedlam.

Suddenly I looked up to see a soldier riding toward me. Through the smoke I could see his eyes, blue like mine. He was laughing. His sword was not drawn; he was here now not to kill but to take a prisoner. Then he was upon me, hooves thundering. I threw myself aside, felt the wind of his passing, and the shake of earth beneath the hooves. I scrambled up, amazed that

I was still alive, could still stand. Hardly knowing what I was doing, I took my little food knife from its place at my belt. He wheeled about, came at me again. Again the thunder of those mighty hooves, the dust and wind, and then his arm swinging down to take me. I slashed out with my knife, missed, and somehow he got my arm and hauled me up onto the horse in front of him. I struggled, my legs dangling under the horse; I heard screams—mine, I think—then I was up and was lying facedown across the saddle, his hand crushing down on the back of my neck. I saw earth flashing past, bodies, blood, a horse fallen. My knife was still in my hand, and I slashed backward, blindly, awkwardly. I must have got the man's thigh, for he gave an awful yell and loosened his hold on me. Again and again I slashed at him, felt blood gush warm over my hand. The horse reared, screaming, and I fell. I hit the ground and rolled away. I heard the hooves again, tried to get to my feet, to run, but pain shot through my right foot. I staggered, fell. He was coming back again, a terrible look on his face. On my knees I waited, saying a prayer to the Allfather, my fingers closed about the amulet from Sheel Chandra. The soldier slowed the horse, dismounted just in front of me. I could smell the sweat on him, the blood. Limping, he came a step nearer and drew his sword. I heard the sound of it, smooth and full of death. He put the point just beneath my chin.

Dimly, I was aware of another soldier coming from the side, almost from behind me, riding hard, not holding the reins but riding while he raised his bow. But he was not aiming at me. Incredibly, he was aiming at the soldier with the sword. He released the arrow. It hit the soldier in front of me, going right through his chest. Blood sprayed over me. He fell slowly, to his knees first, his sword hanging loose in his hand. I saw the look of shock on his face, when he saw who shot him; then he fell face forward, his head almost against my knees, and lay still.

I stared down at him, numb. When I looked up again, my rescuer was gone. Had I imagined him? As in a dream I looked across the fallen, burning tents, the chaos, the destruction. So many soldiers. And soldiers killing, not the Igaal, but other soldiers. And there were Hena warriors, their strange mud-caked hair smooth and gleaming through the dust, fighting alongside the Igaal warriors who were still standing. It was madness. Everything was madness. I got up and staggered away, fell across a dead Igaal youth, and got up again, furious at the pain in my foot. It lamed me enough to get me killed. I noticed then that the center of the battle had moved, the fight changed. It was all Navoran soldiers fighting now, out on the flat bit of ground between our tents and the gorge. Every soldier with a captive was cut down, or hauled off his horse in close combat. Taken Igaal tumbled from their captors' horses, ran for their lives, unnoticed by the soldiers too busy fighting other soldiers. Many of the soldiers were fleeing, dust billowing out of the gorge as they left. Navoran horns were blaring. Above the battleground the buzzards cruised, waiting. Beside me, a woman stood sighing and praying. Her shoulder was bleeding. Others gathered beside us, men as well, and soon there was a large crowd of us, bloodied and hurt and some moaning in pain, or sobbing. Most of us were silent, staring through the drifting smoke, watching in disbelief as Navoran soldiers fought their own.

I wanted to go to the healing tent, to begin the huge task that lay ahead of me there, but I could not walk on my hurt foot. So I stayed where I was, leaning a little on a man next to me. After a time we realized that the fighting had stopped. Yet hundreds of Navoran soldiers remained. One of them shouted an order, and there was silence, but for the moaning of the wounded and the dying still out there. All around the edge of the battlefield huddled the captives who had been rescued, supporting one another. They must have been as astonished and bewildered as we were. The soldiers stayed there, still on their horses, on that patch of ground in front of the gorge, but for one.

One man came to us, riding slowly. His bronze breastplates gleamed in the sun; the plume on his helmet was red. Under his armor his uniform was blue-gray, and across his upper body, formed of two wide sashes tied diagonally, was a vivid blue cross. He must have left his sword behind; he seemed unarmed. Halfway to us he stopped and dismounted, and knelt beside a fallen Igaal warrior. The Igaal was still alive. Astoundingly, the soldier helped him up onto his own horse and brought him over to us. Very gently he helped him down, and two women rushed forward and led the Igaal man back among us. The rest of us stood silent, stunned, unsure.

The soldier took off his helmet and wiped his forearm across his sweating face. His hair was the color of corn.

"Can anyone here speak Navoran?" he called.

I tried to speak, but my mouth was too dry from dust and fear. So I said nothing but limped forward, slowly, until I came to him. I looked up, and shock went through me.

He was clean-shaven, boyish looking. Even through the sweat

and grime, I saw the crooked zigzag scar on his chin. His green eyes danced, and he smiled.

"So, we meet again, Shinali woman," he said.

It was Embry.

23

For long moments I could not speak.

He dismounted and came closer on foot. "You do understand Navoran?" he asked.

"Yes."

"Will you please tell all these people that they are in no danger from us."

I turned and faced the Igaal people, silent and bewildered behind me, and repeated his words. Then I said to him, "You fought your own people, to save us. Why?"

Sighing heavily, he nodded. "We are not part of the Navoran army. We were once, but not now. What happens to my city and my Empire, under the Emperor Jaganath, sickens me. And it sickens my men. We deserted, formed an army of our own, and we fight now against the forces of Jaganath. Our aim is to one day bring his reign to an end." He turned, and his arm briefly took in the Hena warriors. "These fine warriors joined us four months ago," he added. "We all fight for the same thing—freedom."

That, too, I translated. When I looked back at the man Embry, he was staring at me strangely, as if he knew me, and not just from the river that other battle-day.

"I have three surgeons among my soldiers," he said. "They'll work with your Igaal healers, to save as many as we can of the wounded."

"I'm the healer here," I said. "I, and a woman called Chimaki."

Again he looked at me, one eyebrow raised. "You remind me of another healer I knew, a long time ago. He was . . . Never mind, we'll talk later. We have much to do. My men will help put up the tents again, those that are not too damaged. Is there somewhere we can put up a large tent for a hospital?"

I gestured toward the small healing tent. The rows of waiting wounded could be clearly seen, and many more still lay about where the battle had raged.

"You can put up a tent beside our small one," I said. "There's plenty of fresh water there, and it's cool under the trees."

And so it was that, when I mended and bound up the wounded, I worked beside three Navoran surgeons. While a large Navoran army tent was being erected for a hospital one of the Navoran surgeons bound my ankle for me, for it was only sprained. When that was done, I got the pouch of surgical instruments Salverion had given me and went to the hospital tent. Chimaki was there, supervising the women who would clean our instruments between healings, and bandage up the wounded when the surgeons and I had finished with them. I asked her to find what news she could of Ishtok and Ramakoda and others we loved. She was gone a long time, and an awful fear ran through me, though I felt that Ishtok was alive. I tried to put my fears aside and fixed my mind on the healing work before me.

Our healing-mats were in a semicircle around the tent, so we could face one another and talk if we wished. The Navoran surgeons worked standing up, makeshift tables made for them out of the largest wooden chests from the tents, covered over with clean mats. The surgeons had their own packs of Navoran instruments and were surprised when I produced the instruments Salverion had given me, and set them out on a mat on the floor, for that was the way I preferred to work. By the time we had washed our hands and threaded our needles, there was a long line of wounded waiting, beside those I had dragged here.

At first I had only the simple injuries to heal, for Embry's soldiers carried in the hurt, and I think they presumed I was unskilled. Because the wounds I healed were simple, I did not use the skill of blocking nerves, for it would have taken vital time; I simply cleansed and sewed up, as the Navoran surgeons did. Sometimes they spoke to me, asking if I needed help with certain things, but they soon realized I was doing well enough. Soon after we began our work, a man was brought in who had two arrows in his chest, and an appalling belly wound. It was Chro, brother of Ramakoda and Ishtok. Screaming he was, and four soldiers were struggling to hold him down for the surgeon. Stopping what I was doing, I went over and asked if I might speak with Chro a moment, before they began with him. The surgeon working on him looked annoyed but nodded and stepped back. "Be quick," he said.

I bent over Chro and placed my forehead on his, my fingers behind his head. He did not know it was me there; he struggled and fought, and they still had to hold him. It was hard to concentrate, for I was distracted by his howls for mercy, and the moans of those waiting, and the general noise all around, and most of all by my own fears for Ishtok; but I managed at last to find the way into Chro's mind, then down into the deep nerve pathways. He slumped on the makeshift table, his eyes still open and aware, but his body relaxed and calm. Seeing me, he smiled faintly and his lips moved in thanks. I said a blessing-word on him and went back to my own place and picked up the needle again, for I was sewing up a sword cut.

I was aware, then, that they all were watching me—the three surgeons, and the soldiers who were there to hold Chro down, and the soldiers in the tent doorway who were waiting with the next four to be healed. One of the older surgeons said, "Where did you learn that skill, woman? I've only ever seen it done once, by a Citadel healer, before they all were murdered. Who taught you?"

"My mother," I said, truthfully enough, and carried on.

After that they often asked me to stop the pain of those most badly wounded, before they worked on them.

Of all the days I had known, that day was the longest. I do not know how many wounds we mended, how many arrow wounds we packed with salving cloths, how many bones we set in splints. I do not know how many people helped us, who brought water for us to wash and drink, who put food into our mouths while we worked on, who cleaned up the injured a little before we saw them and bandaged them afterward, who brought clean binding cloths, and replaced the mats we worked on when they were soaked in blood. At some time, between healings, someone crouched beside me and put a cup of water into my hands. I looked up to see Ishtok, uninjured. For the first time all day, I smiled.

"It's good to see your face," he said, lightly touching my cheek. "The gods were surely with us this day. We have much to talk about, later. Thank you for what you did for Chro. The Navorans say you are a marvel." As he took my empty cup the next wounded warrior was laid on the mat in front of me. I picked up a clean blade and forgot all but the work of healing.

The rest of the day was a blur, bloodied fighter after bloodied fighter brought to the mat in front of me. Some were Igaal men or Igaal women, some Navoran soldiers from both armies, though not many from Embry's, and there were Hena warriors. Once a child was brought to me, who had fallen from the mountain path and broken his leg. And still the wounded came, one scarcely off the mat in front of me, before the next was laid there. Someone—I do not know who—took away the bloodstained instruments each time, and put down clean ones, Navoran instruments and Igaal knives all mixed up. I suspect they were only washed and not boiled, but it could not be helped. They tell me that sometime that day Embry came to watch me work, but I do not remember it.

At last I became aware of a voice calling, "Only nine more, and you're done."

And then—incredibly—the healing-mat was empty. I looked up. There were lamps around us, for it was evening, and two of the surgeons were leaning over their tables, their heads bent. One was lying on the ground, heedless of the blood and gore. He looked asleep.

Then one of the surgeons roused himself and came over to me and took my wrist in the Navoran handshake, a sign of respect between people. "It was an honor to work with you, Igaal girl," he said.

I told him I was Shinali, and he shook his head and walked away. I heard him say to a companion, "I thought they were all Igaal in this camp. But there are Shinali, too. Perhaps this is the beginning of the Eagle's rise."

I was too tired to put him right.

For a long time after, I slept, though I had terrible dreams, and once I woke to feel Ishtok's arms about me, and his lips against my ear, telling me to hush, that all was well. When I woke fully it was morning's middle the next day, and I was alone in the tent. I went outside and found that our Igaal camp was now a place of makeshift shelters, for few tents had escaped the burnings. Alongside the Igaal shelters were many rows of small brown tents belonging to Embry's army, some of them painted with Hena signs. People had lit fires and were cooking food. Beyond the camp, back along the shore toward the gorge, Navoran soldiers were digging pits to bury their dead, and on the far lake shore the Hena and Igaal were holding their funeral rites. The sky was full of buzzards. But there were two fires over there, and I guessed that, like my people, the Hena burned their dead.

There was a strong wind, fitful like the *shoorai* wind, and dust scudded along the plain where yesterday people had fought.

Dogs and children rushed about, unruly and wrought up, disturbed by the changes in the camp and the tension in the air. I looked up at the sky, saw the clouds streaming like banners in the high gales, and felt my own heart stirred by huge, unseen forces.

When I looked down again the man Embry was walking toward me. He wore no armor, but over the tunic of his uniform he still wore the blue sashes in the form of a cross. All his men wore those blue crosses, though I recalled that the soldiers in Jaganath's army did not.

"Good morning, Avala," he said.

"I suppose it is," I said, "but for the funeral rites. We owe you thanks, Embry. If it were not for your help yesterday, most of the Igaal men in this camp would be slaves in Navora by now, or else dead. Thank you."

"I'm owed no thanks," he replied. "I remember a day when I raided this chieftain's camp and took slaves to Navora. I have many wrongs to put right."

"You were not wholly bad that day," I said. "There was a Shinali girl you did not betray. For that I thank you, with *sharleema*."

He smiled then, and his face suddenly appeared younger. "I remember you well. I could not have betrayed you. Your father was my friend."

"I know. That day I saw you in the pool, I told my mother what you looked like. She said you were one of the guards at Taroth Fort, and that you were very kind to my people. But how did you know that I am Gabriel's daughter?"

"The mystery of a blue-eyed Shinali wasn't hard to figure

out. I knew it straightaway, for you look very like your father. The same forthright look, a bit stern at times. And you have his eyes, and his gift of healing. I watched you work yesterday for a while. The surgeons told me you healed with ways taught only at the Citadel when it was at the height of its power, before Jaganath closed it, sealed up its gates, and threatened death on anyone who entered. We were told that he had burned all the books in the libraries, and murdered all the Masters and their disciples. The place is derelict now, but I'm glad some of the teachings survived. Of course, when I was with your father in Taroth Fort, I didn't know he was a healer from the Citadel. I found that out later, when I took his message to the Empress Petra."

"I would like to hear about that," I said, "but first I must go and see how the wounded are."

"My surgeons are with them. Let's talk, you and I. We have much to discuss."

So we sat in the shade of the trees by the shore, not far from the healing tents, and there he told me of his meeting with the Empress.

"Your father had written a letter to the Empress Petra, and I was asked to deliver it," he said. "Weeks before, Gabriel had told me that if ever I was given anything to deliver to the Empress, I had to guard it with my life and deliver it to her personally, into her own hands. He didn't explain more, and I didn't know what he meant, until I was asked by the fort commander to take the letter to Her Majesty. It wasn't only a letter; there was a ring with it, a little silver ring in the shape of a snake, made in the first letter of the Empress's name.

"I met Jaganath at the palace—if meeting him is the way to describe it. Before we even spoke, he knew where I was from, and what I held. I'll never forget the way that man looked at me. I felt skinned alive, all my bones exposed, and my heart and brain. He knew everything. He demanded the scroll and the ring, though I had both concealed under my tunic. I defied him. I saw . . . things. Demons, I suppose. Shadow-creatures. Your father had warned me about them, about Jaganath, and told me he was a master of illusion. So I ignored the beasts, ignored Jaganath's commands, ignored the guards, fought off two of them, outside the Empress's door.

"By God, I felt sorry for her! I'd seen her a year earlier, at an army parade in her honor. She'd been a beautiful woman then, but something had worn her down. She looked haunted, terribly afraid. I don't know what your father wrote to her, but when she looked up from his words, she was a different woman. She looked joyful, strong, though she was crying, too. She said that all that Gabriel asked would be done, and told one of her personal guards to escort me safely from the palace."

"How long have you had your own army?" I asked.

"A year. The day I saw you hiding in the river, that was the day I began to plan my move to create a renegade army. By chance—if there is such a thing as chance—I was promoted, put at the head of a battalion. Men grew to trust me. It did not happen overnight, but steadily, over months, as I proved myself. I kept my ears open, listened for talk of dissatisfaction with Navora, chose my men and my time. It was not difficult, for by then many were speaking openly against Jaganath. Seven hundred of us rode away from Navora and never went back. Since then we've been on the move, defending a few Hena tribes, and now an Igaal tribe. But the time for these minor battles is almost over."

"What do you mean?" I asked.

"Your father told me about the Time of the Eagle. We need that time, Avala, and we need it soon. We need to end Jaganath's reign, before he destroys everything our forefathers ever built up. He has only a handful of people who are loyal to him. I suspect that if—when—it comes to the final fight, most of the soldiers in his army will surrender. The sooner we can bind these native tribes together, the better. My army will fight with the armies of the Hena and Igaal, and with the Shinali. Together we will make a formidable force against Jaganath. Does Mudiwar know of the Time of the Eagle?"

"Yes, but he is adamant that he will never risk battle with Navora, and wipe out his people as the Shinali have been almost wiped out. He swears he will never take part in the Time of the Eagle."

"Well, he has a point. You don't know how close your people came to being utterly destroyed, in Taroth Fort. And they would have been, but for what your father did. I never met another man like him. He loved your people and your mother, more than he loved his own country, his own life. He told me a lot about the Shinali. That's where my sympathy with them began, back there in Taroth Fort. And it's where I began to be disillusioned with the Navoran Empire. Seventeen years is a long time to be disillusioned, to crave change. I admire your people for their

312

patience, Avala. It's long been a secret fear of mine, that one day the Shinali will lose that patience and decide to march on Navora on their own, with nothing but their courage and their dreams. God knows, I've been tempted to march on Navora myself, at times, with what army I have. Waiting is the hardest thing for an army, Avala. To be trained for something, to be certain of the rightness of it, yet to have to spend a year—maybe many years yet—waiting for the perfect hour to act, is like living with a frenzied horse about to bolt."

"We have a very great priest, Zalidas," I said. "He keeps our dreams alive, but he keeps our hearts true to the prophecy, above all else."

"Tell me about yourself, Avala. How is it that you are here with the Igaal? I've learned to speak a little Hena, which is similar to the Igaal tongue, and many of the Hena with us have learned to speak Navoran, and I understand, from things I've heard, that you are a slave. Is that true?"

I told him my story, omitting the part about Ravinath. But when I had finished he gave me a shrewd look and said, "You're leaving something out, Avala. You speak Navoran extremely well, with the accent of the educated. Where did you learn it?"

To my relief at that moment we were interrupted by one of his soldiers. "I'm sorry to interrupt, sir," he said, "but the Igaal chieftain is calling for a meeting, and you're needed." He added, to me, "You're needed, too. Mudiwar wants you to interpret, I think."

The council mats were placed behind the camp, on the flat grasslands where the goats grazed. Mudiwar, Ramakoda, Ishtok, and

313

the other men of his family, as well as some of the Hena warriors and a few of Embry's soldiers, were sitting there. There was a place for Embry and me beside Mudiwar, and we faced all the others. There were perhaps five and twenty Igaal altogether, and twenty soldiers, with the five Hena men who were of Ishtok's pledge-family. I was the only woman.

Mudiwar was sitting straight and still, his fine old face stern, his staff upright in his hands.

"I begin this day with a word to the soldiers of this man's army," he said, his voice carrying easily in the still morning air. "Tell their leader, Avala, that I thank him for his allegiance with us, and for making yesterday a victory day. But I do not understand why soldiers fight other soldiers. Such men of our own tribe, fighting Igaal, would be killed as traitors. Tell me why this thing is done."

Apologizing for the chieftain's bluntness, I repeated the words to Embry, in Navoran. He smiled a little and nodded, and bent his head and thought a while. At last he looked up and made this speech:

"You are the chieftain of a great tribe that belongs to a great nation, Mudiwar. I, too, am of a great nation, but our chieftain, the one we call the Emperor Jaganath, is an evil man, with magic ways that no one can fight against. He is destroying everything good, that most Navorans love—destroying justice, and mercy, and peace. I and my men, and the Hena who fight with us, wish to see him overthrown. Only then will the great city of Navora be freed from his evil control, and will your Igaal tribes, and the Hena and Shinali, also be free.

314

"Until now, your people have not been raided often for slaves. This will change. The city of Navora has been twice ravaged by plague. The population has diminished, and many people have fled. The city walls have been strengthened and rebuilt, not to keep enemies out but to keep the people in. The situation is desperate. There are not enough people to grow food, to repair roads, to farm, to work in the coal mines. Everything is in short supply. Jaganath has demanded that his army supply more and more slaves, so that the city can be run efficiently. Even the ships in the navy are sailed by slaves, under very hard Navoran commanders. The wounded here from Jaganath's army have told me that there are new orders to treble the numbers of slaves taken. My soldiers won't always be here to defend you. While we're here Jaganath's army attacks somewhere else. He has a double purpose in raiding your tribes: not only does he replenish his supply of slaves, but he also keeps your nation weak and divided, so you will never become the great army he fears. He will attack you again and again, tribe by tribe, until, like the Shinali, your people are diminished and powerless, or all dead. Your only hope is in the Time of the Eagle. The Hena tribes are already willing to join us in battle against Jaganath's army. We await only your agreement, and the allegiance of the Igaal tribes; then the Time of the Eagle is here."

Full of hope, I finished my translation, and looked to Mudiwar. He chewed on his lower lip, and at last replied, "He can't wipe us out, that mad chieftain of yours. We Igaal are like the sands by the sea, the stars in the sky."

"So were the Shinali, once," Embry said.

Mudiwar gave a bitter laugh. "And whose fault is it that they're nothing, now?" he said. "They made a mighty big mistake, tangling with the Navorans. I won't follow in their footsteps."

"Those words are not worthy of you, my father," said Ramakoda, "since Navorans sit among us, and since it was they who helped us win the battle yesterday."

"If it wasn't for Navorans," growled Mudiwar, "there wouldn't have been a battle in the first place. It seems to me that the Navorans are a treacherous lot, divided and fighting among themselves. Half want to kill the Shinali, the other half wants the Shinali to help them to kill their own Emperor. If they want the Time of the Eagle, let them have it. They can all tear one another to pieces. To my mind, the world will be better off without them."

I did not interpret Mudiwar's last speech. I said to him, "My chieftain, you did not hear what Embry said. It is not half the Navorans against the other half. It's a very few Navorans in power who are treacherous and wrong, and who—"

"It's not your place to speak in this council," said Mudiwar. "You are here to interpret, that is all. I heard the man Embry very well. I have said it before, and I say it again: I will not take part in your foolhardy war against Navora. I do not wish to hear about the Time of the Eagle again. And despite my tribe's misplaced gratitude, Embry and his soldiers have not helped us in our trouble, but made it worse. Now their great chieftain knows some of his soldiers have deserted him, and he knows where they are, and he'll soon send his entire army here to wipe them out—and us along with them. We would have been better off if some of us were taken as slaves, than to have the whole military force of Navora called down upon our heads. And we can't even move camp and flee north, with so many injured. An ordinary slave raid would have been better than this."

"Our gratitude is not misplaced, my father," said Ishtok. "My Hena brothers are here, and they are not afraid to stand with the Navorans against their Emperor. They were not ungrateful for Embry's help when they were raided, but joined him, after."

Full of wrath, Mudiwar turned on him. "Afraid? Afraid? You think I'm afraid? By Shimit, I'll have you horsewhipped for that! It's not fear that drives me, you mad fool—it's sound judgment. My first task as chieftain is to protect my people. To keep alive . . ."

He stopped, distracted. We were all distracted, for at that moment there was a commotion at the place where the gorge opened into our valley. A group of Embry's soldiers had been out scouting, making sure that Jaganath's army was not returning with reinforcements, as Mudiwar feared it would. Now they had come back, pulling a horse after them, its rider unconscious across its back. Ramakoda excused himself from the council and ran to them, along with other members of the tribe. Soon there were urgent shouts for Mudiwar, and for me. The chieftain banged his stick on the council mat, ending the meeting, and I helped him to his feet. Together we hurried to the man the soldiers had brought in.

By the time I got to him he had been laid on the ground. People were gathered about him, some weeping, some praying, some saying angry things. They parted to let Mudiwar and me through. When he saw who it was, Mudiwar gave an awful cry and fell to the ground, his arms about the man's shoulders. He wept, saying over and over again, "Chetobuh! Chetobuh, my son, my son!"

In tears, Ramakoda bent over his father. "Let Avala look at him, my father," he said. "If anyone can mend him, she can." Over his father's head, Ramakoda looked at me and said, "Chetobuh was taken in slavery in the time I was away after the lion, when you found me. He must have escaped from Navora."

Several people helped Mudiwar up, and he stood supported by Ramakoda while I knelt by the escaped slave.

His injuries were horrendous. Near death he was, starving and naked, and with awful stripes over him, as if he had been whipped all over his body. One of his eyes had been gouged out, and his tongue had been cut away. Barely conscious, he moaned and sobbed terribly, and he twitched and trembled from the agony he was in. Immediately I passed my hands down over his face and along the back of his neck, easing his pains. When he was quiet, I stood up.

"I'll do my best for him," I said to Mudiwar. "Have him carried to my small healing tent."

Lovingly, Chetobuh was picked up, and six people began carrying him along the shore. As I went one of the Navoran soldiers who had found him said to me, in a low voice, "He will have defied the Lord Jaganath in some way. Such slaves always had an eye gouged, or their tongue cut out. This man must have been braver than most, to have had both punishments. Also, he's the first slave I know who has escaped. I suspect he stole the horse from the farms on the edge of the Shinali land. He was wandering in the mountains west of the Ekiya when I noticed him through my telescope. I wish you well, healing him, Avala; he's suffered the worst kind of punishment, and we see only the outside. God knows what the Emperor's done to his mind. Even if he survives, I suspect he'll be mad."

24

Even great prophecies are not set in stone, but depend
on human beings to work them out and fight for them
and bring them into being.

—My mother, Ashila

The healing of Chetobuh was the hardest I had ever done, and called on every skill I had learned at Ravinath. Chimaki helped, and old Mudiwar insisted on watching, though he rocked back and forth in grief, and wept openly. Ishtok sat with his father, and he, too, wept, tears running down his cheeks like rain.

First, I cleaned out Chetobuh's eye socket, for it was badly infected, and I laid new skin across, cut from his chest, to protect the exposed tissues within. Then Chimaki and I washed all his stripes, and I cleaned the infection from those as well. In parts his ribs and the bones of his back were exposed, and I guessed he had been whipped many times. His tongue I could not mend. But the hardest part of his healing was the easing of his mind. That I did not attempt until the rest of him was anointed with ointments, and securely bound. Then I sent everyone out, though Mudiwar protested.

"I'm going to walk in his memories," I explained. "I may live through some of them, with him. No matter what you hear, what I say, please do not come in. Do not allow anyone to interrupt me. It would be dangerous for me to be disturbed."

Mudiwar nodded. Then he went out, and he looked very old, bent, and in despair. I was surprised, when he lifted the tent flap and went out, to see that it was dusk.

Alone but for the unconscious slave, I sat and pressed Sheel Chandra's amulet to my forehead.

The Master was lying in his bed, a blue and golden coverlet drawn over him. He looked peaceful, but his skin was gray. Salverion was sitting with him, his hand on Sheel Chandra's chest, perhaps healing him. I stood aside, dismayed that Sheel Chandra was ill, and loathe to disturb them. Then I saw Sheel Chandra lift his right hand and look in my direction. "My friend," he said to Salverion, "our daughter needs me." His voice sounded weak.

Immediately Salverion got up. For a few moments he touched Sheel Chandra's brow, then he left the room.

Slowly, I drew close to the bed. Sheel Chandra's hand dropped back on the covers, and he closed his eyes.

"I'm sorry to disturb you, Master," I said. "I'm so sorry."

Without looking at me, he smiled. "Ah, beloved, you could never disturb me," he said. "Don't be afraid. I'm not ill, just very weary."

I knelt by him and took his hand in both of mine. His skin was cool. He felt solid, real to me, though I did not know if my presence was so real to him, or if I was only like a dream.

"How went the battle, dear one?" he asked.

I was surprised that he did not know. Then I suddenly knew why he was so exhausted. How powerfully he had shielded me, when I had gone out onto that battlefield time and time again, dragging the wounded away! Perhaps a hundred times that day I might have died, but for him. Weeping, I pressed my cheek against his hand. I felt suddenly unspeakably favored, blessed beyond words. "Thank you, Master," I said. "Thank you for all the times you held off death yesterday."

"It was my joy to do that," he replied.

"We won the battle. Others fought on our side, with us." I told him of Embry and his soldiers, and the Hena warriors who had joined him four months ago. "The armies are ready to gather," I said, "though Mudiwar still will not believe in the Eagle's Time."

Sheel Chandra said, very softly, "Forces are indeed gathering, Avala, and the time is nearer than you think. But what else is on your heart?"

"A slave," I said. Briefly, I told him of Chetobuh, finishing, "I must walk in his memories, and heal his mind." I stopped, unwilling to ask the favor I had come for.

But he knew it anyway, and said, "I will shield you while you do it, my dear. It is wise of you to seek my help, for it is very hard to heal the memories of someone so tortured. When you walk in his memories you will carry a white light, and that will protect your heart and mind, and ease his."

"But you are already tired, Master."

"Even as we speak, Taliesin is on his way here, and he will help me. All will be well, dear one. Go in peace. Your hour is come."

Though I was mystified by his final words, a great peace went through me. I stood, and bent, and kissed his cheek. His pillow smelled of lavender, and his silver hair spread out upon it was silken soft. "Thank you, with *sharleema*," I said. "I love you, Grandfather."

Then I felt myself drawn away, called through utter darkness; I felt the coldness of stone, of mountain air, and heard the wild night winds howling across the plains. Then there was a softness of leather, a warmth, and the scent of my healing tent with its herbs and ointments. Out of the dimness, I saw the white bindings about the slave Chetobuh. He was asleep.

I took a deep breath and said a prayer. Then I bent my forehead to his.

When I raised my head from Chetobuh's, the birds were singing outside, and it was morning. During the healing, not knowing where he was, he had tried at times to sit up, to flee, and I had held him in my arms and rocked him, as one would rock a distressed child, and that was the way we still were. He was asleep again now, but I was trembling, weary after the long, appalling journey through his mind. I felt I had lived a whole lifetime in one night and seen horrors enough to last for many lifetimes.

Waking, Chetobuh tried to speak, but the sounds were unintelligible, rough and guttural in his throat. "Hush, hush," I said, kissing his brow. "All is well, now. You are home. I am Avala, healer from the Shinali. Your father is just outside, waiting to see you. Ramakoda is here, and Ishtok, and your sister, Chimaki. They all are well. Chro is here, hurt from a recent battle, but alive. Navoran soldiers sided with us in the fight, and are good people. You are safe."

He sobbed, and I rocked him, weeping with him, feeling the

blood seeping through the bindings on his back. I would have laid him down, but he shook his head and clung to me like a child. A long time I simply held him, healing him, loving him. Never had I seen a human being so broken. In his great anguish he seemed to hold all the pain of every slave ever taken captive. In him, through him, I had seen the worst that the Navoran Empire could do; and it seemed to me that in his brokenness lay the suffering of us all. And so I held him and wept—for him, for every slave in Navora, every slave in Navoran mines, on Navoran roads, in Navoran ships. And as I wept a rage rose in me, white-hot and overwhelming, a rage that could not be ignored, or left unsatisfied; and I laid Chetobuh down, and in that rage I went out and looked for Mudiwar.

The funerals were over, the skies clear of smoke and the ugly birds. The place seemed almost normal. Mudiwar was on a feasting-mat, and his family was with him, with Embry and his officers, and the Hena warriors. Hardly able to breathe for the huge things that were in my soul, I went to them. Seeing my face, they fell silent. Mudiwar put down his knife. There was utter quiet. I remained standing, a little way in front of Mudiwar's mat.

"He is well?" Mudiwar asked. "My son, all is well with him?"

"He is alive," I said. "His scars will mend, maybe even his mind. But all is not well with him. All is not well with any of us—not with you, not with the Navorans, not with the Shinali, not with the Hena." My voice rose, I hardly knew what I was saying. I was crying, overwrought, consumed with rage and an overwhelming desire for justice. Mudiwar tried to stand, began to warn me to keep my voice down, to control myself, but

Ramakoda put his hand on his arm. I spoke on, and even the children were quiet, listening.

"Nothing is well in this land," I said. "You think you are free, Mudiwar. You think your people are free. But how can you be free while a man like Chetobuh lives, and suffers what he has suffered? All night I have walked in his memories, seen things I had not imagined human beings could do to one another— things too terrible to think on, to talk of. Things Chetobuh has lived through and survived. Through him, I've seen them.

"I've seen slaves carrying stones to build a Navoran road, one of them a woman in childbirth. She was whipped, forced to continue working even while the child was coming out of her. Even then she was beaten, forced to abandon her newborn, to see it trampled on the road. I've seen children strung up and burned alive, as punishment to their parents for angering the Emperor. I've seen how rich Navorans in Jaganath's palace used little children, and then had their broken bodies thrown on the fire pits outside the city, even before they were dead. I've seen women who have been raped, beaten, humiliated, over and over again, as prizes to the soldiers who had gone on raids. I've seen slaves punished for the smallest errors, because they could not understand the Navoran commands shouted at them. I've seen a man skinned alive because he dropped a knife while serving the Emperor Jaganath. I've seen slaves stripped naked and made to crawl through the drains under the city, to clean them out, to break the ice in them in wintertime. I've seen slaves chained down, their eyes gouged out, or their tongues dragged out with iron prongs and sliced off, because they saw things they should not have seen, or protested, or spoke up for one another. I've seen how any who attempted escape were spiked out on the ground and left alive for the birds and wild dogs to finish. I've seen—"

"Stop!" cried Mudiwar, covering his face with his hands. He was leaning over, his head almost to the ground, distraught.

"No, I will not stop!" I cried. "Because I haven't just seen slaves, strangers unknown to us, whose plight might distress us for a day, and then be forgotten. They are your people, Mudiwar—*your people*! Your sons, your kinsfolk, your tribe, the ones you are responsible for, to whom you are protector and chieftain and father. They are the kinsfolk of the Hena. They are our dear ones, precious and beloved.

"And you say, Mudiwar, that it doesn't matter if a few of your people are enslaved—that so long as most of them are free, you consider yourself a good chieftain, a good protector. Yet are you? Are you truly a chieftain to those enslaved? Who else can they call to for rescue, if not to you? What hope have they, if they have no hope in you? If even their own chieftain doesn't care about them, who else will?

"You say you won't march on Navora, because your people are already free. I say that while one slave, one Igaal slave, remains suffering and broken in Navora, not one of us is free. And while one slave cries for his chieftain to come and rescue him, and that chieftain does not, then I say that chieftain is not worthy of his place."

I stopped, breathing hard. There was total quiet in the camp. Mudiwar's face was gray, and he was staring at me with an expression I could not read. I said, more quietly, my anger spent, "You may come and visit your son when you wish."

I turned and began walking back to my healing tent.

"Avala!" It was Mudiwar calling me.

I turned back. He was struggling to stand, Ishtok on one side of him, Ramakoda on the other. "Come here, before me!" commanded Mudiwar.

I obeyed. People parted to let me through. We were the only ones standing, the chieftain and his two sons, and I. Out of the corner of my eye I saw Embry sitting nearby, his blue sashes blowing in the wind. One of the Hena warriors, who knew a little Navoran, was interpreting my words to him. Suddenly I felt ashamed of my outburst, and more than ashamed, for surely now I had lost all standing with the tribe, and committed a heinous offense.

Mudiwar stood up very straight and signed to Ramakoda and Ishtok to stand aside. Proud, erect, Mudiwar said, "You raised your voice to me, Shinali slave. Worse—you say I am not worthy of my place."

I opened my mouth to ask for his forgiveness, but he raised his hand, stopping me.

"You say I am not worthy," he repeated, "while one Igaal slave calls to me for help and I do not go. Yesterday if you had said these words to me, I would have had you punished, for it is a high crime for a woman to insult her chieftain. But today you say those words, and my son Chetobuh says them through every wound he bears, and I must listen.

"A long time ago, Avala, you first spoke to me of the Time of the Eagle. Yesterday our friend Embry also spoke of that time. Our Hena friends speak of it. It is time I, too, listened to the call of your prophecy, to the call for freedom and right."

He stopped a moment or two, and we all were silent, waiting.

My heart hammered, and I could hardly breathe, for suspense and hope.

Mudiwar said, speaking quiet but clear: "And so I will join with the Shinali and with the Hena and with Embry and his men. I will fight in this mad Time of the Eagle. But I will not fight so that the Navorans will be rid of a tyrant. I will not fight so that the Shinali get back their bit of land. I will not fight even for the Hena, though a tribe of them I honor. I will fight because I am chieftain, and my people are wronged. I will fight to free my people who are slaves."

25

For a heartbeat there was silence. Then everyone was jumping up, cheering, laughing, dancing, hooting wild war cries, jubilant. People hugged one another, trampling the remains of the feast, Igaal and Hena warriors and Navoran soldiers all embracing like old comrades. Mudiwar's sons were hugging him, almost knocking him over, and Ramakoda was kissing the old man's balding head, fierce and smiling and triumphant. Then Ishtok was hugging me, laughing, crying, saying something I could not hear for the clamor. And all the time amid that mighty tumult I thought, with astonishment, almost with disbelief, *It is come! The Time of the Eagle is come!* Then joy-wildness swept over me, overwhelming and glorious, and I thought of my mother, of Yeshi, of old Zalidas and all my people, their time come at last. I thought of the ones I loved at Ravinath, and lifted the amulet from Sheel Chandra and pressed it to my brow, and knew that he would know.

Then quietness fell, and I realized that old Mudiwar was standing with his arms raised and that he wished to speak. Pushing aside the trampled baskets and dishes, we sat down again. Mudiwar too sat, very erect and dignified.

He said to me, "Avala, tell my words to the man Embry and his soldiers, for this is talk of war, and must be clear to all."

So I interpreted, and the words he said rang like a summons.

"I say we need to march soon," Mudiwar said. "Before the Emperor in the stone city gathers his army together against us and Embry's army, we need to move. While our hearts burn, and while my son Chetobuh's wounds are still fresh to goad us to act, we must move. Before the next full moon, we must move."

A cheer went up, but Embry lifted his hand, wishing to speak. "I honor your words, chieftain," he said. "But it will take time to gather up the tribes. It will take maybe until the middle of summer. There is much to be prepared for. And the Shinali, too, must be called to arms."

"Within three days," said Mudiwar, "I can have all the Igaal tribes gathered together. My pledge-son, Ishtok, can ride to the marshlands with these Hena kin of his, and they can gather up their tribes. In four days we can be ready with an army of twenty times a thousand warriors, ready for battle. Is that soon enough for you?"

"How can you call all the Igaal tribes together so soon?" asked Embry. "They are scattered over hundreds of miles."

"There is a plain in the middle of all the Igaal lands," said Mudiwar. "It is where we meet for the Gathering of all our people, at the beginning of every other spring. On that plain where we meet is a dead forest, many trees very tall and tinder dry. Long have we had a plan, that if ever the need arose for all the tribes to gather urgently, that forest would be set on fire, and make a great beacon-light that can be seen from all our lands, and that will draw every tribe swiftly to it. That dead forest is but a morning's ride from here."

"That is well and fine," said Embry, "but even the Lord Jaganath, with all his powers, cannot find the Shinali. Even if I sent out fifty scouts, it may take all summer to find them."

"I can find them by day's end," I said, and could not help smiling at the look on Embry's face. His soldiers talked quietly among themselves, and there were a few chuckles.

"I will vouch for her powers," said Mudiwar, "for she found us, after being away from us for more than a year, and only the gods could have told her where we were."

Embry said something to one of the Navoran soldiers, a big red-haired man with a wild beard and a nose like a hawk, and for a few moments they talked quietly together. Then Embry said, "It seems that you are right, Mudiwar, and we can indeed march within the next few days. But we must work out a battle plan, and choose a leader whom all—Shinali, Hena, Igaal, and Navoran—will follow. There must be total unity among us. But first we need to know where the Shinali are. Even leaving tonight, it may take many days to bring them to us, and to tell them the plan. I hope they will be ready."

Suddenly the children on the edge of the camp began to shout, and people started running. There were calls for Embry, and some of the Igaal men came running from the tents with their bows. We had visitors. Looking along the riverbank toward the gorge, I saw one of Jaganath's soldiers riding in, slowly, with a small group of Igaal captives walking beside him. The Igaal people walked free, and before long they were running, and the

331

soldier did not prevent them. People ran out toward them, and there were hugs and glad cries.

Embry went out to meet the soldier, and they talked on the edge of the camp. We saw the man draw his sword, and several Igaal arrows were aimed at him. But he placed the sword on the ground and knelt down, with his hands folded on his brow. When he stood, he and Embry shook hands in the Navoran way, and embraced, and Embry gave him back his sword. The man got on his horse and rode away through the gorge again, and Embry came back to us. He was smiling broadly, and there was a lightness in his step. He came back to the council mat and said to Mudiwar, while I translated, "Those soldiers who fought us yesterday, they wish to come back and join us. Every one of them."

Mudiwar gnawed on his lower lip, and looked suspicious. "How can we trust them?" he asked.

"Their commander—the man I just spoke to—was my friend when I was still in Jaganath's army," Embry said. "His name is Oren. He would have joined me then, but his wife was very ill and he did not want to leave the city. She died in the winter. He's a fine soldier and a great leader, and his men are loyal to him— more loyal to him than to Jaganath. They are ready to surrender to me and my army, and to fight beside us all in the Time of the Eagle."

"You trust him, this Oren friend of yours?" asked Mudiwar.

"I'd trust him with my life," replied Embry.

"Would you trust him with the lives of my tribe, my children?" asked Mudiwar, still unsure.

Embry smiled. "Oren was obeying orders yesterday. Now he

returns the Igaal captives he took, unharmed. If we accept him and his men, we have on our side almost six hundred more Navoran fighters. There are other advantages. Oren and his battalion were not sent to this valley; they were on their way north to seek out tribes for slaves, when they saw the entrance to the gorge. On a chance, one of the soldiers was sent to investigate. He spied your people, and so the slaves were taken from this tribe. Jaganath does not know that we are here. So far as he knows, his raiding party is still riding north. If you accept the surrender of these soldiers, your camp here remains secret. I trust my friend, Mudiwar. There is no treachery in him. But your caution is understood, and if you wish, your warriors may search the soldiers and keep all their weapons, while they are in your camp."

"They may join us, on that condition," said Mudiwar.

For the rest of the day our camp was in chaos, but in a good way. Although the soldiers surrendered all their weapons, even their small eating knives, old Mudiwar was still deeply suspicious. However, I talked with Embry's friend, Oren, and saw the colors of his soul about him, strong and true, full of courage and a hunger for justice. I saw the same colors in his men, and sensed the liberty they felt, to be out from under the yoke of Jaganath. I recalled things told to me in Ravinath, how many Navorans would welcome the Time of the Eagle and the new life it would bring, and saw the evidence of that hope in these soldiers. From my talks with them, I discovered that not one of them had volunteered for the army, and many had been told that, if they refused to fight in Jaganath's name, family members would disappear, or homes would be confiscated, or sons imprisoned on false charges. "Life was always hard under Jaganath's rule," one old soldier told me, "but after the bulai fever hit the city last summer, killing thousands, it's worse than ever. Over the winter there were food and fuel shortages, and the city's water system was contaminated. People starved and died of disease, while at night the palace lights burned and there was music, and Jaganath and his lords feasted. People are at the breaking point. There have always been rumors of the Time of the Eagle, and people whispered of it with dread; but now they are in the temple every day, praying for it."

That afternoon I went to Mudiwar's tent, got the map I had made at Ravinath, and walked along the lake shore toward the gorge, where, undisturbed, I could seek out my people. At times I walked on ground stained by blood, and every now and again passed a garment torn off in battle, or a bloodstained shoe, or a broken arrow. Strange feelings went through me—a huge, immeasurable joy, that the Time of the Eagle had come, and that all the nations were so ready for it; but I also felt a deep apprehension over the looming battle that would end all battles. I had tasted war now—had seen it and smelled it and heard it and been in the midst of it—and was more certain than ever that I did not want to fight, but only to heal afterward. Yet how could my people go to war this last momentous time, and I not be with them?

Torn, confused, I sat on the stony ground near the mouth of the gorge and spread the map out on the ground. My hands trembled as I selected stones and placed them on the corners, so the wind would not blow the parchment away. Then, sitting very straight and still, I made my being calm, and looked at the map through half-closed eyes.

Along the great rivers my spirit flew, through the mountain gorges of the far north, over the borders of the Hena and the Igaal lands. But my people were not there. South I came, down through the snow-topped ranges, and down farther yet, toward our old Shinali lands. And there, in a canyon deep in the Napangardi Mountains, I felt a throb of life. I went along that place again, down a wide flat valley with a river, aware of the dizzy height of canyon walls all around. Then, in a vast natural cavern hidden by the sweeping cliffs, I felt the presence of my people. About halfway between Ravinath and the coast they were, and—as the eagle flies—only five miles from their old homeland. It seemed strange that they were so close to the place where the battle would be fought, almost as if they knew the time had come.

Nearly all the people were out on the flat ground in front of the cave. Shooting targets had been set up on sticks, and everyone strong enough to draw a bow was lined up in ranks, bows in hands, and Yeshi was going back and forth in front of them, shouting instructions. Beyond them, on the cliff face, a huge eagle had been painted in black. Under the eagle sat old Zalidas, more wrinkled and frail than ever, his hair pure white, yet with the strength of his dreams about him like a light. Very still he sat, dignified in full ceremonial and priestly garments, holy signs painted on his face. He was watching the archers, and his lips moved, as if in prayer.

As I looked at him, at the orderly ranks of archers, at the eagle painted on the cliff, a joy went through me, a wonderful astonishment, and I realized what they were doing: my people were preparing for war. Hardly able to contain my joy, my gratitude, I crouched in front of Zalidas. His lips became still, and his eyes widened. He was halfway in the other world, half entranced. With all my will, I passed to him two words: *four days*. I repeated the words several times, but Zalidas gave no sign that he received them. And then another idea struck me, though I did not know if it would work, or if I could do such a thing within a vision such as this: I decided to make an illusion of an eagle in flight, that would be seen by him and all the tribe.

Standing, I looked along the canyon, past the towering cliffs, and called up an image of my people's sign. At the head of the canyon my eagle began its flight; it swooped low, gliding right over the heads of the archers, its wings almost sweeping their bows; then it turned and came along the cliff, past Zalidas, who was standing now, transfixed, his hands raised in salute to the giant eagle that passed, so close to him that the wind of its wings lifted his white hair; then it gave four loud cries, soared away, and vanished into light.

Everyone there saw it. For a few moments they stood looking up, and some of the little children ran to their mothers, screaming; but the young people gazed up in amazement, the old ones began chanting prayers, and Zalidas cried out in a loud voice, "The Eagle has come! Four days! Four days we have, and then

336

they will join with us, our allies! Shoot well, my children, shoot well with your bows! Soon you will be on the battleground, fighting for our lands!"

I lifted my head, and saw that the *shoorai* wind had blown bits of grit and sand across my map. It was near evening. I looked along the shore of the lake to where the camp was and saw that several big cooking fires had been lit, for the usual pits were not large enough to contain meat for all that great company. Mudiwar and Ramakoda were still sitting on the council mat on the grass, with Embry and some of his soldiers, obviously still talking battle plans.

Shaking the dust off my map, I rolled it and began walking back, trying not to look at the signs of battle beneath my feet, for they spoke too clearly of the greater war to come. Despite the joy that my people were in readiness, I could not understand the heaviness on me, the feeling that although the Time of the Eagle had come, my part in it was somehow skewed, out of tune with who I was. I could not imagine picking up my bow and firing an arrow through the wondrous chambers of a man's heart, even if that man was the soldier of the Emperor Jaganath. But neither could I imagine not marching in that mighty army, not being alongside my mother, and Yeshi, and all my people I loved, when they fought their last great fight for freedom. I felt torn, painfully divided.

Back at Mudiwar's tent I put away the map and went to the healing tents. So many wounded, there were! In long lines they lay, tough Navoran soldiers alongside Igaal women and men and

Hena warriors. Most were recovering well, and many were leaning up and talking to one another. They called a greeting to me as
I went among them, and seemed cheerful enough. Some were in
pain, and those I knelt by for a while, my hands on their nerve
pathways. One Navoran soldier, a youth not much older than
myself, was dying. As I sat by him he gripped my hand, his eyes
full of suffering and fear. I eased his pain and held his hand while
he made the journey to the shadow lands. When he had gone I
closed his eyes and sat there by him with my head bent, sorrow-
ing, wondering. Someone in the stone city loved him as son,
brother, maybe husband. How could his death make anything
right?

I went out and asked two of Embry's men to come and carry
the youth away for burial, then I went to my own small healing
tent, where Chetobuh lay apart from the others. Ishtok was with
him, and stood up when I entered.

"You look weary," he said, coming close. I leaned my head on
his shoulder, and he put an arm about me and kissed my brow.
"Did you find your people?" he asked.

"Yes. They are in the Napangardi Mountains, less than a
morning's march north of their old homeland. They are preparing for battle. Will you go and tell Embry for me? Your Navoran
is good now, and he will understand. I want to sit with Chetobuh
awhile."

"I'll be glad to tell him." Then he drew back a little and
cupped my face in his hands, looking at me. "I thought this day
you would be a high lot happy," he said. "But you are sad. Why?"

"Because I hate war, Ishtok. What was done to Chetobuh
here was wrong, the very worst kind of wrong. But does killing

a man, even one of the men who did it to him, make it right? And how many killings will it take, to bring justice and peace? Our small battle here yesterday was bad enough. How many wounded are there? How many dead were buried and burned and sent to the skies today? How many, Ishtok?"

"There were more than two hundred wounded," he replied. "Dead, there were fifty and two of Jaganath's soldiers, nine of Embry's men, twenty of my people, and five Hena."

"Too many," I said. "There has to be another way, Ishtok."

"Another way for the Time of the Eagle to come?" he asked, surprised. Seeing that I was serious, he added, gravely, "It is your people's dream that is fanning this fire, Avala. Your vision that has fired up my father, and Embry, and the Hena, and even the Navorans. If you want another way, you'll have to find it."

His lips brushed my cheek, and he went out.

I sat by Chetobuh and placed my hand on his brow. He was slightly feverish, and in pain again. I stopped his pain, and gave him water to drink. But he seemed distressed, and waves of fear came from him. Pitying him, I said gently, "If it is well with you, I will walk with you through your thoughts, your fears, and ease them. Will you agree to this?"

He nodded, and I bent over him until our brows touched. Images rushed over me—the rooftops of the stone city, with their slender pointed towers and noble domes, and courtyard gardens. I was looking down from a balcony high on a wall, and knew it was the palace. Then there were long passages of polished black stone, floors with beautiful mosaics, vast rooms with fountains and trees in gigantic pots, and ceilings painted blue with silver stars. And over all a brooding, fearful presence.

Then a glimpse of a robe, brown and ordinary, and the back of an old man's feet, shuffling as he went along a dusty floor. The light grew dim, and I saw the whole of the old man, his simple robe, long such as the Navorans wore sometimes, and his white hair. He carried a small lamp. Down narrow stairs he went, and I followed. Blackness engulfed us. There was a sense of being enclosed, of stone all around, close and suffocating, and an unbearable fear of being buried alive. I thought of white light, and it was there, lighting up the old slave's back, making a bright halo of his hair, and turning his small lamp to a dim yellow glow.

Through deep subterranean tunnels we went, winding and steep. Sometimes we came to vast caverns with three or four tunnels leading away from them, and the old man ahead chose one without wavering, and we followed. There were crypts where ancient dead lay in rotting binding cloths, and caves with dusty pots of arrows and spears, and the remains of fires from times long past. At times the passages were so small we stooped to pass through, and I felt the hammering of Chetobuh's heart, his awful fear at being so deeply underground. Then we heard a deep booming through the rock, and soon after came out into a cave and saw gray cloudy skies, and the sea thundering on rocks far below. Chetobuh sobbed with relief.

I lifted my head and rubbed my forehead. I ached from the tension of our long underground journey, and realized my palms were sweating from the fear I had shared. But Chetobuh lay peaceful, sleeping, his lips curved.

I remembered a story my mother had told me, of how my father, too, had escaped the palace through catacombs, guided by a friend who knew them well. Did many know of those tunnels, I wondered? They went from the underground palace store-rooms to the coast. I wondered how many slaves had dared escape that way, risking being lost, starving to death alone and in the dark. And while I wondered, the thought occurred to me that if people could escape the palace that way, they might also go in. Then other thoughts came, tumbling over one another, urgent and compelling—snatches of conversations in Ravinath, things Taliesin had said, about how Navora was built on slavery, and if every slave rebelled the city would fall within hours.

As if struck, I sat bolt upright, an amazing idea rushing over me. What if the slaves were armed, the city taken from within, Jaganath captured, his stronghold conquered, all within a single morning? Would there be a need, then, for the huge battle? Maybe not. But then, hard on the heels of hope, came the cold realization that if the slaves rebelled, Jaganath would summon his army. The slaughter would happen anyway, but the city itself would be the battleground, and the slaughtered would be the slaves, the very ones we wanted to rescue. No, I told myself, I was being irrational, desperate, dreaming. But the idea of a slave rebellion blazed strong in my mind, and I tried to think of ways it could be done without Jaganath calling on his army to subdue it.

For some strange reason, I remembered some of the poems Delano had read to me in Ravinath, his stirring battle epics of conquests of past times. Lines of his poems came to me, verses I had loved: a story of a small band who, by trickery, overwhelmed an entire army; an account of a bold uprising when surprise and cunning won against impossible odds; a tale of a king deceived, his army drawn to a false fight while his city fell, undefended. As I remembered the stories of cunning and deceit and pure bravery I wondered whether Jaganath, too, could be drawn into a false fight. Could he be deceived? I thought of what Embry had said about waiting being hard, and how he had been tempted at times to march on Navora before the Time of the Eagle, taking his chances with the small army he had. Could Jaganath be deceived into thinking that the Shinali had become impatient, that they were marching alone, without the other nations?

And then the ideas came, huge images flying like dreams into my mind, many at once, yet each one clear and whole and astonishing, until, within the space of a few heartbeats, I had the whole stupendous plan. For a while I sat there, breathless, hardly able to believe that such a plan had been given to me. But it was there, bold and blazing in my mind, and I had to take it to Embry, even if he laughed and called it mad.

Half afraid, astonished at my own audacity, I went outside to look for him. People were sitting on the mats, eating the evening meal. It was dusk, and the first stars were out. Embry was sitting with a group of his soldiers, and some of the Hena warriors, next to Mudiwar's mat. I went over and stood at the edge of his group. Embry looked up and smiled.

"Come and sit down, Avala," he said. "I wanted to talk with you. Ishtok told me where the Shinali are. I looked for you, to discuss the matter, and couldn't find you."

"I was with Chetobuh," I said. Two of his soldiers moved to make room for me, and I sat between them, facing Embry across

342

the bowls of food, suddenly shy, unsure of myself among these experienced soldiers. How real was an idea in a poem, against their combined years of battles and conquests? Hesitantly, I said, "I've had an idea. It's probably a bit wild."

"I like wild," said Embry, with a grin. "Beside, you've already given one inspired speech; from the look on your face, I'd say there's another coming up. Spit it out. I'm all ears."

I said, "Navora can be taken from within. There are catacombs leading into the city. You know of them?"

Embry nodded. "Those catacombs are treacherous," he said. "Very few people know the way through. I don't know anyone familiar with them."

"I know the way," I said. "The slave Chetobuh escaped through the catacombs. The dread of them still torments him, and I've walked there several times with him, through his memories. I could find the way through."

Embry put down his feasting knife. I saw some of his men lean forward, and they all stopped eating. "Go on," said Embry.

I said, "I've been told that most of the people in the palace are slaves. I also understand that if all the slaves rebelled, the city would fall very quickly. If a group of your men went in through the catacombs, they could secretly arm the slaves, and organize a rebellion."

"It wouldn't work," said one of the soldiers. "Jaganath would have his army into that city so fast, the slaves wouldn't have time to fall down before they died."

"Not if his army was already occupied," I said, "already involved in a battle outside the city. It wouldn't be the great

343

battle with all the tribes, just a small battle, at first. A diversion, a false battle to confuse and distract. You said something to me the other day, Embry, about my people being patient as they wait for the Time of the Eagle. You said that sometimes you've been tempted to march on Navora before the right time. What if we deceived Jaganath into thinking that we are all impatient—you and your breakaway army, and the Shinali people—and that we are marching on Navora without waiting for the unity with the Hena and Igaal?"

I waited for another objection, but there was none.

"This is my plan, if it will work," I continued. "At dawn, just as the slaves revolt, my people, with your forces, will enter through Taroth Pass, and march down across the Shinali land toward Navora. They will surely be seen, and Jaganath told. But thinking it is to be only a small battle, he will send out only part of his army to deal with it. Your army, with the Shinali, will meet Jaganath's few thousand, and then, just as they join in battle, the full force of the combined tribes will come in through the pass and pour across the plain to support our side. It will be too late for Jaganath to do anything. Even if the rest of his army is on the way to the city by then, to put down the slave uprising, he will have to divert them to the real battle. It takes time to send messages, to change orders. It will be too late; his army will be divided, confused. Jaganath's soldiers—the smaller force facing the twenty thousand warriors—will realize they are hopelessly outnumbered, and will surrender. By the time our tribes reach Navora, the city also will have fallen. Since most Navorans are already looking for the Time of the Eagle, we'll be welcomed. The battle will be over, the Eagle will have settled its wings, and most of Jaganath's army won't even have got to the fight."

For long moments there was utter silence on our feasting-mat. I had not noticed, until then, that some of the soldiers on nearby mats had overheard my plot and come near to hear more. Lamps had been lit and placed on the mats, and in the leaping red light the soldiers' faces were tense and expectant as they waited for Embry's response. Embry rubbed his chin but said nothing.

"There is another reason this will work," I said, "another reason we need the battle in two stages. My people don't have horses, and will have to march to the battleground and fight on foot. They can't start the battle at the same time as the Hena and Igaal warriors, who will move fast and fight from horseback; my people would be left behind, still marching onto the battle-ground while the battle is halfway through. My people need to go first, they need to begin the fight. That's their right."

Breathless, I waited for Embry's word. At last he said, "By God, Avala, where did you learn battle tactics?"

"In Navoran poems," I said.

One of his soldiers laughed, saying, "Delano! She's been read-ing Delano! By God, I wish he was alive to know his poems inspired this last battle!"

"We don't know, yet, that they have," muttered Embry. He turned to the red-haired soldier next to him. "What say you, Boaz?" he asked. "Do you think this wild idea might work?"

"It's insane," growled Boaz. "Utter lunacy, too far-fetched to be credible. Of course it'll work."

Some of the soldiers cheered. We noticed that the feast was over, and we were the only group left on the mats. As I stood to go Embry said to me, "I'll think about this idea of yours, and talk it over with my men. When the plan's finalized, I'll need you to translate while I talk with Mudiwar. It'll be a late night, I'm thinking. The sooner we are on the move, the better." He took my wrist in a Navoran handshake, adding, "Thank you. Your father would be proud of you, this night. One day the whole Navoran Empire will know your name, warrior-woman."

I said as he turned away, "I'm not a warrior, I'm a healer."

26

There is a day, a moment, called the Fullness of Time,
when the threads in the All-father's great earth-weaving
are drawn together for one mighty purpose,
and all things are connected, all hearts made ready.

—Saying of Tarkwan, past Chieftain of the Shinali

Mudiwar called for his gong to be brought, and he banged it to summon the tribe, though most were already there. I was waiting with Ishtok; his Hena brother, Atitheya; and Boaz, the big red-haired solider who was Embry's second-in-command. Boaz's gruff voice and name were familiar to me, and I remembered that I had heard them both down by the river that fateful day I had hidden in the pool. Then, his companions had warned him about speaking treason. Now he was deep in treason with more than words, and an excellent fighter for his new commander. The weariness I had heard in his voice that day was gone now, and there was a fierce joy in him. He was a big man, scarred and tough. Beside him, Atitheya could not have been more different: he was tall and slim, almost elegant, with a beautiful face and manner. He wore his hair in many long fine ringlets twisted with red mud, that swung and clattered when he moved. Despite his gracefulness, I heard that he was a ferocious warrior. A little way beyond us were our horses, saddled for the journey, their saddlebags bulging with gifts from Mudiwar to Yeshi.

347

Mudiwar lifted his arms and everyone was silent. "This morning," he said, "we witness the departure of Avala of the Shinali, and my pledge-son Ishtok, our Navoran warrior-friend Boaz, and my Hena son, Atitheya, as they go to the Shinali nation with our pledge of allegiance, and our plan for war. The love of us all goes with you. May Shimit bless your journey, till we meet again."

To my great surprise the old man embraced me. "My word that made you a slave," he said, "it is wiped out this day. Go a free woman. And from this day forth, there will be no slaves in my camp, nor ever shall be again."

I kissed his cheek and thanked him. "I will tell our chieftain, Yeshi, of your greatness," I said. "He will be proud to call you his ally."

Then I said farewell to Ramakoda in the Shinali way, and his eyes were wet as he said, "Before this day's end, Avala, the beacon-fire will be burning on the Igaal Gathering-ground. By dawn tomorrow all our tribes will have gathered together, and tomorrow we will begin the two-day ride to Navora. Take courage, sister of mine: the Eagle's Time has come."

I said good-bye to Chimaki, and to Chetobuh. As I said farewell to Embry I felt a deep anxiety in him. "I hope you were right, and that your people are where you say they are," he said as he gave me the Navoran handshake. "And I hope they are indeed ready for this fight. Because if they're not, we'll march without them. Now that this war has started, there'll be no stopping it, for anything. I hope you understand that."

"My people are ready," I said. "The world is ready."

Lastly, I went to Ishtok's oldest Hena brother, who was to ride to his people within the hour and send out messengers to rally as many of the Hena tribes as possible. To him I made the Shinali farewell, my hand on his heart. He said to me, "Our hearts are indeed together, Shinali woman. Our priest, Sakalendu, has been already spreading word of battle among the Hena tribes. We may not have time to gather all our tribes together, but those who are ready will make a fair army. Together we shall ride to freedom."

Then we travelers got on our horses and were ready to go. Mudiwar's people stood all around, their garments blowing in the wind, their faces solemn and proud and glad. Among them stood the Hena, with their painted clothes and mud red hair. And there were Embry's men, their blue sashes bright and brave in the morning sun.

Boaz rode to the front of us, and the people parted to let us through, and we moved off. But suddenly Boaz drew his sword, raised it high, and cried out in a voice that rang around the mountains: "For freedom! For the Eagle's Time!" He rode fast, and as we followed in his dust I heard the people cheering behind us. Once I looked back and saw Mudiwar supporting his son Chetobuh. I remember thinking, in the middle of that soaring joy-wildness, how strange it was that the Igaal allegiance to the Time of the Eagle had hung, in the end, not on anything I did, but on the escape of one broken Igaal slave.

Then we were in the gorge, riding hard, and Ishtok was making mad fox-barks to spur his horse on. I joined him, and we rode, laughing, barking, racing with Atitheya, all of us behind the zealous red-haired Navoran with his drawn sword fiery in the sun.

Outside the gorge a strong wind blew in from the west, bringing the chill of the last snow that remained on the mountaintops, and clouds of sandy dust. To our right flowed the great Ekiya River, which we would follow south until it turned right into the gorge where I had first met Ramakoda; and in the foothills of the mountains we would make our way around to the place where my people dwelled.

We rode with our cloaks across our faces against the stinging dust, but after a while the wind dropped and the air grew warm. We threw off our cloaks and enjoyed the sun. We were covered in dust, as were the horses, and I could not help thinking that it was a good camouflage. Often I looked through my telescope, noticing that Boaz used one, too, searching for signs of Jaganath's soldiers. We had the whole plain to ourselves, and the snow-topped mountains, and the gleaming ribbon of the Ekiya River. The wide world was beautiful and bare under the summer skies, and my heart sang that at last I was going home—and going with a glorious call to arms.

By evening we were passing beneath the jagged shadows of the mountains that hid Ravinath. Looking across the ranges to the higher peaks beyond, I saw how the pinnacles were strangely shaped, slender and arrow straight, and I knew they concealed the towers. I touched the amulet I wore, and thought of Sheel Chandra. Just for a moment, though I did not even raise the amulet to my forehead, I saw him. He was standing with all the Masters, as they had stood that morning when I was with them and they shielded my people, and he was chanting in that son-orous voice of his. The image passed, had been fleeting like an arrow, yet I knew that they all knew and already had begun their protecting work for the day of battle.

We kept to the foothills until nightfall, when we camped in a small, grassy ravine. We lit a fire and ate the meat we had brought with us. As he looked at the flames Ishtok said, "Our beacon-fire will be burning now, the tribes already gathering. In two days they'll be at Taroth Pass."

Boaz told us details of the plan he had worked out with Embry, and I interpreted his words for Atitheya and Ishtok, though Ishtok understood many of them.

"On the day after tomorrow," Boaz said, "three of our men will enter the city, disguised as market gardeners with vegetables for the palace kitchens. They'll organize the slaves' revolt. That evening you'll be taking us in through the catacombs, Avala. I'll lead the company. There will be fifty of us, and during the night we'll arm the slaves, then support them during their uprising the next morning at dawn. The timing of the revolt is crucial; it would take only one slave entering Jaganath's presence knowing the plot for rebellion, for Jaganath to smell the treachery and end the uprising before it's begun. Secrecy and surprise are vital, and all the planning must be done at the last possible moment."

"He truly can read what is in people's heads, this terrible chieftain?" asked Atitheya.

"Yes, he can," said Boaz. "I've seen men whipped for what they only thought in his presence. That's why he's so powerful—he knows everything. Every last secret. But that's not what makes him so terrible. That man can make you think you're on fire, and it's so real you can smell your own flesh burning. I know; I talked to someone he did that to. They never got over it."

"Who is going to take Jaganath prisoner?" asked Ishtok.

351

"Well now, that's the biggest challenge in this whole campaign," said Boaz. "Personally, I'm hoping that the moment the old tyrant realizes his reign is finished, he'll commit suicide. Otherwise I suppose I'll just have to go and fight the biggest battle of my career, and lock him in his throne room." He grinned, but I saw the waves of fear go out from him, and they seemed strange, coming from such a mighty soldier. He added, to Ishtok and Atitheya, "You two won't be coming through the catacombs with me. At dawn you'll be with your own tribes, waiting to go in through Taroth Pass to support the Shinali and Embry's men, after they've begun the first stage of our attack. Your warriors will be led by Oren. When he gives the signal for you to join in, for the second stage of the attack, you'll have to ride like the wind."

"The palace, I'm going there with you," said Ishtok, and Boaz looked shocked. Ishtok added, his eyes meeting the soldier's, his face resolute, "I swore to Avala, I would be with her on Eagle's day. I swore it, with *sharleema*."

"I honor your vow, Ishtok," Boaz said, "but this is a battle we're going to, not a wedding party. Your father will need you." Ishtok opened his mouth to speak again, and Boaz said, in a tone not to be defied, "This matter is closed." Then he went on, "I want you and Atitheya both to remember, in the battle, that when Navoran soldiers kneel with their hands crossed on their foreheads, it's the Navoran posture of surrender. Spare them. Embry will be telling this to all the tribes. This is a battle to free slaves and to liberate nations from a tyrant, not to slaughter as many Navorans as you can. Most Navorans will welcome you, if you give them a chance. We're marching to free a city, not destroy it. Now we should get some sleep. We've an early start in the morning. We need to find our Shinali brothers and give them the call to arms. We have two days to get them into shape for battle; two nights from now we enter Navora through the catacombs, and the Eagle will be well and truly in flight."

The sun was barely up when we set out. We walked our horses, for the foothills of the mountains were stony and rough, and between the rocks brown tussock grass sprouted up in clumps, hiding the holes of rabbits and foxes. It was noon when our way turned right into a steep ravine, so narrow and rough that we went in single file, leading our horses. Boaz went first, and we picked our way slowly, deep into the Napangardi Mountains. After a while we came to a little stream, and we rode again, following its shore.

As we neared the canyon where my people dwelled, an unspeakable joy rose in me. Knowing it, Ishtok reached out his hand, and we rode close, our fingers entwined. Atitheya noticed and smiled to himself and said something to Ishtok I did not hear. We went around the base of huge sweeping cliffs towering like sheer curtains of rock, and passed fold after fold, always bearing slightly to the left. To our right, across a flat, grassy plain, were other mountains, steep sided and with snow in the peaks. The stream we had been following tumbled across the plain and under trees. It was a hidden place, sheltered from the winds, and very quiet. Then I smelled smoke and knew my inner seeing had been true.

Boaz held up his hand and signaled for us to dismount. "If I go marching in there, fully armed and unannounced, I don't think I'll get a warm welcome," he said, grinning. "I'll wait here. Avala, you go to them first, with Ishtok and Atitheya. When you've greeted your people and have told them briefly what is happening, then call me."

I nodded, and Ishtok, Atitheya, and I dismounted. Leading the horses, we rounded the last bend and saw the cave.

It was immediately in front of us, across a short stretch of dusty ground where children were playing and a group of hunters skinned two stags. Beyond them women tended a fire in front of the cave, and the smoke from it rose straight up and was lost in the dizzy heights of the cliffs. Against the wall near the cave two men sat talking, laughing together. One of them was my chieftain, Yeshi. Across the flat ground, on the plain, the archery targets were still set up, though no one practiced there at the moment.

My heart thundered as we stepped out from the shadow. The children were the first to see us, and they stopped playing and pointed. One of the boys called to the men sitting near the cliff, and they stood. At the same moment the hunters stopped their work, and the women by the fire turned and looked at us. We walked on, out into the pale sunlight, the air breathless about us. Even our footsteps, and the dull thud of the horses' hooves, were quiet in that place.

Yeshi came toward us. As he neared us he saw my face and stopped. A look of astonishment came over him, and he half turned and called out, while still looking at my face, "Bring Ashila! Quickly!"

And then she came. My mother, wearing a dress of pale wool

painted with stars, her feet bare, her smile like the sun. My mother, beautiful and with a gray streak in her hair, walking slow, unsure if it was really me. Then she began to run—we both ran— and then we were hugging each other, both of us laughing through our tears, and she was saying a prayer of thanks to the All-father, and touching my face, my hair, as if not sure it was truly me. At last she pulled away a little and looked on my face while she made the Shinali welcome.

"My heart and yours are in harmony," she said. And how soft her voice sounded, with its beautiful Shinali accents! Then we hugged again, and I could not speak for bliss.

Then my chieftain, Yeshi, came up, and I knelt before him and touched my head to the dust, and he lifted me with both his hands and embraced me and made the Shinali greeting.

"We thought you were dead," he said, "and here you are back from the shadow lands, happy and in good health. Ashila always said things were well with you, but we thought it was a mother's empty hope."

I turned and called Ishtok and Atitheya. Still leading the horses, side by side, they came to us. Their faces were grave, slightly apprehensive.

Then Ishtok came forward, and I said, with pride, "This is Ishtok, youngest son of the Igaal chieftain, Mudiwar. And with him is Atitheya, younger son of the Hena chieftain, Serdar. They come as ambassadors from their people, with messages for you, Yeshi."

Ishtok came and knelt before Yeshi, as I had done.

Rising, he said, "To Yeshi, chieftain of the Shinali, and to all the Shinali nation: my father, the chieftain Mudiwar of the Igaal Tribe of the Elk, sends greetings, and the vow of allegiance in the battle for the Time of the Eagle."

Then Atitheya, too, bowed to Yeshi and said, "My father is Serdar, chieftain of the Fox Clan of the Hena nation. This day he does not have it in his knowing that I am here, but they know who are also members of his household, and they swear their allegiance. In days soon to come, my father will also know of the Time of the Eagle and come with all his tribe, and with as many Hena tribes as will join with him, to stand beside you in the fight for freedom."

As he looked on those young men a light seemed to pass over Yeshi's face, and he drew them to him and embraced them like sons, and wept, and was not ashamed.

"With all my heart," he said, "I thank you. I honor you and your tribes. I offer you my love, and the love of all my people."

He turned and beckoned a man forward. It was Zalidas, just as I had seen him in the vision of the other day, bent and feeble, limping—but it was Zalidas still strong with visions, with sublime faith. Yeshi went to the old priest and embraced him, then knelt at his feet.

"You were right, wise father," Yeshi said, his voice hoarse with emotion. "All your dreams were right. I thank you."

Zalidas bent down and said, "Stand up, Chieftain. Of course my dreams were right! And you were right to take heed. Now the time has come, and our people are ready."

Then Zalidas went and put his hands on the shoulders of Ishtok and Atitheya and blessed them. "We have been waiting for you," he said. "In this winter just past I had a vision of you.

Of both of you. I saw you, Ishtok, on our old Shinali land, and over your head there flew a flag with our Shinali sign for dreams. And you, Atitheya, I saw in battle, fighting Navoran soldiers. I knew you would soon come to us. And I knew Avala would bring you. We are ready to march."

He turned to me, then, and I went to him, and he placed both hands on my head. There was no weight in his hands, just a brush like an eagle's feather, the kiss of a great blessing.

"You, daughter," he said, "I saw also in a vision. You wore a red robe such as your father had once worn, and you were in a high place. You have drawn together the tribes and done your work well."

"I did not do it alone, Zalidas," I said, taking his frail old hands and kissing them. "I have been given help by many people."

"I know," said Zalidas, nodding. "But in my vision I saw someone else, too. A Navoran soldier, with hair like flame."

"He is here," I said, loving our old priest, honoring his gifts, and marveling that I had ever been afraid of him or doubted him. How well he and Sheel Chandra would get on, when they met! I said to Yeshi, "A Navoran soldier came with us, a friend and fellow-fighter with Embry." Briefly, I explained about Embry's army and about Boaz waiting around the last bend in the cliffs.

"You had better be getting him," said Yeshi, "this Navoran friend of ours."

So I went to bring Boaz, and that big man came with a grin wide as his face and laid his sword at Yeshi's feet and swore allegiance to him and to the Time of the Eagle. And so Boaz, too, was welcomed and embraced and blessed.

I took Ishtok to my mother, and she welcomed him in the

Shinali way. "I have been living with Ishtok's tribe, Mother," I said. "Ishtok is my truest friend. He took me to our Shinali land once, and we ate a meal on it."

"You have been looking after my daughter well, Ishtok," my mother said, smiling. "Caring for her heart, as well. I thank you, with *sharleema*. You will have many stories to tell at the feast tonight."

Then Yeshi said, "Come—you must be thirsty and tired. We will drink and eat, and celebrate, for this day we have been awaiting a long, long time. But you, Avala, go first, and meet all your friends and family."

Word of my arrival, and of the Igaal and Hena ambassadors I had brought with me, along with the wild-looking Navoran, flew around the people, and by the time we reached the cave, everyone knew. I had to explain nothing and simply enjoyed all the other welcomes, the embraces, the cries of joy and surprise.

The first of the welcomes was from my grandmother, with her lovely white hair and soft old cheeks and scent of herbs she used to keep fleas out of her clothes. Always she had used those herbs, and the scent of them, the comfort of her embrace, was one of my childhood's most pleasant memories.

"I've missed you, Grandmother!" I cried, hugging her, in tears. "I've missed your wisdom, at times."

"It seems to me that you've had quite enough wisdom of your own," she said.

Then Santoshi was hugging me, and we laughed and stroked each other's hair and face, and could not speak, for emotion. I was welcomed by all the others crowding around, and it was good, so good, to see the old familiar faces, and the young ones, to hug the girls who were like sisters to me, grown up now as I was grown up, changed yet not changed, more sure of themselves, taller, two or three with babies on their hips. Others showed me the wedding tattoos on their wrists, and pointed out the youths they had married. Some of those I remembered as little girls were women now, blushing and curious as they looked sidelong at Ishtok and Atitheya, the first people from outside our tribe they had ever seen up close.

The Shinali youths, too, had changed. They were men, and the ones who had been gangling boys when I left were tall and handsome now. And suddenly even the familiar seemed strange— the men seemed suddenly alien, with their long hair decorated with bone beads, and their faces bare of tattoos. With shy smiles they all gave me the Shinali greeting, many of them shaking their heads in wonder that I had come back, touching my hands and my face to make sure I was real. Then I noticed Neshwan standing in the shadows. He had changed little, and the mocking curve was still about his lips. I went to make the Shinali greeting to him, and as I pressed my hand against his breast, he said, "Are you still afraid to fight, Avala?"

"I have fought battles already," I replied, "in my mind and in my heart. And I have been in the middle of a battle with swords and arrows and fought hard to save the wounded and the dying. No, I'm not afraid, Neshwan."

He said, with a sudden smile, heartfelt and admiring, while he made the welcome, "Your heart and mine are in harmony."

359

I went back to my mother, and we went outside with our arms about each other. Ishtok and Atitheya were meeting the elders of my people, being welcomed like kinsmen long awaited. As for Boaz, he was already showing some of the Shinali men how to thrust and parry with his huge sword, clapping them on the backs and encouraging them in Navoran, though they understood few of his words.

"That young Igaal man, Ishtok," said my mother as we watched him, "he loves you a high lot."

"He hasn't said a word to you," I replied, smiling. "So how can you be seeing that?"

"He looked at your face once, when I was giving him welcome," she replied. "It was the way your father used to look at me."

27

That night's feast is engraved forever on my mind. Never had I known such joy among my people, nor heard the old battle songs sung with so much fervor, nor seen Yeshi so empowered. Even Zalidas seemed to grow in the light of that big fire on the flat ground outside the caves; he sat straight, his majestic old face beaming, and many times I caught his gaze on me. As I looked about the faces that I loved, at my mother next to me, and Ishtok on my other side, and Atitheya next to him, I thought how generations of my people had longed for this night, this beginning of the unity, and I marveled that all things had come together in such wondrous ways.

While we ate I told my mother of my life with Mudiwar's tribe, of its joys and difficulties, and of how I had not been able to persuade the old chieftain to join our Shinali cause. I told her about Chetobuh, and how he had been the one to finally give Mudiwar the reason to march on Navora. When I mentioned walking in Chetobuh's memories, my mother gave me a questioning look, and when I had finished speaking she said, shrewdly,

"You weren't the whole time with Mudiwar's tribe, then. You went somewhere else, and got the knowing of powers only your father's teachers knew."

"She was away from my tribe for more than a full turning of the seasons," said Ishtok. "But she won't say where she went."

My mother looked at the silver ring I wore, with the seven stars of the Citadel, and when she looked at my face again, there were tears in her eyes. "Zalidas was right about you, too, in his vision," she said. "He saw you dressed in red, the color your father wore. He is always right, Zalidas. Even when you first disappeared, he said things were well with you, though Yeshi and all the tribe thought you were dead. Yeshi feared that the soldiers had come back and taken you, and would return in greater numbers to attack our camp, so we moved. After a time I, too, thought you were dead, but then, in that first winter you were gone, I felt that your spirit came to me and gave me peace. I knew, then, that you were alive and well."

"I've been very well," I said. "But tell me of you. Of the Shinali."

So she told me of their hard journeys, and of the time the Navoran soldiers discovered them near a wood one winter, and yet miraculously passed by; and of the last few weeks.

"Two full moons ago," she said, "we were camping very far north, in the mountains on the edge of the Hena lands. One night Zalidas had a dream of days not yet born. Before sunup he woke all the tribe, and told us of it. His face shone while he spoke, and the light was on him from the realms of the All-father. The eagle was in flight, he said, and the tribes of the Hena and Igaal were gathering. He said that Navoran friends were gathering, too, though none of us could understand that, at the time. He said we must be ready, because when the eagle summoned us for war, we must be swift. So the next day we began the journey here, to these caves, to be close to our land, close to Navora. Each day since then we have been preparing, making arrows, sharpening our spears, making strong our bow arms. Every person more than twelve summers has been practicing archery every day, nearly all day. Each night we have sung our old war songs, our freedom songs, waking up the spirit of our strength. And one day we all saw a giant eagle and knew it was a sign. Then, just as Yeshi was satisfied that we were ready, you came."

At that moment Yeshi stood up and lifted his arms for silence.

"Boaz is wanting to tell us the plan for battle," he said. "Will you tell us his words in Shinali, Avala, so we have it strong in our knowing, what we must do."

People were silent, intent, while I interpreted Boaz's words. While he spoke, talking of my people's march to Taroth Pass tomorrow, to meet with Embry and all the tribes, I realized that this was my only night here, with my people; that the next time we met it would be on our Shinali land, and the battle would be over. I looked at the faces about me and wondered how many I would see again, alive. I looked at my mother, at Ishtok, at their faces shining in the firelight, full of hope and courage; and a fear fell on me. I finished interpreting, then went and sat down again.

A woman began singing, her words silver clear in the still night, soaring with the flames against the stars. A Shinali love song she sang, and we all were utterly quiet, listening. While she sang I lifted the amulet to my brow and sped my thoughts across the heights and saw Sheel Chandra in his room.

Majestic he was as he meditated, his eyes closed, his beautiful old face full of peace, yet strong, so strong. Before I even touched his hand or spoke his name, he said, "We are prepared, beloved. When the battle rages, we will be there, in our minds, shielding and protecting. When you do what you must do, we will be there, in our minds, shielding and protecting. When the city is free, we will be there ourselves, restoring and rebuilding, leading the great reformation of our Empire. Go in peace; the All-father is with us."

I opened my eyes and lowered the amulet, and saw Ishtok's face as he watched me, his eyes wondering and afraid.

"You've seen a vision," he whispered.

"I've visited a man," I replied. "You'll meet him one day soon."

The woman was still singing, and when she finished the last word hung about the cliffs and lingered long in our hearts. Then, spontaneously, all the people began singing a famous war song, and when that was finished there were other songs, and stories, and several youths got up and did a war dance just outside our company, where the firelight met the dark.

The moon was high when we went to bed in the caves.

I slept between my mother and Ishtok, with a small lamp burning near our heads. During the night Ishtok moved out of his blanket and slipped under mine, and put his arms about me.

"I'm sorry I can't be with you tomorrow," he whispered. "I vowed that I would, and I am breaking my word."

"It's being broken for you," I said. "Sometimes even vows have to bend to greater things. I know your heart will be with me."

"But it's not right—you've had two vows to you bent to greater things. Mine, and Ramakoda's."

"The All-father had other plans," I said.

We lay without moving, our faces close, lips almost touching. He slept, but I lay awake a long time, looking on his face in the dimness. As I felt his breath go in and out across my skin I thought what a wondrous thing it was, the human breath and heartbeat and life, and how easily and swiftly, with one sword stroke, it all could be finished. Weeping, I kissed his lips and eyes while he slept, and thought how beloved he was to me; and with all my being I covered him with light, and shielded him, and prayed for his safekeeping.

"Line up, all of you!" ordered Boaz. "Let's see how well Yeshi's trained you for battle!"

He had moved the archery targets farther out and halved the size of some of them. All those who would fight had gone out with their bows—men, women, and all the young people twelve summers old and upward. Even some of the old warriors were there, though I doubted Yeshi would let them march on Navora, since some were crippled with illnesses, and there were three who were half blind. Still, they all wanted to impress Boaz, so they lined up, and the first row drew their bows, their arrows notched, ready.

Ishtok and Atitheya had been invited to show their skills as well. They were in the first group to shoot, and I saw the Shinali girls watching them admiringly. Ishtok was excellent with a bow, steady and sure; but Atitheya had a shooting style all his own. He turned to his target and drew his bowstring with an ease and gracefulness that was stunning to see, and his shot was always perfect. Many of our Shinali shooters were almost equal to him in skill, and Boaz was impressed. I overheard him talking with Yeshi, saying that his Shinali warriors were to be commended for their skills.

"All times, I am keeping my people's arrows sharp, their bow arms full of strongness," said Yeshi, in his broken Navoran. "This battle to come, all we were born for it."

"Later, I'll tell them the weak spots in Navoran armor," said Boaz. "They must make every arrow count. The battle will be all yours for a time—yours, and Embry's—until the Hena and Igaal arrive. It'll be a hard fight." Then he caught sight of me watching, and came over.

"You don't have a weapon, Avala," he said.

I replied, "I won't be fighting in the battle."

"True, not beside your people," he said. "You'll be fighting in the palace, beside the slaves and us. Do you have any skill with a bow?"

"I have a high lot of skill with a bow," I said. "I've hunted often, for food."

"Good. Ask Yeshi for a weapon."

"I will not fight," I said. "I'm a healer."

"Ask him for a bow!" repeated Boaz, his face growing red, his big voice raised.

Behind him, the people stopped their archery practice and turned to look at us.

"I will not," I said. "I will not shoot an arrow into a man one hour, and the next hour cut it out. I will not do it. And you will not command me."

The redness in his face changed to white, and his blue eyes

blazed with wrath. "By God, you shall take a bow!" he said. "And you shall take commands from me, else I'll not have you among my men."

"Then I wish you well, going through the catacombs," I said.

He swore and for a while stood glaring at me. At last he said, through clenched teeth, "And what will you do, healer, while you wait for us in the palace? Roll up bandages?"

"No," I replied. "I'll go and capture Jaganath."

"Excellent!" he said, still furious. "And after that you can go and raise Salverion and the other Grand Masters from the dead. We could do with their wisdom, when we build the new Navora." He stormed off, muttering to himself, "God help me! Right when I need warriors, I get landed with a peace-loving lunatic!"

In the afternoon I was to leave with Boaz, to meet up with Embry and his soldiers in a concealed valley near the entrance to Taroth Pass. Then, with fifty of those soldiers, Boaz and I would ride on to the coast, and that night enter Navora through the catacombs. Embry would wait for the arrival of the Shinali people, who would march with Atitheya and Ishtok to Taroth Pass under cover of darkness. Meanwhile, if all was going well, the Hena and Igaal tribes would be gathering, ready to ride to the plain just east of the pass, also after sunset. By tomorrow's dawn every one of us would be in our place, ready.

For the first and only time, I wished I were staying with my people, to fight with them. As I watched the men and women painting their faces for war, saw them dancing, and heard the thunder of the drums echoing around the cliffs, all the old battle stories of my childhood came back, and for a time I was wholly Shinali, my soul afire for the battle for our lands. Ishtok knew, and came and stood by me.

"You'll dance with them in the Time of the Eagle," he said, "when they celebrate on your Shinali land. We'll both dance. But now Boaz is asking for you. It's a long ride to Navora, and it's time you left."

Boaz must have forgiven me for defying him earlier, for he was amiable, though gruff, as he brought my horse to me, already saddled for the journey, the saddlebags packed with food. Then, too soon, it was time for the farewells.

The drumbeats ceased, and the people stopped dancing. Soon they, too, would leave on the march to Taroth Pass, to be there by nightfall.

Yeshi came, and he and Boaz exchanged last-moment words. Yeshi was in full war paint, naked from the waist up, and beads of sweat ran down the glistening colors. He made the Shinali farewell to Boaz, pressing his hand against the soldier's chest.

"Time to end the dancing, my friend," said Boaz. "You've an eight-mile march to Taroth Pass. Leave soon after us. You know where to find Embry and his soldiers, concealed just the other side of the pass. At nightfall you'll be joined by the nations of the Hena and Igaal. Fight well in the morning, brother. Be strong like the Eagle." He made the Shinali farewell, and got his palm covered with blue paint. He wiped the paint off down the front of his cloak, proud, as if he wore it like a badge.

Then Yeshi said farewell to me, and my mother and grand-mother came forward. My grandmother blessed us and kissed both my cheeks. She would be staying here in the cave with the other elders, to mind the children until they were sent news. Then I said farewell to my mother. Fearsome she looked, with her face painted blue and red, and her bow across her back. We made the Shinali farewell, and she said, "I'll be seeing you on our land, my love, in the Eagle's bright morning." Memories of the battle at Mudiwar's camp swept over me, and I gave her the ring of the seven stars, a link with the powers at Ravinath, and shielded her with all the force of my mind. "I love you," I said. "Fight well."

I said good-bye to Atitheya, and then turned to Ishtok. So fine he looked, so brave and steadfast! The Shinali youths had painted his face in bold stripes of blue and white, and there was the Shinali sign for dreams painted above the Igaal tattoo on his brow. As my hand touched his breast in our Shinali farewell, he placed his own hand over it. Neither of us could speak. Then, though the eyes of all the tribe were on us, he kissed me.

"Oh, for pity's sake!" muttered Boaz, from behind me. "Go and fetch your horse, Ishtok! You may as well ride with us. That mad woman is going to need your protection, since she refuses to carry a weapon."

Ishtok ran so fast to get his horse that everyone laughed. I looked at Boaz and was surprised to see that, despite his disgruntled frown, there was affection and humor in his sea blue eyes. Before I could say anything, he turned and mounted his horse. I got on mine, and then Ishtok was back, and we were ready to go.

Before we went, Yeshi made one final, brief speech, and

Zalidas said a prayer. My sight was blurred as I looked across my people, their painted faces radiant with hope, their spears and bows shining. It struck me that they all wore blue paint, the brave Navoran color for freedom. There could not have been many more than a hundred Shinali warriors altogether, yet I knew that already the tribes of the north were gathering, and the shadow of the Eagle's wings lay dark across the lands. For such a time as this my father had died, and I had been born.

I turned and trotted my mare alongside Ishtok, and the huge warhorse Boaz rode, and we left.

Fast we rode, close to the foothills, southward toward the coast. It did not take long to reach the pass, and Boaz took us into a hidden valley on the far side. We rounded a sharp bend in the mountain rock and saw the ordered ranks of Embry's army. At their head stood the fifty men who would ride to Navora with Boaz, picked for their knowledge of the palace and of Jaganath's ways. To my surprise and joy, Ramakoda was there with Embry.

Greeting me warmly, Ramakoda said, "We have fifteen tribes arriving here tonight, Avala. Eleven thousand warriors. I know of ten Hena tribes, seven thousand warriors. Maybe more yet to come. They'll all be here by nightfall. I came to inform Embry."

I said, "Thank you, Ramakoda. Thank you, with *sharleema*."

"We'll be thanking you, tomorrow," he replied, with a wide grin. "All of us, and all our freed kin."

Then Embry greeted us, looking worried until Boaz informed him that the Shinali had indeed been where I had predicted they would be, and they were admirably prepared for battle. But I heard Boaz say, in an undertone, "But there are only a hundred and fourteen Shinali warriors marching, sir, some of them women, some not far out of childhood. I had hoped there'd be seven times that many. It'll be a hard fight, that first stage of the battle."

"We'll manage it," said Embry. "All we have to do is deceive Jaganath into thinking that we are the entire force against him. So long as he sends no more than four thousand against us, we can hold our own until the Hena and Igaal arrive. You'll have a harder time, arresting Jaganath himself." He added, with that boyish grin of his, "Have him tied up and ready for trial before I arrive, will you?"

Then the fifty who were coming through the catacombs mounted their horses. Surprised that Ishtok was going with us, Embry asked why, and Boaz replied, loudly, "Because that stubborn Shinali soothsayer is a pacifist, that's why, and needs a guard."

"I'm glad to hear it," said Embry, with a smile. "I was going to suggest that Avala stay in a safe place until the fighting's done. We'll need her healing skills, after."

Boaz asked, "The three disguised as market gardeners, they've gone into the city?"

"They left this morning," said Embry. "If they're successful, if they've arranged for the palace slaves to meet you in the cellars to be armed, by dark tonight they'll place a white flag near the end of the old coastal road, where it peters out into the Citadel hills. If there's no flag, we'll have to manage without

371

the slave uprising, in which case come back to fight with us in the battle."

Boaz nodded, and Embry came and said good-bye to me. As he shook my hand the Navoran way, he said, "Sovereign God go with you, Gabriel's daughter. I'll see you in the morning of the Eagle, in the surrendered city of Navora."

Then we rode out. Before we turned toward the coast, I stopped for a few moments, looking across the empty grasslands. I expected to see the combined forces of all the Hena and Igaal, raising long lines of dust across the summer plains. But the lands were still, empty, with no sign of human life. Seeing where I looked, Boaz stopped beside me. "They'll be sticking close to the foothills," he said. "Surprise is still our best ally. Jaganath won't know what's hit him until they all pour in through Taroth Pass, across your land. Never fear, Avala; there are close to twenty thousand Hena and Igaal out there, waiting for their moment. By midnight tonight, this plain outside Taroth Pass will be black with a sea of warriors—your people, and their allies."

The sun was setting by the time we reached the coast. We were not going through Taroth Pass, but through a narrow cleft between the mountains and the cliff, that led through to an old coastal road that skirted the Shinali plain. In single file, leading our horses, we passed through the rocky cleft and out onto the road. By then the first stars were out, and on our right stretched the Shinali lands, purple in the dusk. We went only a little way down the coastal road, then descended a steep track in the cliffs onto a sandy beach. We rested the horses, letting them drink at a stream that trickled down into the sea, and there the soldiers refilled their metal water containers.

As we ate the food we had brought I asked Boaz what weapons they were taking to the slaves, for I saw none.

"Knives," Boaz replied. "We have about seven hundred in our saddlebags, just small eating knives given by our battalion, but lethal enough if slipped between the right ribs. The slaves will have to conceal their knives in their clothes until the signal is given for attack. They're searched after every slave-duty for anything they might have stolen, that could be a weapon. They'll not be searched as they report for work, and we'll be seeing them just before then. Soon after dawn one of my men will sound a trumpet from the top of one of the palace towers. The trumpet will sound over the entire city; every slave, within and without the palace, will hear it."

"The city slaves, the ones outside the palace, will they also be in the rebellion?" I asked. When he nodded, I said, "But who will arm them?"

"Our three harmless gardeners," replied Boaz, with a grin. "They'll have been busy this afternoon, taking vegetables from the farmers to the city markets, too, along with knives. Always the wealthy send their slaves to buy produce. The city slaves will also be ready. Now, we must move on. With luck we'll be at the catacombs an hour or two before midnight. We'll rest in the palace cellars while we wait for the slaves."

That hasty ride along the hills to Navora was a time burned forever into my memory. With every heartbeat I was aware that, far behind us, my people were on the march; and that in the foothills of the mountains all around the wide Igaal lands, the tribes were also on the move. This day's long ride would change history for us all.

It was a clear night, and a chill wind blew straight into our faces. Suddenly Boaz signaled us to stop. I realized that the flat stones of the road had given way to grass, and just ahead, gleaming faintly in the starlight, streamed a white flag.

"It's all on!" said Boaz quietly, but I caught the triumph in his voice. Past the flag were dark hills, and Boaz told us to dismount and tether our horses in a little wood not an arrow shot off. Each man took from his saddlebag a pack that he strapped onto his back: the knives for the slaves. Boaz divided us into ten groups, and we were to go, one group at a time, through the hills and around the wharves to the city. "You'll have to cross the river," Boaz said, "but it's only knee-deep about half a mile inland, and can easily be forded. Keep close to the city walls, and where the river enters the sea, look for a track down to the cliffs just below the corner of the palace. Somewhere there is the exit of the catacombs. It's a big cave just above high-tide mark. We'll gather there. The sea's rough at the bottom of those cliffs, so take care. A fall would mean death."

I interpreted his words to Ishtok, though he had understood most of the instructions. Then the first group departed. We watched their black forms vanish into the dark shadows of the hills, then, after what seemed an age, the next group left. Ishtok and I were in the group with Boaz, and we left last of all. As we crept over the brow of the last hill, I saw the harbor spread out before us, its waters pale as steel under the crescent moon, its wharves and ships lit with the red glow of burning torches and lamps. A ship was about to leave, for we could see lights moving along the wharf beside it, and already the great sails were being unfurled. Beyond the water was the city of Navora, its walls towering black against the star-studded skies, and within the walls I saw the glimmering domes of roofs and towers. A thrill went through me as I remembered the painting on the wall at Ravinath. But it was not all pleasure, this first experience of my father's city; the wind brought with it alien and unpleasant smells, and in the dark the city looked ominous, forbidding. I remembered that the evil there, that my father had glimpsed and denounced, now had full hold.

In single file, with myself in the middle and Ishtok just in front of me, we ran down the grassy hollow to the river. I smelled it before I saw it. I found out later that it bore away all the city's sewage and waste, including the corpses of nameless beggars and unwanted babies, and the various smells mingled with a strong reek of rotting fish. I nearly retched as we stepped into its murky flow, and I noticed that two of the men with us held the ends of their cloaks over their noses and mouths. The water was only knee-deep, muddy in parts, and Boaz held my arm as we crossed, almost lifting me off my feet. To our right, beyond the shadow of the city wall and too exposed for us to use, was a stone bridge.

Moving in line again, we went up onto stones into the total blackness immediately under the city walls. They soared above us and seemed to lean down, to slowly fall. I hated being under them. I could smell moss and damp stones, and in places could hear water trickling down. Here, sheltered from the roaring of the wind, we seemed to make more noise, and even our breaths sounded loud. I was thankful that behind us men were shouting on the wharves, occupied with the ship that was pulling slowly away, its sails full and gleaming. I could see the black shapes of other ships moored beyond it on the moonlit water, and the outline of a small island in the center of the bay. I stumbled on in the dark, and Ishtok reached back and offered me his hand. In the black moon-shadow, I could barely see the white paint on his face, or the white plumes on the helmet of the man in front of him.

As we neared the end of the city wall I heard the thundering of the sea against the cliffs, and our way became rocky and steep. We rounded the corner, and the force of the sea wind almost blew me off my feet. But here the moon glimmered on the rocks, and we could see well enough. Even so, it was a terrifying climb. Deafened by the crashing sea not far below, at times feeling its spray stinging like cold rain, I clung to Ishtok's hand and stumbled on. Occasionally I glanced behind me to make sure the last two soldiers still followed; I saw the face of the one immediately behind grinning up at me, gleaming with salt spray. We climbed steeply over rocks slippery with seaweed from higher tides, with the sea foaming and thundering over the jagged rocks below. I shook with fear and cold, and was unspeakably relieved when at last I was unceremoniously hauled up onto a flat place, and found myself in a large cave.

The men were laughing now, relieved that we all were safe, shaking the salt water from their plumes and drying their faces on their cloaks. The paint had run on Ishtok's face, and he wiped it off on his sleeve. Then, suddenly, everyone fell silent, their eyes wandering uneasily to the four pitch-black holes leading inland from the back of the cave.

Boaz came and put his hand on my shoulder. "Well, lass," he said, "I know it's been a long ride, and a hard climb up the cliff; but if you're ready, it's time for you to play your part."

28

Shivering, facing the back of the cave, I closed my eyes and shut out everything but Chetobuh's memories, and the way through the tunnels that I had walked with him. I thought of how my father, too, had escaped through these catacombs, and I wondered if I could possibly attune myself with his memories, if they could somehow come to me from the realms of the All-father. And as I stilled my mind and prayed, something happened that I can hardly speak of, for wonder. But I have to tell it, for it is part of my story, part of what happened when we entered Navora that momentous morning.

I cannot say I had a vision, or was aware of entering a trance, or saw images or heard anything spoken; but I felt a warmth, and a presence came to me, as real and solid as the rocks around and the soldiers who crowded behind, and I knew, with everything in me, that as long as I stayed with that presence all would be well. The presence was so intense, so clear, that, though I saw nothing, I knew he stood just in front of me, a little to my right. I knew it was a man, and I knew he loved me, and I knew I could trust him; more than that I will not say, for even now what happened remains a sacred mystery to me. With my eyes wide open I walked to the entranceway of the tunnel on the far left. I stopped, waiting, as aware of the soldiers behind me as I was of the presence in front. One of the soldiers spoke to me, but though I heard his words clearly, for my senses seemed intensified, I could not reply. I was bound, all of me, with the One who led. I heard Boaz tell the men not to speak to me, and to be silent. Then I heard flints being struck, and the dim glow of candlelight spread across the tunnel entrance. With the soldiers and Ishtok pressing behind, I walked into the blackness.

The way rose steeply and was rough. Often I stumbled and had to steady myself by putting out my hands, and my palms brushed damp walls slippery with moss and slime. I was conscious of the people following me, of their fear and uncertainty, and of the dank foul air, and the intolerable weight of mountains of rock on top of me. There were times when the walls seemed to press in, to crush and to suffocate, and I came close to panicking. But most of the time I was wrapped and shielded in incredible peace, unaware of everything but the beautiful and strong assurance that Another led me.

Sometimes I saw, almost lost in the dimness, long crypts carved into the tunnel sides, with corpses laid there, wrapped in pale, rotting cloths. Some of the tombs were carved deep, and there were many people laid there. Our dim lights shone faintly on ancient pots and the long shafts of spears and arrows. Sometimes I became aware that I could barely breathe, and that an awful stench thickened the darkness, and I stepped over decaying bundles on the tunnel floor. Once I realized we were passing through a huge cave, and I glimpsed paintings on the walls, broken pots on the floor, and stones marking out ancient hearths. A few times, when I felt most afraid, there came to me a scent like spice or incense, that reminded me of Ravinath, and gave me courage.

Suddenly, unexpectedly, I came to a hardness in front of me, like a door. At the same moment the guiding presence withdrew. Both things frightened me, and I shook myself, as if waking up, and cried out.

Someone pushed past me; it was Boaz. "It's all right, Avala— it's just something concealing the entrance," he said, pushing it carefully aside. It was an old wooden screen. As it was moved aside light seemed to pour over us. It was only a torch flaming on a wall outside the tunnel, but it seemed bright after the blackness we had been through, with our meager candles.

We stepped out into a large room that was really a cavern with rock walls, but it was filled with urns and statues and bits of furniture such as I had seen at Ravinath. Lamps burned on the walls, in readiness for our arrival. It was an underground palace storage room, and, from the stale air and layers of dust on everything, I guessed it was seldom entered. As we crowded in, there were quiet words of jubilation, and the soldiers gripped hands with one another the Navoran way, with fierce joy. Grinning, Boaz thanked me. Ishtok, too, was smiling, though there was a tension about him, and I realized how much he hated being underground.

Then they were busy removing the knives from the packs ready to hand out, and Boaz talked at length to one of the soldiers, giving him orders about the signal for the revolt. The man left, running quickly up a narrow flight of stairs to an upper part of the palace. I noticed the smooth curve of a Navoran horn in his left hand.

After he left Boaz said to me, "During the slaves' revolt you'll wait here. If we're successful, I'll send someone to fetch you." He added directly to Ishtok, "Stick with her, and don't let her move from this place. If no one comes with news—if the whole battle goes against us—go out with her through the catacombs, and get as far from here as you can. She's the daughter of Jaganath's worst enemy, the man he hated more than anyone else. She must not be captured. Do you understand?"

Ishtok nodded, his face pale.

The preparations made, we all grew quiet, tense. It was warm in that room with so many of us crowded together, and at last I stopped shivering, and my damp clothes began to dry. We had no idea of time, and it seemed that long hours of the night crawled by. Many of the soldiers rested, wrapped in their thick cloaks on the stone floor, or sitting on the broken pieces of furniture.

At last came the muffled sounds of many bare feet on the stairs, and in moments all the soldiers were on their feet, alert and ready. The first slaves arrived, crowding in among us, their lamp-lit faces glimmering with hope and a desperate eagerness. It shocked me, though I don't know why I had not thought of it before, that there were women among them, and some slaves barely out of childhood. I heard their murmurs of gratitude, and the solemn voices of the soldiers telling them how to use their knives to kill quickly and cleanly, and to wait until they heard the signal, the blowing of the Navoran horn. Hands slipped the weapons inside tunics and under cloaks, and the slaves left. The last of them had barely disappeared when the next group arrived. The ghostly scenes of those hundreds of slaves being armed, of the darkness and the secrecy, the looks of hope and liberation, the whispered thanks, are pressed forever into my mind. It was terrible and it was glorious, that plotting of death and of freedom.

When they were all gone Boaz said, "We can't hear the signal from here. When the revolt begins, one of the slaves will call us. He'll use the word 'Freedom.' Some of the slaves will set the palace on fire, to distract the guards. When the fighting starts, use your swords for defense only. Remember that most people here want this revolt to happen. Most of the people you fight will be your friends. Jaganath has few true supporters. So if anyone surrenders, show mercy. The hardest part will be to take Jaganath. God only knows what horrors he'll call up, to defend himself. I want him taken alive for trial, but if you can't withstand his powers, kill him.

"May Sovereign God be on the side of good people everywhere, and may this be the dawn of freedom for us all. May victory be ours, in this Time of the Eagle."

"For the Time of the Eagle!" they all said and drew their swords and raised them point uppermost in front of their faces, like a salute.

Soon after that there was a shout, echoing down the stone stairs and ringing around the walls above our heads: "Freedom!"

Then the soldiers were running, streaming up those narrow stairs into the palace, and I thought on how the hopes of nations went with them. When they were gone an awful quiet was left.

Ishtok took his bow from his back and placed an arrow in readiness. Then he sat on the edge of a dusty table, to wait. He looked toward the stairs, and I could not see his face in the dimness, but I sensed the sudden, overwhelming disappointment in him, that his people were marching into battle and he was not with them. I might have felt the regret myself, had I not another battle to fight.

"Don't get too settled," I said. "We're going into the palace."

"You can't," he said. "Boaz's orders."

"I've got business with Jaganath," I replied. "Are you coming with me, or not?"

Slowly, he stood up again, his eyes searching my face. "You are joking, aren't you?" he said.

"No, I'm not. I'll go alone if I have to."

"You can't! All the things we've heard of him, of the things he does, his evil! How can you fight him? You don't have those powers! Besides, Boaz gave me orders. If Jaganath takes you prisoner . . ."

"Come and stand here, by me," I said.

He obeyed, though a fear was in him. And then, for the only time in my life, I created an illusion just to impress: I lifted my right hand, palm upward, and sent up from it a flame, tiny at first, that increased until it was a column higher than a spear; a perfect fire, blazing fine and strong against the ancient stones all around. I breathed on it, and the fire faded, spread out like glass, a shining wall between us, high as the lofty roof, and hard as steel.

"Touch it," I said.

Hesitantly, with fear, he leaned forward and touched the glass. He knocked on it with his knuckles, and it hummed softly like a metal gong. I melted it, and his hand went through as if it were smoke. He withdrew his fingers and wiped them on his tunic, as if something from the image clung to them. I blew out my breath again, and the illusion vanished.

Ishtok was shaking.

I lifted the amulet Sheel Chandra had given me and held it out. "The man who gave me this," I said, "is called Sheel Chandra. He is the one man in the world who equals Jaganath in power. Sheel Chandra taught me how to spin images out of nothing. He taught me to fly in my mind, to see my people wherever they are, as he taught me to see you when your Hena family visited. I can shield my thoughts with a force greater than that simple illusion you just saw. And I know that this hour, in these very moments, that great and powerful man, my teacher, will be shielding me with powers far stronger than anything Jaganath can conjure up.

"I don't ask you to face Jaganath with me, Ishtok. That is my battle, and I will not be alone in it. But I would be grateful if you would make it possible for me to get past his guards. Your arrows are swifter and farther-reaching than Navoran swords. I know I ask you to fight some of the strongest guards in the Empire, and I will understand if—"

"Of course I'll clear the way for you," he said, with a tense smile. "I would rather do that—fight Jaganath's personal guards faithful to him—than fight unwilling soldiers in his army, men like Embry and Boaz. I'll be glad to go with you to your battle-ground."

Briefly I lifted Sheel Chandra's amulet to my forehead, and

saw a white light full of goodness and wisdom and power. In absolute trust, I took off the amulet and put it about Ishtok's neck. Then we ascended the stairs into the palace.

We came out in a kitchen deserted and dim. We walked through, and almost slipped in the blood of a dead guard just outside the door. There were more passages and ascending stairs, and with each step the darkness grew more gray. We came out in a small courtyard made of white stone. Above, the skies were turning pink, their blush reflecting in polished pillars and paving stones. There was no grass. Across the courtyard was a wide pillared walkway with gracefully arched doors leading to rooms and passages beyond. There was a pool in the middle of the courtyard, and a fountain. It was unbelievably serene. Yet we could smell burning, and a column of black smoke was rising from somewhere beyond.

Again I recalled Chetobuh's memories, his knowledge of the palace layout. He had served Jaganath himself and knew well the way to the royal rooms. I was surprised at how familiar the palace seemed to me. Ishtok followed me so close behind, I could hear his quick breaths. He had an arrow in place, and I could feel the tension in him, but no fear anymore. Neither was I afraid; I had an incredible sense of peace, of being shielded and guided, and felt only eagerness to at last meet face-to-face this man in whose presence lay my true battleground.

We went down white stone passageways, through arched and curtained doors, through splendid rooms with domed ceilings painted with silver stars, and up flights of stairs. In many of the doorways guards lay with their throats cut. We pressed on, past pillars of black polished stone, along carpets of stunning design.

Smoke was thick now, swirling about the high pillars and in the curved ceilings, and billowing out the elegant windows. Everywhere curtains burned, fiery fragments falling from windows and doorways. Carpets smoldered, and wooden furniture flamed against blackening stone walls.

From somewhere close came shouts and screams, and the sound of blades clashing. Suddenly there was a man, his back to us. He heard us and swung around, his sword drawn. He wore black, with a red horse embroidered on the front of his tunic. Before he could take breath, I heard the swift wind of an arrow, and the guard fell, pierced through the heart, his sword clattering on the polished floor beside him. Ishtok got another arrow, and we hurried deeper into the palace. Twice more we were accosted by guards, and those, too, Ishtok left dead. We saw many more guards in black, lying dead or dying, some with knives in their backs. The floors around were stained with blood.

Finally we passed down a hallway of gleaming black stone. At the end of it was a pair of high doors covered with gold. Six guards lay in their blood outside them, with the bodies of three of Boaz's soldiers. I held up my hand, and Ishtok stopped.

"Wait here," I said.

"I'm coming with you."

"No. He would try to get to me through you. He would do terrible things to you, just to break me. I can't protect both of us. This is my fight, Ishtok; I was trained for this."

Unwillingly, he nodded. I went close to him and raised the amulet about his neck. Unutterable peace flooded over me. "If ever you are in need of help," I said, "raise this to your forehead. You will see a vision of an old man. Do as he tells you."

I kissed him, then said a prayer, and faced the golden doors. Pushing them open with both hands, I passed through. Beyond them was an archway heavily curtained. I pushed aside the drapes, and went in.

The room was full of fire. The sight of it, the sound of its roaring, the pungent smell of smoke, almost beat me back; but then—perhaps because I was protected—I realized that there was no heat. Then I saw that the red carpet beneath my feet did not burn, and that the white marble floor on either side remained untouched by the fire, though the flames licked and poured along it toward me. It was a strong illusion, and I knew that to believe in it even for a moment would be to feel its heat, to die in its intensity. Remembering all that Sheel Chandra had taught me, steeling my mind, giving doubt no place, I stepped into the flames. I cannot describe the feeling of walking in that illusion, the strangeness of the effect of heat beating all about me, of intense forces lifting my hair and brushing my face, indescribable radiance licking my skin, leaving me almost breathless; yet there was no heat, no burning. On I walked, and soon the illusion of fire faded and vanished away, and I saw near my feet, lying contorted, as if they had died in utmost agony, the bodies of two soldiers. One of them was Boaz.

Kneeling, I put my hand on his neck. There was no pulse. Neither was there a mark on him, though he had died screaming, with an arm across his eyes, horror and anguish in his face. For a moment I was almost undone, moved by sorrow and the enormity of the evil that had defeated him. I checked the other soldier, saw no mark on him, either, though he was dead. Gathering up my courage, I said a prayer for their souls, and stood up and faced the way ahead. All the fire had gone, and the room shone in the early sun that poured in through tall windows on my right. The red carpet went on only a little farther, and at the end of it was a golden chair with cushions of purple velvet. On the chair sat a man.

He was leaning with an elbow on the arm of the chair, his elegant right hand stroking his oiled and curled beard. He was olive skinned, handsome, with very black eyes. He smiled a little as if he were amused and said, in a voice as soft as silk, "Welcome, daughter of Gabriel Eshban Vala."

Slowly, again shielding myself with light, knowing that what I saw now was indeed reality, I approached the throne of the Emperor Jaganath.

He was a striking man, in a dark and evil way. Though perhaps more than sixty summers old, he appeared younger, potent and forceful. Smiling, still stroking his beard, he watched me approach. His fingers glittered with jewels, and his long robes, the color of emeralds, were richly embroidered with purple and gold, and there were gems sewn into his sleeves. His hair was shoulder length, curled into ringlets, and a narrow band of gold was about his brow. So lordly he was, so majestic in many ways, that I had a strong urge to fall to my knees before him. I remained standing. With my whole inner force I protected my mind, envisaging a helmet of light, and a radiant unseen armor all over me. Above everything, I did not want him to know my thoughts, to know of the full force of the tribes gathered against him. Here, now, in the arena of my mind, I faced the biggest battle of my life.

"I trust you haven't come to arrest me," he said quietly, with a charming, deadly smile. "Others have tried that, and you passed their corpses. The mind is an awful and marvelous weapon. The men you saw were killed by their own fear. It never fails to astonish me, the power of belief. But you are well aware of that. You must also be aware of the fact that it is impossible for any person on earth to overpower me."

"I have not come to arrest you, Jaganath," I said. "That is the task of the new rulers of the city. But I will take you prisoner and make you incapable of resisting them."

He laughed softly. "You're a true Shinali," he said. "Mad with dreams. I know that your people are on their way. The watchmen in the highest tower spied them the moment they came through Taroth Pass. Also, I saw them myself, in the mind of the soldier Boaz, before he died. I saw you, in his mind. I know all about you, Avala. Everything."

He lied, I knew. I said nothing but kept my protection strong, unbreakable. He went on, still in a quiet, sardonic way, "I know all things, see all things. I know that your people march with deserters from my own army, led by that traitor Embry. When the battle begins you can watch with me. You will see your people slaughtered one by one, exterminated like rats on their own land. Even as we speak, I have my army on the move—six thousand men, fully armed, marching out to meet them. And how many on your side? A thousand?

"Did they grow impatient, your people, Avala? Were the Hena and the Igaal too set in the ways of old enemies, to become your allies? Was the nomadic life too hard for the soft Shinali? Was the great prophecy too long in being fulfilled? Did they decide to march anyway, aided only by Embry's treacherous little troop?"

Here it was, the truth, the hidden heart of what he wanted— information about the one thing that threatened him, his one

390

almighty fear. I saw it in his eyes, his suspicion of a trap. His lips curved, but his eyes were piercing and watchful, and I had the uncanny feeling that something cold and supernatural crawled about the edges of my mind, probing, seeking a way in. I closed myself against him, and spoke out my own little deception.

"We have a priest," I said, "who is a great visionary and seer. He had a vision in which he was told that even the greatest prophecies cannot come to pass without the willing agreement of those destined to fulfill them. He was told that even the All-father cannot cross the free will of any human being. And that willing agreement we could not get from the Hena and the Igaal, for they remain our bitter enemies. But in his vision, our priest heard that another people would rise up to become our ally, and with them we must fight, and with them the Time of the Eagle would come. Then, soon after our priest's vision, we were found by the man called Embry and his Navoran army. And so we march, and the Time of the Eagle has come."

For a few moments the Emperor was silent, watching me, seeking out a chink in my armor. I remembered Zalidas in a trance, his whole being caught up in the splendor of the other world, and that much I let Jaganath see, and no more.

Satisfied, the Emperor said, with a kind of glee, "Your poor, foolish priest! Your poor, foolish people! You all have been deceived. You see, Avala, I know the power of the old prophecy. Prophecies don't change. Your people *were* meant to join with the Hena and the Igaal. Then, and only then, can the prophecy be fulfilled. I know. Today is not the day for your people to march. Today is not the Time of the Eagle. Today is the day of doom for your people. They are cursed, for their stupidity and their blindness and their impatience."

"You lie," I said, pretending doubt. "You know nothing about prophecies, about sacred visions. You deal in illusion, in what is false, in deceit."

"Do I? Where do you think I learned my powers, Avala? I was one of the most powerful Masters at the Citadel, in days gone by. I had a great friend, Sheel Chandra. We were equal in power, he and I. But I left the Citadel, chose to be free, to use my power unhindered. Sheel Chandra was weak, he chose to remain there, his abilities tied up in knots by their petty laws and regulations. He taught your father. I would have been your father's teacher, if he had had the courage to walk out of the Citadel and ally himself with me. Gabriel could have been the greatest man in the Empire by now, next to me." His voice fell, became soft and seductive. "I loved your father, Avala. He was my great enemy, but I loved him. I loved his courage, even when he opposed me. And I love your courage. I honor it, as I honor your skill in seeing through my illusions. It was no small thing you accomplished, walking through my fire."

I said nothing, waiting for the next insidious attack.

Suddenly he lifted his head as if listening. Then he smiled, not a mocking, cruel smile, but one with joy. "Avala!" he cried softly. "This day all your dreams are fulfilled. There's someone here who wishes to see you."

His voice, his eyes, his pretended joy, entranced me. Breaking his hold, I tore my gaze from his and looked instead at the wall behind his throne. There was a painting there of the city of Navora. And beside the painting, radiant as the morning sun flooding across him, stood my father.

So real he looked, with his crimson robes and green sash, and his red-gold hair curling on his shoulders, every strand clear and vivid in the sun. And his eyes—how they looked on me, so full of love, of joy! He spoke my name, and I knew, I knew, that was how his voice had sounded! He held out a hand toward me, palm up, the hollow of it filled with light. He was grave and glad, fierce and full of peace, and beautiful, all beautiful. I longed to run to him, to touch his hand, his face, to feel his warmth. Yet I knew that if I did he would change into something unspeakably ugly that would break my heart and haunt me for the rest of my life.

I said to Jaganath, "That is not my father."

The Emperor gave a soft laugh, though his eyes on me turned hard, like the eyes of a snake. The illusion vanished. "Your father would be very proud of you, Avala!" he said. "He, too, was highly suspicious of me. You're very like him. Idealistic and passionate, with a little power. But you're also foolhardy and shortsighted. He crossed me, and died for it. The same fate will be yours. You made a big mistake, seeking me out. What did you hope to achieve? To confront me with my wrongs, the way your father did? To kill me, maybe? No—you won't do that. You have an aversion to violence. A horror of it. A fear. You're like your father, Avala. Weak. Spineless. Double-minded. Do you know what drove him to your Shinali people? To your mother? It wasn't love, Avala. It was guilt. Fear."

I longed to answer him but closed my mouth, shut all myself against him. If just for a moment I believed him, he would have a hook into my heart and into my mind.

The Emperor went on, his voice velvet smooth, full of cunning. "I'll tell you why he was guilty. He stole something from your people. Something priceless, a great Shinali amulet. He was only a boy when he stole it. He stole it from a wounded Shinali woman, and he left her there to die alone in the mud while he ran away with her amulet. And that was what drove him to your people—his guilt. He was a weak man, unworthy of the huge honor our Empire placed on him. He was never worthy of the Citadel. Never worthy of being taught by the Masters there. I wasn't surprised when I knew he'd abandoned them, betrayed his Empire and his own family, and gone to hide with the very people he had stolen from. And you are the same, with the same feeble-mindedness and hypocrisy. Like him, you're torn between two nations. Like him, you'll betray one of them in the end."

The armor, the armor over me. How close he came to tearing it apart! He said other things, but I did not listen. I was somewhere else, in a high place, my head on Sheel Chandra's knee, and his hand was on my head, shielding me. When I was aware of the Emperor again, he was getting to his feet.

"I'm going to watch the slaughter of your people," he said. "If you wish to take me prisoner, you'll have to follow. I presume that is still your plan?"

"At the right time," I replied.

He looked amused. "Let us watch the slaughter first, Avala. Then we'll play your little game."

He went to the corner of the room and through a curtained doorway. Beyond the curtains were more stairs. Like the stairs in the tower room at Taroth Fort, they wound upward, spiraling. Jaganath stood on the lower step, half turned, as if expecting me to be too afraid to follow. When he saw that I was with him, he smiled darkly and beckoned, then faced the stairs and ascended them. I followed. He called down over his shoulder, in a friendly tone, "No need to fear, Avala. No more tricks, no more illusions. Reality will be hard enough for you to bear now."

"I'm not afraid," I said.

We came out in a rounded room with green carpets and a wide window. It had no glass, but thick wooden shutters were folded back and fixed against the stone walls. A large telescope stood by the window. Beyond, the skies were silver blue, the horizon streaked with a few clouds of pure gold. I was surprised to find it still early morning; already the day had seemed long.

The Emperor stood before the window, looking down. "Come and look," he said. "It's a wonderful view. We're at the top of the highest watchtower in the city."

I went over, as far from him as possible, and looked down. Far below was the city, parts of it smothered in smoke. Flames leaped from buildings, and the streets were full of people scurrying like ants. I could see, on the far side of the city, the closed gates in the walls, the road behind them blocked with people and carts and horses, frantic to get out. There was confusion everywhere. Beyond the city walls were the green hills, the farms far to my left. It was hard to see; distance, and the new-risen sun, blurred my sight.

"That instrument by you is a telescope," said Jaganath almost kindly, not knowing I was familiar with such things. "Look through it. Through that small eyepiece, there, near you. It will make things that are distant seem very close."

I looked through the telescope, and the farms, the Shinali lands, leaped into my view. Across the lands, just past the garden where our house had once been, a small army approached.

There were Embry's soldiers on horses, and they rode in formation, making a long V-shape about ten horses deep. Behind them, shielded by them, marched a group of people on foot. The Shinali. My mother, and Yeshi, and—

"Move the telescope," said Jaganath. "Move it down a little, see what is closer, what is waiting for them."

I did as he said. A black shape fled beneath my sight; I saw the sown fields, the Navoran houses. I had moved the telescope too far. Slowly, carefully, I went back. Back to the blackness on the earth. And saw that it was soldiers on horses, vast lines of them, many, many horses deep, standing along the edge of the Shinali land, waiting. I gazed along the lines; saw the plumes, the shining armor, the glint of sun on deadly Navoran crossbows and swords. Thousands and thousands of them.

I gazed at Jaganath. He was still smiling, leaning on the window edge, his jeweled fingers idly playing with the gems that hung about his neck in chains.

"As I promised," he said, "we will have a good view of the extermination of the Shinali race. They'll be cut to pieces on their own land. You can go and burn the bits, after. If you're lucky you might find your mother's head, maybe even more of her. And when you've finished burning what's left of your nation, I have other uses for you. Your father robbed me of the pleasure of executing him; I shall have that delight, instead, with his daughter."

I shut out his voice and looked across the Shinali lands, over the top of the telescope. The day was beautiful, calm. Far, far in the distance, I could see the blue of the mountains, the river snaking like a bright thread toward Taroth Pass. There was no sign of any warriors, and my people were only an arrow flight away from war. For a few heartbeats, fear tore through me. Had something happened to detain the tribes? Had Jaganath tricked me, after all, and had the main part of his army already gone out, in the night, and slain the twenty thousand? Were my people all about to die?

Then, near Taroth Pass, I saw a faint smudge like dust, or smoke. I looked through the telescope again, in my excitement aiming it too far, then too close. Struggling to calm myself, to conceal my feelings from Jaganath, I looked across the lands. I caught a glimpse of red-brown towers and walls. Taroth Fort. I moved the sight down, to the right a little, to focus on the pass. It *was* dust I had seen—dust that rose from hundreds and hundreds of riders. Through the narrow pass they came, pouring in across the Shinali lands like a brown flood, spears and knives and bows bristling through the dust. More came, and more! They rode fast, spreading out across the Shinali land on both sides of the river, steadily approaching the small army they had come to fight beside. The land was covered with horsemen, teeming with them, rank upon rank of warriors. It was the entire Igaal nation, surely—that, and the Hena!

I looked up from the telescope, joy-wild, laughing, crying. "It is come!" I cried. "The Time of the Eagle is come!"

30

Jaganath was already rushing for the instrument. I moved aside, all fear gone. I saw his face unbelieving and dismayed as he gazed down at his army hopelessly outnumbered, at the battle he could not possibly win, the first sign of his defeat. After a few moments he stepped back.

From behind him I looked across the lands below; only a few minutes more, and the Hena and Igaal nations would be with the Shinali, and the battle would be all but over. I did not need the telescope to see that Jaganath's army was already in disarray. Some were standing firm, fighting Embry's men and the Shinali warriors, but many were already fleeing from the hordes that bore down on them, that were more than halfway across the land. But even then, with victory for my people certain, I protected them with all the force of my mind. As I did so I slowly became aware of a vibration in the air, a power that gathered, deadly and inexorable, beside me.

I looked at the Emperor. Terrible he was, motionless as he gazed down across the battleground, all the power within him bent upon one final act of utter destruction; and that power streamed from him like shadowed forces, dark tendrils that flowed out across the morning air, and down, down upon the fighters far below. It was an evil he wove, the harnessing of demon-strength, something terrible beyond swords and muscle and army power. I knew he was sending the dark forces to the battleground not to win—that was impossible now—but to wreck what havoc he could upon the Shinali race he hated. And I knew, too, where my next fight lay.

I became very still, all my mind turned on that great skill I had been taught, of going in my spirit to where my body could not. So quickly I went! Suddenly the turmoil poured over me, the clashing of steel on steel, and battle shouts and screams. Horses neighed in terror, and the swift sound of arrows flew all around. At first everything was confusion, chaos; then I saw that I was with my people, and they were fighting fiercely in a close band, firing their arrows over the heads of Embry's men, who protected them, or through the spaces between their horses. I saw my mother and Yeshi. And then time seemed to slow down, to almost stop; I saw horror on Yeshi's face as he reached behind him to take another arrow, his hand going wild, clutching at the air, though there were still many arrows. Then I saw my mother, felt her despair and shock as she reached for her arrows, seemed to find nothing there. Around them others from my tribe showed the same panic; for them their arrows, too, had vanished. In battle they were helpless. And they stood there, their bows useless in their hands while Embry's men fought closely all around, defending them. But even they were in strife, their eyes full of agony as some of them flung away their swords. The swords glowed red-hot. And then I knew Jaganath's trick.

And as I knew it, I was aware of him with me, in the midst of the battle. I almost saw his form; it was wavering, his skin and robes and all of him gray like a man made of shadow and smoke, a great wind streaming his tattered shades about him; and I—I was myself, yet not myself, a spirit-form that clung to him to keep him close, yet fought him, too. Even then he seemed not to be aware of me. But I raised my right hand and made a sword of light, as potent and real as the armor I wore; and I poured its brightness across the illusion of empty quivers and the red-hot swords, and gave back truth. But I gave an added force: the swords I changed so that their blades glowed with an unearthly power that would not only strike terror to the eyes of their enemies but also give courage to the hands that held them; and the arrows my people found again—those arrows, too, flamed with a holy light and left light where they flew, so the battleground became crisscrossed with paths of fire. And all the time a thunder shook the earth, a mighty clamor came nearer and nearer, and I heard the high, wild battle cries of the approaching warriors from the north.

My people were still in a close band, surrounded by Embry's mounted soldiers, and around all of them were the troops of Jaganath's men. But many of Jaganath's soldiers had got through the close circle, were closing in on the Shinali. I saw my people shoot their horses first, forcing Jaganath's men to fight on foot. Many of the soldiers were armed only with swords, useless against the arrows of my people; yet some had the deadly Navoran crossbows, which could shoot farther than our arrows, and many times I shielded Shinali warriors, causing the arrows against them to fall against a wall of light. Sometimes I fought with them, wielding my sword of light, warding off what would have been fatal blows from Navoran blades. I saw the looks in my people's faces, as it came into their knowing that they were protected; and they were transfigured, empowered, almost joyous in their battle strength. One after another, Jaganath's men fell, pierced with Shinali arrows, or sliced through by the swords of Embry's men. I saw Embry fighting like one possessed, his left hand tight on the reins of his horse, his sword leaving great arcs of light where it swung.

And then the thunderous tide of Hena and Igaal warriors arrived, closed about them, long spears and curved knives flashing in the morning sun; and soon that tide overran all, and Jaganath's soldiers were utterly overwhelmed. Navoran horns blew their signal for surrender, and hundreds and hundreds of soldiers knelt down on the churned ground, some risking trampling by the enemy horses, and placed their hands across their foreheads.

There was a Shinali cry for peace, and it was taken up by all the warriors until it rang across the land and back from the mountains, and slowly the battle ceased. For a time it was just men on horses milling about the thousands of kneeling, surrendering soldiers. There was a trumpet call, and Embry's soldiers, and twenty thousand warriors, all turned to face the west, the road to Navora. Then Embry, holding high a bright blue Navoran banner, led the warriors away, and they streamed down the road between the farms, trampling the nearest crops, and then poured, an irresistible wave, down the wide white road toward the city. And on the battleground, on the place where my people would begin a new life, were strewn dead horses and severed limbs and abandoned weapons and the corpses of soldiers and warriors beyond counting, and the surrendered men still kneeling, and the wounded crawling on grass that was black with blood.

Then the shadow-form with me turned on me with an almost unbearable hate; I could not look at its eyes. It turned all its force on me, pouring over me shades too terrible to describe; yet they could not touch me, for the light that was over me. It seemed then that a strong wind pulled me back, and I was drawn up and up, and then knew myself to be standing again beside the window ledge, with the defeated Emperor beside me. For a long time neither of us moved or spoke, but I sensed the awful rage in him, the intolerable defeat, the desolate wish for death.

"Do not even think of jumping from the window," I said.

"You have no power to hold me," he said. "I am the Lord Jaganath, Emperor of the Navoran Empire. I will not be taken prisoner; I will die first, by my own act."

"I am Avala," I said. "Daughter of Gabriel Eshban Vala, the man whose death you caused, whose brother you murdered. I am daughter of the Shinali, the people whose land you stole, the people you would have wiped from the face of the earth. I am Avala, and in the name of all these that I love, I take you my prisoner."

He turned toward me, his lips curved, mocking, his whole

bearing proud, even in what he believed were his last moments. And then I captured him.

I did not even need to touch him. Just a slender shaft of light, no thicker than my little finger, sent from my mind to play on his skin on the back of his neck, then going in, swift and fine, like flame, following the nerves of his spine, blocking them, stopping all feeling. He did not realize, at first, what it was; but he rubbed the back of his neck as he looked at the ground hundreds of feet below, intending to leap. He moved toward the window ledge, stumbled, fell. Crawling, he dragged himself to the ledge, gripping it, trying to pull himself up. He could not. His fingers locked on the stone ledge, stayed there. He tried to speak, but his words were slurred. Then his whole body slowly collapsed, and he sank lower onto the floor, inert and feeble inside his fine garments, like a grand puppet whose strings had been let go. But he could still move his head a little, and he gazed on me, the most terrible hatred in his eyes.

Quickly, I blocked the tiny blood vessels to his brain, muddling his thoughts, crippling his ability to concentrate, to gather up the forces necessary to create illusions. Confused, his powers scattered and undone, he tried to move, his face red from the effort, and sweat ran down him. Then he wept, probably from sheer rage; I felt no regret from him.

"You were right," I said. "The mind is an awful and marvelous weapon. But the body, too, is a marvelous thing. All it takes is a little pressure on a nerve or two, a tiny tear in a vital part, and a man can be rendered totally helpless, paralyzed. It will wear off eventually, but not before Embry comes with his soldiers, and they carry you off to your trial."

I sat on the edge of the wide window ledge, not far from him, to wait.

After a time a mighty roar reached the city, and there was the sound of the vast wooden gates being hammered upon; then they crashed and splintered, and across the city came the sound of Navoran horns, and the cries of the countless warriors, and the clamor of that huge army entering the city.

Looking down, I saw, in the distant streets, Embry's blue banner, and under it the soldiers with their blue sashes, and the blue-painted Shinali, on foot and orderly before him. And behind them, high because they were on their horses, were the ranks and ranks of Hena and Igaal warriors. I saw them halt not far into the city, as many people rushed down the streets to welcome them. I saw the crowd struggling past Embry and the Shinali, to be picked up by the Hena and Igaal warriors on their horses, and I realized they were the liberated slaves, united at last with their own. Soon the warriors rode away, taking their freed kin with them, and after their going the place seemed deserted. Parts of the city closest to the palace were burning, and the dark smoke drifted across a few bloodied bodies in the streets, smashed statues, and broken fountains. The uprising of the slaves in the city had not been without its cost.

Then Embry and his soldiers came on toward the palace, on foot with my people and some of the Hena and Igaal. I heard the clear, silver tones of Navoran horns blowing, and a distant voice raised in proclamation. Then Navoran survivors of the slave revolt began to come out of the houses. Seeing the Navoran soldiers, and hearing the announcement, they must have been emboldened, for soon the streets were crowded. I heard a great applause, and cries of welcome. They came, my people and the people of Navora, and Embry's liberating army, along the smoke-blown streets to the palace gates below. As they approached, more and more people joined them, and more, until they poured out from every street and house, singing and cheering. They reached the palace, and then the cheering ceased, and there rose a mighty chant. Insistent and compelling and full of hate, the chant rose on the smoky morning air to our high window, and I heard the words clearly: "Jaganath! Jaganath! Death to Jaganath!"

I glanced at the man crumpled at my feet. Hearing the cry coming up from below, he raised his eyes. He looked confused, weakened, like a man who had drunk too much *kuba*. But his black eyes were still aware, and now they filled with fear.

At that moment I heard footsteps on the stairs, and leaped up just as Embry entered, with Ishtok. Behind them were several soldiers. Embry's face was taut with fear. "Where's Jaganath?" he demanded, not noticing the crumpled form behind me.

"Here," I said. "At your feet."

In silence they crowded in, and Ishtok came and bent his forehead to mine, his eyes telling his relief. Behind him, the soldiers gathered, swords drawn, their points to Jaganath's back.

Embry crouched down and looked into his Emperor's face. Then he glanced up at me, his eyes worried and questioning.

"He's totally paralyzed," I said. "He'll stay that way until dark,

405

I'm thinking. Don't be afraid; I've lessened the blood supply to his brain, too. He can't perform any tricks. You'll have to carry him out."

Embry stood up. He came over and shook my hand the Navoran way. There was blood on him, but not his own, and his face shone with sweat and triumph and tears, for he had seen those who lay on the red carpet in the throne room below. But he smiled as he said, still gripping my hand, his voice hoarse with emotion, "Greetings, Avala of the Shinali, on this morning of the Eagle!"

He said something else, but I was watching Ishtok. He was standing directly in front of the Emperor, his face bewildered. Turning to me, Ishtok asked, "This man, he's the one they all feared? The great Jaganath?"

I nodded. Slowly, Ishtok crouched down, his face level with the Emperor's. Jaganath's head was bent, his oiled and perfumed ringlets falling over his face. Slowly, Ishtok lifted his hand, gripped Jaganath's hair, and pulled back until the Emperor was looking straight into his eyes. With his free hand, Ishtok withdrew his knife. At the same moment Embry and his soldiers moved, their swords raised, but I held up my hand. They stopped, watching.

A long time Ishtok just looked at the Emperor, reading his face, the terror in his eyes. He placed the point of his knife against the soft flesh above the Emperor's right eyelid. In Navoran, Ishtok said, "I am Ishtok, son of the chieftain Mudiwar of the Igaal Tribe of the Elk. My brother Chetobuh, you cut out his eye, his tongue. Whipped him close to death."

Unable to speak, Jaganath stared at him, his eyes like those of a man about to die, unready and overwhelmed by terror. Ishtok went on, "Now power is mine, to pay back for my brother. But I will not, for doing such a thing, it would make me less than a man, less than a maggot, equal to you. That is a thing I hope I never am."

He let go of Jaganath's hair, and the Emperor's head dropped forward. Sheathing his knife, Ishtok stood up and came back to me. Jaganath groaned slightly and sweat rolled down his skin.

Going to stand in front of Jaganath, Embry said, "My lord, Emperor Jaganath—in the name of Sovereign God, and in the name of Navoran justice, you are under arrest. You will be tried this very hour. The citizens of Navora are gathered in the courtyard below, as well as the slaves who still remain, along with the chieftains of the Hena and the Igaal, and the Shinali. They will be your judges."

Embry nodded to his soldiers, and six of them came forward and picked up Jaganath, ready to carry him out. I caught a glimpse of Jaganath's eyes on me, brimming with helpless rage and hate, and I thought how the indignity of being carried out must have wounded him almost as much as the loss of his Empire.

As the Emperor was carried down the stairs, Embry said to me, "Most of your people survived the battle, Avala. Your mother is fine and is going to the Navora Infirmary to help heal the wounded. Some of my soldiers are clearing the battlefield now. I know you will want to be with your people, but there's work here in Navora, if you will do it for me. There are many wounded in the city. As soon as the soldiers still in the army barracks realized that the Hena and Igaal were coming, they rushed here to defend their families. They found the slaves in revolt, and there was much hand-to-hand fighting. There have been many deaths, and many hundreds wounded. I've already dispatched my three surgeons to set up a hospital in the city, in one of the large houses with plenty of room and clean water. Many slaves are still here to help you—I mean, ex-slaves. They are not Hena or Igaal, but from other conquered nations. They'll be returned to their homelands eventually, by ship. But first, there's much else to be done. One of my surgeons is waiting for you in Jaganath's throne room, to take you there. Will you do that for me?"

"Of course," I said.

"You come with me," said Embry to Ishtok. "Most of the citizens welcomed us, but there's still a lot of fear and confusion in the city. Until order is properly restored, I need every soldier I can trust. I'll also need you to translate, for your people."

"I'll be glad to help," said Ishtok.

I noticed how Embry looked suddenly very weary, and not only from the battle. There was a weight on him, the mantle of a supreme, almost overwhelming responsibility.

"You have much to do, Embry," I said.

"It's one thing to fight a battle and free a city," he replied. "But the hardest work is yet to come—ending Jaganath's reign, finding a new leader, restoring the greatness we once had, rebuilding the Empire. I'm a soldier, not a politician. I wish, with all my heart, I had the Citadel Masters to help. I badly need their wisdom, their great influence."

"You will have them," I said, and the look on his face, the joy and the relief, were wonderful to see. "They will be here, soon," I added. "Sheel Chandra and Salverion, and seventy others with them. You are not alone, Embry. Not one of us, in this great morning, has been alone."

He looked away, out the bright window, and wiped his hand across his eyes. He said something—a prayer, perhaps—then looked back at me. "You don't know what it means to me, to know that they all live," he said, his eyes wet. "It also explains a lot of things. I'll go in peace now, and leave you to begin your healing." He nodded to Ishtok, and turned to go.

Before he left, Ishtok turned to me and, with joyful solemnity, made the Shinali greeting. "It's a fine morning, free Shinali woman," he said. Then he kissed me and went out with Embry.

For a few moments I stood at the high window and looked across the surrendered city, at the sea of shining faces below, at the blue flags and garments waving, and fathers lifting their children high on their shoulders to see the defeated tyrant, and slaves shaking their fists, joy-wild and free. From amid the cheers, I heard snatches of Shinali songs. Beyond the crowds, over the walls of the courtyard, the terraced streets of the city also teemed with people, all cheering. From somewhere across the tiled roofs and white domes and towers came the tremendous ringing of bells.

On an impulse, I looked one last time through the telescope, beyond the bloodied Shinali lands, to Taroth Pass. And I saw a group of people coming in, wearing crimson and gold, and over their heads, streaming high in the bright morning wind, was a long white banner emblazoned with seven silver stars.

Fourth Scroll

House of Belonging

31

The Navoran surgeon and I hurried through the crowded streets. He was one of the healers I had worked beside after the attack on Mudiwar's tribe, the one who had shaken my hand after, and his name was Rhain. He was still wearing his armor, though not his helmet or his sword, and there was blood sprayed down the front of him, and on his face. He took my arm to prevent our being parted, and I glimpsed, over the heads of the pressing, cheering throngs, high pillared buildings of white stone, splendid and shining against the smoky skies. We hurried up long flights of white steps, through narrow market alleys with stalls of bread and vegetables, striped awnings fluttering above; then crossed a crowded city square with a towering pillared temple on one side. Soon we were passing high walls with big gates of wrought iron, beyond which I glimpsed stone courtyards with fountains and statues and pots of plants and small trees. We came to wide, walled streets where there were few people about, and the houses I saw through the gateways were like palaces. Then we turned into a street where dozens of injured walked or were carried, all of us heading in the same direction. We came to a place with double gates thrown open and went through into a wide courtyard. All around us were wounded people—fathers with children in their arms, husbands and wives supporting one another, other injured ones walking, or being carried on make-shift stretchers by friends, many of whom were also bleeding. We were all going up toward a grand house, many-storied, with sloping roofs of red tile, and slender towers and elegant balconies.

"This will be our hospital, for a few weeks," explained the surgeon, taking me quickly through the gathering crowd, across the courtyard, and up steps to a high porch flanked by pillars. I found myself in a wide entranceway, also crowded with injured people arriving. On the wall above us I glimpsed a huge mural of wharves and ships, and slaves in chains. Rhain hurried me on. About us were people hurrying with bundles of blankets, layers of fine white material, and elegant bowls containing water. Some had minor wounds roughly bandaged. We came to a long narrow hallway, and Rhain opened a door. Waves of pain rushed over me.

The room was huge, with high windows along the far wall, looking out onto a courtyard garden. All the furniture—beautiful tables, chairs, lamps, and rugs—was piled up along another wall. All over the white stone floor were injured Navoran citizens, some moaning, some lying silent, shocked, others sitting, rocking while they wept. Some clutched bloodied cloths to their faces or eyes, others had deep cuts to their hands or arms. There were many with stab wounds, and they lay silent, hands clenched to their chests, blood running out between their fingers. The white floor was smeared with blood.

"This is just the first lot," said Rhain. "As you've seen, there are plenty still arriving. You'll find scalpels and needles and everything else on one of the tables over there. There are four of us healers, and we'll have help from Navoran citizens who aren't wounded. We'll be brought more supplies, blankets and bandages and suchlike. Just do what you can, the worst injuries first."

"Where will you be?" I asked.

"In the next room along, if you need me. There are four rooms like this, and they'll all be packed with wounded by tonight. We'll be getting the injured from the battlefield as well, once the Navora Infirmary is full."

"These people were all hurt in the slave revolt?" I asked, appalled.

"The worst cases have been taken to the infirmary, where they've got proper operating rooms. We've got the easy cases. Don't look so shocked, Avala," he added, gently. "We estimate there were about five hundred citizens injured in the revolt. Considering Navora has a population of forty thousand free people, we got off very lightly. Good luck."

Then he was gone, and I faced the rows of the wounded looking up at me, their faces suddenly suspicious and afraid. I went and knelt by an elderly man at the end of the row nearest me, saw that he had only a minor cut to his hand, and told him he would have to wait. The next person was a woman with a stab wound in her shoulder, not fatal, and I stopped her pain and moved to the next. It was a man with a slice through his abdomen, and he clutched the wound with both hands, unable to speak for

415

his agony. His eyes implored me. I knelt and stopped his pain. Then I said, "I'll get water and a needle and thread, and do my best for you."

And so I began the most difficult healings first. A woman came who had been a slave, and she cleaned the knives for me, and threaded the steel Navoran needles, and brought me water to wash my hands between patients. Others came to help, binding those I had sewn up, and making beds for them on mattresses that had arrived. A team of helpers washed the floors of blood, and gave water to the sick and to me. It was almost like the healing after the battle at Mudiwar's camp, but here there were no flies, the wounds were free of dust, and most were relatively simple cuts, easier to mend than the ravaged battle wounds of barbed arrows and swords.

Once, during the morning, I went and stood outside for a few moments of rest, while I ate some bread and cheese. I was in the courtyard garden, and a fountain played there, the sound of its waters reminding me of the fountain at Ravinath. I remember that I looked up and saw flocks of seagulls wheeling and screaming in the deep blue skies; and suddenly there seemed to be a change in the atmosphere, an intense stillness, a peace, as if a huge tension in the world had suddenly been let go. The moment passed, and the gulls whirled and shrieked again, and the world spun on. I knew, then, that Jaganath was dead.

As I went back into the house, bells peeled out across the city, and I heard a distant roar like many thousands of people cheering. Knowing what it meant, some of the wounded cheered, some had the strength only for a whispered prayer or a smile of sheer relief. I did a strange thing, for me, an impulsive thing born out of the huge feelings in my heart: I stood in the middle of that great sunlit room, with the wounded about my feet, and sang a song I had learned at Ravinath. A Navoran song it was, a song of freedom and justice, words of the poet Delano put to music by the finest musician in the Empire. I don't have a very good voice, but maybe it was the high ceiling, the smooth stone walls, that made my song ring clear and true, for people were utterly silent while I sang, and some were in tears. The Navoran surgeons came to stand in the doorway to listen. When the song was finished, one of them came over and embraced me. "I know those words you sang," he said hoarsely. "The poet Delano. Always I have loved his work. Thank you."

I picked up another bundle of clean needles and knives and carried on with my healing. And it seemed, after that, that the air was cleaner, rarefied, the sunlight somehow brighter as it streamed in the high glassed windows and shone back from polished white walls and burnished tables with their gleaming instruments, and danced on the clean white bindings on those who were healed. I thought often of the amazing light at Ravinath, and of the Masters, knowing they would be in the vast Navora Infirmary, bringing wholeness to the battle-hurt. I thought of my mother, with her beautiful face full of tenderness as she mended the Navoran soldiers and wounded warriors, working alongside those greatest of healers that I loved. Though our work was terrible in many ways, and the agony of the wounded was my pain, too, I felt that a great web of healing was laid like a light across the once-tormented city, bringing a restoration, a peace. And there was another thing I felt, in that grand Navoran house: I felt the presence of my father often, as if in these rare and extraordinary days, the veils were thin between the worlds, and he stood near, a supporting and sublime witness to the days for which he had laid down his earthly life.

By mid-afternoon I had treated all the seriously injured and had begun to help the many who were left, the ones with simple cuts and minor injuries. My most constant help was a girl slightly younger than myself, with red curling hair and green eyes. Her name was Elanora, and she had a lovely nature, caring and gentle, yet tough, too, for she did not shrink from anything we had to do. She mopped away blood as I worked, and helped me wash out wounds, and cut threads as I sewed up. She never once asked to rest, and stopped to drink and eat only when I did. I asked her if she had been a slave.

"No. I live in the house next to this," she replied. "My father owns the university."

"Was anyone in your family hurt, during the revolt?"

"No one. Our slaves—we had ten—would never hurt us. We treated them well. When the rebellion started, they locked us all in the cupboard upstairs, with the brooms and cleaning things. They said it was to protect us. My father was furious and tried to fight them, but the gardener was a big man, and he picked my father up and threw him into the cupboard with us, and he fell into the mops and buckets. I think Papa would rather have had a knife stuck in him."

We laughed and began binding up a woman's arm.

Elanora chatted on. "All our slaves are free, now. Two have gone back to the Hena, but the rest are from Amaran and will have to wait to go back on a ship. My mother's been crying all morning. She hates cleaning and cooking, and says we'll have to do everything ourselves now. But one of the slaves, my favorite, an old woman called Sarwan, she says she'll stay. My mother's still not happy; she says we'll have to pay Sarwan for her work and will have to ask her nicely to do things, or she won't do them. We won't be able to yell at her anymore, or order her around."

"That won't be so hard," I said.

Elanora grinned. "You don't know my mother," she said. "It'll be a huge challenge for her."

We finished the binding, and went and washed our hands. Already a new pack of instruments had been washed and set out on a tray for us, and Elanora brought them to the next person we would heal. For a moment I looked about the room, saw it orderly now, and clean. Many who had been treated had returned to their homes, but those who needed to stay for ongoing care were lying on mattresses in straight rows. Tables had been set up along the center of the room, with drinking water and bowls of washing water and plates of soap, and many piles of clean towels. No doubt many of the houses around had contributed what they could for our new hospital.

In the evening I told Elanora to go home and rest, for I would need her again in the morning. She went, but I worked on, helped by someone else. At some time in the night a Navoran soldier came to see me. I was sitting binding up a child's foot while a freed woman held a lamp for me.

"Take a rest," said the soldier. "It's after midnight."

"I'll finish here, first," I said.

"Don't argue. They're bringing cartloads of soldiers and warriors from the battlefield. The infirmary's overflowing and can't deal with them. There were thousands injured, many of them soldiers surrendering, trampled by the horses. People from the farms have roughly bound them up and stopped the worst bleeding, but these ones coming to us have had no proper medical care. Rest now, for a few hours at least. There are bedrooms upstairs. The people who owned this house have fled the city. Jaganath's supporters, probably." He grinned as he added, "Sleep in whichever bed you like, and enjoy the silk sheets."

I washed my hands and face and did as he said, for I was deadly tired. On the way to the stairs I passed the other rooms outside the one in which I had healed, and pushed open the doors. Inside, flooded over by moonbeams, were rows upon rows of people, most of them cleanly bandaged by now, lying on mattresses. Alone, Rhain still worked among them, his weary face golden in his lamplight. Slowly, I went up a long flight of stairs.

It was dark upstairs, and I had forgotten to bring a lamp. The first room I came to was small, with a bed near a wide window seat. I could see stars outside. For a while I sat by the window, looking out at the warm summer night and the three-quarter moon shining on the distant sea. The windows were of glass, and I pushed one open, and smelled the fresh, salt-laden air. From the city below I heard music, sometimes cheers, sometimes angry shouting. I thought of Embry and sent him peace. Ishtok, too, was in my mind—had been there all day, safe-wrapped in thought, protected by my powerful amulet, beloved. Smiling at the memory of his face, too tired to move, even to take off my bloodied clothes, I lay down where I was, peaceful, warm. I slept, and dreamed of a young boy with red-gold curls and eyes the color of a summer sky. He wore a carved Shinali bone, and his face was strong and beautiful.

The next morning I explored upstairs, looking for cupboards of clothes, so I could change into something clean. I found several other bedrooms, much grander than the one I had slept in, and a small room with enough clothes to dress a tribe. I found a simple long blue dress, and changed. I also found a splendid bathroom with marble walls and a large bath sunk into the floor. I did not know how to fill the bath, but I found a deep bowl full of cool water, and soaps, and had a wash.

Refreshed, I went downstairs and discovered that many of the ones I had healed yesterday had gone and been replaced by soldiers and tribal men and women from the battleground, the ones for whom there had been no room at the Navora Infirmary. Many had appalling injuries, and there were a large number who had been trampled and were near death.

I drank a cup of sweet Navoran tea and ate a small meal, then someone brought me a white apron to wear to protect my clothes, and a tray of cleaned instruments, and I began my work. Again, my faithful friend Elanora helped and stayed until afternoon's middle. I admired her a great deal, for the battleground injuries were not easy to look upon. The sufferers near death I released from pain, so they could go in peace to the shadow lands. I was grateful that there were many people from the surrounding houses to help, and those dying ones were not alone in their passing. Even young Navoran girls, barely more than thirteen summers, bravely sat with those who were dying, holding the hands of once-wild warriors. Elanora, too, was staunch, and only once, while we were healing, rushed out to get sick.

At last we finished mending all the people in that big room, and I thought, with a huge weariness and relief, that I had finished; but one of the surgeons came and told me to go to the courtyard outside, and that he would join me there shortly. In dread, I went. And there, with flies buzzing over them in the afternoon heat, were a hundred or more soldiers and tribesmen waiting to be healed. Some were in the shade, sprawled on the white stone steps, leaning against the pillars, or under the branches of the potted trees outside; others lay in the sun, flies crawling on their wounds and about their eyes and mouths. Already many of the wounds were infected, and people needing the toilet had gone where they were, unable to move. The stench was unbelievable. My heart went out to them, in pity; it was a day and a half since the battle, and they still awaited help.

Elanora looked desperately tired, and I suspected she had picked up a fever of some sort, from one of the soldiers. I told her to go and rest and was relieved when she did not argue, though I would sorely miss her help. I went into the house, had a few mouthfuls of food and a drink, got some clean instruments and bandages, then returned to the hot and fetid courtyard.

I do not know how I managed to carry on, except that sometimes, in the midst of that terrible suffering, there came to me a peace, a sense that I was not alone, that left me strengthened in my mind and in my body.

Some of the soldiers newly arrived brought news from the other parts of the city. One seasoned old Navoran fighter told me, as I picked bits of bone out of his shattered knee, that

Jaganath had been tried and executed yesterday.

"I heard that he was arrested by a slip of a girl," the soldier said, grinning at me through the flies buzzing about his face. He brushed them off, mingling blood with his sweat. "It's the biggest wonder of the last two days. Not sure I believe it, though."

"What other news can you tell me?" I asked, smiling.

"Jaganath's advisors and aides are in prison, awaiting trial for corruption, murder, and other felonies. That I do believe. There were more criminals ruling the city than there were in the prisons. I guess that'll change, now that Jaganath's been beheaded."

"There will be many changes," I said. "The Time of the Eagle is a new beginning for us all."

"True," he agreed, "and some of us in Navora have hoped for it. But there's a lot of fear. When they were bringing us in from the battleground, the road was jammed with rich Navorans fleeing with their family treasures, no doubt because they thought everything would be seized. Or maybe because they were Jaganath's supporters. They'll be in the ports along the coast by now, buying berths on ships bound for other countries. And I've heard there's rioting in parts of the city, and looting. There's an army commander in charge. He's put up proclamations saying that nothing will be confiscated, that people are to stay calm. This is a time of restoration, of liberty for everyone, including slaves, he says. I reckon that'll mean anything but liberty, for some Navorans, especially the rich. Some of them have never lifted a finger to help themselves. I'm glad my wife was always industrious. Has her own business, you know, weaving cloth. Always busy, even though she can't walk. Accident when she was a child." He added, with grim humor, "We're going to be a good pair, she and I. I don't suppose I'll be galloping about, either, when I get home."

I began binding splints about his knee. "Not for a few months," I said. "And then you'll be galloping with crutches."

He gazed intently into my face, curious. "You speak Navoran very well," he said. "I've been trying to figure out who you are. Slaves from Amaran have dark skin and blue or green eyes, but if you were a slave you wouldn't have these healing skills. I give up: where are you from?"

"I'm Shinali," I said.

"Shinali! My enemy! By God, wonders never cease! What's it like to stick spears in people one day, and sew them up the next?"

"I don't know," I said, finishing my work with him and standing. "I wasn't fighting yesterday. At least, not on the battleground you were on."

"Why aren't you on the Shinali land, with your people?"

"I am with my people," I said, and went to kneel by a stricken Hena warrior.

Evening came, and still I worked in the courtyard, while Navoran people from nearby houses brought pitchers of clean water and washed the instruments and tore up fresh bandages. Then lamps were brought, and I carried on. My hands shook, and I was terribly thirsty. Sometimes I was brought water to drink, and food, but I could not eat. At times in my weariness the suffering of those I healed seeped into my mind, and I had to shield myself against their pain. Sweat ran into my eyes, and I could barely see. I called for more lamps, and the flames drew big moths that fluttered about me while I worked. It was a long, long night.

The skies were growing gray when I heard voices at the gate, and thought more wounded were being brought in. Unutterably weary, I knelt by a Shinali woman with a Navoran arrow in her chest. Waves of her pain came over me, and I bent my head a moment, guarding myself. She was suffering horribly and I marveled that she had survived this long.

"I have to take the arrow out," I said. "I'll stop your pain first."

I glanced at her face, saw it smeared with blood and sweat and blue paint. Her hair was plastered across her eyes, and I lifted my hand to brush it aside. Then I saw who she was, and dismay and grief went over me. She was my friend Santoshi.

Moaning, whispering her name, I bent over and kissed her face. Lifting a hand, she touched my wrist. "Don't cry," she said, faintly. "I'll live. Zalidas said." Sweat poured down her, and her flesh was yellow gray and feverish.

Unable to stop my tears, I moved my hand over her face, around to the back of her neck, seeking out the great nerve pathways to her chest, her laboring heart. But I was weary, overwrought at seeing her like this, and my inner powers were faltering. At last her pain eased, and I placed my hands about the arrow shaft, ready to pull it out. A girl knelt close to me with a lamp, but she was looking away, shaking so much that the black shadows from the flame leaped and wavered, and I could hardly see. The arrow was deep, had gone in on an angle, piercing Santoshi's lung and, I suspected, also tearing her diaphragm and liver. Overwhelmed by the enormity of the healing she needed, I closed my eyes for a few moments and prayed for strength. When I looked up another pair of hands were about mine, steadying them. Old hands, strong and sure and beautiful, hands I knew and loved.

I raised my eyes. Salverion smiled, his serene old face radiant in the lamplight. "We'll heal this brave woman together," he said. "Then we can heal the rest, and after that you can sleep as many days as you like. The hardest work is almost done."

Tears rolled down my cheeks, and I brushed them away. "She's my friend," I said.

"I know, my dear." He put Santoshi into a deep sleep from which she would not wake, no matter what pain we caused, then placed his hands on the arrow shaft again, about mine. "Now," he said calmly, "on the count of three, we will withdraw this arrow. Are you ready?"

It took a long time, that healing, but throughout it Santoshi's heartbeat stayed strong. I noticed, over Salverion's shoulder, that the Navoran surgeons came in quiet moments to watch the Master, whispering among themselves, their faces awed.

While we worked, and Santoshi stayed in her deep sleep, Salverion told me, "I worked with your mother in the Navora Infirmary. She is well. When she knew I was coming to help you, she asked me to send you her love. So I do. They are very busy there, with more than two thousand wounded taken from the battleground. In the city I met the man in charge, Embry. A friend of yours, I believe. Sheel Chandra also sends you his fondest greetings. He is very tired, but well. He is staying with an old friend of his, a lawyer. The house is not far from here, actually. We have many friends in the city, people of integrity and wisdom, who will help Embry as he brings law and a new order. At the moment there's a fair bit of chaos, and Embry's had a hard two days."

"He would have been delighted to see you," I said.

Salverion laughed softly. "He welcomed us all as if we had come back from the dead. His pleasure at seeing us made me feel very humble. By the way, while I was with Embry I met a young Igaal man. He was wearing the amulet Sheel Chandra gave you, and spoke of you with great affection."

"Then you have met Ishtok," I said, smiling. "I gave him the amulet for protection. He cleared the way for me to go to Jaganath."

"I heard about that," Salverion said. "The whole city's talking about it, how Jaganath was taken prisoner by the daughter of his old enemy. Some say she took him all alone, using supreme powers her father gave her; others say that her father was with her, and they both stood in a light that was shining and unconquerable."

"I think the stories are both wrong," I said. "She took him with many great friends beside her. There were Salverion and Sheel Chandra and Taliesin and Chetobuh and Ishtok and Embry and . . . Well, it's a long, long list."

"A long list, indeed," he said, his eyes sparkling. "Jaganath didn't stand a chance."

The sun rose in the clear blue skies, and the courtyard grew hot. Salverion and I finished our work on Santoshi, and she came through it well. Before we left she opened her eyes and thanked us, and a girl brought a drink for her. "Have Santoshi taken into the house, and put in a clean bed," I said. "Stay with her every moment. If her pain returns, call me."

I knelt and kissed Santoshi's face again, and Salverion and I together said a prayer over her, then we turned to the others who still needed help. Some of the wounded soldiers, realizing who Salverion was, touched his robe as he went past, then lay back, wonder on their faces. During that bright morning the Navoran surgeons came one by one to Salverion, taking his hand in the Navoran way, and giving him words of welcome and love. One of them, speechless with emotion, simply knelt at his feet, and was lifted up and embraced.

Rhain said to me, during a brief break for food and water, "You seem to know each other well, you and the Master. They say that he and the others from the Citadel were living in the mountains, in an old hidden city they called Ravinath. A place that might have been found by a Shinali woman, in her wanderings."

"It was a place that found me," I said.

He grinned and said, "Well, that explains a mighty lot of things."

It was past noon when everyone in the courtyard had been tended to. Salverion and I washed our hands, took off our filthy aprons, and ate a meal. I was weary to the point of dizziness, and Salverion's hands shook—something I had never seen before.

"I've found a little room to sleep in," I said as I helped him up the stairs. He was pale, and we rested twice on the long stairway. "It has a bed, and a window seat. I'm happy with the window seat, and you can have the silk sheets."

"I'm so tired," he said, leaning on me, "that a pile of straw in a horse stall would be heaven, right now."

In the little room, I pulled back the sheets on the bed for

Salverion and helped him on. I removed his shoes and covered him. I thought he fell asleep immediately, and kissed his cheek before I lay down on the sunny cushioned seat under the window. But as I closed my eyes he said, "I know this house, Avala. I've been here before."

"It must have been a long time ago," I said.

"It was," he said. "I remember it for the big mural in the entrance hall, of the ships moored at the wharf. The house was owned by a very famous sailor and merchant. I came here to deliver a parchment scroll to his son, a letter to say that he had been chosen to train as a healer with me, at the Citadel."

I sat up, staring at him through the sunbeams. "This is my father's home?"

"It was. His mother sold it not long after he came to us, and bought her farm on the edge of your Shinali lands. But this was Gabriel's childhood home."

I lay down again, lost in wonderment. "I dreamed about him last night," I said. "He was a young boy. He was wearing a Shinali amulet."

"It was not merely a dream," said Salverion. "He did wear a Shinali amulet. He never took it off."

I said, very low, "Jaganath told me about it. He said my father stole it, that he helped my people because of guilt. He told me things about my father that I don't believe. Things I don't want to believe. But my mother said that my father had a secret that he never told her. Do you think he had a secret guilt? That he stole the amulet?"

Salverion said, "A secret guilt? Perhaps. We all have our secrets, our guilts. I don't know how your father got the Shinali amulet,

Avala. But I do know this: that the amulet became a driving force in his life, forging his dreams, changing his heart, setting him on that high road to his great destiny among your people. How he got that amulet, whether he stole it or was given it, is not important. It came to him, was meant to be his, and that is all that matters. And there's another thing I know, which I must tell you quickly before I fall asleep: Jaganath will have done his utmost to rob you of your love for your father, which is one of the great driving forces in your life. Don't let it be said that the old goat succeeded."

"He didn't," I said.

Two heartbeats later Salverion snored, and I smiled to myself, and waited for sleep. But although I was unutterably tired, the stillness of the great house, the smell of its polished wood and stone, the memories locked within its walls, kept me awake. A long time I gazed at the wooden ceiling with its shining beams, knowing that my father, too, had looked up as I had done and listened to the silence, and dreamed his fine Shinali dreams.

32

I have been thinking lately of my childhood, and the home we had,
and of the things that shaped me into the person I am. You know,
Mother, that from childhood I have felt a bond with the Shinali
people. I cannot tell you what first began that bond, but it became
the strongest thing in my life, stronger even than the desire to heal.
It was a bond that drew me to their land, to Ashila. With her the
bond became love, sublime and beautiful and above all else.
The Shinali have a prophecy about an age to come, called
the Time of the Eagle. The prophecy is also known in Navora,
by a few brave enough to believe in it, the Empress Petra
among them. I have a feeling that the time is close. If I can
do anything to bring about the Eagle's Time, to bring
to Ashila true and total freedom, to make restitution
for what my nation has done to hers, then I will do it gladly.

—Excerpt from a letter from Gabriel to his mother,
kept and later gifted to Avala

All the next day Salverion and I worked, and near evening
Elanora returned. She still looked pale, but she said she
was well, and that there was something in the city I needed to go
and see. She added, seeing my worried look, "It's not work, Avala,
it's something wonderful. I've asked Rhain if you can go with
me, and he said you must. But you'll need to wash, and change
your dress."

So I did as she suggested, and soon she was leading me through
the streets. Gradually our way became more and more crowded,
and before long we were pressed in by a large multitude all going
in the same direction as ourselves. There was an air of festivity,

of great excitement and anticipation. I asked Elanora where we were going, but she only smiled and held on to my arm tightly, so we would not lose each other in the throng. It was sunset, and the huge pillared buildings of the inner city soared rose colored against the skies, and the shining white stone of the towers and domes seemed almost translucent. Up wide flights of steps we went, along streets lined with pillars, and under noble arches so high and graceful it amazed me that human beings had built them. Sometimes Elanora pointed out splendid buildings and called their names to me, but I could hardly hear her, for the noise of the crowd.

We came at last to a vast open space, the city square, and there we all stopped, pressed close in a gathering that must have numbered many thousands. In front of us was an imposing white building reached by a short flight of stairs, and at the top of the stairs was a wide space like a stage, lit by fiery torches. By then it was almost dark, and the torchlight glimmered red on the pillars all around, and on the faces of those around me. For the first time I studied the people about me and saw that they were from many nations. I saw Hena with mud-caked hair rubbing shoulders with Navorans and smiling at them, and people from my own tribe pressed close with Igaal warriors. There were fathers with children in their arms, and young people from many nations smiling shyly together, or trying to talk with gestures, admiring one another's painted clothes or jewelry. I glimpsed Shinali friends, and waved to them, but we could not reach one another, for the closeness of the crowd.

Suddenly a great hush fell, and I looked up over the hundreds of people in front of me and saw two people walk onto the lamp-lit floor at the top of the wide white stairs. One of the people was my beloved Sheel Chandra, and when the Navorans in the crowd recognized him, they went wild with cheering. A long time the cheering and applause went on, and Sheel Chandra waited, humble and gracious, in tears, his face alight with that beautiful smile of his. For him, too, this was a time of freedom, of coming home. At last he lifted his arms, and people fell quiet. Then he beckoned to the person with him, an Igaal boy about ten summers old, and he stood with the child before him, his hands on the lad's small shoulders, and said, "Thank you. Thank you, and welcome. I am Sheel Chandra, and my young Igaal friend here is called Olikodi. He is now free, but he was a slave for many seasons, and learned to speak Navoran well. He will interpret my words for those who cannot understand them."

The lad interpreted the words so far, his voice high and clear in the calm night. Then Sheel Chandra welcomed us, naming each nation represented, and made his speech. And while he spoke there was a light about him more than the light from the burning torches, more than the light of the stars, and I think each one of us watching must have been aware of it, for there was not a stir, not a murmur, in all that huge gathering. Sheel Chandra spoke about the Time of the Eagle and how it was a time for a new beginning, a time for peace and tolerance, a time for love. He also spoke of forgiveness. It was a beautiful speech, simple and profound, and he ended with the words, "Forgiveness is not a feeling, but an act. There is a very great thing I would ask each of you to do: I ask that you turn to a person near you who is not of your nation, and greet them, and wish them peace."

For a few moments no one moved, and the stillness seemed immense. Then a beautiful thing happened. Every single person in our great company turned to someone next to them and spoke a simple greeting—and not only spoke, but embraced them as if they were kin, and kissed their cheeks. All through that huge city square, under the stars, it happened over and over again—the quiet embracement, the kiss of peace, and not just once for each person, but many times, until we all had shown this tiny act of forgiveness and love to many of those who once had been our enemies. It was more than Sheel Chandra had asked, more than I would have dreamed possible; it was a holy thing, an impulse of hearts, true and powerful and unforgettable.

At last we all were still and very quiet, and Sheel Chandra spoke a prayer. Then he left, holding the Igaal boy by the hand, and the flaming lamps were put out. Into the covering dark came the sound of Shinali pipes, heartrending and beautiful, and soon they were joined by Navoran instruments, and then a woman's voice. A tiny light moved in the darkness at the top of the stairs; we saw the singer, a young Hena woman carrying a small lamp. Still she sang, her voice pure and strong and incredibly lovely. There was another light, another voice, and an Igaal man joined her, and then a Navoran woman singing. Other singers came, bearing other lights, and their voices wound about one another in the night, rich and harmonious.

After the singers the lamps were lit again, and some Navorans danced to Igaal drums, and it was wild and wonderful, and strangely like our own Shinali dances. Elanora whispered to me that it was the famous Navoran fire-dance, performed by the most renowned dancers in the Empire. Then there were the finest dancers from my Shinali people, and from the Hena and Igaal; and the drums throbbed and the music filled the night, and all of us watching clapped and stamped, and sometimes the dancing was so breathtaking that we all cried out without knowing that we did, and we applauded and called and whistled until our voices were hoarse and our arms ached.

After the dancers came more singers, and some of the musicians from Ravinath. There was glorious music, chanting, and songs so sublime they made many of us weep. Some of the words we could not understand, for the singers were ex-slaves from far countries, singing the old folk songs they had loved. I remember one song a young girl sang that was so hauntingly poignant that, when I looked around at the people about me, I saw that they all were swaying in time to her song, lost in the wonder of it, bound by its beauty. It was wonderful to see that freedom of the slaves, not only the freedom of their bodies, but also the freedom of their souls, which let them sing again, and sing with joy.

It was an awesome night, and I hold it in my knowing as one of the finest of my life. My only wish was that I had been with Ishtok, and I hoped that he was there somewhere, for I wanted with all my heart to share it with him.

Afterward, without speaking but with our arms about each other's waists, Elanora and I went back to the house that had been my father's; then she went on to her own home, while I went upstairs to my little room to sleep.

But until dawn I lay awake, marveling at what I had witnessed, at what I had been a part of; for I knew that what I had seen was unique in the troubled history of our world, and that centuries of injustice and hate had at last been transcended by love, and the Navoran Empire was forever changed.

Eight days I stayed in the hospital in my father's childhood home, for a fever broke out among the sick, and we were afraid that it might spread to the rest of the city. Salverion kept checking people's mouths for signs of the bulai fever, which was so deadly, but he found no evidence of it. Those who had no fever, and had someone to look after them, were sent home, and all those from the courtyard were carried inside. Santoshi steadily got well, and the fever passed her by, but she could not be moved and stayed in the hospital. I had someone with her constantly, though she chided me, with the old smile I remembered, for giving her special care.

Slowly the sick who remained got well, but it was a busy time. I heard that my mother still worked in the Navora Infirmary, where they, too, battled fever among their patients. Sometimes people brought me messages from her, verbal assurances that she was well, and full of joy to be healing with an amazing man called Taliesin. But mostly, during the fever-days, visitors were not allowed, in case of bulai fever, and we were cut off from the rest of the city. I thought so often of Ishtok, and longed to see his face again.

During this time I went to visit Sheel Chandra, still staying not far away, with his friend. I found him sitting in a chair in the sun, resting, looking out across a garden of fountains and statues and potted trees and flowers. He looked frail, yet his arms were strong as we embraced each other, and I spent a blissful hour sitting at his feet the way I had in Ravinath, my head on his knee.

We talked of that amazing night in the city square, with its profound healing and harmony, and of how the whole city had been changed. But I sensed a sorrow in him, and he told me that over the past two days he had been called upon to act as one of the twelve judges at the trials of Jaganath's supporters and family. "There have been many executions," he said. "I grieve for the guilty, Avala. They knew no better, some of them. Others had acted out of fear of Jaganath. But they all had committed terrible crimes—all, save one. One we allowed to go free. She was Syana, Jaganath's youngest daughter. I believe your father healed her, many years ago, when she was a little girl. She was the only one who defied her father on behalf of the slaves, and had suffered for it. As for the rest . . . I can only say I'm glad it's over. Now begins a new order. Arrangements are being made for the people of Navora to elect a Council of Seven, who will jointly rule the Empire in the future. They wanted me to put my name forward for election, but I declined." He sighed, though a sudden humor leaped in his great dark eyes. "I'm getting too old for all this excitement, Avala," he said. "I want peace. I want to go back to the Citadel. But there's much work to be done there, too. Salverion and I went there the other day. All this time it's been neglected, the gardens gone to ruin, the vineyards overgrown. The place is damp, the murals on the walls are cracked and peeling, the floors covered with leaves and dust, the fountains full of slime. It made my old heart break. It will be restored, but that will take time."

"I have heard that the Citadel was once even more glorious than the Navoran palace," I said.

"It was. And it will be again. But it will be different, this time.

We used to have very strict rules there, Avala. Only men for disciples, and they were not permitted to visit their friends or families for seven years, except in dire emergencies. We demanded total dedication, perhaps unfairly. This time there will be women as well as men taught there, and husbands may live there with their wives, and people will be able to visit their families as often as they wish. There will be gifted disciples chosen not only from the Navoran Empire but also from the tribes, from the Hena, and Igaal, and Shinali. It will be a great day, when we open its doors to all."

Then we talked of other things, of Jaganath, and my battle-hour with him. We spoke about Ishtok, and the Shinali. Sheel Chandra told me that the bloodied land was cleared of battle signs, the funeral pyres had finished burning, and a new Shinali house was being built, a single large underground dwelling like the last, with a thatched roof.

"I found out something about your Navoran grandmother, and your Shinali land," Sheel Chandra said. "Years ago, when the Navoran authorities put the land up for sale, she bought over half of it and persuaded her farmer neighbors to buy the rest, so that the plain could be kept free for when the Shinali returned. She's a far-sighted and wise woman. And a brave one."

"I look forward to meeting her," I said.

Sheel Chandra began to look very tired, and I stood up to go. As I kissed his cheek I said, "I could have accomplished nothing without you. I can never thank you enough for everything you've done, for everything you are to me."

"You thank me just by being in my life," he said, smiling.

* * *

438

Kneeling down by the mattress, I put my arm about the shoulders of a Navoran soldier and raised his head so he could drink. His fever had almost gone, but he was very weak, and I held the cup against his lips while he drank. Afterward, I laid him down and smoothed the bandage about his head, slipping my hand behind his neck to ease the pain that still lingered. He smiled a little and thanked me.

"When will you go, Avala?" he asked. "It's ten days since the battle. Salverion's gone off to clean up the Citadel, and everything's peaceful in the city. Surely you must want to go to your own land. My cousin came to see me this morning, from his farm on the edge of your land, and he said they've finished the Shinali house."

"I'll go soon," I replied.

I stood up and stepped between the orderly rows of mattresses with the people resting in the sun, with clean white sheets over them. Some reached out to me as I passed, asking for water or relief from pain, and I knelt to help. Others simply smiled or greeted me by name. Many of them talked quietly together or read or played Navoran games given to them by the people of the city. I saw a young soldier and an Igaal youth playing a Navoran dice game, their heads bathed in sunlight, one head flaxen, one dark. They were laughing. In a joyful kind of peace, I went out into the wide entranceway, past the huge mural of the ships. In the doorway I stopped.

Ishtok stood there in the porch, leaning on a pillar, waiting. His back was to me, and I did not recognize him at first, for he wore a green Navoran tunic over narrow white trousers, and a wide leather belt studded with jewels. His gleaming blue-black hair curled over his collar. Hearing me, he turned around. For long moments we looked at each other.

I went out and stood in front of him, close, and touched my hand to my chest, and then laid it on his breast. I could feel the beating of his heart. "My heart and yours are in harmony," I said.

He covered my hand with his own, holding it there. He smelled of flowers and smoke, and he looked excellent and fine. Lifting his other hand, he stroked my face, his touch full of tenderness. Suddenly he gave a low, hoarse cry, and kissed me. Long, long, we kissed, until someone whistled behind me, and then there were other whistles, and hoots, and cheers. The kiss finished to a burst of applause, and, still in Ishtok's arms, I turned around. About fifteen soldiers and warriors stood in the entranceway, leaning on their crutches or on one another, watching us.

"Well, it looks like we're about to lose our favorite healer," said one of the soldiers to his companions, with a wide smile. "Guess we can all throw away our crutches now, and confess we've been well for days, and trot off home."

They all laughed, and I took Ishtok's hand and introduced him to everyone. They all welcomed him, then went back inside. Only a Hena boy stayed, and I realized he knew Ishtok well, for they hugged, glad to see each other.

"Have my people gone home without me?" the boy asked, and Ishtok shook his head. "Some of your people, and some of mine, have stayed on the Shinali land, to wait for you injured ones. They wanted to come and see you but were told there was a fever here, and they could not. But never fear; they won't leave without you."

Rhain came to the porch, and I introduced Ishtok to him. As he shook Ishtok's hand the Navoran way, Rhain said to me, "Well, I guess we'll just have to struggle on without you now, Avala."

"I'll go only when I'm not needed here," I said.

"We'll never stop needing healers like you," he said, with a smile. "Go to your own people, Avala, with our blessing. You have done over and above all that we could have asked. But say good-bye to everyone before you leave."

So I did, and Ishtok came with me, shaking hands, talking with Hena and Igaal people he knew, waiting while I embraced people and said my good-byes. I had not realized how fond I had become of these ones I had healed, who had been a part of the whole great healing of Navora. Lastly, I said farewell to Santoshi and told her she would be well looked after, until she was strong enough to be taken to our people; and I thanked the surgeons, and Elanora, who had come back and worked untiringly.

Then Ishtok and I linked our fingers and, walking close, went down the white stone steps of the healing-place that had been my father's house, and left for the Shinali land, and home.

We made the journey home on Ishtok's horse, for it was more than fourteen miles to the Shinali land from the city, and I rode behind him, with my arms about his waist. It was bliss, that ride, and many times I hugged him, my cheek pressed against his back. He allowed the horse to walk, and as we passed through the city toward the main gates we went by terraced houses with red tiled roofs and white towers splendid and shining in the sun. We went through marketplaces with their bright awnings over stalls piled with fruit and vegetables, and once Ishtok dismounted to buy some apples for us. He gave the man gold for the fruit, and when I asked where he had got it from, he said, grinning, "Your mother. She has the most amazing stash of Navoran gold. Said it was your father's."

Laughing, munching on the apples, we went on through the Navoran streets, the horse's hooves making a tranquil clip-clop on the cobbles. The streets were peaceful, and people walking there often greeted us or waved and seemed surprised when I answered them in Navoran, wishing them peace. Sometimes we were overtaken by horses pulling fine chariots, and we drew aside as they clattered past, bounding over the stones.

"The center of the city is a high lot grand," Ishtok told me as we went down the wide sloping street to the gates, where the houses were small and plain. "I've been there most of the time, going to the houses with messages from Embry, telling people not to be afraid and what was happening, and who to ask if they wanted information. Many of the people were afraid, thinking we'd rise up and kill them all, and take their city for ourselves. Atitheya has been busy, too, interpreting. He knows enough Navoran now to be a help. We've been living at the palace." He turned and smiled at me over his shoulder, and added, "I've been sleeping in a Navoran bed, with slippery blankets. And I've swum in an inside lake, naked."

"I see you've helped yourself to some Navoran clothes, too," I said.

"Embry gave us all new clothes, since we had only the clothes we wore to battle, and most of those were stained with blood. He's got a lot of gold, too. Jaganath's. He's put someone he trusts in charge of it, so it won't be stolen or wasted. Much of it will be given to the hundreds of slaves who still remain, either to pay for their voyages to their own countries, or to set themselves up in homes and businesses here, if they wish. But he's also bought us what we need."

"Well, the green tunic suits you," I said. "Imagine it. Mudiwar's son, living in the palace at Navora."

"Not anymore," he said. "We've got a Shinali house to sleep in, tonight."

"What's it like, our house?"

"Very big. It's the size of six of our tents put together. My father is most impressed. He and Yeshi are good friends now, and my father's given him his most valuable horse."

"He's still here, your father?"

"Him, and one or two others."

"Who?"

"You'll see. Your mother's at the house, too. She went there last night. And all the Shinali elders and children, who stayed in the cave in the mountains during the battle, they're there now. Everyone's home, Avala, waiting for you."

We passed between the high city gates, broken now, and out onto the wide stone road leading up to the massive Navora Infirmary. The infirmary was gigantic, its mighty dome gleaming against the hills beyond. High towers, also domed, flanked the steps up to the vast porch. Past the infirmary was a road lined with trees, that led to another towered building, smaller, very elegant. Then the road began winding through hills, and we passed trees and orchards and gardens where waterways glinted in the sun. We went over a bridge, then the road divided into two; it went left toward the farms and our land, and bore right past a stone with a word carved on it: CITADEL. Across the hills, over the treetops, we glimpsed towers as white as milk. The sight of them tugged at my heart, and I thought of Salverion there, and Sheel Chandra, and all the others I loved, making it their home again.

The road was no longer paved but was beaten dust. As we went on we saw a cart coming toward us, drawn by four white horses. A beautiful cart it was, painted blue, and covered with white cloth marked with silver stars. Six men guarded it, one wearing a long robe of crimson.

"Delano!" I cried, almost falling off Ishtok's horse, in my excitement.

Delano and I dismounted, and hugged, laughing. "Well, what a welcome!" he said. "We're on our way to the Citadel, with the first cartload of treasures from Ravinath. Some of the books. And we've delivered something for you, to your Shinali house."

"Thank you. Oh, it's good to see you again!" I said. Turning to Ishtok, I said, in Navoran, "This man, Delano, makes the best words in the world. Delano, this is Ishtok, the best carver among all the tribes."

The poet and carver shook hands the Navoran way, then Delano said, "You must come and visit us at the Citadel, both of you, when we have it back in order. We'd be honored if you would bring some of your carving to show us, Ishtok. We've seen one thing of yours: the cup Avala used at Ravinath. I know many of us would like to see more."

We said farewells, and he went on with his treasures to his restored home, and Ishtok and I went on to ours. Not far ahead were fields of wheat, and walled pastures where cattle and sheep grazed. As we passed the farms, it was hard to believe that a place so peaceful could have seen, not many days before, the passing of thousands of warriors and soldiers. There was no sign of them now, except that the low walls to the pastures were broken in places, and some of the land was trampled where the road had been too narrow for the great throng that had passed through. We went along between fields of wheat, and then I saw it: my land, and my people at home there.

In silence, I dismounted, and took off my shoes, for this was sacred soil, bought with a dream and a prophecy, paid for with blood. Ishtok got down and walked beside me.

At first the ground was trampled, grass and churned soil made dark by blood, and as we crossed a little bridge I could see, out on the northern side of the river, dark mounds of stones where funeral fires had been. But as I walked, the land became as it was the day Ishtok and I had walked on it, so long ago, before Ravinath; across the river was the garden with its brave Shinali flag and before us was our new Shinali house.

So peaceful it was, with only its thatched roof visible above the ground, and a smoke-hole with smoke going up, blue and straight into the cloudless skies. Women washed clothes in the river, and some men were cutting up a deer. Sheep grazed farther out on the plain, but about the house hens scratched and clucked. A goat was trying to eat the thatched roof and was chased off by children. Beyond the house were herds of horses, and a large

Igaal tent, and many smaller pointed army tents painted with Hena designs. But the most wonderful dwelling of all was the Shinali house, golden on the land, not on it but within it, a part of the earth we had lived for.

In tears, choked up with joy, I took Ishtok's hand. "It's beautiful!" I said.

Then people saw us and began calling for my mother and for Yeshi.

And, oh, the ecstasy! I cannot even begin to tell of it—of the welcome they gave me, my mother, looking young again, radiant, back on the land on which she had met and loved my father, and fought for twice; and Yeshi, and my grandmother, and old Zalidas, crying in his joy, taking both my hands and kissing them, and blessing me; then there was Ramakoda, his smile fairly splitting his face, coming to give me a hug that nearly broke my ribs; and he brought his sons to meet me, twin boys ten summers old, well and fine, and freed at last from their captivity. One was the lad who had interpreted for Sheel Chandra on that great night of celebration in Navora. There was Mudiwar, trying to look dignified, making the formal Igaal welcome, then giving up and embracing me; and Chimaki, and little Kimiwe, and Chetobuh, gentle and smiling and almost healed; then the Hena came, led by Atitheya, solemn as he welcomed me the Hena way, with a kiss on each cheek and on my forehead. I met the Hena priest, Sakalendu, to whom I owed, for his prophetic dreams, the preparation of the Hena tribes for the Eagle's time, and who greeted me with honor and with warmth, as a fellow-seer. Lastly, there were the greetings from the freed slaves, people I did not know, who loved me. I was in tears by the end of it, overcome.

446

Then, with my mother on one side and Ishtok on the other, with all the people standing around, silent, glad, I was taken to the Shinali house. Ishtok took off his boots, but my mother and I were already barefoot. Then we went down the earthen steps into the cool dimness inside.

The interior was huge, almost an arrow flight across, beautiful; a home large enough for all my tribe. The excavated walls were lined with mats woven of flax, worked with stunning designs. Above our heads, high curving wooden beams held up the thatch, and the floor was covered with carpets from Mudiwar's people. The central fire was edged with a wide hearth of flat river-stones, on which stood silver bowls, gorgeous pottery, and jars of fine Navoran knives and spoons. Around the walls of the house, on a raised platform, were the beds, many spread with rich Navoran rugs, and colorful tasseled cushions for pillows. Wooden chests, also gifts from Mudiwar, stood at the foot of many of the beds. At the foot of one bed, not far from Yeshi's, was my wooden chest from Ravinath. And above the place where Yeshi slept, shining on the flaxen walls, were our tribe's treasures: my father's sword, and the letter from the Empress Petra.

A long time I walked around, looking, marveling, admiring. Then I went and put my arms around my mother. "So this is the dream," I said, "the home you all wanted to return to."

She laughed. "It was never quite this grand before," she said. "The farmers helped us build our house, and the people of Navora sent cartloads of blankets and food and clothes, and cooking things. Mudiwar sent word to the women minding the Igaal children during the battle day, and they came, bringing the carpets and the chests. Embry sent us wonderful things from the palace, which he said were a small compensation for what had been stolen from us, times past. We have more now than we ever had before—and peace, with it." A sorrow came into her eyes and she added, softly, "There is only one thing missing."

I thought of the presence that had led me in the catacombs, of the moments of rare peace and empowerment that I had known these last days; and I said, with absolute certainty, "He has not been missing, Mother."

Ishtok and I sat by the river, our backs against a tree, and looked across the land. A night wind blew, bringing the smell of smoke from our feasting-fire. The people were still sitting about it, and the firelight made their shadows leap across the ground and dance over the low thatched roof. We could hear laugher, and snatches of pipes and songs came to us through the smoky air. Past the house, across the place where the battle had been, winked the lights of the farmhouses. Above, the stars were brilliant, and Erdelan hung low over the Citadel hills, close to the round and rising moon.

"When my mother and I were with Grandmother Lena, today," I said, "she told us she was the one who had made the garden here on our land, where the old Shinali house had been. She placed the banner over the garden, as a sign that the land was ours and that one day we would return."

"How did she know your Shinali dream-sign?" Ishtok asked.

"When my people lived here before, after my parents had met and my father had returned to the Citadel, Lena sent her younger children to our Shinali house with blankets and gifts. My mother sent back a gift for my father, a dream-sign made of grass, and told the children to be very sure to pass on the meaning of it. That was how Lena knew what the dream-sign was, and what it meant. She wanted to be friends with the Shinali. When my people were imprisoned in Taroth Fort, she took them medicines and fresh food. Only one time she was permitted to visit, and it was the first time she met my mother, and the last time she ever saw my father. She also met Tarkwan, our great chieftain. I feel that I have known Lena a long time, and not just from today. I already love her well. She's wanting me to take you, next time I visit her. What did you do while I was there?"

"I looked at carvings from Ravinath. Three more carts came through on their way to the Citadel, with stone carvings wrapped in cloth. They stopped and let me look at one of them. It was a white stone image of a boy, a high lot beautiful. I would give anything to be able to carve like that. Especially stone. I'm looking forward to carving again, when I have time of my own. When I don't carve, I feel that I don't breathe."

"Time of our own," I said, sighing. "How long since we've had that!"

"What will you do, tomorrow?" he asked.

"Tomorrow I'm going to walk right around the edge of our Shinali land."

"It's a long way to walk," he said. "It's not just this plain anymore. It's all yours again, Embry said—all the land from the west coast to the Napangardi Mountains, to the northern lakes. If the Navorans want to keep the crops and herds they've got there, they'll have to pay you for the use of the land."

"Perhaps I'd better ride, then," I said, "and see only part of our land tomorrow. I'd love you to come with me. Have you finished helping Embry in the city?"

"Yes, I'm free now."

"That's a truth."

He laughed softly, his breath tickling my ear. I was sitting with my back to him, leaning against him. He was holding me, and my arms were over his. I could feel the fine smooth material of his Navoran sleeves, and the jeweled cuffs.

I asked, "What will you be doing, now that you are free?"

"I'll go riding with you."

"I wasn't meaning just tomorrow. I was meaning after that." I added, suddenly unsure, with a rush of apprehension, "When your tribe leaves. What will you do then?"

He took a deep breath. "There's a woman I love," he said. "Part Shinali, but mostly Navoran. A long time have I loved her. But she had a high destiny, a work to do. When last we spoke of it, she was not sure what that work was, and I'm not sure now if it's finished. I told her, once, that if she wanted me she would have to speak first, to say when she was ready. I'm still waiting."

"I think the first part of her work, the task to do with the Time of the Eagle, is complete," I said. "The rest of her work is to be a healer. I think she is ready, now, for the man she loves."

"She only thinks she is? Can she not be more certain?"

"Very well," I said. "Will you be my husband, Ishtok, son of Mudiwar?"

"Shimit's teeth, Avala!" he cried, jerking upright, so I almost fell on the grass. "That was my arrow, to shoot! I only wanted a little encouragement!"

450

I rolled on the ground, laughing, and he fell on top of me, holding me down, chuckling while he kissed my neck. Then he kissed my face, my eyes, my mouth. I put up my hand and covered his lips with my fingers. "No more kissing," I said.

"Why not?"

"Because you haven't answered my question."

Raising his head, he looked down on me, his eyes glimmering in the shadow of his hair.

"I, Ishtok, son of Mudiwar," he said, "agree to be your husband, Avala, daughter of Ashila of the Shinali and Gabriel of Navora—on one condition. I must be allowed to live here with you, on your Shinali land, near the stone city."

"Why that condition?" I asked.

"Because I want you to know that you don't have to come and live with me in my father's tent. I already have two tribes, two homelands; another won't make much difference. But you—you have waited all your life to be here. Here, on this land, and in the stone city, your heart belongs. So this is where we'll stay, if you wish. Wherever in the world you are, that is my home."

"You're a rare man, my beloved," I said.

"That's very nice, but is the ban on kissing finished?"

"No, not just yet," I said, my eyes beyond him, on something marvelous. "Keep very still, Ishtok. Don't move. Ah—it's wonderful!"

"What? I haven't done anything, yet."

"The moon! You have the full moon sitting exactly on your right shoulder."

He smiled. "How blessed I am!" he said. "The moon on my right shoulder, and the sun within my arms."

451

"You haven't got the sun within your arms, Ishtok; you've got me."

"I've got my day-star, my light, the reason for my life," he said, and gave me a kiss that left me breathless.

My mother put the garland of wheat and wildflowers on my hair, and retied the sash about my waist. I was wearing a Navoran dress, tawny gold for joy, with a crimson sash for love. The front of the dress was threaded up with dark blue cord, and the sides were slashed to the thigh. I wore a white Igaal skirt under it, the most beautiful I had seen, patterned deep in the hem with exquisite cut-out designs. About my neck was a Shinali necklace of bone, wondrously carved, that had belonged to Yeshi's only sister, who had died many years ago, and which had not been worn since, until now. With the necklace I also wore Sheel Chandra's amulet, which Ishtok had returned to me.

My mother held me at arm's length, looking me over carefully. At last she said, with tears in her eyes, "You are beautiful, my love. Turn around, show yourself to your grandmother."

I turned, and my grandmother nodded as if satisfied, and came and kissed my cheek. Over her shoulder, I saw the other old women of the tribe, their faces smiling, full of love.

From outside the house came the low sound of many people

talking. I knew the feasting-mats would be laid out, the feast pre-pared, dishes of gold and silver from Navora spread out upon the flax. And there would be another mat, the most beautiful of all Igaal carpets, out on a flat place by the river, where Mudiwar's family would be standing, waiting. And a young man would be standing with them, waiting for me.

I turned again and faced the door, and my mother. I trembled a little, but only from joy.

"Are you ready?" my mother asked.

"I am ready," I said, and we walked up into the radiant even-ing light.

Silence fell, and people stood up and looked toward me. All along the riverbank, and out onto the plain, were fires, and the feasting-mats. And the people—so many there were! There was half a Hena tribe, and all of Mudiwar's family as well as the Shinali. So dignified they looked, in their beautiful painted and patterned leather garments, their best. There were Salverion and Sheel Chandra and Taliesin, and others from the Citadel, their long robes splendid in the setting sun. There was Embry and many of his soldiers, impressive in full uniform, and there were people from the farms, among them my Navoran grandmother and her family.

As I approached, the people all parted, and I walked between them to the mat by the river. I was barely aware of those all around, of the flames, the fiery skies above; there was only that long walk across the shining grass, to him.

In that great silence I came to him, and he was standing with the sun's last light full on him. Fine he was, in his Igaal garments of palest deerskin, and with the garland of wheat and flowers upon his hair. He, too, wore a Navoran sash, crimson like mine, and his boots were Hena boots, painted with elaborate designs. Smiling, he held out his hand, and I went to him. He pressed his brow to mine in the Igaal greeting, then we both sat down on the carpet, facing each other, our hands touching.

There was a rustle of garments as all the people sat down, except for the priest, Zalidas, beside us, and Mudiwar behind Ishtok, and my mother behind me.

Then Zalidas sang a prayer, his voice wavering in the bright evening wind. When the prayer was finished he came and said a blessing over each of us, then placed two bowls on the mat between us. In one was a piece of bread, symbol of homeliness and earthly life. In the other was a yellow sauce mixed with bitter herbs and sweetened with wild honey, symbol of forgiveness of past hurts, of love, and acceptance of whatever the All-father might bring to our lives. Ishtok broke off a piece of the bread, dipped it in the sauce, and put it into my mouth. I ate, then fed him. The bowls were taken away, and it was time for us to make our promises to each other. They were simple words, heavy with meaning, and we had them strong in our knowing. I spoke first.

"Ishtok, son of Mudiwar, I promise to hold your dreams, your happiness, your heart's peace, as high in importance as my own. I will help you to become the person you were born to be, free and strong and true. This I swear, in the All-father's Name."

He made the same promise to me, only promising he would help me to become the woman I was born to be.

Then Zalidas said to all those present: "People who love Avala and Ishtok, will you promise to help them keep their vows to each other, and to make their home a place of peace; and when their children come, to help teach and guide them as if they were your own?"

All the people said, in one voice, "We swear it."

A tray was brought with Zalidas's holy painting-things. I put out my left hand, palm down, and Ishtok put out his, beside mine. A sacred thread was wrapped about our hands, and then Zalidas painted signs on the backs of our wrists. Tomorrow, the signs would be tattooed into our skin, our marriage-signs, there for as long as we lived. Our signs were identical: an eagle within a circle, signifying freedom and strength, and the perfect fullness of time. As Zalidas painted the signs the sun sank lower, turning the wet black paint on our wrists to the color of fire.

As the stars came out Zalidas sang the final prayer. An old Shinali benediction he sang, a thanks for all things, and this time his voice soared, mingling with the music of the river and the sound of the wind as it swept across our land, and all of us who knew the song joined our voices with his, and the prayer became an anthem of triumph and of peace. Long after we stopped singing, the song seemed to hang in the air, transcendent and sublime.

Then Ishtok put his arms about me and kissed me, and we were wed.

My mother was the first to congratulate us, then old Mudiwar, and Grandmother Lena. After that everyone else came up, and Ishtok and I had never been so embraced and kissed in our lives. There were so many people, I cannot name them all—every one of them precious to me, every one of them having played a part in my life, and made me who I am. Ishtok and I were still greeting friends when the drums sounded, telling us that the feast was laid out.

Out by the river we ate, with the firelight leaping high against the stars, and everyone talking at once, and laughing, while Ishtok and I gave each other loving glances in between rare bites of food, both of us too excited and overwhelmed to eat. When the feast was over the musicians brought out their pipes and flutes, and the Igaal musicians joined them, and we danced. Mad and wonderful dances they were, a marvelous mix of wild tribal leaps and twirls, and the more sedate Navoran moves. With all the noise and talking and laughter, I barely heard the Citadel musicians when they first arrived, but soon the strains from their beautiful stringed instruments soared high above all else, and we celebrated and danced to the best music in the world. Then Delano read a poem he had written for us, and one of the Navoran singers sang for us, and Salverion made a speech about love and unity and the power of healing, which had us all in tears.

As the moon rose the talk grew quieter, and the children were taken to bed in the Shinali house. People were sitting in groups, tribes and nations all mixed up: I saw Sheel Chandra sitting with little Kimiwe on his lap, his beautiful old hands smoothing the burn scars on her face; Taliesin looking happy as he and his wife talked, mainly through signs, with a freed Igaal slave; Embry and his soldiers joking with Igaal and Hena warriors; Shinali girls blushing as they talked shyly with the lovely Atitheya; Zalidas and Sakalendu communing together, their heads close, doubtless sharing visions of the Eagle's Time; Santoshi, still weak and supported in her husband's arms, talking with Chimaki; and,

457

across the dark grasslands, children from the farms coming to watch and being invited to join us.

Late in the night my mother and I had a happy time talking again with my Navoran grandmother. We sat with her on the edge of the firelight, and she told us stories of my father. "All his life he loved giving gifts," she said. "When he was a child he was always bringing me home flowers or fruit, sometimes just a leaf he had found, that he thought looked beautiful. It always gave him great pleasure, to give to others." She looked at me, her beautiful blue eyes brimming with affection, and lifted her hand and briefly touched my face. "But the greatest gift he ever gave me was you, Avala," she said. "And I have something for you, a wedding gift. All the letters your father wrote to me while he was at the Citadel are in your tent, for you to read in the days to come. I have worn the pages thin, reading them. They are yours to cherish now."

Overcome, speechless, I hugged her, and kissed her soft cheek.

Around us, guests were beginning to leave, for it was well past night's middle. Ishtok came for me, and we went together to say farewell to our friends. But many guests, mainly the younger ones, stayed on, talking and laughing around the fires. My mother came to us, and said, "You two may go now. Your tent is ready. Don't say any more good-byes; just go." She kissed us both and whispered something to Ishtok that made him nod and smile.

I looked across the dark land toward the mountains, where a little tent stood alone, its sides glowing amber from the lamps within. It was Ishtok's and my marriage-tent, ours to sleep in for the first ten days of our lives together. I glanced at Ishtok;

for once he looked a little shy. But he took my hand, and kissed my mother's cheek, and we began the long walk across the dark grass to our sleeping place. To the sound of Navoran music we went, and some of the guests called out to us, and we waved to them, laughing, self-conscious. At last we came to our lamp-lit dwelling, and went in.

Ishtok lowered the tent door, and we were alone.

It was the first time we had been alone since the evening out under the full moon, two days ago, when I had asked him to marry me. In our Shinali house he had slept with the young men and I with the women, and it seemed strange now, to be just the two of us.

For a while we stood, looking around, our hands linked. The tent was luxurious, some of its furnishings Igaal, some Shinali, some Navoran. Everything in it was crimson or white or gold. On the floor was one of Mudiwar's best carpets, and there were elegant Navoran lamps burning on stands, and a long carved wooden clothing-chest, a gift from Ramakoda. On a flax Shinali mat were set out food and drink, and a golden bowl for washing, with soft Navoran towels. And on the floor in the center of the tent, splendid with tasseled cushions and rich red Navoran coverings, was our marriage bed.

I looked at Ishtok; he was watching me, his beautiful eyes luminous and moist. For a while we gazed at each other, and then he took off our garlands of flowers, and put them on the carpet. He began to caress my face, and I felt his fingers trembling. For the first time I felt awkward with him, and shy. For all the beauty of our lamp-lit tent, it was unfamiliar, the situation strange, and I wished we were out in the summer grass, under the stars and

459

moon. I thought perhaps Ishtok knew how I felt, for he drew me to him, very gently, and simply held me awhile. From outside came the sound of merriment, and then Shinali music, haunting and lovely.

"Can I tell you my heart's truth?" he asked softly, kissing my hair.

"I hope you never tell me anything else," I said.

"Our sleeping place here is very fine, but it feels strange to me. I'm wishing we were out in the hills, the way we were the other night, and that I had the full moon on my shoulder again, to help me dazzle you."

"You don't need the moon," I said. "You dazzled me the first time I ever saw you. But if you want the moon, we can go for a walk."

"Heart's truth? You don't mind if I don't sweep you into bed straightaway?"

"Heart's truth, that bed seems strange to me, too. And I feel wrought up still, after the ceremony. I'd like to walk and talk awhile, before you do any sweeping."

He suddenly hugged me, relieved. "Thank the stars for that!" he said. "I'm taut as a bowstring, myself. I don't think I'd be a very satisfactory lover right at this moment."

Letting me go, he bent and gathered up the rich red covering from the bed, and picked up a jar of wine and a hunk of the bread. "Let's sleep outside," he said, grinning. "But we'll take plenty of food. I'm starving. I was too nervous to eat before. Is there anything you want to bring?"

"Only a satisfactory lover?" I asked, struggling to look devastated. "I was hoping for a little bit more than that."

"You won't be getting a little bit of anything," he said, "if I collapse from starvation. Will you bring some of that venison? And more bread, please."

"I can't believe it!" I said. "Aren't you the man who once said that one kiss from me was worth starving for?"

He faced me, his dark eyes full of humor, his arms full of blankets and edible supplies. "A kiss I can accomplish, on an empty stomach," he said. "But a full satisfactory performance, I think not."

Laughing, I gathered some food into a cloth and bundled it up, and we crept from the gorgeous tent out into the summer night. West we went, behind the Shinali house, and on toward the city, and found a place in the hills beneath the Citadel, where we could look across the Shinali land and the ebbing fires and the gray dawn creeping up over the mountaintops. There, wrapped in the blanket, we drank and ate our own wedding feast, and then, with the newly risen sun spilling gold across our grass green bed, we loved for the first time; and I was no more awkward or shy, and he was a high lot satisfactory.

That summer was a high time in my life. It would take another scroll to tell of all that we did, Ishtok and I—to tell of our visits to the city, our wanderings through the houses of art, and Ishtok's awe at the statues and carvings there; of dinners at Taliesin's house with his wife and family; the nighttime performances of Navoran music in the huge city square; the evenings we walked around the path on the summit of the city walls,

461

our arms about each other, admiring the thousands of city lights below; to tell of our visits to the Citadel, of the hours we spent marveling at the huge murals being restored after years of neglect, and the overgrown gardens and vineyards being replanted, and helping Salverion and Sheel Chandra in the vast libraries, radiant even in their dust; to tell of happy times with my Navoran family, on my grandmother's farm; the jubilant feasts in our big Shinali house, the grand festivities before the Hena tribes and Mudiwar's people went back to their own territories, with promises to visit soon; and the days we rode to the edges of the Shinali lands and saw the Nyranjeera Lakes and after that the sea thundering on the western beaches.

It was a glorious and peaceful time, a time of heart's-ease, of inner healing, for all of my people, and for Navora. Only one thing was wanting, in that time, for me; I longed to be working again, to be healing, using the skills I had learned from my mother, and at Ravinath. My mother was the tribe's healer, and though I helped her when our skills were needed, there was not work enough for us both. Some days I went to the Navoran Infirmary and helped the physicians there. But always when I passed the road to the Citadel, and thought of the Masters there, of that great place still being restored, my heart ached.

The trees put on their fiery autumn garments, and the winter winds came, and in the warm Shinali house Ishtok and I lay at night in our furs and loved, and listened to the river-song and the wind as it sighed across the land.

The first snows came, and we had a visitor.

Afar off he was, when we first saw him, his swift Navoran

chariot bounding over the snow-powdered lands, and glinting in the winter sun. Ishtok and I ran out to meet him, though we could not see at first who he was, for he wore a long fur cloak and hood over his Citadel robes. The chariot stopped beside us, and he got down, and we threw our arms around him.

"Salverion!" I cried. "What a wonderful surprise! Have you finished all your work now, at the Citadel?"

"Well, it's restored, if that's what you mean," he said, smiling broadly. "But the real work—that of teaching again—is about to begin." He pulled off his winter gloves and gave them to the driver, still waiting in the chariot. "Go on, please, and wait outside the Shinali house," he said to the man. "I'll walk the rest of the way, with my two friends."

The man shook the reins, and the black horse trotted on, taking its chariot with the seven silver stars blazing on the sides. When it stopped outside our house children ran out to see it, and the driver lifted some of them up, to take them for a ride. Their excited shrieks were loud in the still air. Beyond the thatched roof with its thin column of smoke, beyond the sheep in their stone shelters, the mountains were white and blue, their shadowed valleys the same azure as the sky.

"I hope you'll stay and feast with us tonight," I said, tucking my arm about Salverion's. Ishtok walked on his other side, grinning with pleasure, for he, too, had grown to love the Grand Master.

"I'd like that very much," said Salverion. "Actually, I've come on business. I've brought something for each of you." He stopped walking, and gently withdrew his arms from ours, and reached into a scarlet bag he carried over his shoulder. He took out two scrolls, each carefully rolled and tied with a ribbon, one green for healing, one silver for the arts, each sealed with blue wax.

"I want you both to think very carefully about what is written in those," he said.

Before I opened mine, just seeing Salverion's face, the fondness in his eyes, I knew what it was. I wept, could hardly speak for joy. I put my arms about his neck and kissed his cheek.

"I don't need time to think," I said.

Salverion smiled, his gray eyes twinkling. "I seem to remember your father saying those exact words," he said. "But you have a husband to consider, Avala. He may not be willing to live at the Citadel with you, and do carvings and sculpture for the next seven years—even if you can visit your home here whenever you wish."

I looked at Ishtok. Struggling to contain his happiness, he said huskily, in Navoran, "Carving I would love to do. And my home, it is always where Avala is."

Smiling, Salverion put his arms about our shoulders, and we began walking to the Shinali house. My mother stood on the snowy ground outside, waiting for us, knowing in her heart why Salverion had come, her face serene and glad.

Beyond her, between the dwelling and the sacred mountain, the wheels of the Citadel chariot left a pattern in the snow of looped and interlacing lines, like the symbol for Shinali dreams; and the voices of the children rang, full of joy, across the white and radiant land.

The End